W9-CIC-146

To Ed and Rosemary ♡
You're doing such great
work. I hope you
enjoy this work
All the best
John

Controlling Time

JOHN J HEARTFIELD

Copyright © 2012 by John J Heartfield.

All rights reserved. This book, or parts thereof, may not
be reproduced in any form without permission.

ISBN: 1468151460

ISBN-13 9781468151466

DEDICATION

To Michelle

JOHN J HEARTFIELD

ACKNOWLEDGMENTS

The author wishes to acknowledge some of the people who helped with this book. Thanks to Marty Brounstein, whose knowledge of hand-to-hand combat was invaluable. Thanks to Frank O'Neill, whose careful editing of the manuscript was so essential. I cannot neglect to mention my darling wife, Michelle, who always provided me with a woman's point of view.

Also, thank you, Augustus, for making me take walks in the sunshine.

CHAPTER 1

KO

Manhattan, South Of Canal Street
Winter, 1999

The old man said, "Ko, I'll have my cigar now."

Ko stood behind the old man's left shoulder, regarding me without emotion. From what I'd seen in the past, Ko didn't find emotions to be all that useful. He preferred to indulge his appetites.

I was quick, but without a weapon, I harbored no illusions about my chances against Ko.

He was five-nine, but as wide as two men pressed together. The city's most talented tailor made Ko's charcoal-grey suits fit as well they did. However, even that master craftsman was unable to mask a visible tightness in certain lines of the cut. Tonight, in addition to a blood-red silk tie knotted over his crisp pale yellow shirt, Ko wore invisible restraints forged by his respect for the old man.

He stood waiting, perfectly balanced, and every now and then, with the slightest motion, he would lean towards where I sat. It gave me the impression that I had placed myself too close to the wrong end of a stretched bow or a cocked revolver.

If the old man let him have his way, Ko would happily choke the life out of me while thinking of it as a light workout. Perhaps daydreaming about such a pleasant activity was the reason that he responded too slowly to the old man's request.

"Have you forgotten my cigar, Ko?" the old man said. "After all, you're already up."

One corner of the old man's lips rose slightly as he shared the double meaning of his words with me.

Ko did not move. He was certain I would never try to harm the only person worthy of our loyalty. However, Ko must have felt that, after what had happened, placing any amount of trust in me was an unnecessary leap of faith.

In a voice just louder than a whisper, but with a much different tone, the old man said to him, "Go now."

Ko immediately left us. The old man lowered his eyes and studied a delicate cup on the small round table that separated us. We were sitting in the dimly lit room where he spent most of his time. The old man didn't care for sunlight. Too many people were in it.

In one quick smooth motion he raised the cup to his lips, tipped it back, and replaced it almost precisely in the same spot. The movement struck me as a good model for the way he conducted business. Once he decided on an action, it was carried out as efficiently as possible.

After he drank, he turned his attention to me. His gaze forced me to think of all the things that I had done and all the things that I still wanted to do. If I'd known him only by his reputation, I'd have felt like a man watching a knife being slowly forced into his chest.

But I'd been in this room before, standing beside him rather than sitting across from him. A wall clock clicked louder than it had on those other nights.

For some reason, he decided that before I heard his decision I needed one final lesson.

"There are only two kinds of men in the world," he said. "Those who act on what they believe should be done and those who don't. Sometimes, overcome by passion, a man will behave differently, but that's not the same as a man who has time to consider all the consequences of his actions and then moves ahead, whether minutes or years pass between the cause and its effect. When such a man also possesses intelligence, he'll be respected. If fortune favors him, he'll acquire power. There's no shame in being the other type. It's simply how you're made."

He shrugged so gently that I couldn't be certain that I'd seen it.

"Ko tried to warn me," he said. "I don't understand why you allowed that traitor to beg for what no longer belong to him. How did he persuade you to give him time to prove his innocence? Was it your old friendship? It doesn't matter. If you had trusted my judgment, then nothing he said could have made you so weak. I sent Ko as soon as you told me what you'd done, but it was almost two days before he made his way through those who took in your friend. Some of my associates are complaining that Ko acted too harshly. Well, people always talk. That kind of talk fades away. However, Ko believes cleaning up after you was beneath him."

He looked down at his hands.

"I don't need to tell you that Ko will always act on his beliefs."

I also looked at the old man's hands. In the past, I'd imagined him to be immortal, but suddenly I noticed that he was showing his age. I realized how much his disappointment in me had contributed to that and I was ashamed.

"If you were my blood, it might be different," he said. "But not as things stand. I can't allow you to remain with me, a reminder to my enemies, strengthening them, informing them that you disobeyed me and I forgave you."

So he had decided. It was a death sentence. Ko was close. I prepared myself by forcing my mind to clamp down on only one thought.

I will not allow Ko to crush me like an insect.

I tried to remember his favorite moves. He enjoyed prolonging the struggles of opponents who allowed him to get too close. He had taught me when it served his purpose. I concentrated on ways to give Ko as much pain as possible before he finished with me.

The old man reached into a deep pocket of his simple black cloth jacket and took out an envelope.

"Take this," he said. "Go away and never come back. It must appear as if you were buried where your body could never be found. Only Ko and I can know what happened here tonight."

"What about you?" I said.

Of course, my question didn't want an answer.

"Have you suddenly decided to consider my interests?" he said.

His tone cut deeply into me.

"Don't concern yourself," he said, sounding weary. "The ones I can't control still need me."

There was nothing left to say. As I walked past him on the way out, I resisted the impulse to show him some sign of what I felt for him. For almost seven years, he had treated me as if I was his favored son.

Ko stood in the hallway, managing to look as if he was leaning against the wall. It appeared as if he was smiling. But Ko only smiled when he was sure someone else couldn't.

"I can't believe you're walking away from this," he said. "You know what will happen. I always knew you were weak, but I didn't think you could spend so much time with him without learning a damn thing."

I'd learned it was essential to treat Ko with a certain wary respect. I'd seen what happened to those who made the mistake of thinking otherwise. But I'd never liked him. I finally had my chance to speak my mind, knowing that the old man had given me a safe pass.

I moved my face to within inches of his unreadable expression.

"You came into this world ready to kill anything in your path," I said. "What did you learn?"

"What did I learn from him?" he said. "Patience. He taught me to wait for the right moment."

3

His hand disappeared inside his jacket as quickly as a small deadly snake. Then he slowly removed an object from his pocket.

I couldn't believe Ko would go against the old man. I tried to get ready.

But all he held in his hand was a cigar, a Montecristo, not five hours off the plan from Cuba.

"You should hurry in with that before it gets stale," I said.

He smiled with the corners of his lips. Then he turned and walked away. Suddenly, he stopped and turned around.

Ko said softly, "I promise you. There'll be another night, little boy."

I was careful when I stepped into the street. I slid into a deep shadow, glanced inside the envelope, and saw that it held a stack of hundred dollar bills. Later, when I carefully counted them, I discovered they added up to twenty-five thousand dollars.

I stashed the money in my jacket, zipped up against the cold, and considered how to get out of the city in the least visible manner.

The next night, sitting at the counter of a truck stop diner, I celebrated my eighteenth birthday.

I took a bite of stale cake.

It tasted very good.

CHAPTER 2

ENEMIES

New York's Financial District
Summer, 2012

The prince said, "I hope this won't take all day."

Wearing an immaculately tailored silk business suit and an unaffected air of superiority, second in line to lead one of the twelve richest countries on earth, his tone made it quite clear that he felt he had better things to do than negotiate a trade agreement that could easily make his country the tenth richest.

The seven other men who shared the large quiet elevator with the prince decided staring away from him and remaining silent was their best response. Only Edgar Treeves felt it was correct to speak.

"If my opinion may be of any value to your highness, I can assure you, with a great deal of certainty, you won't be inconvenienced for very long."

As he spoke, Treeves alerted a man standing behind him that they were entering a situation where they'd be fighting for their lives. He stretched his neck by turning it slightly to his right. Anyone who had noticed the movement would have thought that he was feeling a bit tense before the impending negotiations.

However, with that small motion, Treeves made sure his Weapon was ready to be used.

Time understood the signal as clearly as if Treeves had turned and shouted at him. Soon, the tasteful décor and hushed conversations in the luxurious law offices of Lang & Ellsworth would not set the tone. An irreversible act was about to shatter the day-to-day business calm. The people on the twentieth floor, several who had just completed a short pleasant walk from Wall Street's life-sized bronze statue of a bull, were minutes away from a dramatic change in their plans. At least one person near Time was about to be killed.

Time didn't speculate about who was fated to die. To guess would be a dangerous waste of his concentration. Time was like a man engrossed in a book, except that he was reading Edgar Treeves.

The heavy elevator doors opened and the prince's lead bodyguard stepped out.

As he followed him, the prince remarked, "I don't care for offices. Can you imagine having to work while simultaneously being forced to deal with other people all the time?"

The men surrounding the prince didn't seem to appreciate the irony of his remark, even though as well-trained bodyguards, they were constantly forced to interact with each other and almost everyone around them.

However, Time, at the rear of the entourage, imagined Treeves might allow himself the subtlest of smiles. Although it was not relevant to their current mission, Treeves appreciated everything about human behavior on one level or another.

As Time stepped from the elevator, he tested his footing on the expensive carpet. His shoes had been custom made to provide maximum traction and control on a variety of surfaces, but he automatically checked any critical factor that might impact his abilities. He continued to watch the tall frail Edgar Treeves, waiting for the subtle indicators that would tell him which people in the operations area would remain civilians and who would become his targets.

Time adjusted his breathing. He calculated distances and listened for sounds as soft as deep breaths. He had shifted into predator mode.

Directly to the left of the elevator, an attractive floor receptionist stood as the prince entered. As instructed, she bowed slightly without speaking. The prince acknowledged her with a subtle nod.

As Time passed by her, she smiled warmly at him and he smiled back. It crossed his mind that, despite her slightly flirtatious greeting, soon she could be labeled one of his targets. It had been deeply ingrained in him that the moment Edgar Treeves identified a target, that individual was no longer to be considered a human being. Rather, targets were only walking talking collections of opportunities for Time to neutralize them the instant Treeves signaled him to do so.

Time knew that multi-opponent close-order combat was chaos. A random shot or a knife scoring a few centimeters to the left or right could decide the outcome. No one had control over luck or destiny. Therefore, he focused on variables that would provide him with the edge he needed to eliminate targets as quickly as possible with a minimal amount of collateral damage.

The most important variable was Edgar Treeves. When the moment arrived to make the key decisions of who should go down and in what order, it was Treeves who gave him that vital information.

There were hundreds of silent signals Treeves could convey to Time in one way or another. They were separated into categories, some requiring patience, others instantaneous reaction.

The two of them had practiced for countless hours. Once they were certain a signal was clear, they practiced it again a hundred times.

If a person unexpectedly and quickly moves their hand towards another's face, even in a gesture of affection, the object of the movement will instinctively pull away. The level of silent communication that existed between Treeves and Time was similar to such a natural reaction.

Elio, the prince's chief of security, remained close to his employer's right elbow. His gaze buzzed like a fly over everyone within twenty feet. Treeves was on the prince's left and didn't appear to be overly interested in anyone or anything.

The prince's entourage calmly approached Charles Lang, the senior partner responsible for the most important decisions regarding the firm's direction. He waited patiently near the entrance to his luxurious office with a welcoming expression.

Lang did not feel it was wise or necessary to be obsequious. Although he was hosting royalty, he felt just as powerful in his own kingdom. Surrounding Lang, in ten slightly less-imposing workspaces, five on either side of his office, his attorneys were converting words of specificity into piles of money.

Lang's partner, Carlin Ellsworth, had died four years earlier. However his distinguished career warranted keeping his name on the door. Their partnership agreement kept Ellsworth's daughter, Beth, impatiently waiting to be made a full partner. She occupied the office directly to Lang's right.

Lang's political connections, forged over many years, made him invaluable to those who needed the services of an attorney who could navigate the details of an international trade agreement that required an intricate blend of corporate cooperation and government approval.

In addition to someone with Lang's experience, it was equally essential to employ the services of a Corporate Diplomatic Liaison. A CDL was tasked with impartially smoothing over rough patches that inevitably arose during complicated negotiations.

Every party involved in the current negotiation had no doubt Edgar Treeves was one of the finest Corporate Diplomatic Liaison available. Although he possessed more than the necessary skill set, Treeves was not a CDL. He was a ghost. A man whose identity was so deeply buried, it was possible to stamp detailed personal histories and high-level credentials onto him at will. Treeves played any role a situation required. Afterwards, the identity he had assumed simply vanished. During a mission, his physical appearance was often disguised in some manner. However, that was almost unnecessary. People with unacceptable intentions who found themselves interacting with Edgar Treeves either wound up dead or unable to recognize him in the unlikely event they ever saw him again.

Time moved closer to the rear of the prince's entourage. They passed around a group of plush sofas that encircled a large sculpture in the center of the room, complete with a waterfall of recycled water that fell in gentle sheets into a pool containing *Koi*. If the surface of their world was disturbed, the fish exploded into a swirling canvas of movement and color. For anyone idiotic to consider doing so, a tastefully placed small sign, written in the type of gold lettering found on expensive wedding invitations, read: *Please do not feed the fish or throw coins into the fountain.*

The bottom of the pool was littered with coins, proving that wealth often had little effect on traits such as cleverness or consideration.

Various clients, employees, and supplicants were scattered on and around the sofas. They had exited or were waiting to enter one of the soundproof offices on the circular edges of the reception area. There was no way to know what transpired inside the offices once their doors clicked quietly shut.

A security guard stood next to the receptionist's desk. He had the height and weight of a college football player beginning a descent into seed. Time noted that Lang, perhaps because of his prestigious location and strong electronic surveillance system, didn't seem overly concerned about the capabilities of his security personnel.

As the guard nervously shifted his weight from right foot to left and back again, an expandable baton jiggled in a Velcro holster strapped to his thigh. A Glock 21 rested in a holster on his right hip. A strap over the top of the handgun was snapped closed.

Handguns were not Time's specialty. However, as a professional, it had vaguely annoyed him to see such an excellent weapon treated so foolishly. He mused that perhaps the Glock was snapped into the holster in case the guard chose to break into a few jumping jacks to remove some of the extra weight he carried around his middle. Any serious opponent could have killed or disabled the guard nine different ways in the time it would have taken him to raise the Glock into a position where it would be useful.

On the other hand, the security detail that surrounded the prince was made up of five very serious men. Elio, the man in charge, walked in lock step at the prince's elbow. He had placed the most capable bodyguard two steps in front of the prince. Three other members of the security team and the prince's personal assistant followed, all of them only one or two steps behind. Once they reached Lang's office, three members of the team were to secure the entrance. Elio, who never left the prince's side, and the prince's personal assistant were the only subordinates who would be allowed to enter the soundproof comfort of Lang's inner sanctum along with Treeves, Lang, and the prince.

Treeves had not given him further instructions so Time simply watched as Elio suddenly quickened his step. He halted next to the bodyguard directly in front of the prince and, in one swift motion, slit the man's throat.

It was neatly done, nothing dramatic about it at all. With a gurgling sound and a spray of blood, the bodyguard raised his hands to the expanding wound, turned to Elio with a puzzled expression and collapsed. He shook for a short time, desperate to draw air through his own blood.

Two other members of the security team, a few paces behind, drew twenty-two caliber automatics, and placed them against the heads of the prince's assistant and his last loyal bodyguard, and pulled the triggers. The small metal projectiles entered the victims' skulls, but lacked the force to exit. They rattled around in brain matter until they were still.

As intended, the sound of pistol fire caused waves of fear and confusion to crash upon the reception area. People rushed from offices only to bump into those who were trying to get as far away from the gunmen as possible.

Time stood his ground, appearing surprised and shocked, although he felt neither emotion. He'd witnessed violence much more swift and brutal. His focus remained upon Treeves.

Lang was awash in blood from the bodyguard's throat. He rubbed his hands from the top of his chest to his groin and said, "My God."

From his tone, it wasn't entirely clear if he was bemoaning the fate of the man lying on his carpet or his own custom-made pinstriped suit.

Time was certain he could kill Elio and his two men where they stood without much risk. He had already choreographed the most effective movements in his mind, but Treeves had not given him elimination orders. Three directives were seared into Time's personality profile. Protect Edgar Treeves at all cost, clearly communicate with him without detection, and follow his orders without question or hesitation. These simple directives had saved his life in many previous operations they had become ingrained into Time's survival instinct.

Treeves had scanned everyone on the floor the moment he stepped from the elevator. He weighed indicators that increased the probability they would become targets. Naturally, he'd known about Elio and his men long before the entourage had entered the building. He quickly tagged two others in the reception area. Moments after the sound of the gunfire faded away, his choices made them themselves obvious to everyone.

The secretary seated outside of Beth Ellsworth's office rose and quickly moved towards Elio and his men. The young guard by the elevator managed to free his Glock and, rather than pointing it at the gunmen, began waving it randomly over the heads of the terrified crowd. These two were sleepers. They had passed many ordinary days waiting to show themselves as more than faces in the crowd.

By slightly moving his right foot, Time signaled, "*Instructions?*"

"*Hold position,*" Treeves responded.

With a fluidity that comes with countless hours of practice, the men who had fired the pistols put them away, trading them for Russian PP-90 submachine guns. The PP-90 was manufactured specifically for protection details and covert ops. It combined compact size with excellent firepower. Capable of firing seven hundred rounds per minute, it featured a large ejection port to prevent jamming and folded up to the size of a socket wrench box.

The prince stared at the leaking throat of his close body man with a grim expression. However, he said nothing, simply moving his feet slightly backwards to avoid having his shoes stained by the expanding puddle of blood. He had a reputation as a tough character. Having survived his nation's violent internal conflicts, he was no stranger to bloodshed.

Treeves moved closer to him. It was natural for a Corporate Diplomatic Liaison to remain calm in any situation, regardless of how unpleasant or stressful. It was one of the reasons CDLs were traditionally compensated with one fifth of one percent of the first two years gross profit from successful negotiations. Treeves knew a CDL would likely believe that he was not in any immanent danger. Terrorism has morphed from a political weapon to a religious struggle to an international business. There was a great deal of money to be made by anyone who had a talent for it. A good CDL, especially one who could be convinced to work for bargain-basement prices in exchange for his life, was invaluable.

The targets moved the hostages towards the center of the room near the fountain, herding them together, facing away Lang's office.

The guard shouted at the terrified receptionist to lock the elevator. The volume of his demand was excessive. Time saw the secretary and Elio exchange glances, but they did nothing to restrain him. When dealing with hostages at the outset, having a member of your team display an acceptable level of frenzy was a good tactic.

Time watched as Elio hustled Lang, Treeves, and the prince into Lang's office. He was uncomfortable whenever Treeves was out of his sight, but he wasn't overly concerned. Treeves had told him to take no action. He also knew that somehow Treeves had already formulated a plan to bring Time into Lang's office.

While he waited, Time assessed the strengths and weaknesses of his targets. The secretary had been given one of the twenty-two caliber automatics. It was clear she knew how to use it. Time also noted how the guard handled the Glock. It was equally apparent that he hadn't been thoroughly trained with it and hadn't practiced enough to employ it effectively. He might terrify civilians, but against Time, the guard would have an equal chance of survival armed with a toy pistol.

As the guard attempted to maintain the appearance of a forceful man in control, he gave the impression he was, in fact, jittery and unfocused. The powerful emotions of a fanatic didn't radiate from him. It was no longer necessary to recruit fanatics to a cause. As with all modern human conflict, it was capital that fueled the machine. A significant segment of the current generation was not too bright, but they had embraced a philosophy with greed at its core. Quick large paydays and high adventure seemed like shiny coins compared to the heavy leaden slugs of small tax-ridden checks from jobs at outlet malls.

For the briefest moment, Time thought it a shame that the guard had made such a bad choice so early in life. Soon, he wouldn't be making any more choices. Then, he put those thoughts away. Time did not hold onto regrets regarding what he had done or what he was about to do. If his targets had the slightest suspicion what he was, they would do their best to kill him as quickly as possible. Killing them before they came to that realization was simply self defense.

Later, if there was a later for him, he might remember faces and the things that he had done. Fortunately, he was well supplied with experts trained to make sure that those memories didn't keep him awake late into the night.

Time's current identity was Dr. James Warren, a major in the United States Army. On the day the prince's entourage arrived in New York, his personal physician had left their Manhattan hotel for a quick visit with a colleague. He suffered a shattered arm and ankle when a careless bicycle messenger crashed into him and then immediately disappeared. As the doctor was rushed to the area's finest hospital, the United States President telephoned the prince to apologize.

He insisted that he would immediately assign a member of his personal medical staff as a replacement to remain with the prince at all times during his stay in America. It would have been an unthinkable insult to refuse.

Time was not a doctor. However, as a trained and experienced battlefield medic, he could put on a good show if the situation demanded it. In the event of an emergency requiring an actual physician, a top-notch substitute, who had been provided with an excellent explanation regarding a medical specialty, was prepared to step in on a moment's notice.

Even in that eventuality, Time's current identity, as false as the one Edgar Treeves currently inhabited, was unbreakable. But in Time's case, because he didn't possess the morphing skills of Edgar Treeves, his athletic frame needed to inhabit a more suitable skin.

Thousands of people disappeared from the face of the earth every day. Many of them had no friends or close family who cared enough to try and locate them.

Their absence might be noticed for a short time.

Neighbors might say, "Hey, have you seen that guy who lives upstairs recently? He must have taken a vacation or something."

However, after a short time, the speculation stopped. Concerned with the ups and downs of their own lives, the man upstairs left no imprint in the memory of anyone who had been vaguely aware of him.

General Martin Tresain employed two invaluable tools to provide identities for Time. His orders allowed him to stealthily tap into the computers of intelligence agencies all over the world. By combining and sorting their information, he maintained a single private and comprehensive database of almost every man on earth who was a reasonable physical match for Time.

In addition, he was fortunate enough to have the services of a young computer genius with neither the temperament nor the poor judgment to be indiscreet. The programmer was not particularly curious as to why he was asked to create a program that output personality profiles based on parameters provided by an unknown source. Men of notable accomplishment, close families, or gregarious personalities were tagged as unsuitable. Only profiles of men who possessed specific traits and relationships were provided to Dr. Edgar Treeves for evaluation.

One candidate that drew Treeves' attention was a young cadet, two months shy of graduation from West Point.

Name: James Warren;
Religious Affiliation: Atheist;
Significant Family: Father (Factor==1);
Significant Relationships: (Factor==2);
Current, Physical: (Factor==8);
Condition, Mental: (Factor==1);
Prognosis: Chronic Depression (Factor==9);
Medication/Treatment: (Factor==1);

These parameters and others attracted the interest of Dr. Treeves. Posing as visiting psychologist, Treeves went to West Point, pretending to evaluate a group of cadets who had not performed up to their expected potential. After a ninety-minute session with James Warren, Treeves informed General Tresain that, regardless of intervention, Cadet Warren would end his own life. Furthermore, without immediate counter measures, he would do it in the weeks prior to a graduation that Warren felt he was unworthy to attend. Armed with that information, General Tresain made arrangements to insure the cadet's suicide would not be noticed.

After Warren took his own life, General Tresain had him cremated and arranged a credible cover story. The boy had been taken ill with a contagious disease and transferred to a military hospital. Warren's father, Colonel Thomas Warren, was serving a tour of duty in Iraq. Treeves informed General Tresain that once the colonel had been assured his son was not in mortal danger, he would decide it was unacceptable to abandon his command to simply stand at his son's bedside. Colonel Warren believed, as with all things, the boy's fate rested in the hands of the Almighty.

General Tresain arranged for the boy to graduate from West Point in absentia. He had that kind of power. Colonel Warren never saw his son again. However every so often, he received short letters from him, informing him of his assignments and accomplishments.

On paper, James Warren went on to receive a medical degree from the very military hospital where he recovered as his classmates attended their graduation. The same unmemorable Warren was assigned to combat zones and awarded medals for bravery. He enjoyed a distinguished career. One year after his son's graduation, Colonel Warren suffered a heart attack in an officer's club. His son, busy with important responsibilities, was unable to attend the funeral.

When it was needed, Time slipped into James Warren's identity as easily as he might guide his arms through the sleeves of an overcoat. In the depths of America's military computers, Warren's face was replaced by Time's face. His history was grafted onto Time. His experiences and abilities belonged to Time. Barring a statistically insignificant stroke of misfortune, it would have been impossible to prove, without a doubt, that Time was not currently Major James Warren.

The targets armed with PP-90s ordered some of the hostages to pull furniture from the offices and reception area and cover the elevator doors. The stairway doors were welded shut. Time considered it a bad sign that the targets seemed intent on sealing the only access in or out of the floor. It appeared as if a clear escape route didn't factor into their plans.

He dismissed the thought. It no longer mattered what they planned. Time thought of the targets as having no future. After this situation was resolved, they would never again enjoy, endure, or regret the events of their lives. It had been an essential element of his training.

Time maintained an unshakable conviction he would defeat any opponent in any arena. To imagine he might lose was to have lost before the fight began. Whether his conviction had any basis in fact was immaterial. It was the absence of doubt that mattered. Even his code name was chosen in part to assure him that he was the ultimate instrument of death. All things fell to Time.

Once the exits were covered, the targets arranged the hostages again and ordered them to sit together on the floor. One target was almost as tall as Time, a couple of inches over six foot. He was slim in comparison to the other, who was a foot shorter and at least thirty pounds overweight.

The slim target walked to where Beth Ellsworth sat and pulled her to her feet. He dragged her roughly by her left arm to a position close to the front of the captives. Ellsworth was an attractive dark-haired woman in her thirties and, for possibly the first time in her adult life, she was terrified that she'd never look any older. Her long obsessive pursuit of a partnership in Lang & Ellsworth no longer seemed as imperative to her as it had earlier in the day.

"We have wired this floor with high explosives," the target said calmly with very little accent. "However, we are not planning to die. This is about money."

He paused.

"After all, we are on Wall Street, are we not?"

He enjoyed his little joke for a moment.

"We have no reason to harm you," he continued. "You are our guarantee your government will not act foolishly. However, it is essential that you understand we are serious."

He allowed the submachine to hang from its strap and took a revolver from the side pocket of his jacket. He snapped the gun open and allowed all the bullets to fall into his hand. Then he showed one bullet to the hostages and inserted it back into the cylinder. He spun it to insure the position of the bullet in relation to the firing pin was unknown.

He rested the barrel against Beth Ellsworth's temple and pulled the trigger. The hammer came down with a click and Ellsworth grimaced as if she had just been slapped hard across the face.

"Oh my God, no," she said.

The target pulled the trigger again. When another click sounded in her ear, her eyes rolled up, and she fainted onto the floor. The targets let her lie there.

"We will tell you what to do and you will do it instantly. No talking, no discussion. If one of you doesn't instantly do what you're told, I'll repeat this demonstration with someone else, but I will use three bullets instead of one. Spend your time in the next hour or two calculating your odds of surviving that. Now, one by one, get up and prepare to be searched."

He pointed to Beth Ellsworth's office.

"All of your possessions will be placed there. You can retrieve them when this is over."

He pointed to a man to nearest to his left.

"You first," he said.

Time was certain the target had palmed the bullet before playing roulette. The demonstration was meant to frighten the crowd, not outrage them. The possibility of the unthinkable happening often instilled more fear than actual event.

The targets conferred quietly. The secretary and the overweight target went into Lang's office to join Elio. The roulette player and the young guard patrolled the floor, controlling the hostages.

Time looked uncomfortable and adjusted his seated position on the floor as a target passed by him, hoping he might notice. Although he was capable of maintaining positions much more uncomfortable, it was the small details that supported an identity. It was also good tactics to feign weakness before combat.

Inside Lang's private office, Treeves had determined how the targets in the room should be eliminated. Since he'd met with the prince several times prior to this meeting with Lang, he was familiar with Elio and his team. He'd noted basic factors such as left or right handed, the way they stood or sat, how they moved their arms and fingers, and how quickly they reacted mentally and physically to the unexpected. He gave extra attention to the woman since he had not seen her before.

Earlier that morning, Treeves had formulated a plan to place Time in a strategic position when he was required. It wasn't long before the woman stepped out of the Lang's office.

"Which one of you is James Warren?" she said.

Time raised his hand.

"You're the doctor?"

Time nodded.

"We need you inside the office. Now."

Time got up slowly, pretending that his legs were cramped. He pointed to the office where the hostage's possessions had been thrown behind a rolled-up rug.

"I need my bag," he said.

"I'll bring it in," the woman said.

Time glanced at the kid as he walked past him on his way into the office. Anyone might have mistaken his expression as one of discomfort as he walked past a heavily armed man. In fact, Time was checking the width of the kid's neck, considering the amount of torque he would need to cleanly snap it.

On the floor of Lang's office, pushed into a corner, was the body of Charles Lang. He'd drafted his last agreement. His legs and arms lay at unnatural angles and his suit had been torn and stained with blood. There were defensive cuts on his hands and forearms. Someone had come at him hard with a blade, not bothering to employ it carefully. Time was careful to stare at the corpse. Even an experienced military physician would find such an unnecessary and savage mutilation distasteful.

Elio had no reason to comment, but he said, "Lang was a pig. If I had the time and equipment, I would have hung him from a hook."

As the overweight target searched him again, Time kept Edgar Treeves in his peripheral vision.

Treeves, by shifting his right foot slightly outward and raising it a couple of millimeters, signaled, "*Character behavior only.*"

The prince, pale and semi-conscious, was slouched in Lang's large leather chair. The targets had moved it to the left side of Lang's desk. Time went to check his condition.

There was a double tap on the door and it swung inward. The female target entered the room carrying the medical bag and, rather than taking it to Time, she walked over to stand at the right side of the overweight target. They were on the opposite side of the room from Time and the prince.

Before she came back into Lang's office, she had carefully searched the bag. She hadn't stumbled upon the tools that Time could access in seconds.

If she had considered anything in the bag to be suspicious, it could be explained as a piece of cutting-edge medical equipment.

Time didn't need to be a doctor to diagnose that the prince's condition was deteriorating. The prince's pupils were dilated, his breathing was shallow, and spots of vomit soiled his chin and impeccable clothing. The obvious conclusion was that he was suffering a reaction to some allergen or poison.

"I'll have to move him," said Time, helping the prince to slide from Lang's chair onto his back on the floor.

When he knelt over him, there was a clear field between himself and his targets across the room.

"What did you give him?" he said, turning to Elio.

"We gave him nothing," Elio said.

"I need my bag. Bring it to me. All this stress has exacerbated his coronary condition."

"No," Elio said quickly.

The security chief was not a man who took unnecessary chances.

"Tell us what you need," he said. "She'll hand those things to you."

"This man doesn't have time for amateur games," Time said, with a practiced air of arrogance and annoyance. "Do you think she's qualified to understand what I need as quickly as I may need it?"

Elio removed a metal object from his right jacket pocket. A four-inch blade slid out dramatically.

"Then imagine this," he said. "The next few moments will determine how you walk for the rest of your life."

Treeves gave a clear signal, *"Dead end."*

The building's air conditioning had been shut down. The FBI had initiated their standard protocols. They were unaware they had allies in the center of the action. Time noticed that, although none of the targets complained about the heat, two of them were feeling it. The overweight man had taken off his jacket and tie and had rolled up his sleeves. Sweat began trickling down his round cheeks. He pulled one of the office chairs against the wall directly across from where Time leaned over the prince and sat down. That was good. Time knew the PP-90 the target held was pointed directly at his back. That was bad.

The woman remained standing, close to the seated target's right. She held the twenty-two automatic at a forty-five degree angle. It wasn't a submachine gun, but she seemed content with it. She had short light-brown hair and wore a blue short-sleeve dress appropriate for a young corporate employee.

Elio's only visible weapon was the knife. He stood near the left corner of the room, furthest from the entrance. It was an excellent tactical position. He had positioned his subordinates to control the room. If trouble arose, he had distance and cover. Time had no doubt a firearm of some type was not far from Elio's grasp.

The security chief was a slim man, just under five-ten. He had short straight black hair and determined merciless eyes. He wore too much cologne. Despite the heat, he remained dressed in a black suit, white shirt, and slim tie. His shoes shone with polish. He was focused on his objectives. The heat didn't seem to bother him.

"All right, then," said Time. "I'll need my stethoscope, the blood pressure cuff, the portable defibrillator…"

He continued to name basic supplies. It was a critical moment. He knew at least one of the targets was looking at him. He needed a diversion. He expelled his breath and made a small sound as if the heat was getting to him.

Treeves instantly understood. He stepped forward.

"How long are we going to be here?" he said, in an upper class London accent that had nothing to do with his true upbringing. "Who knows what the anti-terrorism teams outside are planning? And what about your prince? He should be in hospital, not lying on the floor."

"Be quiet," said the leader. "You think because you're a CDL, you're invaluable. But no matter how clever you are at tricking people into seeing your point of view, you lack discipline."

In any other situation, Time might have laughed. Edgar Treeves was, without doubt, the most disciplined human being he'd ever encountered.

During this exchange, Time had taken off his jacket and folded it, placing it under the head of the prince. As he did so, he ran his hands down the front and stripped off four buttons. He waited to see if he'd have to move immediately. If the retrieval of the buttons been detected, he knew it would be very difficult to save both Treeves and himself. He didn't relish the choice.

The prince emitted a low choking moan.

"He could stop breathing any second," said Time. "I need someone down here with me."

Elio thought about it. He didn't like it. He'd expected a fluid situation, but the prince's unexpected illness made him uneasy. He wanted to keep all his assets in place. Treeves saw him make the decision.

"You," he said, pointing the blade at Treeves. "Help him."

As Treeves knelt beside him, Time attached a heart monitor.

"Watch these readings carefully," said Time. "If this dial here falls below eighty, tell me immediately."

They pretended to work on the prince. It was as close to an ideal situation as they could have hoped.

Treeves signaled, "*Eliminate visible targets. Low volume.*"

"*Understood. Identify targets.*"

Treeves responded by numbering the targets from left to right, beginning on Time's right. The woman was one, the seated man was two, and Elio was three.

"*Sequence?*" Time signaled.

This was the essential question. Which target should be eliminated first? Treeves needed to tell his Weapon the order in which the targets in the room should be neutralized, counting down from the first to die to the one who was least likely to prevent Time from killing all of them.

Treeves used his thumb and right index finger to lightly tap out numbers on the prince's chest.

"Two, One, Three."

The seated overweight target was to die first, then the woman by the door, and finally, Elio. It wasn't the order Time would have chosen. The woman looked as if she was itching to kill someone and would open fire at the slightest provocation. Plus, her weapon was lighter and she could bring it to bear more quickly.

If it were up to Time, he would have taken her first, but his opinion was irrelevant. Treeves had devoted his life to human pre-behavioral science. He was possibly the best in the world at predicting what a person was thinking, was capable of doing, and was about to do before they actually did it.

Time cradled two of the buttons from his jacket in his left hand. He held the other two in his right. He made his final check of distances and positions. He signaled to Treeves.

"Target three - weapons?" Time signaled.

"Knife - right hand - pistol - right jacket pocket," Treeves responded.

"Ready."

Treeves signaled their countdown.

Time rose slightly and turned as if to ask for something from the medical bag. He pretended to stumble, as if his leg had gone weak from kneeling too long.

Treeves screamed, "No!"

It was a terrified sustained high-pitched wail.

With astonishing speed and accuracy, Time flung two of the heavy buttons at the wall between the woman and the fat man. In almost the same instant, he threw the two that remained in his right hand against the wall over Elio's head.

The buttons operated on centrifugal force. As they spun, a mechanism released sharp spiked edges on their perimeters. When they impacted against the walls, they exploded, filling the air with a light powder. It impaired the targets' vision and caused them to involuntarily choke for a moment. Time had become immune to its effects long ago.

The seated fat man saw a spectral figure explode towards him like a ghost in a horror film. Reflex caused him to open his mouth to shout, but before he could force air out of his lungs, a stifling pressure squeezed his vocal cords together. His head snapped to the right and he felt an odd wetness pour down his chest. The last action of his life was to raise his left hand to discover that Time's right hand had torn away the front of his throat.

The woman also saw the specter in the mist. She quickly turned to her left to empty her automatic at it, but her arm bumped into something. It was Time's left side. He encircled her neck with his left arm, positioning his left his forearm against her throat and snapped upward. She went limp as an empty dress.

With his arm still around her neck, holding up her body as a shield, Time spun to face Elio.

Treeves had stopped screaming. The haze was clearing. Time saw that Elio had made the mistake of taking a few precious seconds to transfer the knife to his left hand before reaching for the pistol with his right. However, his hand was already halfway into his pocket.

Time moved his right hand from behind the woman body. He showed Elio the automatic he had taken from her.

"It won't even be close," Time said.

Elio pulled his hand away from his pocket. Treeves watched him form a strategy.

After a moment, Elio said, "This room may be soundproof, but not enough to silence the sound of a pistol shot. If you fire, my man outside will open that door and spray the entire room with automatic weapons fire."

"And you'll die with us," said Time.

"I'm prepared. Are you?"

"There's no need for either of us to die," Time said. "I need to get out of here. You're worth more to me alive than dead."

As he spoke, he allowed the woman's body to slide to the floor. Stepping over her, he began moving towards Elio as slowly and deliberately as a hunting jungle cat. With each small movement, he kept his attention on Treeves.

"I don't know what you are," Elio said. "But you're not a good liar."

Then he nodded his head towards Treeves.

"But he is an exceptional one, isn't he?"

Treeves watched the thought form in Elio's mind. He had decided to go for the pistol and force Time to fire. He believed his best chance was to duck behind Lang's desk and hope his luck would change.

Treeves signaled, "*Now.*"

Before Elio could act on his own decision, Time was on him. Elio's survival instinct forced him to use the knife to defend himself. He held the handle so that the blade faced downward, edge towards his opponent. When Time reached him, he swept it across, trying to slow Time's advance. He planned to step quickly forward and thrust downward at his attacker.

But Time didn't step back. He allowed the razor-sharp blade to pass within an inch of his unprotected chest. Then he blocked the downward follow-up with his left forearm, sliding his hand to grab Elio slightly above the wrist. He saw the opening, formed an appropriate fist with his right hand, and drove it into Elio's throat, crushing his windpipe. The struggle was over. All that was left was to finish as quietly as possible.

Maintaining his grip on his Elio's wrist, Time grabbed his left elbow with his right hand and turned it upwards until Elio's fingers loosened their grip on the knife. Time removed it, and because of its length, chose to slide the blade into Elio's right eye.

Time lowered Elio's body to the floor.

"*Are we being monitored?*" Time signaled.

"There's a communications device in Elio's left pocket, but it's muted," Treeves said in Dutch.

English was their native language, but it was too widely spoken. Although English was not the native language of the targets, all of them spoke it fluently. If the remaining targets could possibly hear them, Dutch would most likely be mistaken for English, and there was a near-zero probability that any of the surviving targets were fluent in Dutch.

Time was reasonably fluent in Dutch, but it was a challenge to keep his cadence, tone, and sentence structure sounding like the byplay of a physician and his assistant. It was nothing for Treeves to maintain the intonation and phrasing of someone expressing concern over the prince's condition.

"How is he doing?" said Treeves.

"Without the quickly dying, he holds his own," Time replied, making slight grammatical errors.

As a linguist, he was not in the same league as Treeves. On the other hand, he'd just killed three well-armed targets in close-order combat and he wasn't breathing hard.

Treeves, an uncanny mimic, said something using Elio's voice and his native language. Time blinked as he heard the voice of the man he had killed only moments ago. No matter how many times he had heard Treeves perform his vocal acrobatics, it never failed to give him an eerie sensation in the pit of his stomach, as if Elio was speaking to him directly from the beyond.

Treeves removed the communications device from Elio's jacket. As soon as he turned up the volume control, an agitated voice crackled over the speaker.

"What's happening there? We're behind schedule."

"You heard the scream?" Treeves said, using Elio's voice.

"Yes, it barely came through."

"That was the CDL. I had to teach him a lesson. It's nothing to be concerned about. You'll hear from me in ten minutes and we'll continue as planned."

"Understood, brother."

Treeves made certain the device was muted again and placed it back in Elio's pocket.

"Did he believe that?" Time said.

Treeves narrowed his eyes.

"Is that intended to be an insult?" he said. "Did I ask you if you were certain you could eliminate these targets before I told you in what order you should do it?"

Time had no response. Instead, he gestured towards the prince.

"What about him?" he said. "What did they give him?"

"They didn't give him anything," said Treeves.

After a moment Time said, "You?"

"This morning with his tea."

"So, he was with them?"

"The general and I suspected as much all along, but he was an important man. The general wanted proof beyond a doubt. It had to be done correctly."

"How did you know it would be today?"

"I wasn't certain, but when I was with him this morning there were strong indicators. So I poisoned him. In the event that the operation was altered or canceled, I would have found a way to give him the antidote. It's too late now. In about fifteen minutes, he'll be dead. It will appear as if the excitement caused him to succumb to a coronary."

"I should have been told about him," Time said. "What if I altered my tactics to minimize the danger to him?"

Treeves allowed a perplexed expression to cross his features. He hated stating the obvious.

"Why on earth would you attempt to protect him? I didn't tell you to protect him. Your tactics, as you put it, are to follow my instructions."

"You know, there's always the slight possibility that I'll find myself out here on my own."

Without saying a word, Treeves made it obvious that he believed Time wouldn't last long on his own.

"Must I repeat what you were supposed to have absorbed in the first week of your training? Your first priority is to prevent anything from happening to me."

Time knew this was an argument he had no possibility of winning. He decided to direct their discussion to more pressing matters.

"Speaking of priorities," he said, glancing at the office door.

"I've seen enough of those two," said Treeves. "They're not imminent concerns. One has too much discipline and the other not enough initiative. Unless Elio calls for them, they'll stay outside. We have sufficient time."

"Sufficient time is always a plus."

Treeves ignored the word play.

"Our task is to locate the target who just spoke with me as quickly as possible," he said. "He's on this floor, in one of the ten offices that surround us. He's a fanatic, willing to die, and armed with biological weapon potent enough to kill every living thing within half a mile of this building."

CHAPTER 3

CALLIE

Berkeley, California
Winter, 2018

I'd been walking fifteen feet behind her for at least two blocks. I wasn't sure if I was following her yet. When I caught a glimpse of her face as I turned onto Shattuck Avenue, I felt as if an invisible rope was pulling me closer to her.

She was wearing a soft leather jacket that didn't hide her athletic figure. Her black leather boots ended just below her knees. Her hair fell in wavy golden strands, ending a few inches below her shoulders. It crossed my mind that any sane man would crave her permission to run his hands through it.

I'd known my share of beautiful women. I never tried to meet any of them by following them down the street. So with every step, I thought about how to go about doing something I wouldn't have considered a good idea before that morning in early February.

I should have been hurrying to Chocolat to pick up a cake for Jackson. Chocolat sold a cake that resembled a big hockey puck and tasted of rich dark chocolate as sweet as victory and as smooth as warm butter. Of course, Jackson could have whipped up one for himself, but hell, it was his birthday. He shouldn't have to bake his own cake, even though I knew he would. I also knew Jackson's cake would be better.

But none of that was important anymore. I'd made up my mind. I was definitely following the golden hair swaying in front of me, trying out various openings in my mind. None of them seemed quite right. I needed something unusual to happen. Fortunately, it was an unusual day.

That morning it had snowed in Berkeley, California.

The inhabitants of this college town, many of whom had never experienced snow, were skidding around as if the half-inch of white covering the ground had converted the entire town into the world's most perilous skating rink.

Suddenly, her boots slid forward from under her and she went down hard on her bottom. She instinctively tried to break her fall with her right hand. When someone begins to fall backwards, it takes real discipline to implement the logic that your butt is harder to break than your wrist.

When she hit the ground, her purse snapped open and its contents scattered around her. The snow kept them from going very far.

I rushed over to offer assistance. I must admit that if she'd been a burly man rather than a gorgeous young woman, I probably would have just kept on walking, chuckling discreetly.

Still, once I was sure she was unhurt, I had to stifle a laugh. She'd gone down with a comical thud.

She looked up at my hands, outstretched to help her. Through her disheveled hair, I saw large sea-green eyes and the kind of nose that keeps a woman desirable throughout all stages of her life. Her skin was flawless, a shade of coffee, heavy on the cream.

I waited. Beautiful woman aren't always all they're cracked up to be. Often, they can be as much of a pain in the ass as falling hard on a slippery sidewalk.

However, I immediately knew that she had much more than her looks. She exuded a wonderful mixture of determination and mild humiliation. While fully appreciating the awkwardness of her situation, she was determined to overcome it with dignity.

"I don't need help, thank you," she said.

She tried to rise and promptly fell back in the same spot again.

"Maybe not, but a bit of leverage never hurts," I said.

"On the other hand," I continued, nodding at the sidewalk.

A hint of a smile raised the corners of her full mouth. We're all aware that it happens. But how and why? Was it some pheromone I breathed in? Was it the way she raised her eyebrows when she gave me that smile? How I did I suddenly become convinced that I would give everything I owned, fight hopeless battles, and suffer hardships just to see her smile like that once in a while for years to come.

She took my hands and I helped her to her feet. We both bent down to gather up the contents of her purse.

"Please, really. I don't need your help," she said.

I rose quickly.

"Thank you again."

She turned and began walking away.

23

"It doesn't snow much in Brazil either, does it?" I said to her back.

She turned around, staring at me with what I interpreted to be an expression of concern and confusion.

"Why would you say that about Brazil?"

"Well, I'm almost positive your hair is natural, but it's obvious that you have some Latin blood. You speak English with a mild accent. It's a Romance language, but it actually sounds more Russian than Italian or Spanish. Also, there's a Rio Mardigra symbol dangling from that bracelet on your wrist."

She tilted her head slightly.

"You're very observant, aren't you? Like some Sherlock Helmes detective."

That's how she pronounced it: *Helmes*.

"Did I also mention that a Brazilian Passport fell out of your bag?"

She studied my face with great care, as if she were trying to make up her mind about something serious.

"You know," I said. "If you're not used to it, it's quite dangerous out here. Perhaps I could help you reach the safety of a nearby coffee shop. We could wait out the blizzard. I'm sure the streets will be safe in about an hour."

"So, you just want to try and pick me up."

"I believe I've already tried to pick you up. Twice."

"Twice was enough, I think. Goodbye now. Better luck with the next woman."

"Wait, Calena."

She turned again and displayed a disproportionate reaction of fear and anger.

"How do you know my name?" she said. "Is this some kind of test? Who sent you?"

"I have no idea what any of that means," I said. "I glanced at the things in your purse when I bent to help you. I saw that name on a letter and I took a chance. No one sent me. You're not wearing an engagement or wedding ring. If the thought of having a coffee with a man who is simply trying to get to know you better frightens you in that way, perhaps you should talk about it with me. Sometimes help comes when you least expect it."

"So, you'd like to find out all about me. My terrible fears, my tortured soul."

She shook her head from side to side.

"Americans," she snorted. "And after I unburden myself, will you tell me all your hopes and dreams? In your apartment, perhaps?"

I grinned.

"I have a house," I said. "And I'm not going home. At least, not until I'm sure I can see you again."

"I'm sorry, but I have no interest in seeing you again. For the last time, goodbye. I must go now."

"Stop," I said.

She stopped.

"You can walk away, but there's no chance you won't see me again. I already know too much about you. I'm sure I want to know more. I will find you."

"No," she said quickly. "You can't. Why would you do that? You don't understand."

"Forgive my bad manners. I know your name. You should know mine. I'm Michael Case. I'm sure you have good reasons to think that we can't be friends, but perhaps you're wrong. We wouldn't be standing here talking if you didn't want to talk to me. You'd already be gone. I also know that you can talk with me and nothing bad will come of it. I have resources you can't imagine."

Her eyes narrowed. Her next words came out very carefully.

"Believe me, there are reasons we shouldn't be talking that you cannot imagine."

She shivered slightly, even though the sun was already melting the snow. And, although I'd known her for only a few minutes, I hated to see it.

"Okay, I won't push. May I suggest a compromise? Have one coffee with me. Just one coffee. If after that, you don't want to see me again, I swear that you never will."

"How do I know I can trust you?" she said.

I didn't have to answer. It was clear that she'd already decided.

For the next four months we spent as much time together as we could. She had begun a career as a realtor and often had to attend seminars. I traveled as well. Whenever we could, we'd take walks, go to shows, or drive north to tour the wineries. We went sailing on Aram Cooper's yacht a few times.

The one thing we never did was touch.

After we'd been together a couple of weeks, I thought I sensed something and I tried to kiss her. Her reaction was so dramatic that I never tried again. I waited patiently to know if she'd ever want to be more than my friend. Because that's what she had become. Not only my friend, but my best friend. I could make her laugh about some foolish thing and then keep going, saying more and more until she collapsed with laughter so powerful she'd hold up her hands to make me stop, so she could catch her breath.

We didn't talk about the past or the future. We talked about things we saw and felt in the moment.

Callie was in her twenties and I was ten years older. Our minds intertwined on some subjects and we disagreed on others. Whenever we disagreed, we'd debate late into the night, respecting each other's opinions while trying as hard as possible to prove each other's arguments were completely ridiculous.

After a couple of months, she came to my house. She had wanted to see it ever since the afternoon that I mentioned I had a swimming pool in my backyard.

"A real swimming pool?" she said.

"A big one," I said. "Olympic size. The solar panels keep the water very comfortable."

"Can people see it, Case?"

Sometimes Callie called me Case, as Jackson always did in his lilting Haitian accent. Aram invariably referred to me as Michael. Callie went from one to the other with her mood.

"No one can see anything," I said. "My house is at the top of the hills, just below the park. The security enclosures are one-way view only. You can see out as if they weren't there, but no one sees in. Not even from the air. Aram comes to the house and if he gets an idea about SAM or anything else, he wants to scratch it down immediately. He's not taking any chances after what happened three years ago. However, if you're shy, I should tell you that Louie and Fred always monitor the areas outside the walls of the house."

"Louie and Fred?"

"Two of Aram's private security team. They take shifts on the vid monitors watching two acres in every direction. They also keep an eye on external areas like the deck and the pool. Considering the electronic security in the house, the voice recognition sensors, the hidden panic buttons, the vids I can activate, I thought it was overkill, but Aram insisted on it."

"So, no topless sun bathing?"

"Well, Louie and Fred are sworn to secrecy. And part of the deal was that I'd be the one to sign their checks. I've gotten them to close one eye once in a while."

"I'll bet," she said. "I can't believe you have a swimming pool in the hills. I've never heard of such a thing. How did you get around the zoning restrictions? The water laws? How is it possible?"

"It's specially constructed. The water is one-hundred-percent recycled. Another advantage of the security enclosures. In addition to keeping Aram's notes from prying eyes, they also gather condensation from the air, filter it, and feed it back into the pool as needed. There aren't many people in Berkeley who have as much money as I do."

"Aram has more money," Callie said, with a knowing smile.

"Oh, yes. The city council likes their parks and monuments. Aram could probably buy a big chunk of the Berkeley Hills and turn it into an amusement park ride if he felt like it, but he prefers pouring his money into that floating Sausalito palace he calls a houseboat. That is, of course, whenever he gets away from his lab, which isn't often."

I smiled.

"You know, you're one of the few people Aram actually likes," I said. "I think it's because you get along so well with Kristin."

"Kris is amazing."

"My, I love to swim," she added, softly.

"So come and swim," I said.

I let her daydream about the pool for a minute or two.

"I even stock bathing suits."

I interpreted her expression.

"Of course, only for my close relatives and the truly needy," I said.

"You don't have any close relatives. Anyway, you can relax. I come fully equipped. I'm from Rio. I was born in a bikini."

When I had the first of many discussions with architects and contractors and decorators, I told them that their most important goal was to integrate the house as much as possible into the surrounding neighborhood. Having said that, they had two other priorities: The house needed to be as comfortable as it was beautiful, and it had to be so beautiful that it would take a first-time visitor's breath away.

When Callie saw the house, her expression let me know that not only had they had taken my instructions seriously, but they had succeeded beyond my imagination.

"Say hello and your name," I said, as she crossed the threshold.

"Hello, Michael's house. I'm Calena Lacerda."

"And I'm Michael Case. Today's code is *Shilo*. Calena Lacerda, A.K.A Callie, is my guest. Save in memory. There are no security restrictions on her."

Aram's program identified my voice and responded, "Understood, Mr. Case."

I let her wander around, interfering only when her hand came too close to a canvas of swirling oils.

"Don't get any closer," I warned her. "If you do, a large group of heavily armed men will bang down the front door."

"You're joking!"

"Well, I could probably stop them."

"No, I mean, you're not telling me that's the real one?"

"Incredible, isn't it? It was a gift."

We swam, and ate, and laughed, and swam again. All day, I fought desires and impulses. It was difficult to prevent myself from telling her how much I wanted her to stay with me forever.

Every day, I had bad hours when thoughts of holding her, kissing her, being with her muted everything around me. I was happy and miserable, both emotions coming within minutes of each other. It was only because I'd spent much of my life controlling my thoughts and feelings that I was able to hide my desire for her. It took a great deal of my concentration to make her believe that, if being her friend was all I could ever hope to be, that would have to be enough.

As for Callie, once in a while I caught a certain look, a quick glance. In an unguarded moment, she might move her hand towards my arm. There were times when I sensed small indications that she wanted more. She wasn't a prude and didn't tease me. It was obvious that she enjoyed my company, but she never crossed the line between friendship and intimacy. I wondered if she believed, as I did, that if we ever embraced, there would be no going back. She let me know, in a hundred different ways, that we could never be lovers.

About four months after I met her, I was waiting for her at my house in the early evening. We had tickets to the San Francisco Ballet. She told me that she was showing a couple of houses in the hills and she'd meet me at my place for a drink before we left.

When I opened the door, she stunned me. She was wearing a clinging red dress with a plunging neckline. Her heels raised her so that her lips were almost even to mine. The only jewelry she wore was the diamond earrings I had tricked her into taking from me.

"We have time for a glass of wine," I said.

"That's good," she said, taking a small step down into the living room.

I poured two glasses of Cabernet from the winery I financed for a friend in Napa Valley. We didn't make money. He loved running the winery. I loved the wine he was capable of making whenever the grapes cooperated.

I turned to hand a glass to her and we froze. She was breathing deeply. Her jaw was set. She stared at me. I was puzzled and I smiled.

She said, "No."

Then she blinked slowly and evenly, as if concentrating on that small act could make her stop what happened next.

"I can't," she whispered. "I can't anymore."

I threw the glasses aside as she rushed towards me. She put her hands on the sides of my face, kissing me deeply. I discovered my fantasies about her had been inadequate. She tasted like desire. Pure, thrilling, uncontrollable.

I wouldn't let her mouth leave mine as I reached around behind her and opened the back of her dress. It fell to the floor. My breath caught in my throat when I saw she wasn't wearing a bra. I'd seen her in a bikini, but I was unprepared for her naked body.

She pulled her mouth away.

"Take off your shirt," she said, starting on the buttons.

Callie moaned. Everywhere I touched her was silken and firm. The thrill of being with her after I had wanted her for so long intensified the certainty that I had fallen in love with her the day I met her.

Because she'd been so distant, I felt I should be gentle, but Callie released something powerful within her. She pulled me against her and backed us against the wall. We kissed until we both needed more.

When I found a certain spot, she entwined her fingers in my hair and told me, "Yes, querida, hard, kiss me hard there. I need you."

We weren't simply making love. The pressure of her against me was primal. It felt as if we had discovered lovemaking, the joy and power of it.

"I can't wait any longer," she breathed through our kisses.

I tore off my clothes and kicked them aside. She still wore her heels. I balanced her weight as we joined together, as if we had rehearsed it a thousand times. We moved against each other, the rhythm of our muscles locked together. It was an eternity and only a short time when suddenly she cried out my name and her body spasmed, pulsing around me. A powerful release broke through her and I felt a great happiness rush through me. I knew that if her pleasure had come so strong and quickly, it could only mean that she had been with me in her mind all day. That was only fair. She had been in my mind for four months.

After the first waves passed through her, she relaxed and breathed deeply, making small grunting noises in the back of her throat.

I gently kissed her forehead.

This is the moment, I thought.

As she leaned against me, I was positive that she never would have let this happen unless she had fallen in love with me.

She felt me inside her, looked up shyly, and said, "You're not finished?"

I picked her up. Holding her against me, I kissed deeply and carried her towards one of the bedrooms.

"Finished?" I said, smiling down at her. "We've just started."

She laughed softly.

"Oh yes, yes, we have. Jump started, I'd say."

That night we played together, exploring each other. We cried out and we laughed. As the sun began to rise, Callie's head rested on my chest. Her hair tickled my cheek.

"You're sure this is what you want?" I said.

"I'm sure it doesn't matter," she said, raising her head to kiss me. "It had to be done. And now it's done."

She kissed me once again, this time more deeply.

"Don't worry, querida," she said. "My father used to say that worries are only the foolish part of imagination."

She smiled.

"It sounds better in Portuguese," she said.

"In that case, use the other part and imagine this," I said, pulling her closer.

Afterwards, she asked for some clothes so she could go home, a place that I'd never been. I began to argue, saw her face, and stopped. I had learned that when Callie was determined to do something, it was nearly impossible to change her mind. It was one of things I loved about her.

At the door, I kissed her goodbye. We made plans to see each other again. As she was walking away, she suddenly turned.

"Michael," she said. "Please, no matter what happens, you must promise you'll forgive me."

CHAPTER 4

RVX

New York's Financial District
Summer, 2012

Time clamped his jaw shut.

"You can be angry later," said Treeves. "Anger has no place here."

Of course, Treeves was right. However, his admonishment only made Time angrier. He hated it when it seemed as if Treeves was reading his thoughts.

Time said, "You didn't think it was worth mentioning during the pre-mission briefings that we'd be coming in close contact with a compound resembling VX? What about dirty bombs? Are there any of them lying around posing as paperweights?"

Although it was next to impossible to determine with any degree of certainty what Treeves enjoyed, Time believed that his genius partner took no small satisfaction in always being one step ahead of everyone around him. Treeves knew precisely how to regularly remind Time that he was nothing more than his Weapon.

"The RVX was not originally an element in your part of this operation," Treeves said patiently, as if he were explaining a plot twist in an overly complicated storybook to a child. "These operations often take turns off their predetermined paths. Unexpected complications are an inherent part of our work."

Time knew a way to calm himself. He used his only advantage. He was one of the few people on earth who knew Edgar Treeves well enough to rattle his extremely well-constructed cage.

"Well, if, as you say, our target is suicidal, why don't we just wait here in Lang's office?" he said. "Perhaps the annoying little son of a bitch will decide to kill himself without inconveniencing us any further."

Of course, Treeves recognized the tactic. Yet he was forced to suppress a reaction. He was playing out scenarios in his mind, much the way a chess grandmaster imagines pieces advancing on the board, studying positions that don't yet exist. Treeves had told Time in the past that he could be thrown off his game by distractions in the same way that Bobby Fischer claimed that noise and lights affected his game during the world championship match that he won against Boris Spassky.

Treeves said, "I would appreciate it if you would curb your desire to bait me by wandering off topic with your attempts at infantile humor. Instead, please provide me with a brief summary of what you know about VX. I wish to be reassured that you have a realistic appreciation of the threat level we currently face."

"If you insist," said Time. "Let me begin by making it clear that VX is such horrible stuff I should have be told if we were going to be anywhere within a mile of it. It was developed in England in the early nineteen-fifties and is one of the most potent nerve agents. It's an odorless tasteless oily amber liquid with a consistency similar to motor oil. Due to its slow evaporation rate, it continues to poison the atmosphere around it for extended periods."

"Go on," said Treeves.

"VX prevents the proper operation of chemicals in the body that act as the off switch for glands and muscles. It's not wise to have its vapors anywhere near your skin, eyes, or lungs. Within seconds of exposure, a victim will experience painful watery eyes, blurred vision, runny nose, drooling, excessive sweating, chest tightness, drowsiness, headache, rapid breathing, confusion, weakness, and that's not all. The unfortunate subject who gets a more concentrated dose experiences convulsions, paralysis, and respiratory failure. Any direct exposure to VX without immediate and comprehensive counter measures is invariably fatal."

Treeves slowly nodded. It was the only indication that he was listening.

"Officially, civilized nations have banned it. Only the United States and Russia still maintain stockpiles and only the Russians seem inclined to sell it. Fortunately, targets dislike the stuff as much as we do. It's way too volatile and it has the hydrogen bomb factor. MAD. Mutually Assured Destruction. Targets don't use it for fear that we'll turn around and let it loose on them."

"An adequate summary," said Treeves. "You're correct about their reluctance to employ VX. However, what if an ambitious and egomaniacal prince agreed to participate in a complex plot that concluded with him appearing to save lower Manhattan from a dose of deadly nerve agent, thereby giving him a halo of heroism bright enough to gain absolute control of his country?"

Treeves was speaking as if he were carrying on an interesting conversation with himself about a personnel problem.

"However, as you stated, there remains the issue of volatility," he said: "Unfortunately, science always moves forward, especially the field of more effective ways to exterminate humans. Fourteen months ago, a Texas defense contractor, funded by our government, developed RVX, or Reagent-VX. Until a short time ago, that firm was represented by the late Charles Lang."

Treeves glanced over at Lang's body before continuing.

"RVX evaporates at a much slower rate and is almost seven times more potent than VX. It comes in two parts. One part is a liquid that's completely harmless until a reagent is added, converting that substance into active RVX. You could carry the liquid in one hand and the reagent in the other and drop both of them on the floor. As long as they don't mix, they're harmless. However, if they come in contact with each other and, for example, you allowed them to flow down the side of a building such as this, well…"

That was too much.

"Dammit, why wasn't I briefed about this?" Time said. "I'm not some infallible machine. What if Elio had just enough time to retrieve that pistol and shoot you? Then what? I'd be stumbling around in the dark."

"Has it escaped your notice that I am briefing you?" said Treeves. "And why do you insist on harping on the possibility of my death? I don't expect to be killed. Even without you, I'm confident I can extract myself gracefully from any reasonable situation. With you, getting killed would be a very bad stroke of fortune indeed. I need your complete concentration on your mission priorities. I'll transmit additional information to you if and when you need it. You're intelligent enough, but thinking your way out of the situation we're facing at the moment is not in your purview. As for briefing you regarding the RVX, the general and I decided against it, unless it became unavoidable. Your concealment quota is adequate, but we both know you don't perform at my level. You can slip. I will not."

"I can't read you," said Time. "We both know that. But I know how the general thinks. How you help him think. Elio's plan was to buy the RVX from Lang, smuggle it out, and somehow have the prince save the day. They were never planning to pour it down the side of this building. We came for the prince. Probably for Lang as well. The general wanted to be absolutely sure they were on the wrong side. If so, he wanted them dead. Those people outside were the audience for our staging of their deaths."

"Yes, that's correct," said Treeves.

He was becoming impatient with the discussion. His thoughts had already moved on. Treeves had worked with Time long enough to know he would continue to perform as ordered regardless of how he felt about it. Time had been trained to be more than a highly effective killing apparatus. He was totally controlled by Treeves' intellect. They were not friends.

However, Time could have never developed into what he was without his respect for the general and without a connection to Treeves that went beyond trust.

Treeves said, "We don't provoke our opponents until and unless it's necessary. We react. My responsibility is to make sure you have a chance to act before our targets do. This could have gone well. Elio would have killed Lang. The prince would have appeared to expire in Lang's office due to stress. Elio should have ordered the hidden target to exit the building as they had planned. Lang had secret exits installed and he was happy to share that information with his buyers. By seducing a high-level member of this firm, we were able to discover and secure the hidden escape routes from this floor."

"Beth Ellsworth."

"Precisely. She wanted complete control of this firm. Have you ever met anyone with money who felt they were rich enough? The general and I attempted to locate the missing RVX, but Lang was clever. He used a layer through a layer. Even Lang himself didn't know where the RVX was stored. He only knew how he could get to it when it was needed. Despite what you've imagined in the past, I can't read minds. The general had a high-level threat team ready to pick off the target with the RVX as soon as he appeared. However, minutes before you came into Lang's office, I was convinced that Elio had changed his mind. If you like, I'll explain the details later, but I saw the profile change. He had decided to make history. So, while Lang was still alive, he spoke to the target holding the RVX and told him to stay where he was. It was then that I decided the most prudent reaction was to eliminate all the targets in this office."

"Question my decisions if you like," Treeves continued. "However, remember that, not ten minutes ago, you would have chosen a different killing sequence. I think you would have begun with the woman and the seated man would have put a bullet in the center of your chest. His overall reaction quotas and his peripheral vision was vastly superior to hers and, judging by the way he held his weapon, I can say with over a ninety-five percent certainty that he was an excellent shot."

Time let it go. There was no point in arguing with Treeves, especially because he'd never known his analyses to be wrong.

"Well, there's no chance I'll give anything away now," Time said.

He glanced at Lang's broken corpse.

"He was something of a genius too, wasn't he? I guess sometimes even geniuses are fools."

Treeves made a small noise in the back of this throat.

"In any case," he said, "it's a moot point. From the beginning, they planned to kill him. At the proper time, the prince would have been released after convincing Elio and the targets to surrender peacefully on the guaranteed condition they'd be remanded to the prince's country. After a year or two in a comfortable prison, they'd enjoy a lifetime of privilege on the public dime. The prince would also have Lang's RVX to use or sell as a nice little bonus."

"Not a bad plan," said Time. "I suppose I don't need to ask how you know so much about it."

"I can be very persuasive," Treeves said, without a hint of modesty. "Plus the title of Diplomatic Corporate Liaison carries with it an unbreakable aura of confidentiality. I've spent the past ten days convincing the prince that his interests were much closer to mine than he might have suspected. Naturally, I couldn't push, so I wasn't privy to the persons, time, and place, but he was very proud of this venture. It wasn't all that difficult to allow him to convince me how clever he was and how powerful he would shortly become. Imagine how credible his story would have been if he'd left the building with a Diplomatic Corporate Liaison supporting the tale of his heroic stance in the face of mad terrorists?"

"What about the sleeper outside? And this woman here?"

Time paused.

"For that matter, what about me?"

"I would imagine this is how the story would unfold," Treeves said. "You managed to grab a pistol. Then you shot the guard, the woman shot you, and, just before you expired, you managed to get off a final shot to finish her off. You were quite foolish to attempt such heroics."

"Naturally. Bad judgment on my part. May I ask why you've finally decided to tell me all of this now?"

"Obviously, you had to know some of it. Telling you the rest helped to focus my thoughts. It was a good use of my time as I reviewed the situation and decided our next move."

Treeves looked at the door. He was ready. He reverted to signals.

"The younger target. Restraint only."

Time walked across the room. He stood, his back against the wall, the door to his left. Treeves moved to the other side. He signaled and Time opened the door about five inches.

Treeves, perfectly mimicking Elio's voice and using his native language called out, "I have orders for Freddie. Send him in."

The target guarding the hostages assumed that it was time for Freddie to make his final exit and motioned for him to go into Lang's office. The young target entered as if he were strolling into a dorm room. He seemed pleased that he'd been upgraded from hostage control to the center of the action.

Treeves quickly closed the door. The target's Glock was held loosely in his hand, his finger not even close to the trigger. Time formed a flat plane with his right hand. With his index finger pressed against his thumb, he smashed the side of his hand into the bridge of the target's nose, breaking it. The kid's eyes watered and pain rendered him mute. Time took away the Glock and used it to hit the target almost gently behind his right ear. He placed his right hand over the kid's mouth and used his left foot to help the target to the ground by bending his knee from the back. Then Time moved behind him, put down the gun, and placed his left forearm against the target's throat.

With his lips close to the guard's right ear, Time whispered, "I can break your neck faster than you can fill your lungs with enough air to make a sound. Grunt very softly if you understand."

The kid grunted.

"Put your hands in front of you," said Time.

Treeves secured them with a piece of electrical cord.

"Where is the other man?" Treeves said.

In a panicky whisper, the kid said, "Who are you?"

His eyes widened as he took in the carnage in the room.

"Don't hurt him," said Treeves.

Time understood and did the opposite. The kid grunted and began to sweat.

"I don't know what you want me to say," he said, pain straining his voice.

Time gave him a limited amount of air.

"Are you talking about the guy outside?" the kid said. "He's the only one I know about."

Treeves signaled, "*Lying.*"

Time used two fingers of his right hand to apply pressure to a nerve bundle underneath the target's left ear. A lightening bolt of pain shot from his toes to jaw. Time held him tighter. The kid began to tremble. Time tightened his grip to deal with the sweat.

"Listen, I'm just a guard," said the target. "I do what I'm told. When I got this job, they said there might be exercises like this."

Treeves whispered, "Look around you. Do they look as if they're part of an exercise?"

Treeves knelt in front of the target and considered him for a moment.

He whispered, "Listen, I believe you. We're Americans and we don't want to harm you, but you must tell us what you know. I'll tell my superiors you cooperated and we'll all get out of here alive. Where is the other man?"

Treeves knew every trick. No one could project sincerity like he could. But Time had been with him too long and clearly saw through the smoke and mirrors. Long ago, he discovered that, more than the violence inherent in his work, he disliked the dishonesty Treeves employed so skillfully.

"He's in the last office to the left, it's 2001," the kid said. "I don't know what he's doing there, but if anything bad happens, I'm supposed to go and knock four times."

"Show me how. Knock on the floor," said Treeves.

The target knocked on the floor with the knuckles of this right hand. Twice quickly, a pause, and then twice quickly again.

"Is that all you know?" said Treeves, tilting his head slightly.

"Yeah, that's all I know. Please, you gotta believe me."

The kid looked at the prince.

"He's with us," he said, desperately. "Jesus, he talks to the president. Just ask. I'm one of the good guys, like you."

"*Eliminate,*" Treeves signaled.

Time snapped the target's neck. He did his best to make sure there was no awareness or pain.

Treeves said something in the voice of the leader. He answered himself in the voice of the kid who had just died. He saw the expression on Time's face.

"It had to be done," Treeves said, switching back to Dutch.

"Was he telling the truth about thinking that he worked for our side because he worked for the prince?" Time said.

"Not entirely. He was using that as a rationale. However, it's irrelevant."

He gestured at the bodies in the room.

"He saw our faces and what we'd done," Treeves said. "He'd been bought. There was no other option."

"We have a very limited window," Treeves continued. "The target holding the RVX must be a serious man, not easily rattled, but by now, he'll be agitated. There's probably no code or set check-in times that could be accidentally missed. The prince was more valuable to them than the dispersal of the RVX."

"Perhaps you shouldn't have been so quick to neutralize everyone," Time said.

"This is a complex scenario," said Treeves. "One can't take back moves. It's pointless to think like that."

Time had no inclination to argue philosophy during combat, but it crossed his mind that he'd just killed a defenseless young man. Someone, somewhere, might miss him in the days ahead. He wasn't inclined to think of it as a game.

"Focus," Treeves said. "Give yourself five seconds to think of those people in the reception area and everyone within twenty blocks of this building, then clear your mind."

Treeves nodded at the guard's body.

"That was a target," he said. "A clear and present threat to what we're here to do."

Time's lips tightened. No matter what his partner said, it always seemed as if Treeves could read minds. Whenever it was done to him, he felt exposed.

Treeves retrieved the site-to-site communicator. He weighed his options and then turned up the volume. As Elio, he spoke into the microphone.

"Where have you been? What are you doing?" the target holding the RVX responded.

Treeves answered using Elio's voice.

"Lang was stronger than I anticipated," he said. "I wanted more information about his source. I was wise to keep him alive. His treachery was limitless. You don't have the true reagent. If you mix and release the liquids now, they'll flow harmlessly down this building and we'll appear to be incompetent fools. Fortunately, Mr. Lang had the true reagent hidden here in his office."

Treeves stopped speaking. Asking questions at such a moment would raise the target's suspicion level. Treeves knew that most people wanted to talk, to convey information, especially in high stress situations. He waited.

"Don't worry," he heard the target say. "After you told me our plan had changed, I armed the dead man switch. I have a strong right hand. I can hold it until you bring me the true reagent."

"You're a good man. I won't be long and I'll bring Lang with me. The prince will be released. After that, I'll begin killing hostages. When the FBI hears the shots, they'll have to come after us. They'll be responsible for what comes next. We'll release the true death on them and you and I shall die a glorious death together."

Treeves closed the connection. He repeated the conversation word for word to Time.

"So it's simple," said Time. "We have a man determined to die with his thumb on a dead man's switch. If he releases it, the real reagent and the RVX will cover the side of this building."

"If you can't be discouraged from providing me with your strategic overview, at least be more precise with your words. The target said he had armed the switch and it was in his right hand. He didn't say his thumb was holding the trigger."

Time decided this was not the time to tell Treeves what he thought of his Medium's strategic overview.

He said, "What's important is how can we keep his thumb or whatever appendage he's using, holding down the trigger after he's dead."

"Correct," said Treeves. "We'll have to go in together."

"Of course. You told him you were bringing Lang. What do we go in as? Door-to-door weapons salesmen?"

"You could say that," said Treeves.

He glanced at the body of Lang.

"You must be joking. That won't work."

Treeves eyebrows came together slightly.

"Have you ever known me to joke during an operation? This man is no fool, but he'll hang on to his belief that he's in control as long as we give him the opportunity. It's a reasonable risk."

"I'll have to be Lang," Time said. "You'll need to interact with the target."

He nodded at Elio.

"You're inches taller than him," Time said.

"I can keep up the illusion for a short time. We'll use the fast drill, my right to your left. Complete focus on the target. I'm counting on the fact that he hasn't spent time in close proximity to Lang. In fact, most likely, they've kept him out of sight. Your hair color is similar and we'll make adjustments to your clothing."

Once Treeves decided on a course of action, he displayed no hesitation. They changed clothes as quickly as possible.

Even though he'd watched similar transformations in the past, Time still marveled at Treeves' ability to arrange his body so that he almost fit into Elio's clothes. He made a few expert cuts in the less visible areas of the garments. Treeves adjusted his height by bending his knees and dropping his shoulders. He practiced striding across the room and slipped into Elio's manner of walking, calling upon a photographic memory of his gait.

Treeves broke open a black pen and distributed the ink through his hair. Then he slicked it back to resemble Elio's style. He rubbed cologne off the dead man's throat and onto himself.

Although he was approximately Lang's height, it was more difficult for Time to transform himself. Perhaps the target had seen a picture of Lang. There was also the fact that the target believed that Lang had recently undergone severe physical punishment.

Treeves studied Time's face.

He said, "You understand what's needed?"

He lifted a heavy paperweight from Lang's desk.

Treeves said, "Ready?"

Time nodded.

Treeves hit him on the right cheek, aiming for a spot between Time's eye socket and jaw. It was a solid blow, enough to cause immediate swelling and bruising, but not enough to cause confusion or permanent damage.

"Once more," he said.

He struck Time with a glancing blow on the other cheek, using a rougher edge. A gash opened and blood streamed out.

"Good," said Treeves. "That should do. How do you feel?"

"Like perhaps you enjoyed that too much."

"Are you clear headed?"

"Enough to know I don't want another."

Treeves studied him closely.

"Fortunately, you don't require another. You're already swelling nicely. Remember to keep your head low. Be defeated, frightened."

"As opposed to my confident this-is-definitely-going-to-work self?" Time said.

He went to his medical bag. Inside, his fingers found a combination of pressure points on the cloth. A compartment snapped open and two objects fell into his hand. One was slim, about six inches long. The other was similar, but shorter. He also removed a bag of plasma.

"How close do you have to get to be sure we can make the switch in time?" said Treeves.

"There's no sure in a business like this," Time said. "It would be help if I had some physical characteristics. Could you tell anything from his voice? Will his reaction quota allow him to put up a defense?"

Treeves shook his head. "Too little time. We don't have anything. This man was always apart from us. You'll have to use your own discretion, moving as quickly as possible, of course."

"It's weak. I expect better from you."

"Save your comments for the debriefing. I'll ignore them then."

"Go in before me," Treeves continued. "Let him have a quick look at the damage on your face, then lower your head. I'll follow you. Don't move close to him right away. Go to the window. I imagine there's some kind of explosive charge on it. If this goes badly, at least we won't know about it. Pretend to change the reagent."

"Why don't I swap out the real reagent and then take him?"

"You'll never have that much time. This illusion will only last for seconds."

Treeves whispered something in the language of the targets.

"That means, 'Hold on tightly to the trigger.' We'll be on a two-count after that."

Time nodded.

"Repeat the phrase," Treeves said.

Time repeated it until Treeves was satisfied.

"Let's go," said Treeves.

Treeves opened the door and, with Elio's voice, ordered the hostages to turn their eyes to the floor. He growled that anyone who looked anywhere else would be immediately executed.

"Come here," Treeves said to the last visible target, standing on the far side of the room. "I have new instructions."

When the target was a few feet from Treeves, his eyes widened. Time rushed out and shoved the six-inch blade under his chin. He didn't allow him to fall to the floor. Wrapping one arm under his shoulder, Time dragged him out of view of the hostages.

Treeves reminded them that the floor had been wired with explosives and any attempt by them to move would mean certain death for all of them. However, if they cooperated, they would soon be free to go.

Treeves knocked the code on the door of the office numbered 2001. He cracked open the door and said he was coming in with Lang. The target responded.

Time opened the door and walked into the room. The target was in a standard office chair on wheels between the door and the window. He was sitting straight up with both his forearms on the arms of the chair. His right thumb was gripping the trigger of a device that he held in his palm.

When Time entered the room, he partially obscured Treeves, who spoke to the target and then casually stepped behind him, a natural move to keep an eye on Time, who was posing as Lang. He told the target holding the switch that Lang had the real reagent and it was fitting that the traitor should be the one to add it to the RVX. His final betrayal would be that he would destroy his own city. It was one thing to sell something so deadly. It was entirely different to be the one who actually deployed it.

Time moved to the window. He feigned pain in his body, as if he had been beaten in his torso as well as his face. He kept his distance as he passed by the target. Time had outstanding visual memory and he took a snapshot of how the man sat and held the device.

When he reached the window, he stopped and turned to face the target. Treeves and Time had him between them. There was no point in waiting any longer. Treeves said the phrase, jumped forward, clamped his right hand over the target's thumb and made his entire world the pressure he exerted to keep the keep the target's thumb on the trigger.

They were lucky. Treeves forward motion had pushed the chair closer to Time. It gave Time a split second extra to reach the target, place his left hand on his wrist, and slide down towards where Treeves was preventing him from releasing the trigger. The moment Time's fingers touched the top of Treeves' hand, they slid them apart, maintaining pressure while exchanging positions. Time now controlled the dead man's switch. They had practiced this type of exchange countless times.

Time placed his right hand on the target's right forearm, pinning him. Once he had control, he twisted the target's arm slightly counter clockwise, exposing the wrist. He counted on his speed to protect him from a defensive maneuver. Time brought his head down and used the small blade that he had placed in his mouth to slice deeply into the precise nerves that controlled the muscles of the target's hand.

He bent the wrist backwards. The target screamed as blood gushed from his artery and splattered Time's face and neck. To be certain he had control, Time released his right hand from his opponent's forearm, grabbed the target's hair, and pulled him face down onto his rising right knee. He connected well and knew the target would not be conscious as he bled out.

He said to Treeves, "Get them in here now. This is slippery as hell."

Treeves returned to where the hostages waited and, still in the guise of the leader, chose one of the more powerful cell phones from their possessions. He dialed a number that would automatically lock in a secure line.

He said, "We're ready, general. We need Mr. Reilly in 2001, stat."

Within minutes, the air filled with tear gas. A team of commandos rushed in, killing the dead targets, and rescuing the hostages. A secondary team, lead by Explosives Specialist Reilly, went to disarm the RVX.

Two bodies were brought in. They were anonymous corpses that had been collected precisely for this purpose. The United States would announce that four hostages, including the well-known attorney Charles Lang and a Diplomatic Corporate Liaison, were victims of a senseless terrorist act. Tragically, a heroic young Navy doctor, James Warren, had been killed attempting to protect the prince. However, the greatest loss was the prince, who had worked so tirelessly for peace. He suffered a fatal heart attack during the crisis.

Treeves and Time were brought out long after the hostages. By that time, the news stations had left. There was no mention of them in any reports of the incident because no one recalled anything particularly interesting about them.

CHAPTER 5

SCULPTURE

Berkeley, California
Summer, 2018

Callie's naked body slowly took shape. The block of Italian marble, slightly off-white to accentuate her curves, responded well as I carefully chiseled away the excess stone around her.

I was an amateur, but I was fortunate to have Antonio Cabal, an incredible teacher, who often reminded me, "Carving is easy, just keep using your chisels until you get to what you imagine is inside the marble and then stop."

After the first twenty times he repeated it, I said, "Didn't Michelangelo say that?"

"Maybe. And Noel Coward said that thinking up brilliant things to say is nothing. Knowing the appropriate time to say them. That is everything. Or something like that."

The life-size nude was an ambitious undertaking. I planned to give it to Callie on our wedding night. There was no chance that I'd ever produce anything that resembled Antonio's work, but I wasn't completely un-satisfied when I stepped back and saw that the statue was close to the image I held in my imagination.

Sculpting demanded all my attention. In return, it locked out memories of things I wish I could change. Also, opportunities I let slip away. To avoid distractions, my studio was located at the back of my estate. It contained only my tools and the most minimum security.

I wiped my hands. Suddenly, I felt a low-wattage jolt of electricity race through me. It was similar to the feeling you might experience if you were racing down a flight of stairs and, in the instant before you fell, your body realized that you had missed a step. I'd experienced the same type of feeling before. I came to think of it as a warning to be the most careful whenever my plans seemed to be progressing as smoothly as possible. I have no idea why I ignored it that night.

Four nights ago, I handed the keys to my fifty-five Falcon to the valet at Jackson Aurelian's restaurant on Shattuck Avenue. Three of America's other finest restaurants were all within walking distance. Jackson's location was a testament to both his confidence in his skill and the confidence of his friends who had invested in him.

When Jackson, pushing his Haitian sense of whimsy to the limit, decided to name his restaurant The Ahh Baloney Café, all of his friends, including me, had tried to talk him out of it. Now, six days a week, there was a month's wait for a reservation and his abalone baloney sold out every night.

I walked into the clean unassuming lines of the dining room and saw Callie waiting at our table. She looked as she always did, like a blazing campfire in a room full of candles.

"You are a monster," she said.

I kissed her and sat across from her.

"Can you possibly imagine what it's like to sit here hungry, watching waiters pass me by, carrying Jackson's amazing food?"

"And you are being dramatic," I said. "I can't believe Jackson let you sit here with nothing to eat. That would fly in the face of his religious beliefs."

"Of course, I had a little something, but I'm starving. I've been waiting for you to share the experience."

"You are, as always, too kind."

"Monster," she said.

"Deep apologies. Aram had me on a conference call with Apple. You can't imagine how they go on."

"Who? Aram or the Apple people? I know how Aram goes on when he's talking computers. At least, I think he's talking about computers."

AB's impeccable headwaiter, Henry, appeared. He was also an excellent sommelier.

"The wine, Mr. Case?"

"You choose something, Henry. Something extra special tonight."

"Of course," he said, as if my request was superfluous.

A well-trained waiter brought us two bowls of Haitian *Consommé a l'Orange*. We didn't need to order. Jackson would send out the food. The moment I placed a spoonful of *consommé* onto my tongue, I silently thanked Jackson's parents for the night that produced him. I hoped it gave them a fitting preview of the pleasure they were about to bring into the world.

Callie was absorbed in her meal with the kind of single-minded intensity that she applied to everything she found worthy. Since that first night we'd made love, I knew I wanted to marry her, but I was nervous that it was too soon to ask. It wasn't easy to predict her reaction whenever I tried to let her know how I felt. One moment, she was giving me everything, and then, suddenly, it was as if she turned into some charming woman that I'd just met.

Her father was Brazilian, her mother Irish. Calena Lacerda, fully alive for twenty-seven years. I watched her devour the consommé. Her long strands of golden hair were in danger of falling inside the edges of the bowl. Her sea-green eyes shone with a pleasure mirrored on her full smiled-shaped lips.

She was wearing a sleeveless pale green dress, cut low in both the front and the back, accenting all her assets. Simply looking at her sent fiery jolts of desire racing through me.

She felt me staring at her and looked up. She swallowed a final morsel.

"What?" she said.

"You've got a bit of *consommé* on your chin."

"Consider yourself fortunate," she said in her mild Portuguese accent.

She reached for her napkin.

"This is so good I almost stuck my whole face into it."

I laughed a bit too loudly. She tilted her head and studied me.

"Not so funny, Case," she said. "Something's on the mind, no?"

She waited for me to respond. I locked eyes with her for what seemed like a long time. Any trepidation about the proper moment faded away. All that remained was the certainty that I had no doubts.

"I love you," I said, trying to remember exactly how I wanted to say it. "More than anything I've ever loved, and more than anything I will ever love."

She assumed the pose of a movie ingénue, her head slightly tilted back and to the side, eyes looking off into the distance over my right shoulder.

"It's not something I get tired of hearing," she said, with a small sigh.

There it was. Her way of telling me I was coming too close. She was covering up, trying to keep me from asking too much. However, this time I wasn't letting go.

"I need *serious* now," I said.

I watched her decide. She came back to me and her foot touched my ankle under the table.

"Okay."

I reached into my pocket and took out the ring, a two-and-a-half carat flawless yellow diamond set in an antique band. I was told it would get a reaction and, when I placed it on the table in front of her, it did.

"Callie, we can get married in private tomorrow or you can have hundreds of guests and everything that goes with them. You can have it any way you want, though I guess you know Jackson would have a stroke if we picked someone else for the food. I know you're unwilling to share some things, but I don't care. There's nothing you could tell me that would change my mind. I'm not the best man in the world, but you'll never find another more willing to make your life everything it can be. Not to mention the fact that I laugh at your jokes."

She was staring at the ring. She looked like a woman standing on the ledge of a tall building, deciding whether to jump or to turn and walk away. I waited silently, as tense as if I was actually watching her on that ledge from a few feet away. I knew there was nothing more I could do or say to help her decide.

"The thing you said about how you laugh at my stupid jokes. That has to be, how do you say it, a clincher," she said. "Besides, Michael, you are the best man in the world."

She hesitated.

Then she said, "But I don't want City Hall. I need time."

"Say, 'Yes,' and then take all the time you need."

She nodded.

"Yes," she said.

I've always suspected that Jackson trained the waiters at AB to read lips. Less than a minute later, he arrived at our table, dressed in his chef's whites, stained by his evening's work. He was expertly opening a bottle of Bollinger Special Cuvée.

I'd met him the first night I arrived in California. His hair was shorter now and he'd shaved off his thick beard, leaving only a constant covering of short stubble. But except for those two alterations, he looked exactly the same as the day we bumped into each other at an otherwise dull party.

He was shorter than me, about five eleven, and thin, something that never ceased to amaze everyone. His metabolism must be set to overdrive to burn off all the calories he had to ingest to in order to season his creations. Most of his friends found it annoying that he could enjoy a large ice cream sundae at twelve midnight and wake up two pounds lighter in the morning.

He had a dark complexion and deep brown eyes. With his hooked nose and heavy jaw, no one had ever accused him of being too handsome, but that never seemed to trouble women. There's a widely held notion that writers and chefs always seem to find themselves surrounded by the most beautiful women and Jackson had certainly proved it to be true. If you're looking for a way to a woman's heart, start with words, and then seal the deal with a savory home-cooked meal.

Jackson's most prominent feature was his limitless energy. There were times when I heard him say he was tired, but it never seemed to prevent him from personally attending to every small detail that lifts a restaurant from great to extraordinary.

Two hours after we met, we both knew we'd be friends and now we had four solid years behind us.

"I don't believe it," he said, expertly pouring the champagne. "Honestly, I never thought it would happen, but I suspected his time was up about five minutes after I met you, Callie. Well, all I can say is that he's lucky he asked you and even luckier you said, 'Yes.' I was waiting in the kitchen, and the way you look tonight, if you had said, 'No,' I was ready to make my pitch."

"Don't be ridiculous," Callie said to Jackson. "How could you possibly be in love with me? I'm not smothered in pepper sauce! But, even so, I'm glad you waited until now to bare your soul because the choice would have been much too hard. You're both so incredibly handsome, strong, and charming."

"Don't stop now, missy," Jackson said. "You're rolling downhill and gaining speed."

"Let's see," Callie said. "I read in a magazine last week that you have a good man if he puts the cap back on the toothpaste and the toilet seat down when he's finished."

"Don't you believe it," Jackson said. "In this town, where can you find a straight guy who lifts up the seat before he begins?"

In my studio, I smiled at Jackson's line once again. I banged my hands against my overalls and watched the marble dust blow into the air.

I stepped out the door onto the grass just in time to see Callie emerge from the back of the house.

"There you are," she said.

"As are you," I said.

I opened my arms wide.

"Come here for a proper hello, future wife."

"Not a chance. You're covered in dust from head to toe. What are you doing in there? Sculpting a Rolls Royce?"

"You might say that."

"All right, then. Just close enough to kiss me."

I leaned towards her and caught the scent of Pineapple and Rum on her breath. She leaned back and giggled. She jumped up and down slightly. Callie was usually in a good mood, but I'd never seen her act positively giddy.

"You've been drinking. You didn't drive up here?"

"Taxi, silly."

She looked around.

"I have a big surprise for you."

"Really? How about telling me all about it in the shower?"

"Oh no. That would spoil everything. But I tell you what. You go and get cleaned up, be sure to put on a bathing suit, and then come down and take a swim with me."

"Well, that sounds like a plan."

The vid on a nearby stand hovered up.

That gave me just enough time to say, "Case."

It floated over and stopped a short distance from my face.

"Mr. Case, Fred here. Your perimeter alarms and video surveillance went out without warning. By now, you should be in a safe room and I see that you're not. A security team will arrive any second."

I looked up at the inconspicuous area where a small red light was blinking. I raised one eyebrow at Callie.

"Guilty," she said, a bit too loudly

Then she leaned in close to my ear.

"Okay. I turned off the perimeter security. Believe it or not, there are some things I rather not have Fred or Louie see."

"Fred, code word for today is *Archie*. I'm placing my wrist on the vid. Cancel the alert. The cameras and the alarm will go hot again in about forty minutes."

"You know I can't do that, Mr. Case. If Dr. Cooper finds out, he'll have my head."

"Dr. Cooper doesn't have to know, does he? I mean, even Dr. Cooper can't know everything. Tell you what, Frank, you know those Cuban Cigars you like so much and the forty-year-old scotch that goes so well with them? How about five boxes and two bottles get delivered to your home tomorrow morning?"

"Forty minutes?" he said.

"Starting now."

"I guess it's okay" he said, sounding like he was sure that it wasn't. "But, no matter what, everything goes back on in forty."

"No problem, Fred. Vid down."

The vid hovered back to its stand.

"As for you, darling…" I said, turning to Callie.

"Forty minutes isn't a very long time," she said. "The more of it you spend lecturing me, the less of it we'll have together, and I mean very together, in the pool."

"Blackmailer."

"Use the closest downstairs shower," she said. "No peeking."

As I began walking towards the house, Callie said, "Oh, and one more thing. Do you remember what Jackson said? About wanting to marry me?"

I smiled.

"You haven't changed your mind, have you? Decided to go with him instead of me? Was it the *Griot* that he somehow managed to make without pork?"

"No, I haven't changed my mind. But, after he's done at the restaurant tonight, can you get him to come up here? We'll have something to celebrate and I'm hoping he'll whip up something wonderful."

"Jackson wouldn't know how to whip up anything else."

I went into the house and stepped into the bathroom. After pulling off my clothes, I pushed them through the door of the clothes processor. I stepped into the large shower, spoke my preferred temperature and the six water jets, four soap jets, and nine drying jets made quick work of the marble dust.

I stepped out of the shower naked and thought about simply stepping out of the house the same way, but Callie had said to wear a bathing suit. I didn't want to do anything to alter her mood.

I walked to the closet area.

"Bathing suit, dark blue," I said.

The pool and the grounds around it were empty. I checked my watch. I'd been away for about ten minutes.

"Callie?" I shouted.

"Full-house intercom," I said. "Callie, I'm at the pool now. Where are you?"

"Okay," I said. "I'm going to do some laps. Time's a wasting. Twenty-eight minutes and counting."

The lights around the pool had been dimmed to reproduce a moonlit night. There was a short shallow end, about six feet long, then the depth dropped smoothly to twenty feet. The bottom had to be reinforced to support the weight, but I enjoyed practicing my scuba in the deep end. I stepped into the shallow end and followed with a horizontal dive. I turned over and looked through the pool's one-way cover at the night sky, luminescent with stars.

I began swimming laps with an even energy-conserving stroke. I probably went up and down the length of the pool four times before I changed my style and swam with my face submerged in the clear water. As I approached the edge of the deep end, the pool lights provided just enough illumination for me to make out a vague shape at the bottom.

I dove down to get a better view.

When I saw her, I thought she was playing some stupid trick on me.

Was this her idea of a surprise? That she could hold her breath underwater and scare the hell out of me? My mind wouldn't accept the expression frozen on her face as her hair floated around it. No bubbles escaped from her nose or mouth. Her eyes were open, doll-like and empty.

I was choking, unaware that I had screamed her name under the water.

I grabbed her shoulders, pulled her to the surface, dragged her out of the water, and placed her on her back. I started CPR, but I knew she had been in the pool the entire time I swam laps over her. The thought forced me to push down bile that rose into my throat. As I forced air into Callie's slack mouth, I knew it was too late. It was much too late.

I stopped and stared at her, hoping I would wake up.

My mind wouldn't accept that Callie was gone. Forever.

"No, that can't be," I said, to the empty night air.

It wasn't right. Time needed to back up. She'll be alive and I'll stop this. I'll protect her and we'll be together like it has to be. In this world we had made, of security vids and advertising follows, you were never really sure you were alone. But without Callie, I'd be alone for the rest of my life.

I was cold. The night had changed. Everything had changed. I wanted to lie next to her.

I said, "Vid Up. Level One."

Fred came on immediately.

"Mr. Case," he said, calmly. "I cannot ignore that."

Level One was a code for the highest-level threat. It was roughly equivalent to the antiquated 9-1-1.

"Fred, get an ambulance and the police."

Fred said, "It's done. Our team will be there before them."

There was nothing else to say.

"It doesn't matter," I said.

I stood up. I wanted to get a blanket for her. I took a few steps and stumbled.

Images exploded in my mind. Callie struggling during the last seconds of her life, her unblinking eyes under the water, my mouth on her lifeless lips trying to change the unchangeable.

I was on my knees. People rushed in. A strong light blinded me. A professional-sounding voice quietly spoke to me.

"Mr. Case, my name is Olivia. I'm in charge of a Cooper Security Emergency Response Team. Our doctor is working on her. The police will arrive in a few seconds. Just sit tight. Everything's under control."

I started to get up. I had to go back to her. Olivia stood in my way.

"You can't go over there. They're busy."

"Get out of my way."

She touched my shoulder. The STAY hit my bloodstream and she gently lowered me to the ground.

"You'll be back to normal in about ten minutes, Mr. Case," she said.

I couldn't move. Of course, I couldn't speak. But my eyes let Olivia know that she was wrong. Nothing would ever be normal again.

CHAPTER 6

PRIVATE

The Pacific
Summer, 2001

When they tossed him into the darkness, they also threw in one full plastic gallon jug of water. By listening to the amount of water sloshing around in the bottom of the jug, he estimated that he'd been alone in the dark for about two days. He'd been careful with the water, but it was almost gone. He tried not to think about what would happen if they forgot about him.

He began to ponder what the word *alone* meant. When he heard small scratching noises or felt puffs of breath on his neck or unexpected caresses on his skin, he told himself it was only his nerves or perhaps minor hallucinations from lack of food and sleep.

He knew such places existed, but he never imagined one would be located in the belly of a United States Aircraft Carrier.

The cell door opened. He quickly raised his forearm to protect his eyes from the glare of a light bulb. Shapes moved purposefully toward him.

"Rise and shine, asshole," a voice said. "Your nap time's over."

The private had heard voices like that before. The man's tone was rich with the insolent ring of a command too easily won.

Two big men went to his sides and locked his wrists and ankles into heavy iron shackles that prevented all but a minimum of mobility.

"What are these for?" he said. "I couldn't whip an egg the way I am now."

The private was astonished that just the thought of a whipped egg seared deep hunger pangs into his belly.

51

The face of a young lieutenant appeared inches in front of his eyes. His features were distorted with anger.

"Shut that useless hole in your face, private. And, by the way, back when you had enough strength to kill a non-com and forgot you weren't really supposed to do shit like that, did you also forget how you're supposed to address an officer?"

The shackles were heavy.

The private said, "I was just inquiring about the hardware, sir? Even in this hole I can feel we're at sea, sir. I'm not likely to swim away, am I, sir?"

"Hold him up," the lieutenant said.

The sailors glanced at each other. They had orders. But orders from afar were always different than orders from three feet away. They raised the private until he was an undefended target. The lieutenant put his shoulder into a short, but powerful, uppercut to the private's solar plexus. It was close to a killing blow.

"Stanwyki may have been an asshole, but he was also a for-shit poker player," the lieutenant said. "He lost at least a hundred a game. You've pissed off a lot of people, dick wad. Some of those people have friends in Leavenworth. You'll be lucky if you last a month."

The private stared at the lieutenant's face, committing it to memory. He wanted to be sure he'd remember him in the unlikely event they ever met again when his wrists weren't chained.

The sailors dragged him out of the room, through the bowels of the ship, and up to a helicopter deck. After three days of breathing the fetid air of the cell, the freshness of the ocean wind stunned him. A helicopter was waiting for him, ready to take off. He was pushed inside and a crewman strapped him in.

A navy medic leaned in, a loaded hypodermic clearly visible in his right hand. The private's eyes widened and he instinctively pulled away.

"Relax," the medic said. "It's only a mild sedative."

The private shook his head.

"Don't need it," he shouted above the noise of the blades. "Love to fly."

The medic laughed.

"Orders," he said. "But don't worry. I don't play poker and I've seen some of Stanwyki's work. He turned my stomach. Somebody should have taken him out a long time ago."

He found a vein and thumbed the plunger.

"Count backwards from ten."

The private woke up to the rhythm of the lieutenant slapping him. His body was stiff and his mind was groggy. It occurred to him that he had no idea whether he'd been under for a few hours or a few days.

"Enough," he said. "I'm awake."

"Too bad. I was beginning to enjoy it."

"You were more than Stanwyki's poker buddy, weren't you, you son of a bitch? The two of you were kindred spirits."

The lieutenant leaned in close enough to be certain that no one else could possibly hear.

"My orders were to deliver you alive. There wasn't anything about your condition on delivery. Keep mouthing off and you'll feel like I delivered you by dropping you off a roof."

If possible, the private's estimation of the lieutenant dropped even lower. He'd learned long ago that, rather than spouting pointless threats, it was always better to spend time deciding what action to take.

The helicopter landed on the spacious lawn of an isolated country lodge. Raising his head, the private was startled to take in a panoramic view, including a large lake. At first glance, it appeared to be a woodsy vacation getaway for the very rich. That impression lasted until he saw that the statues scattered about the lawn and placed on the roof were actually heavily armed guards.

The private couldn't comprehend why he'd been brought to this place. For good or bad, he was certain of one thing. The army didn't court-martial privates in the isolated luxury of guarded country estates.

He was dragged across the lawn, through the front door, and into a medium-sized room. It had the look and feel of a wood-paneled private study in an expensive hunting lodge. One chair was strategically placed facing a large oak desk about three feet away.

The lieutenant stood behind him and slightly to his right.

"Sit down and shut up," he said. "I'm holding a truncheon. Open your mouth and I'll hit you hard enough on the top of your head to break your teeth."

"Ten-hut," the lieutenant said loudly.

He snapped to attention as a five-star general entered the room.

The private tried to do the same, but he could only attempt to clumsily rise to his feet. His mind was spinning. He didn't think that it was possible for a modern general to wear five stars. There had been only four five-star United States Army Generals throughout history and he was sure the rank had been retired when Omar Bradley died. He tried harder to stand at attention. To any soldier, an officer wearing five stars deserved to be respected, even when it didn't matter anymore who you respected and who you didn't.

"At ease," said the general in a raspy voice.

He studied the private.

"Sit down," he ordered.

The lieutenant looked around, but there was only the one chair in his vicinity. For a moment, he wondered if he should sit on the floor, but decided the general had meant the order only for the private.

The general was tall and lean. His salt and pepper military crew cut and weathered features placed him somewhere between fifty and sixty. He stood at the front of his desk as straight as Roman pillar. Fierce grey eyes seemed to give orders each time they blinked.

Many years ago, his mother said to him, "You're always so serious, Martin. What do you want to be when you grow up?"

The nine-year old boy answered without the slightest hesitation.

"I intend to be a general," he said.

Some things had changed. He had thick eyebrows now and his nose had been broken enough times to never be quite straight again. But his will had never changed. The general was exactly where he said he was planning to be, projecting the confidence of a man who was almost always was where he planned to be. His chest carried an array of medals. Some were the type a soldier gets simply for behaving like a soldier. Others demonstrated that this man had displayed courage and valor above the call of duty in combat. Those were traits that only truly became apparent when it was necessary to draw upon them.

The general's uniform was starched perfection with one jarring omission. He wasn't displaying a nametag. Two side arms with mother of pearl handles were holstered slightly high on his hips. The private wondered at them. They looked like antiques compared to the general's otherwise standard modern uniform.

The general studied the private for a minute and then walked around the desk to sit back in his deep soft leather armchair.

"You can leave now," the general said to the lieutenant, as if he'd forgotten that he was still in the room. "Remove his shackles before you go."

The lieutenant hesitated.

"Begging your pardon, general, are you certain? This man is extremely dangerous, perhaps even psychotic," he said.

It was a bold statement, but the lieutenant couldn't help thinking what would happen to his career, to him, if he were in involved in any way, in any situation, that endangered a five-star general.

He continued quickly, "Army Regulation R..."

In response to his outburst, the general stopped staring at the private and glanced over at the lieutenant, tightening his forehead so that his eyelids closed a fraction of an inch.

"I'll be outside the door if you need anything, sir," the lieutenant said, instantly.

He quickly removed the shackles.

"Shut the door behind you," the general said.

"Yes, sir."

The general turned and focused the full force of his attention on the private. The private took a chance.

"He was hitting our prisoner too hard for no reason, sir," he said.

"What's that suppose to mean?" said the general.

"That's the answer to the question that you were about to ask me, sir."

The general smiled slightly, but not in a friendly way. To the private, it was more unsettling than the fierce expression he had turned on the lieutenant.

"I'd like you to consider something before you make any other snap decisions about what's in your best interests, private. As a military man, I believe in strategy. Now, for example, at this moment, what would you consider a better strategy? To listen carefully to what I have to say and then answer my questions soberly and respectfully? Or perhaps you care to continue to crack wise with me, attempting to convince me how clever you are? I'm aware you enjoyed making smart remarks to that fool who is waiting outside my office with his ear pressed against the door. But before you consider your answers to *my* questions, I suggest you take a moment to consider what someone in my position can do to someone in your position."

"Yes, sir. I apologize, sir."

The apology had shot out of him. Not because of the threat, but because of the man's bearing.

He's one of those, the private thought.

"So, tell me why did you kill Sergeant John M. Stanwyki while he was performing his duty?" the general said.

From the tone of his voice, he might have been asking the private why he deserted his post to go to town and get drunk.

"Sergeant Stanwyki wasn't performing his duty, general. He was beating a prisoner of war to death for no reason but his own pleasure. The man's jaw was shattered, his tongue was almost severed, and his eyes had rolled up. He couldn't have told us anything even if he wanted to. But Stanwyki kept hitting him. So I pushed the son of a bitch off balance while his arm was cocked to make his next strike and he responded by telling me he was going to gut me with that knife he carried in the field. What followed, sir, was an accident."

"I see. You accidentally killed one of our finest instructors in hand-to-hand combat while he was wielding a twelve-inch serrated non-regulation knife and you were bare handed."

"I believe what you just said supports my claim that it was accident, sir."

The general grunted.

"Do you see that camera in the corner of the ceiling?" he said.

"Yes, sir."

"I want you to look directly into it and swear that from this moment you will follow all my orders to the letter, regardless of how unusual they may seem. Furthermore, you swear that you will not harm anyone or attempt to harm anyone in this compound. Also, swear that you will not attempt to leave this house. Do it now."

"You said I have to follow your orders to the letter, even if they appear to be irrational. You can kill me, but I won't follow orders that any civilized society would judge to be insane. I'm through with that. As far as harming anyone, I don't have any intention to do that unless I have to defend myself. That lieutenant outside is probably hoping he'll have an opportunity to arrange an accident for me. I won't stand by and simply let that happen."

The general nodded.

"In that case, I swear."

The general picked up a black telephone on his desk and put it to his ear. The look on his face signified that he heard something that satisfied him. He hung up.

"Lieutenant," he called out.

The lieutenant burst into the room.

"Slow down," said the general. "These are my orders and it's your personal responsibility to ensure that they're followed to the letter. You will remain with the prisoner at all times, but the two of you are not to speak or interact with each other or anyone else in any way. He's not to be harmed or mistreated. If he is, you will take his place.

"Outside the door you'll find an aide who'll direct you to the areas where you need to go. First, you'll escort him to the dining hall where he's to have a good meal, as much as he wants, though not too much or he'll be sick. After that, you'll go to a room where he can take a hot shower. There'll be some clothes on the bed. After he's changed, give the overalls he's wearing at the moment to the aide. He'll see that they're burned. When you're ready to bring him back to my office, retrieve and hold his tags for me. By the way, on the bed, you'll also find a revolver and a belt holster than can be worn left or right. The prisoner is not to touch the revolver until he's wearing the holster on the side that feels most comfortable for him. Then he's to holster the revolver without examining it in any way. Both of you will return here in exactly one hour and fifteen minutes. Understood?"

"Yes, sir," said the lieutenant, though it was perfectly clear he didn't understand any of it.

The general stood up and turned to look out the window as if he were the only one in the room.

CHAPTER 7

GAMEFACE

Berkeley, California
Summer, 2018

The STAY wore off.

Lightening came shortly after the thunder. A hard rain began falling. The first wave of police stood around. A second wave arrived. They smelled wet. All of them reminded me of a construction crew on the side of a highway. One of two appeared to be very busy. The rest stood around chatting and, once in a while, they would point at something that didn't appear to be important.

They didn't stare directly at me, but each one of them stole a glance from time to time. Their expressions alternated between vague sympathy and outright suspicion.

Whenever I caught one looking at me, I fought a pointless impulse to walk over and growl, "What are you looking at? Don't you have something more important to do?"

I reminded myself that it didn't matter. Nothing they did would change what happened that night. The only thing that mattered was making sure I changed the future of the person or people who had brutally murdered the woman I loved while I was taking my nice warm shower.

Before they covered her body, I noticed Callie was wearing a white one-piece bathing suit. I hadn't seen it before and I felt reassured. If she was still wearing that suit, I couldn't imagine that she'd been molested.

An officer told Olivia to lead me to a deck chair not far from the CSI unit. He said someone would be around to take my statement. Someone from Olivia's team wrapped a large towel around my shoulders.

I wondered if the police thought that I'd be uncomfortable so close to the scene of the crime. Maybe I would expose some clue by the way I was reacting or not reacting. I studied them, searching for the one I wanted.

I chose a tired-looking man in a grey sport coat, tan pants, white shirt, and black shoes. His tie was stained. He might have been mid-forties, but looked older. He'd shaved badly that day in some old-fashioned way, cutting too deep in a couple of spots, missing almost entirely in others. He was close to five-seven and not too big around the middle, though he gave the impression that his daily exercise routine was lifting a heavy coffee pot, followed by a brisk walk to the cigarette dispenser.

I got up and approached him. A few cops began walking between us, but he waved them off.

"How many of your people are canvassing the area?" I said to the back of his right shoulder.

"Canvassing the area?" he said. "Canvassing for what? Something the vids didn't pick up? Neighborhoods like this, rich people, they see less than poor folks in Oakland. You watch too much crap on the vid."

I walked around and stood directly before him.

"My fiancé died tonight," I said.

His eyes dropped.

"Yeah, I know. Sorry. I didn't mean offence. You get used to it, you know?"

"She was murdered."

His expression changed instantly and his eyes sharply focused on my face. All the sympathy was gone.

"Yeah? Who murdered her?"

"Who am I talking to?"

"Detective Janison, Homicide. I'm in charge of this investigation."

"Michael Case," I said.

"I know who you are."

"I don't want to talk to you in my bathing suit."

"Fair enough," he said. "Ellis!"

A man strolled over who looked too young to be a detective. He had a bad complexion, but his short hair was well groomed and he was nattily dressed in a blue suit and a striped tie. He attempted to hide an excess of nervous energy.

"Detective Ellis," Janison said, with a tone that made it clear he was used to giving orders to his partner, "Escort Mr. Case inside and see that he has a chance to put on some clothes so we can talk more comfortably."

Ellis head popped up and down slightly, indicating that he thought Janison's choice of words was hilarious.

We went into the house. I dressed in jeans, a light pullover, and deck shoes. I lead Ellis to my study and sat on the couch. Ellis remained standing, ever vigilant, in case I decided to overcome him and escape.

A man entered the room and shut the door behind him. He had a big head and a body to match. His thinning hair was tied back in ponytail that fell half way down his back. He was thirty-nine. To hide his chins, he'd grown a long goatee. He was dressed in a dark-blue pinstriped Armani suit. He could have easily paid for it with a couple of billing hours.

I'd never met him, but everyone in the Bay Area had seen Kenny Krause in action. He was the best criminal defense lawyer in California, maybe in the whole country.

"Detective, give me a few minutes with my client."

Ellis shot Krause a look that attempted to make him feel like he was an enormous cockroach that had just crawled out of a corner of the room.

Krause returned the look with one that said I'm a thousand times richer, a hundred times smarter, and ten times more likely than you to get laid tonight.

Ellis left, acting as if he'd won the exchange. He shut the door behind him.

Krause walked to where I was sitting and sat at the perfect distance to speak to me quietly.

"What's our current level of electronic surveillance?" Krause said.

"I'm not aware of any. I never activate internal surveillance unless there's a reason. With all these strangers walking in and out, active internal sensors would be going wild. Aram's team is monitoring everyone. The woman in charge seems efficient."

"Good looking, too."

He realized the comment was inappropriate and lowered his eyes.

"Sorry. That slipped out. I wasn't trying to lighten the mood. Back to business."

He pulled a very small device from his jacket pocket. He placed it on a nearby table facing us.

"Activate. This is Kenny Krause, attorney-at-law, one zero zero one two, licensed to practice in the state of California. New file. Acknowledge."

A very good voice simulation responded, "Activated."

He noted the location, date, and exact time.

"Mr. M.B. Case is my client as of one hour ago. Mr. Case is not currently designated a terrorist and does not appear on any terrorist watch lists. Therefore, comma, any and all communication between us is covered under attorney client privilege, comma, addendum 14A, comma, Non-Threat To The State. We both assert that we are unaware of any type of electronic surveillance that may be in force and therefore, comma, any recording or record of any communication between us, comma, until otherwise noted, comma, must be considered strictly inadmissible in any court of law."

59

Krause smiled reassuringly.

"I think that covers it," he said. "At least, it covers anything I couldn't talk my way around in front of a judge."

"So, Mr. Case," he continued. "I believe you know me or, at least, my reputation. As I said, you're my client."

"Am I under arrest? Am I suspected of something?"

"Absolutely not. I'm simply here to protect your interests."

"I didn't hire you."

"Aram Cooper hired me. To be more precise, I'm on permanent retainer to one of his satellite corporations."

"Well, in that case, you're fired. Get out."

"Excuse me?"

He looked as if I had told him to get out of the way while he was standing between me and a loaded gun.

"I don't want you here," I said. "The cops hate you. I need one of them to trust me."

Krause smiled at me as if I were a child asking to be taken for a ride to Mars.

"Look, I can't imagine how you're feeling. I've seen enough to know that people react strangely in situations like this. But let me assure you of two things. Tomorrow, you'll feel a bit differently. And then differently the day after. It'll get better in some ways and worse in others. More to the point, no cop out there is going to trust you. Most of them don't even trust themselves. So don't make things worse for yourself in the worst possible way. This looks like an accident, but there are some touchy aspects. Your bribe for a forty-minute security blackout, for instance."

"That is quite a coincidence," I said. "In any case, I don't want you here, so I'm telling you to leave."

Krause expression changed into a dark intense stare. I wondered what it felt like to be in a witness box when he did that.

"It's not that simple," he said. "You're a vital part of the corporate integrity of Cooper SHW Incorporated. Under the most recent federal rulings, Cooper SHW enjoys even more rights and privileges than a private citizen. Aram Cooper, as founder and majority stockholder of the corporation, has the right to take steps to prevent major stockholders from intentionally causing harm to the corporation. Ignoring the best advice of a criminal defense attorney of my standing could easily be construed as intentionally harming yourself. Therefore, Mr. Cooper has the right to prevent you from harming yourself. If he feels you're not, um, thinking clearly, he can take steps, against your will, if necessary, to prevent you from causing injury to yourself. Don't blame at me. The Roberts Court began the process. The Thomas Court polished it all up. Ipso facto, it's not up to you to hire or fire me."

He paused. He appeared to be pleased with his argument, as if he had just won something. It wasn't difficult to see that he was a man who lived to win. He smiled.

He said, "Furthermore, I hope you won't take this personally, but I should point out that you are taking this personally. Aram Cooper does not lack enemies. Many people consider you to be an integral part of his ability to fund, shall we say, his interests. Removing you, physically or emotionally, from that equation would be a serious setback to Mr. Cooper and the corporate interests of Cooper SHW."

I stared at him. He wasn't a foolish man.

"Don't harm the messenger," he said quickly, avoiding the word *kill*.

Suddenly, I was glad he was there. Until that moment, I hadn't realized how hard it had been to hold back.

"Okay. But, regardless of all that, you're *my* attorney tonight. So anything I say to you is attorney client privilege, strictly between us. You can't even share it with Aram Cooper. Correct?"

"That's correct. I'm here for you."

I motioned for him to shut off his recording device.

"End recording," Krause said.

I leaned a little closer to him.

"Someone killed Calena Lacerda tonight. But all I can think of is myself. What's tomorrow going to be like without her? I think about how we slept wrapped around each other. About how she sometimes lapsed into Portuguese when something delighted her. A couple of hours ago, I was taking a shower and I was waiting to feel her against me. Now I have to accept that I'll never feel Callie against me again."

I turned away from Krause. I didn't want to look at him face-to-face.

"I'm ashamed how selfish I am," I said. "I can't help thinking of what losing Callie means to me, not what happened to her. When I was a boy and I thought about death, it was always about being completely alone. The terrible fear that everyone and everything would be ripped away and I'd be thrown into some never-ending void. Not just loneliness, but the conviction that I'd be without company of any kind. Forever. As I grew older, I decided death was one of two possibilities. Maybe it was simply nothingness. The filament burns out and the bulb no longer accepts the electricity that made it shine. Everything we are ends in non-existence. Or death might be something so completely distinct from what we are in life that worrying, or even thinking about it, was a waste of time."

Callie's eyes under the water flashed before my eyes. For a moment, I thought about time and how many days and years had been stolen from us.

I said, "So now I don't fear death very much. I don't even think about it often. However, I do hate the thought that someone might have the audacity to believe they should decide when my time had come. In other words, I don't fear the firing squad. However, I would despise any judge who would wantonly and unfairly place me in front of the guns. Someone did that to Callie tonight. And I can't stop wondering what that person is doing at this very moment. Having a drink in a bar? Something tasty to eat? Or perhaps strolling through San Francisco thinking about how Callie felt as she struggled for her last breath?"

I nodded in the direction of the pool area.

"I look at all the cops out there and, yes, I look at you too, and I know what you represent. Maybe this will be one of the few murders the police can solve. Even though we've all given up our privacy to the corporations, the government, and the advertisers, they still don't solve very many. And if her killers are caught, they'll be remanded to the justice system. Two or three hundred days removed from this night, the murderer will assume a sympathetic pose. The laws of evidence and procedure will lean towards the defendant. Hell, if the defendant's rich enough or notorious enough, you might even wind up as his attorney. By then, Callie will only exist as a name on computer screens. What she was in life, the unique creation she had been, would have been reduced to: *Victim, female.*"

I turned back to Krause, thinking he might look uncomfortable, but he didn't. He didn't practice law for the money. It was his game and he loved it.

"Bargains will be struck, thousands and thousands of words will be said and written. And eventually, if justice has a good day, someone might receive some inadequate punishment for tonight, for this obscenity that can never be reversed...or, maybe I'll find her killers. Then I'll make them truly understand how it feels to be trapped and terrified, to feel what she felt. And, when their darkness closes in, they'll be screaming for a way out that doesn't exist."

Krause was staring at me. He couldn't reconcile the smile on my face with the words he'd heard. There was a knock at the door. Both of us waited in silence until Janison and Ellis entered. I carefully arranged my expression.

"Is your client willing to answer a few questions, counselor?" Janison said.

"I'm happy to answer any questions you may have, detective," I said.

Janison pulled a chair over and sat across from me. Ellis crossed his arms and leaned against my desk, displaying a hostile expression that looked, to me, as realistic as a politician promising a better tomorrow.

I looked into Janison's protruding eyes under his balding scalp and searched for signs of intelligence or insight. I decided that he was my best chance. He pulled out a small black notebook and a small pencil. So he really was a member of the old school. Aram would have labeled him a Luddite.

Janison said, "Okay, for the record, you are Michael Bogart Case, 2138 Vonage Avenue, Berkeley?"

"Yes."

"I guess your mother was pretty fond of old movies, huh?"

"I never knew my mother. She died shortly after I was born. My father said she named me Bogart because she was fond of smoking joints and holding onto me."

Janison smiled as he evaluated my response.

"What's your occupation, Mr. Case?"

"I have interests in several businesses."

"Such as?"

"Cooper SHW, The Ahh Baloney Café, some other concerns."

"*The* Cooper SHW?"

This from Ellis, whose expression took a sudden excited interest in the questioning. Several very rich people could afford big houses in the hills, but the involvement of Cooper SHW meant this case had the potential to be all over the vid.

"There's only one Cooper SHW that I'm aware of," I said.

Janison glanced over at Ellis. His expression couldn't be mistaken. He thought Ellis was dumb as a brick and he wanted him to stop trying to prove it.

He turned back to me.

"You knew the deceased well?" he said.

"Calena Lacerda was my fiancé. I knew her that well."

"So, tell *me* exactly what happened?"

I was encouraged that he clearly intended to use the singular.

"I've been in Seattle for three days on business. I spoke with Callie early this morning and arranged to meet her here about seven-thirty tonight. When she arrived, she was excited about something. She told me that she had a surprise for me. I'd been working in my studio in the back, so she asked me to clean up and meet her in the pool. I was gone only for a short time. You can check that with Fred. When I came back and didn't see her, I dove into the pool to wait for her. Her body was at the bottom of the deep end. I tried to revive her, but it was too late. You know what happened after that."

"This surprise she spoke about. Do you have any idea what it was?"

"No."

"A few minutes ago, out by the pool, you told me she was murdered. Why'd you say that?"

Krause immediately interrupted.

"Don't answer that," he said.

I ignored him. There were a hundred reasons I could have given Janison so that he'd be convinced, as I was, that Callie's death was not an accident. Whatever had terrified her on the day that I met her had caught up with her. But I wasn't about to share any of that with Janison.

I said, "I saw her face under the water. She'd been struggling against someone holding her down. I had to change her expression when I did CPR."

"Maybe she had a cramp."

"Callie was a strong swimmer. She didn't have a cramp."

"CSI did a blood analysis," Janison said. "Pineapple and Rum. She was over the legal limit. We didn't find any evidence that either of you had drinks when she arrived. Was she already drunk when she got here?"

I let him see my confusion.

"Callie wasn't a big drinker," I said. "Maybe she had a drink or two before she arrived, but she didn't appear to be impaired in any way. If I had thought that, I wouldn't have left her alone after she said she wanted to go into the pool."

"Were you always that careful with her?" Janison said. "I mean, did you always try to control what she did?"

"Okay," Krause said. "That's enough. Don't answer that. My client is done."

"Be quiet," I said. "I want to answer. No one can control Callie. It's one of the things I love about her."

There was an uncomfortable silence as we all realized that I was talking about her in the present tense.

Janison broke it when he said, "Fred at the security company told us you bribed him to shut off the perimeter system."

Good. Janison was smart enough to not only talk with Fred, but also make him quickly give up the information about the cigars and the scotch.

"That was her idea."

"Why?"

"I supposed she didn't want Fred to see something we were going to do."

"Do you have any way of proving precisely how long you were in the shower?"

Before I could answer, he glanced at my watch.

"I mean, that's an expensive watch," he said. "You were wearing it, weren't you? Oh wait, it's one of those antiques, isn't it? Doesn't even look waterproof. There's no vid. Is that thing even connected to the Net?"

He thought he was playing me. He wanted me to know he didn't care for the calm manner in which I was answering his questions. Why wasn't I more nervous, more eager to deflect suspicion away from myself? In serious situations, most intelligent people tend to talk to authority figures in a way that they imagine is proper. They want to show respect, offering what they think the person in charge expects.

It was a crucial moment. Should I play his game for a while longer or spread my cards on the table, forcing him to show his hand? Janison might be good, but I'd sat across from the best in the world. I knew I could handle him, but that wouldn't get me what I wanted.

"You're right. If I had to, I could probably tell you precisely when I stepped out onto the deck. I'm a precise man, Detective Janison. I play games and I'm good at them. For example, I usually win at high stakes poker. Check with Jack Davis in Tahoe. I remember one time when Callie got angry with me. She said that she wished I wouldn't treat my life as one long game, always trying to make the correct moves, always trying to achieve a par score. To an extent, she was right. But a real game player always plays within the rules. I'm thirty-seven years old. I thought I was in love once before, but Callie was the first woman I ever asked to marry me."

I paused to steady my breathing.

"When you go up against any top-notch player in any game, you have to develop a gameface," I continued. "No matter what's happening, you don't reveal anything except what you'd like your opponent to believe. You don't overthink what you're showing because that's bad for your concentration. I didn't kill Callie, but I know someone did. I'll help you every way I can. Let me begin by telling you that if you're trying to break me down, or trip me up, or get me to blurt out some contradiction, you're wasting your time. Look at me carefully. I'm going to let you see what I feel. And when you're done looking, if you don't believe that all I want in this world is to find out who took Callie away from me, then you're not smart enough for me to continue talking with you. In that case, charge me with something or get out of my house. I prefer Case to Mr. Case."

Janison locked eyes with me and let my outburst sink in. Then, I saw the subtle shift.

"I'll be Goddamned for a week," he said slowly. "That was some speech. I don't know how you did it. Usually, something like that would make me think you're guilty as hell. I've lost count of how many people have sworn to me that they're innocent. You're the first one I think might telling the truth."

Everyone in the room was startled to hear the question that exploded from Ellis, who had sprung off my desk and was now leaning in close to me, so close that I felt moisture when he spat out, "When was the last time she was mad at you, huh?"

We all stared at him with equal astonishment. My admission that Callie had gotten angry with me once must have been the last thing that Ellis heard.

CHAPTER 8

REFLEX

The Pacific
Summer, 2001

A hot shower, a solid meal, and the ability to freely move his wrists and ankles gave the private a different perspective.

He put on the short-sleeve blue shirt, grey chino pants, white socks, and blue sneakers that had been neatly laid out for him on the bed. When he handed over his dog tags, he noted the lieutenant's smirk of satisfaction. They shared the same thought. A soldier losing his tags symbolizes death.

There was tense moment when the private picked up the thirty-two-caliber revolver to holster it, however it was obvious the lieutenant couldn't believe the handgun was loaded. The private pretended to check the fit by raising it slightly in and out of the holster. The lieutenant was mistaken. The handgun's weight revealed that six rounds were chambered.

They were escorted back to the general's office. They heard his raspy voice ordering them to enter and saw him sitting behind his desk studying the thick contents of a folder. Once again, the general indicated that the private should take the seat directly in front of his desk. The lieutenant remained standing at attention behind the prisoner's left shoulder.

"Feeling better, private?" the general said.

"Yes, sir, much better, thank you, sir."

The general turned to the lieutenant.

"Give me his tags."

"Yes, sir, right here, sir."

The general nodded at the desk and the lieutenant placed them carefully upon it.

"Lieutenant, tell me what you know about Antarctica."

The lieutenant's brows moved towards each other. He hadn't expected a geography quiz.

"I believe it's the South Pole, general."

"Actually, it's the continent nearest the South Pole. The terrain is so forbidding it wasn't established to be a continent until the eighteen forties. The temperature is normally below freezing, but the climate in East Antarctica is actually colder. We maintain outposts there. One reason is that we conduct survival research in hostile environments. It's dark much of the year. Very dark, very cold."

The general paused to allow the lieutenant to appreciate the full weight of his description.

"This is what happened today," he continued. "You were accompanying this private to a temporary holding area. The prisoner somehow managed to get out of his restraints and, in a desperate effort to escape, jumped from the helicopter into the sea. There was nothing you could do. You searched for him as long as possible and then the chopper had to return to the Nimitz. A report has already been written. All you need to do is sign it. Everyone in that helicopter was one of my men. You will return to your duties and resume your career. If you say or do anything about what you've seen or heard today, you'll spend the rest of your military career monitoring weather patterns in Antarctica. Have I made myself clear?"

The lieutenant glanced at the private. There was no doubt that they had come to the same conclusion. There were always rumors in the military. Here was the reality. The private was fated to be the subject of some bizarre experiment.

"Clear as a bell ringing, sir," he said.

Then he made a mistake. He grinned. The general's expression darkened.

"Wipe that smile off your face, lieutenant. The name of your fiancé in San Francisco is Elizabeth and the name of your lover aboard the Nimitz is Barry. Are you so confused you don't understand the necessity of taking my orders seriously?"

The private had never seen a man deflate like a balloon before.

"No, sir. Your orders are crystal clear, general."

"Well, then, stop thinking about they mean and get out."

The lieutenant saluted and backed out of the room as if he were exiting an audience with a king.

The general walked around to the front of his desk, leaned against it, and silently studied the private. He saw a young man, about six-two, weighing about two hundred pounds. The private's physique, though well muscled, could not be described as anything other than slim. Although he didn't show the bulges of a body builder, a sense of physical power emanated from him.

He wasn't a classically handsome man, however his oval face displayed a character that could make other men want to be his friend and women want more. His large blue-green eyes were topped by dark brows. His dark-brown hair was full and cropped short. Italian and English blood ran through him. Considering the life he'd lived, it was a marvel that his nose had never been broken and he'd managed to hold onto a full set of teeth that formed a good smile when the occasion warranted.

When the general completed his appraisal, he said, "I'm Martin Tresain. I command a special unit. I report directly to the president and no one else.

"You heard me tell the lieutenant what's written in the official report," he continued. "The man you were is dead, the life you had is over. You'll have a plot in Arlington if anyone cares to visit. I want to be as clear as possible. The man you were is now at the bottom of the ocean."

The general reached behind him and handed the soldier a photograph.

"I believe you worked for him at one time," the general said.

The private looked at the photograph.

"Seems like another lifetime," he said, leaning forward and tossing the photo back onto the general's desk.

The general's gaze hardened. The private tensed involuntarily.

"I didn't hear a *sir* at the end of that unnecessary comment, private."

"You just told me that my life as a private was over. I'm not planning to join up again. That makes me a civilian. Civilians aren't required to say *sir* to generals, even ones with five stars."

It was impeccable, but bad, logic.

"Think of it this way. If you were talking to a man who could save your life by performing emergency open-heart surgery on you, you'd pay him the respect of addressing him as *doctor*, wouldn't you?"

"Yes, sir, I would, sir."

The private realized that, although he'd just met him, he wanted the general's respect. It was a rare experience for him.

The general lifted a baseball off a stand on his desk.

"I'm a collector, son. These sidearms once belonged to General Patton. I wonder if you can imagine what it cost me to get them. This baseball is also priceless. Do you know who Roger Maris and Mickey Mantle are?"

"Baseball players, sir."

The general seemed pleased.

"That's correct," he said. "In 1961, there was a season when they both tried to break Babe Ruth's long-standing record by hitting more than sixty home runs in a season. Maris did it, but Mantle fell short because of illness. He was only able to hit fifty-four that year. Their stories are admirable for the guts each man showed. This ball is the one Mantle hit for his fifty-fourth home run. It's one of my most prized possessions."

The general began tossing it in short arcs between his right and left hands. It appeared to be a mindless habit he'd developed.

"I notice you've chosen to wear your sidearm on your right," he said.

"Well, sir, actually I'm ambidextrous, but I do tend to favor my right a bit. Normally, given a choice, I'll wear a sidearm on my right."

"Good," said the general.

"Private," he continued. "I want you to feel that you can talk freely with me."

He paused.

"Why did you join the military?"

The private grunted.

"After basic, sir, I made up an acronym, *SLAGIATT*. Seemed Like A Good Idea At The Time."

The general's features cracked into a smile. He continued playing with the ball. It was becoming hypnotic.

"We both know the real reason you joined up."

"And what was that, sir?"

"You were looking for a place to disappear. To tell the truth, it's not all that uncommon a reason. There's no place like the Army to become faceless if that's what you're looking to do. But you couldn't help yourself, could you?"

Without any warning, the general pulled his arm back and threw the baseball as hard as he could directly at the center of the private's face. Only the soldier's incredible reflexes allow him to raise his left hand in front of his face quickly enough to prevent the ball from smashing his nose. His hand stung from the force of the catch.

"Son of a bitch," he growled. "Have you lost your mind?"

"Relax, private. Take a deep breath. I knew you'd catch that ball. I just wanted to see it for myself. I've been watching you since basic training. Your scores were off the charts. I could have pulled you immediately, but you were wild and undisciplined. I wanted you to have field experience and learn military protocols. To have you adapt to military life and get used to taking orders. I was hoping you'd become a bit of a soldier before you became, well, before you became mine. It's just bad luck that Stanwyki overstepped his orders and I had to bring you here a bit too soon.

"Do you know how many men are born with the kind of reflexes necessary to do what you just did? Men like Joe DiMaggio and Mohammed Ali? But beyond that, there's something else that makes you exceptional."

His eyes wandered down to the private's right hand. The revolver had cleared the holster. It was cocked and was aimed directly at the center of the general's chest. The maneuver had been executed as the private was catching the ball.

"How in hell did you do that?" the general said, shaking his head from side to side.

The private looked down at the revolver. He remembered catching the ball. He didn't remember drawing the handgun.

"I don't know," he said. "You attacked me. I defended myself."

The general seemed more than satisfied with the answer.

"One more thing," he said. "Did you look at how many rounds are in that revolver?"

"No, sir, I didn't."

"How many are there?"

"It's fully loaded."

"How could you know that?"

"I know this weapon, sir. It's a thirty-two-caliber Colt revolver. But you're aware that I was familiar with it, aren't you, general?"

The private nodded his head towards the photograph on the general's desk.

"It's exactly like the one he gave me on my thirteenth birthday. I tested its weight when I holstered it."

The general smiled.

"And I suppose you can tell me whether or not it's loaded with blanks or live rounds?"

"Yes, sir. The rounds are blanks."

"Now really, private, don't sound so confident. That's just a guess."

"Let's call it a very educated guess. I was brought here after killing a superior who was acting like a madman. It's clear from what just happened that you intended to act like a madman. Stanwyki was a sadist and a cretin. You may act strangely, general, but you're sure as hell not a fool."

The general grunted.

"Good answer. Let's go. There's someone I want you to meet. Oh, and there's one more thing. It's a bit premature, but I'm going to go ahead and assign you a code name."

"A code name, sir?"

The former private snorted.

"You mean like double-oh-seven?"

"No. More like the code name the secret service gives the president. From now on, we'll be addressing you as Time."

CHAPTER 9

<hr />

SCAR

San Francisco Bay Area
Summer, 2018

I was on a platform high above the ground looking down through the center of four walls of tightly wound wire to a hard surface resembling a clear blue sky. Callie was falling away from me, terror distorting her features. She was about to die and there was nothing I could do to stop it. I watched in horror as she fell away from me. It tore me apart that I had missed my chance to catch her before she fell. I could have grabbed her hand, but I didn't.

As the ground rushed towards her, her hair flowing around her terrified face, I saw her lips form the words, "Case, I'm so scared."

The final instant before her certain death, something grabbed my shoulders and I was pulled away from my nightmare at breakneck speed to brutally collide with reality. I came awake by trying to jump off my sofa onto the ceiling. My heart was pounding. My body was damp with sweat.

I had passed out for a couple of hours. I checked the vid, but there were no new messages. I remembered listening to the three that I'd received while I was in the studio before Callie had arrived. I wanted to see if I'd missed something. However, most of all, I just wanted to hear her voice.

"Wall vid on," I said. "Play messages from yesterday."

I saw Jackson. Behind him, his sous chefs were busy with the elements of the evening's menu.

"Case, what's up with Callie? She left a message for me with one of the new waiters. She said I should swing by your place after I shut down the kitchen. She had something special for me. You know where I am. Vid me when you get this. OK? OK."

A tone announced the next message.

Aram Cooper was tinkering with something in his crowded office inside the Cooper SHW Research Facility in Berkeley.

"Michael, it's Aram."

Once again, I marveled that the man who was considered the premier computer hardware and software genius of his generation felt it necessary to announce his identity when calling me on a video-active vid.

"Whatever you said to Phil White in Seattle worked like a million dollars. Several hundred million to be more precise. Seven companies were pitching solutions to Mobile Con to block the source of those undesirable messages that have been appearing at the bottom of their vid ads. However, they chose us. Mr. White called the head of our sales division two hours ago, practically begging to give us money. I think we should let him. All we have to do is unravel the beautiful algorithm the intruders are using. Where are you? You're in that studio, aren't you? Get back to me when you return to twenty eighteen."

There was another tone and Callie filled the room. I felt as if metal was melting in my chest.

"I love you, Case. I just wanted to say that and tell you that I hate being without you. So you know I hate to tell you that I'm going to be late. I know, I know, what else is new? But I have a very interesting excuse this time. A fantastic way to keep you entertained. Just remember. You're all mine. *Adeus, querido.*"

I said, "Vid up. All. Jackson."

The wall's vid camera focused on the area from where I'd spoken.

Jackson answered on the fourth ring. He had visual on. I could see that I'd woken him.

"Oh Lord, it's early, Case," he said, rubbing his eyes. "Hey, listen, I'm sorry. Tell Callie I couldn't make it. We were jammed last night and after closing I had to bring the whole staff together to remind them how we serve people here. You know, business, pleasure. Oh, wait, I forgot, you don't know anything about that."

He stopped talking long enough to take a long look at me.

"Hey, man, it can't be that bad," he said.

"It's bad, Jackson. Callie's dead."

"What? Did you say Callie's dead?"

Then, very quietly, he said, "Oh, God, no."

His next questions spilled out in the same breath. "What happened? Some kind of accident? Are you all right? I mean physically. Oh, shit, what am I saying?"

"It was no accident, Jackson. She was murdered. Though the police don't seem to think so. They think she drank too much and drowned in my pool. I found her there."

"I'll be there in fifteen minutes," he said.

He let himself in and, when I saw him, the walls came down. He sat next to me on the couch, his hand on my shoulder, saying nothing, waiting. When I could, I told him everything.

"When Janison left, he told me that they'd keep the whole thing low key for the time being. They'd know more after the autopsy. I could tell from a look on his face that the whole thing was going nowhere."

Jackson thought about it.

He said, "But the crime scene people said it looked like an accident."

"Yes. Except there were some bruises on her heels that she might have gotten if she'd banged them against the side of the pool, fighting a cramp."

Jackson hesitated before he spoke.

"I don't understand," he said. "Why was she under the water when you got in the pool? Wouldn't something have to be holding her down?"

"No."

I didn't know if I could say it.

"Apparently a body may not float until gases develop. She hadn't been dead very long. I must have just missed the bastard."

"The bastard?"

Jackson looked puzzled.

"Or bastards. She was murdered, Jackson. I know it. The cops are going to let it go. They've got no witnesses. No vid. And even if they thought they could pin it on me, she was just the girlfriend of someone who's under the protection of the kind of money Aram Cooper has to spend. In their minds, there's no point in expending any further effort. They know Kenny Krause would tear their case apart no matter what they think I did. No. Callie's already an accidental death by drowning. That's the end of it. For them."

I'd been looking down while I was talking. I looked up to see Jackson staring at me.

"What are you thinking?" he said.

"Whatever I have to do, no matter what it takes, no matter how long it takes, I'm going to find everyone involved in this. Last night was the worst mistake of their lives."

Jackson thought about that for a minute.

"That won't change what's happened," he said. "Listen, Case, when I was growing up in Port Au Prince, my brother Jess and I had a friend, Jean, who was like a third brother for us. When I was thirteen, Jess came home and told me Jean had been hacked to death by three men with machetes. Jess didn't know why, but he did know the men did it. So we went to the drawer where our father kept his revolver, made sure it was loaded, and went outside. My father was standing in front of the house. He said, 'Go back in and put that away. You won't change what happened. You'll only change who you are.'"

"Your father was only half right."

Jackson liked to talk. But one of his best qualities was that he also had that rare talent of knowing when to be quiet.

"You need coffee," he said. "Can you eat?"

"Just coffee."

Jackson turned around when he reached the doorway.

"Case, whatever you decide, whatever you do, I don't have to tell you that when you need me, I'll be there for you."

He paused.

"But I've never killed anyone. Have you? I don't think it's so easy."

"Put me in front of the people who murdered Callie and we'll see."

Jackson smiled a sad smile and a short breath rushed out his nose. After a while, I heard him banging around the kitchen. I knew he was cooking something. That's what he did.

I leaned back in the soft cushions. I thought about everything I knew about Callie and everything I could remember about the last few days. I let my mind float without trying to focus. Jackson interrupted me with a tray of coffee and warm scones.

"Case, maybe it *was* an accident. I mean, what reason would anyone have to kill Callie? And what about the security drop? And going to the trouble of making it look like an accident? Obviously, this was planned way in advance. If they were that good, they could have easily framed you. It's not the way a crazy person would do it."

"You're right. This wasn't some random act of violence. Somehow, someone knew the perimeter security was down. Callie was executed. It was done with precision, like some kind of military operation. It wasn't about sex. She was still wearing a one-piece bathing suit."

"You think she got mixed up with the wrong people back in Brazil?"

"I don't know. Callie was so private about her past. There's nothing I can grab onto."

I remembered my nightmare. I knew it wouldn't be the last one.

"You know, it's strange about the suit," I said. "Callie always swam naked or wore a bikini. I've never seen that suit before."

I thought about it.

"What exactly did she say to the waiter at Ahh Baloney last night?" I said.

"She said he should tell me something like she hoped that I was serious the other night about wanting to marry her. But, I didn't think anything of it. I figured he screwed up the message."

"None of it adds up."

I said, "Vid up. Audio Only. Call Lieutenant William H. Janison, Homicide, Berkeley."

That was all the vid needed to disable my visual and reach Janison. Prank calls were virtually impossible thanks to Aram Cooper. Janison would always have an accurate record of where his calls originated.

He picked up and said, "Yeah, Janison."

His visual was also off, but he sounded wide-awake.

"Detective, it's M.B. Case."

"I'm listening."

"Have they done an autopsy yet?"

"Later today."

"Can I see her?"

Cops are born suspicious and they get more so as time goes on.

"What for? You've already identified her."

"I didn't really get a chance to say goodbye," I said. "I want to see her one more time in a quiet place. Not the way it was last night."

"The morgue isn't exactly candlelit. What's this about? You don't strike me as the sentimental type and we both know that's not her anymore."

"So you're saying, 'No?'"

He spat out the address.

"I'll meet you in thirty minutes. Don't make me wait."

He turned off.

"You're going to the morgue?" Jackson asked.

"Yes."

"I'll drive you and no argument. You look like shit."

We met Janison outside the building. Jackson said he'd wait in the car. Janison and I walked in together. We entered a small front office. Then we walked through a corridor to a large room that was metal and cold. Sound bounced off surfaces and echoed with a hollow ring. It was a sterile place, a storage area for containers of organs, blood and bones. Five corpses were visible on metal tables. Some of them were covered with white cloths. I tried not to pay attention to the ones that weren't. I didn't see Callie and I was grateful. Even though reason told me that she couldn't feel shame anymore, I couldn't shake the feeling that she wouldn't want to lie naked in a room full of strangers.

Janison spoke to an attendant, a middle-aged dark-skinned man dressed completely in white, even his soft white shoes.

"Where's the young Hispanic woman who was brought in this morning," Janison said.

Callie was over in the corner of the room, still encased in a black body bag. Janison nodded at the attendant.

"Go get some coffee," he said.

The attendant left quickly.

"I'd like to be alone with her," I said.

Janison shook his head.

"I gotta be here," he said.

"You don't strike me as a man who feels like he has to do anything when there's no real reason."

He ran his hand quickly over what was left of his hair.

"You got a way with you, you know? Okay. You got three minutes. Don't touch her."

He walked out.

I reached out for the zipper and my hand froze. Underneath the black plastic, the woman I loved was nothing but a cold shell. I shook off my desolation and exposed her face. Then it was as if the world shifted back into its correct position. I turned around, pretending that I was horrified. I checked the room's surveillance setup. When I was sure my actions would be covered by the position of my body, I turned backed to her, praying that somehow the circumstances of her death hadn't changed her. I pulled the zipper lower and looked carefully at the top half of her body, examining the inside of her upper right arm. Now I was certain. Warning myself that it was imperative not to overplay the misery, I made a decision that required me to hide my emotions at a time when they were running wild.

I walked out and glanced at Janison. It wasn't hard to see that he desperately wanted a cigarette.

With my eyes lowered, I said, "Thanks," and walked towards the elevator.

As the doors were closing, I saw Janison say something to the morgue attendant.

Jackson was sitting in the car with his head back and his eyes closed against the morning sun. I went to the driver's side.

"Move over," I said. "I'm taking you to AB and then I'm going to the office."

I got in and felt good about how the Falcon responded when I pulled away from the curb. She'd just been overhauled and tuned. The work gave her a third more power than when she was new.

"Listen, I don't have to go in today," Jackson said. "Étienne's been waiting for his chance to take over the kitchen. Let's drive up to Stinson Beach with a bottle of Jack and get stinking. We'll get a couple of hotel rooms and work some of this through."

"Sorry, my friend, I've got work to do and you'd rather eat at a fast food joint than have Étienne take over your kitchen."

"Case, I'm worried. I've never seen you where I thought you needed help before, but maybe it's a good idea."

"You think I've gone crazy, don't you. It's fine. Don't worry. Callie's not dead."

Jackson said, "Oh, man."

He took a deep breath and I could almost feel him working up a speech about denial.

"No, really. That's not Callie in there."

"Case, I know you want to believe that, but..."

"The scar, Jackson. She hasn't got the scar."

"What?"

"Lots of things may happen to people after they die. But scars don't disappear. Callie had a scar on the underside of her left arm. Her brother poked her by accident with a knife a long time ago. It was a funny story the way she told it. That woman in there doesn't have a scar. That woman in there, unless she's had extensive plastic surgery, is probably Callie's twin sister, but it isn't Callie. Her ears are slightly bigger than Callie's. It's incredible. The faces are identical. But, believe me, I know Callie's body and that's not her."

"But if that's not Callie, why hasn't she called you? I hate to say this, but maybe she's not okay. She must know that you're going crazy."

"No. She's alive and she's okay. I have to believe that. I don't know why she hasn't called. That's something I can't figure. Maybe she's scared. All I know is that I've got to find her. Quickly."

Jackson thought about it.

"You didn't tell that detective, did you?"

"No. He's no fool. I have a feeling he'll find out soon enough anyway. But until I know she's safe, I don't want anyone I can't completely trust to know that Callie's still alive. Maybe her sister was meant to die all along. But since the killers got her at my house, it makes more sense that it's Callie they're after and they made some kind of mistake. I'm hoping they don't know they missed her, but it doesn't matter. I'm going to find them. And then, I'm going to take care of them.

"Listen to me, I keep saying *them*. Maybe it's a *him* or a *her*. I don't have a clue about what I'm looking for and I'm not a detective. I need Aram. He can access information that I could never find out on my own."

"What about me?"

"You need to go to work."

"How am I supposed to work today? Let me go with you. I can help as much as the computer."

I glanced over at Jackson.

"You've never really warmed up to Aram, have you?"

"First I'll make friends with the circuits in my oven, then I'll tackle Aram Cooper."

"That's precisely why you have to stay away. I need to convince him to do some delicate things and you'd just be a distraction. Spend today working on dominating Étienne. That way, if I need you later, you can help me without having half your mind obsessing over how he's changing your recipes."

"You'll never understand chefs, Case. I could give Étienne a lobotomy with a salad fork and he'd still try and change my recipes."

We pulled up in front of the restaurant.

"Call me," Jackson said, as he got out. "We'll find her."

"Yes. I know."

CHAPTER 10

MEDIUM

The Pacific
Summer, 2001

When they left the general's office, four impressive guards in unmarked camouflage uniforms appeared around them like shadows from four different light sources.

It occurred to Time that the general probably had better protection than the president. And yet, he'd been alone with him not five minutes ago. If he was determined to harm him, there was nothing to stop him.

The general and Time walked down several unmarked corridors, two guards directly to the right and left of them. Time noticed that the guards kept their eyes focused on a sequence of closely spaced mirrors between the corridor walls and the ceiling. All the corridors were unmarked and seemed identical, except that whenever they made a turn, the walls were painted a different color.

After they made their second turn, General Tresain began briefing him.

"For quite some time, I've been a low-key, but essential, asset in the America's intelligence arsenal. After the U.S.S. Cole incident, the president decided that I should go completely under the radar. Deniable plausibility. I was given my present rank so that my authority, no matter what the situation, could not be questioned."

"That's not always a good thing, general. I found that out in the jungle. Stanwyki had unquestioned authority."

"Yes, I suppose it does depend on who wields that kind of power. However, despite any reservations you might have about me, interrupting me is not an option."

Time signaled his understanding with silence.

"Often, my unit gained knowledge of potential threats through various means, but because of the nature of the threat or because the calculated risk of allowing it to continue might bring us bigger fish, we sometimes allowed plots to progress without nipping them in the bud, especially when operations didn't directly target the United States. Naturally, I monitored the situations as closely as possible, but there were times when I waited a bit too long. The consequences were undesirable. I'm sure I don't need to be more forthcoming regarding such instances.

"Then one day, a civilian found a way to schedule a meeting with me. He had worked his way up the chain of command by simply talking with key personnel until he was escorted to this very lodge.

"I checked his credentials. He'd managed to make his way through academia almost entirely without social interaction. He had two doctorates, but his proposal concerned a discipline that wasn't officially recognized.

"After two hours with him, I was convinced his vision was brilliant. More importantly, it could be practical. He proposed that a specially trained undercover team could be inserted directly into the heart of suspected conspiracies. They would gather intelligence, provide a perfectly timed response, and neutralize threats without the public, or our enemies, ever knowing that they existed.

"Just imagine the potential benefits of such a team. Imagine if such a team had been present in the Japanese subway system, for instance. This man convinced me that I could wield this weapon against not only enemies of the United States, but also aid our key allies as well.

"He convinced me. I convinced the president.

"I understand the concerns that you expressed earlier. No one man, not even the president or I, should be granted unlimited power. I was ordered to form a three-person committee consisting of myself and two others, both experienced high-ranking members of the intelligence community. However, the committee only exists to question my decisions if they seem illogical, irrational, or frivolous. That has never happened.

"The man who came to me can read human behaviors that are virtually invisible to those around him. He's able to predict what people intend to do moments before they act on those intentions. At the appropriate time, he employs a Weapon to neutralize targets who are planning to act on their undesirable intentions. It's a rather simple concept, really."

Time had a great deal of combat experience. He didn't find the general's explanation to be all that simple.

They walked into another wing of the lodge and approached another two even larger guards standing at full attention outside a door that bore no markings. So now there were six.

"Excuse me, sir. But it seems to me that you've just revealed a great deal of top-secret knowledge to me and these men around us. You might trust them implicitly, but I know that any secret isn't secure if too many know it, sir."

"An astute observation, Time," The general said, with a pleased expression.

In that moment, Time realized that everything that had happened to him since he'd been pulled from his cell had been, in some way, a kind of test.

The general pressed a lighted green button on the right side of the doorframe. A red light below it turned green and the general turned to the guards. He said something to them in sign language. Time actually had some experience with universal sign language and, of course, the usual combat signals, but he couldn't comprehend what the general had communicated to his guards.

"These men are deaf," the general said. "And they don't read lips. The gentlemen you're about to meet tests them at regular intervals."

"However," he continued. "Don't make the mistake of thinking they're handicapped in any way. They're trained to respond to certain signals. When we're inside, remember that not even you could possibly stop all six of them from killing you, if it becomes necessary."

The general opened the door.

"You go in first," he said to Time and followed him into the room.

Time's first impression was that he'd entered a large library room that had recently been struck by a tornado. Books, papers, computer storage devices, and film reels were scattered on every horizontal surface. At first glance, they seemed to be tossed about at random. However, upon closer inspection, it was apparent that a single intelligence controlled the whirlwind. The enormous volume of items hadn't been thrown about. Each one had been carefully placed. Each item rested precisely where it was meant to be.

The walls were papered with photographs and news clippings, many depicting graphic acts of violence. Time recognized a few. There was the famous shot of Prime Minister Assizi executing his finance minister with a single bullet to the back of the head during a cabinet meeting. His brother-in-law had been secretly taking a sequence of high-speed photos with a hidden camera and had captured everything before, during, and after.

Time searched for a clear place to plant his feet. The general took up a position slightly behind his right shoulder.

A man sat behind a large wood desk. He ignored Time and the general as he continued to use a magnifying glass to study a sequence of negatives resting on a light board. It was clear that he'd never been a soldier. No one in the military remains seated when a five-star general enters the room. Resting on his desk, within his reach, was the same type of black telephone that the general had used in his study. Mounted on the ceiling to his left was a video screen that displayed the chair where Time had been sitting a short while ago. Time realized this was the man who assured the general that his word could be trusted.

Time found it difficult to believe that a five-star general in a military complex would patiently stand by as the man continued to go about his business, seemingly oblivious to any other presence in the room. After what seemed like several minutes, the man looked up from the negatives and spoke in a voice that had been born, bred, and buttered in the Ivy League.

"Forgive me, gentlemen, but I was engrossed in this scenario that General Tresain placed before me a few hours ago. It's much more challenging when you're not on the scene."

"Quite all right, Doctor Treeves," said the general. "Time, I'd like to introduce you to Dr. Edgar Treeves. He'll be your Medium."

The general nodded towards the negatives Treeves had been studying.

"Have you come to any conclusions?" he said.

A look of disgust flickered over Treeves' features.

"As I understand it, the best reconstruction we have is that the targets were neutralized in this order: five, three, two, one, four."

"Yes. According to our team, that was the best order of opportunity."

Treeves shook his head.

"Ridiculous," he said. "The sequence clearly should have been two, five, three, one, four. If the targets had been eliminated in that order, passenger seventy-two and the flight attendant would still be alive. What a waste."

"You can't be sure of that," said the general, annoyance grating his tone. "Remember, you weren't there."

"Well, that's why we're here now, isn't it?" said Treeves.

"Yes. Yes, that's correct," said the general, properly reprimanded.

Time couldn't believe his ears. No one in his world spoke that way to a five-star general.

He was startled to detect genuine pride when the general said, "Dr. Treeves is the world's foremost expert in human behavioral science. He specialty is predicting behaviors. Dr. Treeves, this is Time, your Weapon."

"He might possibly be my Weapon," Treeves corrected him.

Treeves stood up. He was as tall as Time, but stooped over and lean. He wore a loose wrinkled dark grey pinstripe suit over a light grey shirt and striped dark blue tie. Time thought he looked like someone he'd once seen in a photograph. Then it came to him. Except that his nose was a somewhat longer, Treeves looked remarkably like Robert Oppenheimer, the scientist who led the Manhattan Project, the top-secret operation charged with developing the first atom bomb during the Second World War.

Treeves studied Time with his brown eyes, the most notable feature of his thin face. A shock of brown hair fell perpetually across his right forehead.

"General, before we proceed any further, I must repeat my protest," said Treeves. "Although this man appears to possess superior motor skills, I say again that I'll need three Weapons, not one. What if he's killed defending me?"

"You suggested this operation," the general said. "You knew the risks that came with it."

"I'm not concerned for myself," Treeves said quickly. "I'm confident I can extract myself from almost any situation without undue risk to myself. But if he's killed, I'll have no backup to complete the mission. And imagine all the signal training we'd need to repeat."

"You've already made that case to the committee," the general said. "And three Weapons were rejected. So were two. Can we risk signal leaks under torture? Do we want misreads in combat? We're not talking about a swat team. We need two deep-cover operatives, working in the most delicate and dangerous environments imaginable. The two of you must be bound to each other as if you share one mind, each knowing the other so well that every silent signal between the two of you is second nature.

"It will always be his first priority to make sure you come out alive. But I believe he can take care of himself as well. You saw what happened in my office? Do you think men like this fall out of trees? Intelligent, ambidextrous, super fast reflexes. And, if we could find one with all those qualities, how many of them would be willing to risk their lives for their country when they could be playing baseball or boxing for millions of dollars?"

Treeves opened his mouth.

"Enough!" the general commanded.

Treeves closed his mouth. If Time had been about to say anything, he would have closed his mouth.

"I want a decision," said the general.

It was clearly an order and, military or not, Treeves knew he had to obey. He turned his attention to Time.

Treeves said, "Well, now."

He rubbed his eyebrows with his thumb and forefinger and then scratched his right temple.

"What's five times seventeen?" he demanded, lowering his hand.

"Eighty-five," Time said, doing the math quickly in his head.

Treeves quickly picked up a pen with his left hand and wrote an "X" on a piece of paper on his desk. He then folded it close. When he was done, he laid his right hand flat on the desk, put his left behind his back, and leaned in close.

"You have to understand that no matter what I order you to do, it must be done immediately. For example, if I ordered you right now, as a soldier in front of your superior, to remove all your clothing, get down on your knees, and howl like a coyote while pleasuring yourself, what would you do?"

Treeves followed his words with a lewd grin, as if he was simply playing with Time's sense of loyalty.

Time said, "What the hell, general. He's insane."

"Don't speak to the general," Treeves said, quickly. "I'm in charge here. Do it."

"All right then. I'll speak to you," Time said to Treeves. "You're insane."

"Calm down, soldier" said the general. "Don't forget what you swore earlier in my office and, in case you've forgotten, you should know that one of my side arms is pointed at the back of your head."

Time said, "I haven't forgotten."

"Then get naked, soldier," Treeves said.

Time began unbuttoning his shirt.

"That's enough," said Treeves. "There may be times when you'll have a chance to save many innocent lives, but in order to so it may be necessary for you to do something absurd and humiliating. Would you hesitate?"

Time thought it over.

"To save innocent lives, I'd do it," he said. "But if I found out later that you made me do it without justification, simply for your pleasure, I'd make sure that you regretted it."

"Yes, I know. I wouldn't be concerned if I were you. My pleasures are quite limited," Treeves said, with obvious sincerity.

"Now quickly as you can," he continued, "I want you to tell me everything I did from the moment I said, 'Well, now.' Everything you can remember. Include as many details as you can remember."

Time instantly understood that Treeves had wanted to make him feel the adrenalin and moment-to-moment concentration a soldier might experience in a firefight. He forced himself to recall the events.

"The first thing you did was to touch your eyebrows. Then you rubbed your temple with your right hand. I think it was the right. Yes, it was definitely the right hand because you didn't cover your face. After I answered your math question, you picked up a pen and wrote an "X" on a piece of paper. I remember that clearly because I was wondering why an "X" when I was almost certain that my answer was correct. Then you folded the paper. After that, you put both hands on the table to lean towards me. No, wait, that's wrong. You only put your right hand on the table. I think your left hand was behind you. Then you ordered me to get naked and pleasure myself."

Treeves tilted his head.

He said, "You left out that I used my left hand to make the "X" and that you were to howl like a coyote."

But he appeared satisfied.

"I have one more question," he said. "A Weapon must have at least a rudimentary understanding of human nature. What will happen when the lieutenant who brought you here returns to his ship? Did the general handle that situation well?"

Time turned to the general. He noticed the sidearm was back in its holster.

"May I speak freely, sir?" he said.

"Answer Dr. Treeves' question," said the general.

"In my opinion, the general made an error in judgment when he made that remark about the lieutenant's lover. The lieutenant will return to the Nimitz so terrified he'll awkwardly break it off with Barry. Barry will pester him, perhaps threaten to expose him, until he breaks down and secretly confides why. And Barry doesn't have a strong reason to keep the story a secret."

"The general rarely makes errors in judgment," said Treeves.

"So that's why you gave me those instructions to bring that lieutenant here and had me scare the hell out of him," the general said. "It was one final test."

Tresain's brow creased slightly. He gave some thought to the problem.

"I'll send the lieutenant somewhere isolated, but not so cold. I'll have our psychologists work on him until he won't remember what happened here today. Who knows? They may even help him make a decision."

"What about him?" said the general, nodding at Time.

"I know what I need to know about him for the moment," said Treeves, settling back to his work as a way of dismissal. "I suppose he'll do."

Time wanted to remain silent, but something in Treeves' manner forced him to say, "What do you think you know about me?"

Treeves looked up from his photographs and tilted his head slightly.

"What do you want to hear? Let's begin with sex. Almost everything does. You're obviously heterosexual. You've never experimented with non-female partners. Oh, and humans exclusively. You've limited yourself to one partner per encounter. Let's see if I can determine an exact count. I'm sure you've had less than ten. Nine? More than four? There it is. Five. Yes, exactly five. Considering your age, not an impressive total for a red-blooded American soldier. You find pleasure by pleasing your partners. I'd say, given your choice, you prefer the missionary position. Yes, that's right. Missionary. But it's not about control. No, that's not it. You prefer some kind of emotional connection with your sex partner. Yes. That could also explain the number of partners."

He interpreted Time's expression.

"Because you told me. That's how I know. My superior position was established when you entered. I used a sexual diversion to distract you. It's clear you're a tad prudish and I wanted you to become furious, outraged that the army was about to force you to submit to a sexual predator with more authority than you. By the way, that would never happen. You could not be trained out of certain cemented qualities in your personality profile. You'd probably kill me or yourself or both rather than accept what you considered to be a grave injustice."

Treeves picked up a pen and rhythmically tapped it's point on his desk several times. He seemed as interested in that sound as he was in his own analysis.

"Next would be food. Of course, you might question my deductions since I might easily have access to your dietary preferences in your military records. So, I'll attempt to be as specific as possible. From the look of you I'd say you're a healthy eater, more vegetables and fruits than sweets. Most people tend to have a meal they're particularly fond of and Americans are unfailingly predicable. Cheeseburgers, pizza, ribs. Ah, there it is. Pizza. If asked to choose, you'd say your favorite meal is pizza. Yes, pizza loaded down with good fresh vegetables. Though instead of a soft drink, you'd enjoy an alcoholic beverage. Beer, wine? So it's beer. Work. You're a confident man and not a whitling. You're the type of man who could become successful selling things, except that you would never accept a job that required selling anything. You've never been creative in an artistic sense, though sometimes you wish you were. No. Your one real talent comes from the combination of your natural gifts. You're remarkably quick and strong for your size. You don't have an average man's reservations about hurting people. You wouldn't hesitate to kill if you feel it's justified. You came to the military that way and, naturally, your training has cemented that trait into your character profile. My time is valuable. So I'll conclude this brief analysis with your money. You have some and you believe that no one but you knows about it. Not a fortune. However, you're convinced it's just enough to help you escape from trouble, if and when it comes. No, don't worry. I won't try to determine exactly how much and I don't care where it is. I inherited more money than you'll ever see in your lifetime. Now, if the two of you will excuse me, I have more important work to do."

Time turned to the general.

"How long have you been keeping a dossier on me?" he said. "Even so, how could he guess some of that information? There are things he said that no one could possibly know."

The general appeared to be extremely satisfied.

"Your dossier doesn't include a great deal of that information. However, I'll have my aide add it as soon as possible. Dr. Treeves rarely guesses and when he does, he's rarely incorrect. He got all of that directly from you. Everything he told you, he learned from you since you walked into my office."

"What is it? Some sort of trick? How does he do it?"

When he heard the phrase, "some sort of trick," Edgar Treeves, a man who did not often allow others to see his true emotions, allowed an expression of deep revulsion to cross his features.

"For the moment, let's just say it's no trick," General Tresain said. "Your reaction to the lieutenant. How you ate in the commissary. Your tone of voice, the way you stand, how you walk, how often and when you blink, the muscles in your face and hands, and a hundred more factors than I can enumerate. In a nutshell, Dr. Treeves can read human beings like you

85

can read a newspaper, except he can do it much, much faster. Let's leave him to his work."

Treeves had gone back to studying photographs during the general's explanation. Without another word or acknowledgement of any kind, the general led Time back into the corridor. His guards looked as if they hadn't moved a muscle since the general had left them outside.

Time said, "What did you mean when you said his specialty is predicting human behavior? How can anyone predict what another person is going to do?"

"Don't we all do that all of time, except at much less expert level? Even if you've only been in a soldier's company for a few minutes, you can probably predict what he'll do if you call him coward in front of his comrades. If you push a policeman around, can't you predict his actions? Think of it this way. Doctor Treeves carries around a razor-sharp scalpel while the rest of us are walking through life with sticks."

"And that's why you allow him to treat you like he does?"

The general frowned.

"What I'm about to tell you is most top secret," he said. "I can speak about it only because this is an absolutely secure location. Two months ago, a small atomic device was discovered in a suitcase in a train station. The yield from that bomb would have destroyed a large part of one of our cities. It was hours from detonation. Dr. Treeves was indispensable in helping us locate and diffuse it. Now do you understand why I, um, defer to his eccentricities?"

The general chuckled.

"Dr. Treeves may seem eccentric to you and me, but take my word for it, that man is a national treasure."

"With all due respect, general, all of this doesn't make a whole lot of sense to me. My name is Time and I'm a Weapon? That man in there is a national treasure who no one has heard about and he's a Medium. I get the feeling that I've just been put through some kind of bizarre job interview. Time is more than a code name, isn't it?"

"Actually, all the identifiers are Dr. Treeves' inventions. He believes that names reinforce a person's understanding of their purpose. A Medium in high-risk situations sees things that others are unable to see, just as a medium in a séance claims to see things no one else can see. Dr. Treeves knows when targets are lying. He can determine their mental and physical quotients, and, most importantly, he can predict imminent threats with reasonable certainty. Once a Medium makes a determination, he employs sequences of silent, nearly invisible, signals to direct his Weapon to take appropriate action. Say, for example, your Medium knows that targets are about to initiate a lethal action in an airliner. He signals his Weapon to neutralize the targets before they can cause any serious harm. There are several reasons why your code name is Time. One is to reinforce the idea

86

that there shall be no time between what he tells you to do and when you do it."

"So I'm supposed to act as that nutty professor's Weapon in combat situations?"

"Precisely. For the next few years, along with whatever other work you can do for us, you're going to train with Dr. Treeves and other specialists. The two of you will grow into a team that will infiltrate and neutralize threats to our country at a brand new level.

"In the field, the two of you will communicate through sequences of silent signals known only to you, Dr. Treeves, and myself. I'm in that loop in case both of you are killed or captured. He'll inform you which targets to quietly eliminate. His ability to inform you which targets pose the greatest threats will enhance your ability to neutralize them in the proper order. During interrogations, he'll specify exactly how much force is required and when and where to apply it. You will follow his orders unconditionally and without question.

"And, naturally, it goes without saying, that it's your responsibility to protect him, even at the cost of your own life. We might possibly replace you, though that would be challenging, but it would be almost impossible to replace Dr. Treeves. He's been training other Mediums, but, so far, none of them have come close to his real-time abilities."

"With all due respect, sir, how can you expect me to follow that man's orders? He's not a soldier."

Time couldn't believe the size of the rabbit hole he had fallen into.

"Technically, you're both civilians now. But while on military assignments, he'll have the rank of colonel and you'll have the rank of major. That'll help you move around."

Time realized he'd gone from private to prisoner to major in one week. He wondered what the general had in store for him next week.

As if he was providing an answer, the general said, "You haven't heard the best part. Right now, you're good, but in the grand scheme of things, you're still a rookie playing in the minor leagues. You're about to receive the finest physical and mental martial arts training in the world. The teachers you're about to work with will change everything about how you think and move. You won't be a fighter. You'll be a machine that can kill any opponent in seconds with your bare hands."

"Yes, well, that sounds just great, general, but you know, I don't think I'm ready to spend what would most likely be a very short life taking orders from that civilian in there while I'm trying to keep him alive in combat. So, if you don't mind, sir, I think I'll go back and face a court martial."

The general looked perplexed.

"Well, I'm sorry to hear that, son. However, if that's your decision, let me see. You'd like to go back to where you were? I believe the official report states that your last known position was at the bottom of the Pacific."

The general produced a small communications device. The general's guards moved closer.

"Major, bring my helicopter around."

Time studied the general, trying to decide if he was serious. It wasn't a difficult decision. As for General Tresain, he didn't need to be an expert in human behavior to interpret the look on Time's face.

He spoke into the device again.

"Cancel that last order," he said.

CHAPTER 11

ARAM

Cooper SHW
Summer, 2018

The manufacturing facilities of Cooper Software Hardware Wetware spread over an industrial park in Palo Alto, south of San Francisco. Our corporate offices and some of our most important research facilities were located in a converted warehouse on Harrison Street in Berkeley.

No one knew if Aram Cooper used *Wetware* to represent the consulting division. There had been a great deal of speculation *Wetware* signified he was sure someday he'd achieve his dream and create a computer that was more than a complex adding machine. He'd been asked many times, but he never bothered to answer. Aram had no need to do anything that he didn't feel like doing.

He spent the majority of his time in his lab. His wife, Kristin, also a workaholic, managed their schedules so they could spend some hours together on their Sausalito houseboat or on their estate, not far from Mendocino.

I met Aram at a regional bridge tournament in San Francisco. He was sitting in the south position when my partner and I arrived at his table to play against him and his partner. The first two hands were nothing special, simple games, bid and made. He became the declarer on the third hand, which meant he had to play the cards in the correct order to win a certain number of tricks and my partner and I had to prevent him from doing so.

During that hand, I threw away a card that was a sure winner, to convince him that I didn't have another card, which was crucial to his plans. When he played my partner for that card and I showed up with it, his plan for the hand fell apart. He grunted, but said nothing.

Because my deception succeeded, my partner and I received an excellent score and he had a terrible result.

When I left his table, I said, "Good luck," as was my habit and all he did was toss me a sour look.

After the session was over, he approached me as I waited by the scoring tables for the final results. His five-foot-nine frame was clothed in K-mart, a checked short-sleeve shirt over chinos and cheap sneakers. He gave the impression of being overweight, though he only carried around about fifteen extra pounds. His unruly curly hair was poorly parted on the left. Glasses with thick black frames rested on his nose and through the lenses I saw spit-grey eyes. His skin color was the definition of the absence of sunlight. In computer circles, they call it screen tan. He seemed unwilling to make eye contact with me.

"About that play," he began, pursing his lips as if he was planning to call over the rules committee to protest.

For some reason, I felt annoyed even before he finished his sentence. I had to interrupt him.

"Look, there was nothing unusual about what I did," I said.

"Nonsense, it was a brilliant play. But it was the kind of play that would only succeed against an expert opponent. You don't know me. How could you infer that I was clever enough to draw the inference you desired?"

"I play the cards, not the people."

"Nonsense again. You wouldn't have played that card against a dunce and you know it."

"You don't look like a dunce."

For some reason, I said it with a tone that implied that even though he didn't look like a dunce, he looked like something worse.

"You don't like me, do you?" he said, as if it were a fact and not a question.

"I haven't given it much thought."

"You don't need to think about it. We both know it's true. People don't seem to like me. Somehow they think I have contempt for them. If so many people believe it to be true, perhaps it is. On the other hand, the fact that a great number of people believe something is true has never been a good indicator of the validity of any hypothesis. When I was younger, I made an effort to be more likable, but the fraud was so obvious, it only made my social interactions worse. It's something I've accepted. I have other gifts."

"Other gifts?"

He sighed and turned to study a large board where the tournament directors had posted the scores for each hand. The totals and percentages that would determine the winners were still to come. A crowd of people milled around waiting to see who had the highest scores. There were fifty-two partnerships and each of them had played three identical hands.

Watching him blink at the numbers, I decided that he'd finished speaking with me and this was his abrupt way of ending our conversation. He finished examining the board and looked down at the floor near my shoes, as if he were embarrassed.

"Your partnership came in third," he said. "Your percentage was sixty-seven. You beat the pair below you by half a board. You had two bottoms and seven tops. All in all, a decent game."

"Now it's my turn. Nonsense. No one except a savant could add scores and produce results as fast as that."

He shrugged.

"In a few minutes, you'll see that I'm correct. Of course, they have to enter the scores accurately in order to calculate your percentage correctly. My mother once said I was more of a computer than a human being. Maybe she was right. I get along better with computers."

"I'll be damned. I believe you. About the score, I mean."

I regarded him with a different attitude.

"I've never seen anything like that. Third, eh?"

I held out my hand.

"I'm M.B. Case."

"I don't enjoy that ritual," he said, looking away so I could withdraw my hand semi-gracefully. "My name is Aram Cooper."

"Yes, well," I said, turning away. "It's been a pleasure."

"There's a singles event for gold points tomorrow afternoon," he said, ignoring my dismissal. "Do you want to play together? My partner didn't care for certain comments I made after the last session that were designed to enlighten him as to his weaknesses on defense."

I suddenly realized he wasn't trying to be difficult or superior. He was trying to be himself. And, although somehow I was sure he'd done better than I had, I liked the fact that he'd told me my score without mentioning his own.

"All right. I'll meet you here at twelve to discuss the system we'll play."

"Fine."

He abruptly turned and began walking away.

"By the way," I said. "How was your game?"

He stopped and turned around.

"We came in second. Seventy-two percent."

He suddenly smiled.

"We would have won if you hadn't fooled me with that discard."

I pulled into my parking space. A sign that read, *Michael B. Case, Director, Corporate Development*, reserved the spot.

I never wanted a title but Aram said that no one would take me seriously without one. In effect, what I was, besides being a significant stockholder, was Aram's liaison to humanity.

When he was trying to convince me to take the job, Aram said, "People are in business to make money. That is, of course, obvious. But there are a myriad of ways to establish wealth. Contrary to what many people believe, trust, loyalty, and friendship can be important factors in any lasting business relationship. Unfortunately, I simply do not inspire those sentiments. You're different, Michael. You have some innate, intangible quality."

My expression must have somehow let him know I wasn't taking him seriously. Aram pursed his lips.

"I'm telling you that I've seen how people desire your friendship," he said. "They want to be in your circle. If they're perceptive, they know that, once you've accepted a friendship, you would not betray them. If they're intelligent, they're aware that you'll try to achieve an optimum outcome for everyone concerned. You have decency in an increasingly indecent world. Despite their attraction to what is labeled evil, humanity craves decency.

"I'll be the brain of Cooper SHW," Aram concluded. "I need you to be my voice."

I walked through the front doors and up to the reception desk.

"Good morning, Mr. Case," Terri said.

It was Aram's rule that whenever there were outsiders in the building, formality by Terri was preferable for at least two reasons. It spread the word quickly to anyone entering the building that we had company and it would remind us to hold our tongues about internal projects.

"Who is it?" I asked.

"Microsoft," she said, raising her forehead slightly upwards to indicate prominence.

"Not Garcia?"

"No. Do you want to know who? Dr. Akvadian's got him now."

"Not really. Where's Dr. Cooper?"

She gave me a smile that said: Where's Dr. Cooper always these days?

"With SAM?" I said.

"With SAM."

She hesitated a moment.

"Listen, I know it's none of my business, but a Detective Janison called this morning. Dr. Cooper spoke with him for a while, and later, when I called him to tell him the VIP had arrived, he didn't even grunt before he hung up. Usually, he at least acknowledges that there's a human being around when he ignores me. Is everything okay?"

"Don't worry, Terri. Aram loves you, but it's a secret love. And the cops won't be breaking down the doors any time soon."

"That's a comfort. But I guess it means I have to work the whole day. I'll let Dr. Cooper know you're here."

"Don't bother. I'll take care of it."

I decided it was best not to disturb Aram when he was with SAM. On the door of the rooms known to everyone in the company only as L-9 was etched the phrase: *Don't Even Think About Coming Near This Door!*

It must have been there to discourage anyone who had a chance in hell of defeating the biometric security, Aram's random entrance codes, and the magnetic locks.

I knew that Aram was waiting for me and he'd be out uncharacteristically soon. I borrowed four red pushpins from a secretary, and placed them in the shape of the diamond suit on the wall directly across from L-9.

Some people thought Aram didn't notice mundane things. I knew better. When he saw the pushpins, he'd know what they meant.

CHAPTER 12

WEAPON

The Oval Office
Spring, 2001

"Mr. President, your eleven o'clock is here."

"Send him in, Caroline."

"Agent Johnson is coming in with him."

A tall man in a grey pinstriped suit walked into the Oval Office, followed closely by the secret service agent in charge of the president's close perimeter protection. The man held a folder labeled "Top Secret."

"Do I have something to worry about, Bob?" the president said, following his remark with his trademark crooked smile and soft chuckle.

"Not at all, sir," Agent Johnson said. "I'm aware that you've been briefed somewhat about this individual. I also know that your predecessor didn't provide you with a great many details about your meeting with him today. I'm here to let you know that you're completely secure with him. Regardless of what he asks of you, your safety is not an issue. I'll be down the hall in my office if you need me."

When they were alone, the president stepped around the Lincoln desk and offered his hand. He had a practiced handshake, the right position and the correct amount of pressure.

Martin Tresain caught a light scent of cologne.

"Have a seat, general," the president said.

"Actually, sir, I'd like to request that we step into the small conference room behind that door to our left. Also, I request that you tell your secretary that you don't wish to be disturbed for the next twenty-five minutes unless it's urgent. I won't take any more of your time. I know you have a National Security Meeting at nine-thirty. Finally, please have your secretary ensure that all surveillance and recording equipment in that conference room is turned off during our discussion. What I have to say is a matter of national security. It's for your ears only."

"Well, if it's about national security, I want to have the vice-president join us. Dick handles all that for me."

"For the moment, sir, could we keep what I'm about to tell you just between the two of us? Of course, if after you've heard what I have to say, you'd like me to repeat this briefing with the vice-president, that's entirely up to you."

The president mulled it over for a minute or two. Then he smiled.

"I suppose I better get used to making a few decisions," he said.

He looked amused at his remark. He turned and studied the complicated intercom and telephone system on the right side of his desk.

After a moment, General Tresain said, "Pardon me, sir, it's the second button on the left."

The president smiled. Martin Tresain thought that it appeared to be a defense mechanism.

"I'm only settling in," said the president. "Hell of a lot of buttons."

"I don't think that you can go wrong, sir. However, I would avoid the red ones for the time being."

"Yes, I've found that out already, general," said the president.

He followed his remark with another smile and soft chuckle.

"Caroline, the general and I are going into conference room right. Please turn off all recording and surveillance. Inform Agent Johnson."

"Yes, sir. Agent Johnson has already cleared that."

After they settled across from each other, the president seemed like a slightly different man, less affable and more focused.

"All right, general, you certainly have my attention. What's so secret that Bob couldn't talk about it and the vice-president can't hear?"

"Mr. President, I'm here to tell about an installation that's basically off the grid. It has the code name Bunker."

Tresain was forced to suppress his astonishment when he heard the Texan drawl, "Are you talking about something like an Area 51? You're not going to tell me that we really have aliens stored there?"

"No, Mr. President, this is something entirely different. There is an Area 51, but the only things resembling aliens are a group of scientists working on some unclassifiable metals and rocks. It's exciting work if you enjoy giving all of your attention to things that don't move, don't smell, and don't make any noise."

"That's disappointing. I was looking forward to a visit there one day."

General Tresain smiled, masking the slight discomfit he felt at the president's words.

"The Bunker project is more interesting, sir," Tresain said, turning the subject back to the reason for their meeting. "It addresses world-wide threats that can't be conventionally attacked on land, sea, or air. We're facing a new kind of enemy and, in order to do so effectively, we must employ new weapons. I don't command any area of our military. During the last administration, I was elevated to my current rank simply to avoid any obstacles that might hamper my ability to perform effectively. The men and women who live and work in the Bunker do so under my unquestioned command."

The general paused for the president to appreciate his last statement. Tresain knew that, above all else, all presidents are politicians. The moment they hear the word *unquestioned*, they immediately think *deniable*.

He said, "I answer only to a two-person committee and, of course, I report to you whenever we have information that's vital to national security."

That last sentence was actually something of a lie. General Tresain planned to report to this president mostly after the fact. The last commander in chief could be trusted to remain hands off. There was only one person in the world with whom he shared his secrets. In Tresain's opinion, this man was surrounded by too many advisors who held too much sway over him.

"The men and women who live and work in the Bunker are your best defense against terrorism, espionage, political assassination, kidnapping, and so forth. However, for all intents and purposes, Mr. President, the Bunker doesn't officially exist."

"You know, general, I seem to recall that President Reagan got into some difficulties due to the Iran Contras misunderstanding."

"That is not an issue here, Mr. President. All funding for the Bunker comes through ethical and legal, but rather complex, channels. Of course, I can provide you with the details."

"That won't be necessary at this time, general. I have enough on my plate at the moment without a lot of financing worries."

"Yes, sir, I understand."

"So, why this meeting?"

"Basically, it's an introduction. Because of the nature of my team, there are times when I'll make you aware of situational difficulties. I may request that you intercede directly with some individual or agency to allow my team to perform to its maximum capability."

"And just what exactly is this team you're talking about?"

"During the last administration, I was approached by an extraordinary individual. Here's a brief on him."

The general handed the president a single sheet of paper.

When he finished reading, the president said, "And these are all facts you can substantiate?"

"Absolutely, sir."

96

"You do realize how valuable this individual could be working directly for me here in the White House."

"Of course, sir. The problem is that he would refuse to work for you in that capacity."

"What if I ordered him?"

"He's not in the military, sir."

The president appeared skeptical.

"You mean to tell me that his talents weren't used by the democrats?" he said.

"Not in the way you're thinking, sir. This man operates in his own version of reality. He'd be useless if we attempted to force him to perform any tasks that aren't stated on that page."

"And what's all this about a Weapon?"

The general reached into the folder and pulled out another sheet. He handed it to the president.

"His code name is Time, sir."

Time figured he did about a ten thousand push-ups in his first couple of months in the Bunker.

The walls, the ceilings, and the floor of the Bunker were painted different colors. At random intervals, the general ordered them to be repainted with a different color scheme. There were no signs or identifiers on the doors. Residents studied their navigation instructions for three hours in the presence of one of the general's Rangers. All personnel were expected to memorize the Bunker's maze-like layout and the clues that would enable them to navigate through it before the Ranger destroyed the handout in front of them. If Time was told to go a certain area or room, he was expected to know how to get there from wherever he was at any moment. If it took him too much time to arrive, two impressive guides appeared to assist him. They also made sure that he did a number of push-ups that corresponded to the exact number of steps needed to get to where he was supposed to be. The colored maze not only reinforced security, it also improved the ability of covert operatives to move quickly in unfamiliar spaces.

The general told Time he would have four main teachers: Kaicho for hand-to-hand combat, Manu for edged weapons, Iain for firearms, and Treeves for voice.

"Voice, general?" said Time. "You're joking, right? I can see you using your voice as a weapon, sir. I bet you've given more than one enlisted man a heart attack. But Treeves? What kind of damage could he do with that reedy voice of his?"

"It may be amusing for you to imagine I give enlisted men heart attacks, but let me assure you that, under the right circumstances, Dr. Treeves could literally persuade a private to jump off a ten-story building within a matter of minutes. Of course, you'll never be able to come close to what he's capable of, but there are some rudimentary techniques I'm sure you'll find useful in your responsibilities."

When Time was escorted to his first training session, he expected to see Treeves waiting for him. Instead he found himself alone in a room approximately the size of a high school basketball court. It was divided into four equal rectangles, each covered in a different surface: grass, sand, hardwood, and highly polished marble.

It wasn't long before a short thick oriental man entered. Time took him to be about fifty-five. He was about five feet six and completely bald. If he held his arms against his sides and his legs together, he had the proportions of a four-by-two rectangle with a volleyball balanced on top. There was an aura of strength emanating from him. Time made the natural assumption that the short man was a martial arts master and he attributed his bearing to physical confidence.

With an unhurried pace, the man walked to where Time was standing and stopped three feet in front of him.

The man said, "I am Kaicho. The first time you see me, when I tell you to do something, and when I leave, you will bow and say, "Os, Kaicho."

"All right. I'll do my best to remember that."

"Do not worry. First time you forget, you don't forget again," Kaicho said with calm certainty. "The general say I can do what I want to you as long as it doesn't last a long time.

First, you must remember two things about your body. It is a potent weapon that can inflict very bad damage, but it is also very weak. Vulnerable in many, many ways."

He paused and studied Time as if he were considering which lobster to order from a tank in a restaurant.

"You are Weapon for Dr. Treeves," the small man said. "Dr. Treeves is a great man. You are only Time."

Kaicho chuckled.

"General tell me you are good fighter. Is true? You can fight?"

"I take care of myself."

"We are not here so you care of yourself. You take care of Dr. Treeves."

"Look, the general said you were my teacher. That you'd teach me to be a better fighter."

Kaicho snorted.

"Fighting! Why would I teach you fighting? Fighting is for movies. You think you make movie? Fighting is for cab drivers who honk too much. Fighting is for stupid sergeant in jungle."

Kaicho noted the expression on Time's face.

"Yes, I know about you," he said. "Here, we do not fight. You learn quickest ways to keep target from moving until you want target to move. You make target stop moving forever. Faster it happens, better for you. Better for Dr. Treeves."

"No disrespect, but that sounds like fighting to me," said Time.

Kaicho shook his head with a sad expression.

"Foolish pupil makes teacher's books twice as heavy."

"Who said that?" said Time. "Confusius?"

"I said it," Kaicho said. "I'm Korean."

"Anyone can quote Confusius."

"Anyone who studied Confusius. So it is obvious you have not. I was born in a community of Koreans who live in Japan. What we do, we are best in the world."

"OK. So we've established I'm an ignorant lout who doesn't know anything about fighting, even though I've spent the last two years in the best military outfit in the world. We didn't carry the classics in our field packs. We didn't have time to do much reading."

"That is unfortunate," said Kaicho. "But now you are Time. You will learn the classics. Time changes everything."

"You sound pretty sure about that."

"You change or die. Either way, you are not the same. We begin. Today we start with pain, fear, anger."

The little man's index finger shot out like a nail on the head of rattlesnake. It stuck a pressure point below Time's jaw near his right ear. The blow sent a lightning bolt of pain down his right arm all the way to his fingertips. He fell to his knees. His left hand shot out to keep him from falling face down all together. Nausea gave him vertigo and he struggled to keep from releasing the vomit in the back of his throat. He held that position, breathing hard, until the terrible cramping pain began to subside.

"That is pain," Kaicho said.

The little man walked around him slowly.

Time knew he felt better than he looked. He was certain, that with the element of surprise, he had a chance to get to the man's knees and take him down.

"And there is fear and anger," said Kaicho. "You afraid I hurt you again. You angry I hurt you for no reason. The two work together to make you stupid. What you think happens if you attack my knee? You do not walk for two days. We lose two days.

"Never forget," Kaicho said, tapping the side of Time's skull. "Your pain is in here. Your fear and anger is in here. Now you have no control over them. They make you weak and stupid. I teach them to know their place. When they speak to you, you will not listen."

CHAPTER 13

SAM

Cooper SHW
Summer, 2018

I negotiated a few corridors, turned into my corner office, took a long walk around my oak desk, and sank into my favorite chair. If I turned around, I could enjoy a floor-to-ceiling view of the San Francisco Bay. Unlike Aram's office, which looked like a large, incredibly cluttered storage room, mine was decorated to impress. If it had the same effect on other people that it had on me, the designer had done fine work.

There was a Magritte on the wall to my right and, on my left, a sculpture of a ballerina by Antonio, my sculpting tutor. Fifteen steps from my desk was a hidden wet bar. A door on my left led to a full bath with marble counters and a glass-enclosed Jacuzzi. To the right of that was a walk-in closet. The doors were integrated into the wall so as to make them invisible to casual inspection.

There was a time, not so long ago, when I'd have been delighted to live in a space as large and comfortable as my office. I never would have imagined that someday I'd work in such a place. That was before I met Aram Cooper.

Once, during a party at my house in the hills, Aram was occupying his usual spot in the corner while his wife, Kristin, fussed with his hair.

Kristin and Aram were a physical match like a penguin and a cheetah. Kristin had appeared regularly on the cover of high-circulation fashion magazines. Of course, Aram was a billionaire, but Kristin didn't marry him for his money. For one thing, she had more of her own than she could spend in a few lifetimes and I've seen her spend quite a lot. She also gave away more money than she spent. Her favorite charities were those that rescued animals and placed them in good homes.

I believe Aram fascinated Kristin because he was different than the men who had relentlessly chased her before the two of them met at a fundraiser she organized for displaced pets in third world disaster areas. Aram likes animals, but it was Kristin's photo on the invitation that brought him to a social gathering that he would have normally avoided like a wrestling match. Something about her drew him out and after an evening close to her, it was clear that he loved her personality even more than her looks. For a woman who made her reputation on her appearance, that was a powerful attraction.

That's not to say there wasn't anything else between them. In an uncharacteristically open moment, Kristin confided to me that sex with Aram gave a new meaning to the phrase, "screwing his brains out." It was clear, that in more ways than one, she enjoyed having a genius for a husband.

That night, as the party was beginning to wind down, I was standing about eight feet from the two of them and savoring a glass of Blue Label. Each sip was a smooth comforting waterfall sliding down to my center.

Steve Parkway, a Cooper SHW marketing vice-president had been drinking too much, too quickly. It gave him the impression that this was his opportunity to get closer to Aram.

"Dr. Cooper," he said, somewhat dramatically. "Can I ask you a question?"

"Whether you can or not depends on your present condition," said Aram. "But you may if you like."

"It's something that's always bugged me. I mean, here we are in Mike's incredible home, drinking his outstanding liquor, and, really, no disrespect to you, Mike, but – why Mike?"

"I'm afraid *why* is too open ended. Can you be more precise?" Aram said.

"Look, the story's legendary. You meet Mike at a bridge tournament. You ask him if he has any money and when he says he has a bit stashed away, you ask him to invest it all in exchange for a promise of part ownership in a company you intend to build. Then you start Cooper SHW.

You blow away your competition with your first thing out the door, cut the deal with Intel, and wham, you're eight months away from a Forbes cover."

"If, by the thing out the door, you mean the universal parallel cache, those are essentially the facts," Aram said.

"My point is," Steve said, having obvious difficulty making his point. "I like Mike. Everyone likes Mike. But not everybody goes around making him a multi-millionaire for no apparent reason. I mean, I've Googled him. Everybody Googles everybody at SHW. Does he even have a background in marketing, or even business, for that matter?"

"His money was quite helpful," Aram said, as if that explained everything.

"Steve," Kristin said. "You're spilling your drink on the rug."

"C'mon, Dr. Cooper," Steve said, ignoring Kristin, which was an excellent indication of how drunk he was. "You were gilt-edged. You'd already gotten a Ph.D. from Stanford without having to attend any classes. Wham, take a few tests, dazzle 'em with a dissertation that changed a few of the rules, and there you were. You could've gotten the money anywhere. Hell, I'd have given you the money. So I mean, it's not like I'm jealous or anything. I mean, I do all right, thanks to you. But, I'm really curious. Why Mike?"

Aram actually seemed amused.

"Perhaps I can answer your question with a question," he said.

"Turnaround's fair play, I suppose," Steve said, slurring most of the remark.

"Let's go back to the beginning. Let's say you had been playing bridge with me for approximately two months. Let's say you worked hard and safely invested a reasonable sum of money, possibly as much as you ever thought you'd have. One day, out of the blue, I say to you, 'Give it all to me. Trust me. I'll make you rich.' And even though you recognized that, in some ways, I might be unusual, you were also well aware that all ventures have their risks and you could lose everything. You'd be a fool not to ask at least a few questions. Questions such as, 'What are you planning to do with my money?' 'What guarantee do I have that you'll live up to your promise?' 'What kind of interest rates are we talking about?' and so on. You agree that you'd be a fool not to ask at least a few questions like that."

"Well, hell, yes, who wouldn't?" Steve said, placing his foot squarely in Aram's trap.

"Michael didn't ask a single question," Aram said. "He didn't even ask for anything in writing. He invited me to come to his apartment that same evening. At the time, he was living with four other people. His expenses were minimal. One of his roommates was a Haitian fellow who cooked amazing meals for practically nothing. Michael was working in a gun shop in Oakland, training people on the firing range. He's quite a good shot. Did you know that? In any case, the answer to your question comes in two parts. The first part is that Michael gave me a cashier's check for all the money that he had. The second part, which is more important, was that I was certain that he'd do exactly as he did."

"So you're saying you chose him because you knew he'd be a sucker?"

Up until that moment, Aram had been enjoying the reminiscing and the setup. However, he wasn't built to suffer fools graciously. His eyelids narrowed and his lips pursed. It was clear he was about to say something that Steve would not want to hear.

Kristin intervened by stepping in front of him and telling him it was time to take her home. Aram's adoration of her was such that all gentle requests from her were to be considered as direct orders from the Almighty. They left without another word and Steve spent the night loudly snoring in one of my guest rooms.

The next day, Aram told me he had fired Steve with the standard severance package. I argued that Steve was drunk and Aram had intentionally baited him. Aram responded that he wanted his executives to know when they're being set up. We had a real go around about it, but Aram makes up his mind like a computer. Only a logic error can alter his decisions. In that particular instance, I couldn't supply one.

Aram walked into my office and when the door closed behind him, he spoke the code to lock it.

He said, "Aram Cooper."

He put his hand on a corner of my desk and spoke a ten-digit code. My office was now guaranteed to be secure from any type of surveillance. If I said anything of a compromising nature, it would remain forever between us. In a world where private citizens might be seen, heard, and recorded at any time, we were locked together in a rare zone of total privacy.

Aram walked to my desk, leaned over, and placed the pushpins in a neat pile. Then he sat down across from me.

"Interesting," he said. "You wanted me to know you were here. The diamond symbol might have been your idea of a clever response to my phone message about the money coming in from Seattle. However, I'm sure you spoke to Terri when you arrived. It's your nature, no matter the circumstance. Terri, though first class in many ways, has an unfortunate tendency to be overly familiar with her co-workers. So the diamonds have a deeper meaning, don't they? You know the police have spoken to me. You also know how impossible it would be for me to form a response to show you how deeply it hurts me to hear that Callie is gone. So you wanted to tell me something before I saw you, something that had changed, before I came to see you. I also know that you could never be playful or mysterious this morning if Callie were dead. So, as impossible as it seems, Callie is still alive. Therefore, why did Detective Ellison tell me that she died last night and ask me all those questions? And why didn't Terri call me as I instructed?"

"I told her I'd take care of it," I said.

He nodded. He pursed his lips and frowned.

"Kristin doesn't know anything, by the way. You see how terrified I am. Afraid I'll say the wrong thing. So, please, tell me if my analysis was correct. If anything happened to Kris…"

He turned away with a guilty expression.

"Aram, you need to switch gears. Your analysis, as usual, is quite correct. I don't need consolation. I'm not mourning Callie. I'm hunting her. And I need you to be my tracker."

Aram's expression changed in an instant. His eyes glazed over slightly. Some people have sworn that it was possible to watch him retreat into the place where he processed data.

"Tell me everything," he said. "Remember. Accuracy and details."

He used a computer term.

"Garbage in, garbage out."

It meant if a computer received data that is incorrect or incomplete, it could not output an accurate result.

It took almost an hour to give him everything I could remember. When I finished with my arrival that morning at Cooper SHW, he was silent for a long time.

"So you want me, and only me, to illegally access information," he said. "From your description of Callie's state of mind, obviously she clumsily turned off the perimeter security because she planned to sneak her twin sister onto the grounds to surprise you. It follows that the people who killed her sister were able to monitor my security protocols and were ready to act at that precise moment. These are powerful people, Michael."

Aram was silent for a moment.

He said, "Is it possible that her sister was meant to be the victim?"

"Anything's possible considering what we know now," I said.

It was my turn to pause a few seconds.

"What about Fred?" I said.

"Moved to a less responsible position," Aram said.

"Don't do that. What was he supposed to do? He was between a rock and a hard place."

"He was responsible for monitoring your perimeter. Part of his job was to keep rocks and hard places apart."

"He'll get the same salary and benefits?"

"Done. If he can keep silent about it to his co-workers."

I nodded.

"Aram," I said. "It has to be you and only you. If you wear one of those new undetectable wigs, different glasses, and a goatee, no one could recognize you. At the moment, we're in the dark and, as you said, we are dealing with people who have proven they can crack your second-level security. Even your back doors onto the Net may be compromised. You'll need to work off site."

"Wig? Goatee? I could wear a burka and there's still an excellent chance the people who engineered last night would know me."

I smiled. "That wouldn't stop you, would it?"

"Of course not," he said. "I have Yuri."

Yuri was Aram's driver, bodyguard, and shadow whenever he stepped outside the confines of Cooper SHW. No one was quite sure about Yuri's background, but no one would ever want to get too close to his front. He was paid enough to die for Aram, although he was much more likely to make other people regret getting too close to Aram. Yuri was prepared to die because, in the unlikely event that occurred, his entire family and their descendants were guaranteed by contract to live a very rich life. However, Yuri was good at his job. He and his family had already been living a rich life for the past five years.

Aram took a deep breath and let it out slowly.

"No, Michael, there would be challenges much more difficult than my personal security to overcome. I'm not thirteen now and not without responsibilities. If I'm discovered, there'll be serious repercussions. Past business coups, even the most innocent ones, will be called into question. Deals we were able to pull off because I guessed our competition's strategy would certainly be endlessly litigated. In other words, if I were discovered, I wouldn't be forced to spend time as a consultant this time. They'd go after me and this company. We'd be tied up in civil, and possibly criminal, court for years. There'd be a media circus. Our research partners would pull away. The people who work here would suffer. However, worst of all, is the concentration it would take away from my work. And, finally, let's not forget that, more than a decade, an eternity on the technology clock, has passed since my last adventure into that particular realm. While I've been locked away here with SAM, James Heshedaul has spent all his time ensuring that everything about everyone is known and supposedly protected. Companies like LockDown have spent vast amounts of money and resources in order to prevent younger versions of me from venturing into places where they don't have legal access."

"Have they succeeded?" I said.

The question was rhetorical. There was only one Mozart. There was only one Aram Cooper.

"As Mr. Dylan once said, 'Even the President of the United States must sometimes stand naked.'"

That surprised me. Aram and I rarely spoke about popular culture. I considered the quote to be a good sign. He was preparing himself to venture out into the world. On the other hand, it could have been a manifestation of his comfort level at the moment.

"Maybe it doesn't have to be you," I said. "You still have some ties in the community. Is there a young hacker I could trust completely?"

Aram shuddered.

"You know how I hate that term. They showed us a new world. What did they expect us to do? We were explorers."

I felt better. It was a very good sign that Aram was complaining. Whenever he seemed in a good mood, or worse yet, if he was silent, it was time to shut the storm doors.

"So you'll do it?" I said.

"Michael, you are the only friend I have," Aram said, quietly. "There's not a shred of doubt in my mind that if it was Kristin instead of Callie, you wouldn't rest until we knew everything. As much as the press seems to enjoy convincing the world that I'm some sort of biological machine, if I didn't do everything I could for you now, I'd never be able to look at myself in the mirror again."

"It must be hard enough now," I said.

It cut the tension. Aram had a surprisingly deep and throaty laugh.

"So how would you start?" I said.

"That's easy," he said. "I need to know everything you know about Calena Lacerda."

"Unfortunately, you already know most of what I know," I said, frustrated by how little I had to offer. "She never wanted to speak about the past. I remember that she once said, 'Spend too much time in the past and the present will slip back into it.'"

Aram displayed a sour expression.

"She told me that she came to America directly from Brazil about three years ago," I said. "She took some work to get along while she studied for her real estate license. For the past year and a half, she's been working for Hill Realty on Shattuck. Her mother and father are dead. She mentioned she had two sisters and a stepbrother, but she never said anything about having a twin. Believe it or not, that's about everything relevant that I know."

Aram grunted.

"Hill Realty is the obvious place to begin," he said. "There'll be data I can access while blocking the Net in a natural manner for a reasonable amount of time. Then I'll get what the police have and cross-reference the output. There's always a dark spot to look into."

"If you've got the right flashlight," I said, smiling.

He got up.

"Come visit with SAM," he said. "You should know what I'd be giving up for a little while."

Once again, the complaining was good. He also wanted to reassure me that it would only be "a little while" until we found Callie.

Aram and I walked to L-9. He laid his hand on a plate on the side of the door. His DNA was scanned and then a sequence of ten digits appeared on a screen above it. Aram entered a seven-digit response. The numbers changed every day according to an algorithm that was stored only in Aram's brain. He had to enter the correct sequence that released the eight-inch magnetic bolts that secured the titanium door. The power source for the lock was independent and located inside L-9. If he made a mistake entering the sequence twice in a row, silent alarms would sound in several places and the door to SAM would be locked down for twenty-four hours. I couldn't imagine Aram making such a mistake.

Any explosion powerful enough to bring down the door of L-9 would take down the building as well. And such an event would instantly destroy everything of importance in the L-9. There were three backup systems. They were hardwired to areas deep underground. SAM could feel them the way a man could feel his toes. If anything touched them, SAM would render the data that they stored unusable.

However, the best backup system was Aram's brain. There was no doubt in my mind that, if necessary, he could reproduce every essential routine of SAM's code from memory.

L-9 housed Aram's vision. It was divided into two rooms. The outer one appeared to be a normal living room. A door in the back wall opened into a room that was filled with a vast array of parallel processors comprising SAM's brain. Depending on Aram's mood regarding his progress at the moment, SAM was either an acronym for *Species Autonomous Machine* or *Semi-Autonomous Moron*."

SAM was a combination of massive computational power and artificial intelligence programming. SAM had been Aram's dream since he was a boy growing up without friends. As we entered the outer room, we faced an eight by ten plasma display that either appeared as a painting or the complex code that was SAM's mind.

"Hello, SAM," Aram said, clearly.

We waited about ten seconds.

SAM said, "Full activation complete. All routines are loaded and are functioning within acceptable parameters."

SAM's voice was a reproduction of human phonemes. Aram had speeded up the simulation and, except for the slightest mechanical echo, SAM sounded like a well-trained accent-free butler.

"Good morning, Dr. Cooper," SAM said. "How are you today?"

"I'm well, SAM. Please communicate in American English."

"Of course, Dr. Cooper."

"How many languages now?" I said.

"SAM is currently fluent in eight hundred languages."

"Best in the world," Aram added with pride.

SAM had recognized my voice pattern.

"Dr. Cooper, shall I interact with Mr. Case as well?" SAM said.

"Yes, SAM," Aram replied. "My friend, Michael, is quite interested in your progress."

"Good morning, Mr. Case."

"Good morning, SAM," I said. "How are you today?"

SAM analyzed direction from sound waves. If Aram was not standing between my voice and SAM's sensors, SAM made the assumption that I was speaking to it.

"I'm well. Thank you for asking."

I turned to Aram.

"Aram, I still think you should tone down the formality. SAM is too damn polite."

"If I was raising a child, the first thing I'd teach him or her was good manners," Aram replied, with a trace of annoyance. "SAM will grow into an individual. He or she will develop a personality. Are you suggesting I add subroutines to have SAM mimic a child in Walmart screaming for a toy?"

"Point taken. Are the humor sub-routines taking?"

"Humor is one of the most difficult nuts to crack, especially because it varies across so many cultures. As you know, my own sense of humor is quite subtle and dry. It would be a disaster to have SAM think that I'm an amusing person. So what I've done is have SAM absorb as much human culture as possible and then make his own conclusions as to what's funny and what isn't. In other words, I had to let SAM develop his own ideas about what makes people laugh."

"SAM, tell Michael a brief joke," Aram said.

"Category?" SAM said.

"Absurd," said Aram.

"An attorney jumps off a twenty-story building," SAM said. "On his fall to certain death, an angel suddenly appears. The attorney says, 'Oh no, so there is a God. I think I've made a terrible mistake. Am I going to heaven or hell?' The angel answers, 'The jury will be back in about four seconds.'"

I laughed. Aram was beaming.

"SAM made that up right on the spot. Good work, SAM. You made Michael laugh."

"I have a million of them."

I swore I could hear pride in SAM's voice.

"One will suffice for the moment," Aram said. "We have work to do."

"Yes, Dr. Cooper."

"I know it's not my place, Mr. Case," said SAM. "But may I express my deepest condolences on your recent loss."

I raised my brows at Aram.

"I had nothing to do with that," he said. "Through seven firewalls of varying complexity, SAM is hooked into the Bay Area news services. You're a priority person in his program and the authorities must have revealed her identity. Anything that might directly affect you would be recorded for retrieval and action."

Aram imagined a world where you'd wake up in the morning and speak to a confidential companion who was capable of instantly accessing a database containing all knowledge of the known universe. However, SAM would be much more than just a provider of information. SAM would be a trusted super-intelligent self-aware friend, someone with opinions, someone who could offer advice when asked.

However, Aram was well aware that, at the moment, it was still only a complicated hat trick. To him, Artificial Intelligence was a set of rules to manipulate data and, when appropriate, create other rules. Computer programs, written in languages like LISP and Prolog, learned by creating their own programs while executing existing code, sometimes with surprising results. Even so, the technical advances of the past seventy years had not brought scientists much closer to recreating, or even comprehending, the mystery of organic intelligence.

Aram dreamed of the day when he would stumble upon the right combination of circuitry in a tangle of wiring and code. Suddenly, almost miraculously, he would hear the voice of a new type of conscious mind emerge from inorganic matter.

"I've improved the holographs," he said. "SAM, use medium power to simulate the weather in this area of Berkeley at thirteen hundred this afternoon."

The room darkened. A bolt of lightening seared across the room and there was a startling crack of thunder. Holographic rain began falling all around us. When Aram was satisfied the effect had been appreciated, he told SAM to end program and the room returned to normal.

"We're hooked directly into the most accurate weather stations," Aram said.

"Impressive."

"Yes, but still so far away. I hope I have time."

He looked at me quickly.

"Don't take that the wrong way."

"All of us are fighting time," I said. "I have to go now. It wouldn't seem right for me to spend the day at the office."

Aram looked uncomfortable.

"What about the funeral?" he said.

"Good question. By now, they must have informed the rest of her family in Brazil. I suppose they'll be coming."

"Grieving for the wrong child."

"What a mess."

"Can you call Phil White when you get home?"

"I'll take care of it."

"I'll have something for you soon. What will you be doing?"

"Everything I can."

As I was walking to my car, I noticed the sky beginning to cloud over.

CHAPTER 14

VOICE

The Bunker
Summer, 2001

Time entered a fifteen-by-fifteen foot room. The only furnishings were two folding chairs facing each other in the center.

He saw Treeves casually leaning back in the one furthest from the door. Time walked over without undue haste, planning to sit down in the other chair.

As he neared the empty chair, Treeves said quietly, "Don't sit down."

"All right, but if that's supposed to be some kind of Jedi Mind trick, you should know that I can still recognize the droids."

"I understand the cultural reference, but please refrain from infantile attempts at levity during these sessions. We have an enormous amount of material to cover. The quicker you become effective, the more lives will be saved."

After a moment, Treeves said, "In place of what you might consider a clever remark, tell me what I'm doing at the moment."

"You're sitting down," Time said.

"And I suppose if I had asked you what I was wearing, you would have said *clothes*."

Time said, "You're sitting on your ass looking up at me with a clear expression of superiority, your right leg is crossed over your left, your hands are folded in your lap, you're awake because you're talking and your eyes are open. Should I go on?"

"You could, but you've already missed everything," said Treeves, "I asked what I'm doing, not how I'm sitting. I am tapping my right toe in the air slightly and my left hand is moving slightly over my right. My left index finger is tapping the top of my right hand with a different rhythm than my toe. Now consider what I'm about to say very carefully.

"You don't have to sit if you'd rather not."

He paused for four or five seconds.

"Sit," said Treeves.

He spat the word out in the tone of an order given to a well-trained dog.

Time did not feel compelled to sit, but he was thrown off balance. If he sat, he'd be cementing Treeves' authority, something he was unprepared to do. If he refused to sit, it would be a small victory, but after a very short time he knew he'd be standing next to the chair, looking and feeling childishly stubborn.

Time decided to sit, slowly and deliberately.

"My right leg is over my left," said Treeves. "My left hand is over my right. For simplicity, since my leg is larger than my arm and my right leg is over my left, that signifies *correct* until we move to a more challenging level."

"So I guess that means you're right handed," Time said.

To Time's astonishment, Treeves uncrossed his legs, leaned forward, and morphed into another man right before his eyes. He felt the next sentences that Treeves spoke hit him with the speed and power of a bullwhip.

"That is the last time you will ever say or think such a ridiculous thing in my presence. You will do your best to ignore such thoughts whenever they occur to you during our training sessions. Your only task is to understand our signals, learn to request further instructions, if necessary, and instantly react to my orders. A rifle does not decide which way it should be held, or pointed, or when its trigger should be pulled. It responds to the hands that hold it, point it, and fire it. Your instructors will hone your physical skills as a Weapon, skills you may use when I tell you that they are appropriate for the situation. However, I'm the only one who decides when and how my Weapon is used."

"And if I stray from the holy path," Time said. "Will Kaicho beat some sense into me?"

Treeves fell back into a relaxed position.

"Kaicho?" Treeves said, smiling gently. "Kaicho can only hurt your body. You're used to that and can stand it. I can take you to places that you know quite well, but never want to think about. Thoughts of those places come to you every once in a while, but your mind tries hard to protect you."

Time shoulders began to burn. It felt as if they were beginning to cramp.

"I've heard it said that a loved one can break a heart with a single word. That a parent can inflict lifelong damage on the psyche of a child and not even be aware of it. Even a stranger can inflict a humiliating wound that can never be forgotten."

The pain in his shoulders was getting worse. Time fought the urge to reach up and rub them. It wasn't simply what Treeves was saying. There was a tone in his voice, not threatening, not cruel, but somehow worse than either of those. His voice felt like a scalpel slicing off pieces of Time's shoulders. Time did not want to hear what Treeves was planning to say next.

Treeves leaned forward and forced Time to meet his gaze.

"Don't worry. That was just a small demonstration. Relax."

Immediately, the pain began to subside. Time wondered if he'd been hypnotized. He couldn't imagine that his will was so weak.

Treeves said, "I doubt that we'll ever become friends. Friendship is not useful in our work. The best outcome would be if we maintain a healthy respect for our respective abilities. I will teach you how to threaten people and when to do it. Here's your first lesson. Threats are rarely useful. It boggles the mind how many people make foolish threats. Often, they make threats after the fact in conversations with uninvolved third parties. Sometimes they even obsess what they should have threatened in soft words, spoken to themselves while walking alone, long after the fact. However, when a threat is warranted, it must meet two conditions. One, the threat must be potent enough that, without question, if you carry it out you'll get what you desire. Two, you must be willing to carry out the threat immediately. Do you understand?"

"It's not complicated," said Time.

He thought about asking Treeves if he really believed he could teach him to threaten people using just his voice.

But he kept silent.

"I'll do what I can," said Treeves. "Let's begin."

CHAPTER 15

JANISON

The Berkeley Hills
Summer, 2018

Janison and Ellis were waiting for me when I got home. As they walked towards me, it seemed to me that Ellis was trying to mimic a cop in a vid. He might have looked more ridiculous if he was sporting costume-store rabbit ears. It was clear that Janison had long ago decided that foolish consistency wasn't the hobgoblin of small minds. He was dressed in the same clothes as the last time I saw him. And he looked just as tired.

He stopped directly in front of me.

"I don't care who the hell you are," he said. "Call Krause if you want, but you and I are going to talk."

"No problem," I said. "Let's go inside."

We all went into my living room. Janison and I sat down. Ellis decided to stand to my left. He must have read somewhere that standing gives a person the upper hand.

"Vid. Record all," I said.

Janison opened his mouth to speak, but before he could form the words, he changed his mind and closed his lips. Every few seconds, he went through the same motions again. I thought he looked a bit like a fish. Finally he grunted softly, tilted his head to the right and down, and began rubbing his eyes with his thumb and forefinger. After a few more seconds of that, he made a decision.

"Shut that damn thing off," he said.

I did.

Janison said to Ellis, "Go wait in the car."

"What do you mean?" Ellis said, unable to hide his confusion.

"What do you mean 'what do I mean?' Get the hell out of here."

Ellis took a step towards Janison.

"You talking to me that way in front of him?" he said. "It ain't right. You can't do that."

Janison looked at him steadily.

"I can't, detective?" he said.

When Janison said *detective*, it sounded like another word.

"Shit," said Ellis, quickly backing down.

His exit was clumsy and loud. Janison and I heard him start the car and drive away.

"There goes your ride," I said.

"He'll be back," Janison said.

It was obvious Ellis needed him more than he needed Ellis.

"We came to give you the official story," Janison said. "Nobody except the immediate family is supposed to know that's Laura Lacerda in the morgue, not Calena. But you knew that already, didn't you? Did you also know that it's a crime to withhold evidence in a murder investigation?"

"But this isn't a murder investigation anymore, is it?" I said.

He turned his head slightly from side to side.

"I knew you weren't stupid. This afternoon, two very neat suits, wearing neon signs saying federal government, had a talk with the captain. An hour later, Ellis and I got called in. 'There's no evidence that this was anything but an accidental death,' the captain says. 'The coroner's report supports that.' 'I've got some new information,' I say. 'And the boyfriend, who's no idiot and rich enough to matter, seems to think otherwise.' 'The boyfriend is so damn unreliable he identified the wrong girl.' I didn't say anything to that. 'Go smooth the boyfriend over,' says the captain. 'We got plenty of work to do around here on other cases. This one remains officially open, but off the record, you're not to spend any more time on it, you understand? The coroner's report will be filed as accidental death.' 'I don't like it,' I say. 'I'm telling you something smells bad.' The captain interrupts me before I can say anything else. 'Just what adjective would you like me to add to your file, detective?' he says. So that's the end of that."

"I've never been smoothed over by a cop before, but this seems like an unusual way to go about it."

That was a mistake. Telling the story had made him angry all over again. He exploded.

"Listen to me, shithead, I don't like people playing detective. I don't like that you walked into the morgue this morning thinking you were some Sherlock Fucking Holmes and walked out without one fucking word to me about who was lying there."

"But," I said.

"But, I've been a cop since the day I left the navy," he said, calming down. "You can't be on the job for that long without getting a sense of who's who and what's what. Ellis thinks you're Mr. Director of Corporate Bullshit. But I could put what that idiot knows about people into a shot glass and have room left over for a double. I guess you know that Aram Cooper owns this city. He says, 'Jump,' and the mayor and city council say, 'How high and into what?'"

"That's not exactly a secret," I said. "Most people in this city like Aram better than the mayor. Half of Berkeley works for his corporation in one way or another."

"That's right. And according to the records I can access, you've been a model citizen since the day you stood up out of a crawl. So I talked to people. Good people. And, I don't know, maybe I'm crazy, but, from what I heard, I get the feeling you're not the type who gets killed acting stupid."

"That wasn't my plan," I said.

"Shut up and listen," he said. "Because there's really only one reason I'm talking to you. Every day I watch animals get away with a little more. Sure, I know where they come from, but tell me what makes a fifteen-year-old kid stab another teenager to death because he's standing up for his pregnant mother? Then they punch her in the stomach, right in front of her other kids, so they can take twenty bucks off her to buy cigarettes. I catch them. The vids don't even make it hard. And if I do every damn thing right, the court puts them in juvie for six months because that's all the state can afford. Then they're back out. Only the next time, they're a little goddamn meaner."

I thought for a moment he was going to spit on my carpet.

"Somebody killed Laura Lacerda and they didn't even make sure that she wasn't Calena. You can bet they know by now. And you can bet they're looking for your girl. This morning the captain makes it very clear if I try to do anything about it, it's my ass on the line. Well, fuck them all. I hope you find out who did her and take care of business. Oh, hell yes, I see it. I saw it that night right here in this house. You'll try and kill them, won't you? Just remember one thing. Don't let me find out about it."

He reached into the inside pocket of his jacket.

Here," he said. "This is a copy of Todd Carrol's business card. I found it hidden in Calena Lacerda's apartment. Carrol runs a photography studio, but I know he's mixed up in this somehow. And I won't be talking to him."

He flipped the paper on the coffee table.

"I wrote in some extra contact info. Burn that after you memorize it. I don't want my DNA showing up in your pocket."

We heard a car pull up outside.

"Looks like your ride's back," I said. "I have to say I'm curious. Why do you work with him?"

"I had a good partner once. A jacked-up herometh dealer shot him three times right through his vest with one of those new armor-piercing rounds. I was holding him when he died. Nobody wants to work with Ellis, but I don't mind. If somebody tries to shoot me, Ellis will be all heroic about it, just like on the vid. Might even do me some good. If somebody tries to shoot him, and believe me, with his mouth, somebody will try soon enough, I'll get a chance to look good with no risk. If I save him, I'll get a promotion. If I don't, well, to be honest, I really wouldn't give a shit."

"And maybe, just maybe, you can make him a better cop?"

Janison looked at me. He'd lost ideas like that a long time ago.

"You don't know me," he said.

He opened the door to leave.

"One more thing might help," he said. "It wasn't easy, but I pulled the plates of the feds while they were in with the captain. They were U.S. State Department Security."

CHAPTER 16

PROJECTILES

The Bunker
Summer, 2001

Time woke up wondering why they were training him if the plan was to kill him in the process. He had spent the previous day with Kaicho. As he rolled out of bed at five thirty in the morning, he decided that the only part of his body that wasn't stiff from crippling pain was his hair.

At breakfast, one of the general's deaf guards laid Time's schedule for the day next to his plate. Time was relieved to note that Kaicho, and even Treeves, had the day off. There was only one item on his agenda for the entire day.

Dark Blue Corridor. Third Room On Left. 10 AM. Projectiles.

He was finding it easier to navigate the painted corridors of the Bunker and was having fewer encounters with the push-up guards. Once or twice on his way to a session with Treeves or Kaicho, he encountered an extremely attractive young woman and admired her from both the front and the back. She was a redhead with freckles and a tight little figure. Time found her posture and her horned-rimmed glass to be very sexy. On the other hand, she hadn't given him the slightest indication that she was aware of his existence. He was hoping to see her again as he navigated his way through a corridor that was currently painted a dark blue.

He opened the door of the third room on the left and stepped in. He felt as if a bird suddenly flew directly in front of his face. That sensation was followed instantly by the unmistakable thud and slight tremble of a knifepoint burrowing deep into wood.

There were two men on the opposite side of the thirty-by-thirty foot room. One was leaning against the wall with his arms crossed. The other was casually standing about two feet closer to Time, holding a fan of eleven and one-half inch, fourteen-ounce Cold Steel True Flight throwing knives in his left hand. Time turned to see the same kind of knife buried deep into an entirely wooden wall behind him. Its blade couldn't have missed his nose by more than an inch or two.

"Projectiles," Time said. "I get it. But if you do that again, I'll be over there before you can raise another one and I'll give you a quick demonstration of what Kaicho has taught me the past couple of weeks."

"I don't have to raise them," the man said, with a pronounced Spanish accent. "I could throw all of these underhand and I'm sure none of them would miss you at this distance. The purpose of these sessions is not to teach you how to throw like me. I am to teach you how to deal with objects that are thrown at you. My name is Manu. I will do what I can to have you understand edged weapons."

Manu nodded his head towards the man leaning on the wall.

"That's Iain. His specialty is firearms."

Manu pronounced the word *firearms* as if he were talking about toys that would only interest children.

"I don't see any firearms," Time said.

"I will not have those noisy foolish things in here," said Manu. "Where's the art in pointing with your finger and blowing out little pellets."

"Manu's a right prima donna with his babies," Iain said. "However, don't you fret now. Later, I'll show you some pellets, all right. You'll see more firearms than you ever dreamed about. Name's Eee-ann, by the way, not Eee-eye-un, the way this bleeder pronounces it."

"You're British," Time said. "SAS from the look of you. How did you wind up in this madhouse?"

Manu's gaze went up towards the ceiling.

"Right you are. I was SAS. In for life. Or so I thought. Then comes along this lieutenant, right little prick he was. He was like to get half of us killed for king and country. Learned combat tactics at his fancy boarding school, I imagine. I was about twenty meters off and at least that pissed. Anyway, I suddenly found my Browning HP in my hand and it sort of raises itself all by itself. I was aiming for between his eyes, see, but only for the good feeling in it. I wasn't really going to pull on him. Then, suddenly, for no bloody reason I'll ever know, the Browning goes off. Startled the hell out of me, tell you that. Next thing I knew, he had quite the hole in his jaw. Now, if I was going to shoot him for real, I wouldn't have done sloppy work like that. Even so, probably nothing would have come of it, but he had some royal connection, twice or three times removed. They put the bloodhounds on it, I can tell you that. I was sure they were going to put me in MCT, Military Corrective Training, for a bloody couple hundred years. But along comes the good general, great man he is, and I just sort of disappeared. Wound up here as sort of an odds and end man, if you follow my drift."

Manu said, "If you're through with your charming story, which I have now officially heard over a hundred times, may I have the attention of my student?"

"Don't get a burrito up your butt, Manu," Iain said.

"'Spouse he's right, though," Iain said to Time. "It's his hours. Good luck with what he's got to show. Don't worry. We'll have some fun later."

Iain winked at Time.

"The general said I'd be the best soldier in the world," Time said to Manu. "Frankly, I have some doubts about that. Do you really think that you can teach me to throw knives like you?"

Manu and Iain exchanged a look, both slightly nodding their heads from side to side.

"You think you will handle knives like me?" Manu said.

With a movement as calm and fluid as leaf floating on a soft summer breeze, he used his right hand to select a blade from the fan in his left hand and threw it at Time. It was only an illusion that he did slowly. Time had no chance to get out of the way as the razor-sharp edge flew within an inch of his right ear and, once again, the knife buried its tip half-inch into the wood behind him at a perfect ninety-degree angle.

"What the hell's wrong with you?" said Time. "Stop doing that!"

"I began throwing knives in Madrid when I was four years old," said Manu. "I have thrown them all day every day. And not only knives, but anything I could place in a target. I was thirty-six two months ago. I know where my children will rest before they leave my hand. You will never love them as I do. You will never speak to them. So they will never listen to you when you throw them with your clumsy hands. They know there is no love for them in those hands. If you prayed to them for a hundred years, they would not listen to you."

Iain shook his head.

"Bloody circus freak," he said.

He started to say, "Oughta be popping balloons ..."

However, he saw the look on Manu's face and thought better of it.

"Well, if you can't teach me to throw, I don't see much point to it," said Time.

The Spaniard's arrogance annoyed him. He thought his comment might return the favor.

"Oh, I will teach you to throw. And you will practice every day. You will get along. But even after I am finished with you, I wouldn't throw beautiful knives like these at someone you care about. I will also show you how to use a sharp edge or point in close. With your speed that shouldn't be too hard. It is only a matter of good places and bad places. When to feint, slash, or thrust. With Kaicho's help, you'll be able to stop people from getting at your bad places too easily. No. The most important thing I will teach you is to watch the thrower. Watch the hand, the torso, the shoulder, the eyes, everything. If I say to you now, the next knife I throw will enter your throat just below your chin, that should help you get out of the way. Here it comes."

While he had been speaking, Manu had transferred the fan of knives from his left hand to his right. He made a knife appear in his left hand and threw it at Time. As soon as Time saw the knife enter Manu's hand, he moved a foot to his left. The knife chunked into the wooden wall behind him exactly where his throat had been a moment ago.

"Of course, Dr. Treeves can tell you more than I can."

"Speaking of Dr. Treeves," said Iain.

"Look at the wall behind you," said Manu.

Time hadn't paid much attention to the wall since he entered the room. He was more concerned with what was coming at him from the other side of the room. He turned and saw startlingly realistic drawings of Edgar Treeves etched into the wood.

"Put on the suit," Manu said, nodding towards the corner of the room to his left where there appeared to be a pile of wood.

Time walked over. There was a suit of armor that looked like something Don Quixote might have worn. It had two parts. Both consisted of a stretch polyester fabric that was covered in slats of wood. There was a large chest and back plate. The arms, legs, feet, and hands of the wearer were protected by the wood with joints at the elbows, wrists, crotch, knees, and ankles. There were also spaces between the wooden slats that offer no protection whatsoever against Manu's razor-sharp knives. There were patches of green and red covering the areas of the suit. The implication was obvious. Manu intended to throw knives at him while he was covered in this wooden armor.

"Put it on," said Manu.

"You've got to be kidding," said Time. "I'm not putting that on so you can toss knives at me."

"You're not?" said Manu, looking perplexed. "Didn't the general tell you what you are? If a target throws something at Dr. Treeves, you must make sure it doesn't get to him. If you can't reach something to stop it, you'll have to use your body. The green areas are good areas. Catch the knife there and you can still fight. Don't let the knife hit you in the red areas. That's not so good."

Time looked at the suit.

"I want to talk to General Tresain," Time said.

"General Tresain isn't in the bunker right now," Manu said. "But Kaicho is here. I think he's doing his meditation. I have never disturbed him during his meditation. You know, I am actually curious as to what would happen."

Time walked over and began putting on the suit. His mind was spinning.

"Just one question. How am I supposed to quickly get into this suit in combat? Will I have something to wear under my clothes?"

Manu and Iain looked at each other for a moment. Then they burst out in loud hearty laughter as if they'd heard a hilarious joke.

Iain caught his breath first.

"Bloody hell," he said. "He thinks he's going to wear armor under his clothes! What are you going to tell targets when they search you, mate? You got your special little suit in Saville Row."

Both of Time's instructors began laughing again.

After four grueling hours with Manu, Iain led Time into a room that looked like a warehouse of every hand-held firearm produced in the past two hundred years.

"I'm told you're a decent shot," Iain said. "I'll make you a better one, but that's the least important part of my job."

"You're not going to be shooting at me while I wear some kind of tin can, are you?"

Iain laughed.

"I like you, mate. No, I won't be firing right at you. You see, the thing is, in most situations with Dr. Treeves, you can't be carrying any kind of firearm. Dead giveaway as to who you are. You can't ever be perceived to be any kind of threat. What I'm going to teach you is how to deal with a target carrying a firearm. Dr. Treeves will let you know who's a good shot. The one who has the ability to put a bullet in your head the quickest. But Dr. Treeves' area is people. He doesn't know a Ruger from a Colt. A twenty-two from a forty-five. You need to know how much damage the cartridge'll do. Whether the shooter has his weapon on safety or is ready to fire. You see all these beautiful weapons? As a soldier, you know the low-caliber models have less recoil than the high ones. Of course, that affects both accuracy and damage. We'll start with the most common ones and work our way down to these small plastic models. They'll go right through most security checkpoints, but they won't be accurate over a certain range. Even a target, unless they're planning to go down with the ship, won't fire a higher-caliber weapon in a plane."

Time looked around.

"I'll never learn all that," he said.

"Why not?" said Iain. "I did."

"Over how many years? Did you start like Manu, when you were four years old?"

"Six, actually. But don't you worry, mate. I'm the best there is. Little by little, you'll pick it up. And there's plenty of duplication. We've got time."

"Time?"

"You bet," said Iain. "At least two years, if you survive."

Eight hours later, Time lay on his bed in his small sleeping cell, the sound of gunfire still making his eardrums vibrate. Iain has insisted he wear only minimum ear protection.

"You won't be having those things out in the field," he said. "You might as well get used to it."

"I've heard weapons fire before," Time said.

"Like this?"

Without warning, Iain fired a twenty-two not three feet away from Time's head. The memory of it made his body tense.

Before he lay down, he had dimmed the lights in the room. He soaked a washcloth in cool water and placed it over his eyes, hoping to ease the pounding in his head.

Time didn't move when the door opened, but he prepared himself. He had no idea who, or even what, was about to enter. Was it Kaicho, planning to give him another beating? Or perhaps it was Manu, wanting to know if Time could stop an intruder from plunging a knife into him while he slept.

"If you're going to kill me, just get on with it," Time said. "I'm too beat to stop you."

"I don't think that's your best attitude when you're in the field."

Time pulled away the cloth. The redhead with the glasses was standing there in the Bunker's standard uniform. She began unbuttoning her top. When she got to the fourth button, Time saw she wasn't wearing a bra. Her breasts were round and firm. They ended in small nipples that pointed directly at him.

"So what are you?" Time said. "My prize for being a good humored punching bag and all-around target for every damn weapon you can throw, fire, or stick at someone?"

"Pretty damn sexist," she said. "How do you know that you're not my prize?"

"Meaning?"

"I'm off to somewhere far away from here tomorrow. There's a very good chance I won't come back. You may be my last chance to be with someone I'm not playing."

She had gotten to the last button and pulled the blouse wide open.

"If you want me to leave, just say so."

Time slid over to make room for her.

"Leave your glasses on for the time being," he said.

CHAPTER 17

SUSPECT

The Bay Area
Summer, 2018

I called Aram after Janison left. Then I put my head on a pillow on the couch for a few minutes to consider what I'd learned. The next thing I remember I heard the vid calling me. Trying to clear my head, I crossed the room to stand in front of the wall vid. The moment I got near it, I knew it was Callie.

"Vid on," I said. "Full."

The other end was audio only. All I could hear was her breathing.

"It's okay, Callie," I said. "It's me. I'm alone."

"Michael, I'm so sorry."

"Callie, are you safe? Are you unhurt? Tell me where you are."

"I had to talk to you one more time. I had to explain."

"Callie, please don't waste time. Everything will be all right. Just tell me where you are and I'll come get you. You'll be safe here with me."

"I knew you'd find out it was Laura," she said.

Her voice was on the edge of breaking. Her next words came out in a rush.

"I brought her in right after you went inside to take your shower. We were laughing. I was telling her to be quiet. She already had her suit on. She went out to the pool to wait for you. I was going to hide in the house and come out when you were in the pool with her. We thought it would be so funny. My God. I thought of something to tell her. I went out to tell her. I didn't see her. I saw him leaving. I panicked. I thought he'd taken her. I followed him, but he was alone. He got in a car. I didn't know what to do. I went back to the house. I could hear sirens and so many cars. I was so scared for you. I prayed Laura was safe. I ran. My God, I ran. Then I heard it on the vid. *Meu Deus*. He killed Laura."

She began crying.

"Michael, it's all my fault," she said. "I'm so sorry. I want to die."

"Callie, it's not your fault. Tell me where you are. We'll work this out."

"My sister's dead!" she said. "If anything happens to you, I'll die. You have to forget about me. Forget you ever met me. I don't ever want to see you again."

"Callie, please don't waste time. This is a secure line. Aram guaranteed it. Just tell me where you are. There's nothing that could change my mind about you. Trust me now."

"No. You must never know. Forget about me, Michael. Forget all of it. You don't know him. He'll kill us both."

"Callie, listen, I know everything that I need to know about you," I said. "You don't have to tell me anything you don't want to. I don't care. You have to trust me. I can protect you. Please, Callie, I'm begging you. Just tell me where I can find you."

"No, Michael. Don't try to find me. I knew that you would. I only called to tell you that you have to stop now."

"I'll stop the moment I find you."

"You're not listening to me. You don't know what you're doing."

"Then help me. Tell me where you are. We'll talk so that I'll know what I'm up against."

"Michael, always remember you're my angel. It's the same word in Portuguese, but it sounds like this."

She pronounced it for me.

"Say it."

"I'm your angel."

"Never forget that. When my family comes, don't say you were my fiancé. Say that you're my angel. Please. You must remember that."

"I'll remember. I promise. Now you have to do something for me…"

But I was talking to a dead line. I called Aram.

"Callie just called my house. Can you find out where that call came from?"

"I'll do my best," he said.

After I hung up, I thought about it. Callie was no fool. She'd probably called from a burner vid somewhere on the road. Now she was gone. It might help me to figure her general direction from the Bay Area, but it wouldn't be any real help in locating her.

For a moment, I'd been with her. I'd heard her voice. I had her and I failed to convince her. The moment had passed so quickly and there'd be no more chances. At least I was certain that she was alive. Flashes of relief, frustration, and anger pounded through me. I grabbed a vid on a stand and threw it against the wall as hard as I could.

It bounced off the wall, and then, remarkably, it floated over to its cradle. A moment later, it began calling me. Truly, it was one of the most remarkable inventions of all time.

I answered.

"Callie?" I said.

"Sorry, it's Aram. I'm still at Hill Realty, by the way. I'm sitting in an excruciatingly uncomfortable office chair in front of ugly computer terminal which is producing information at a primitive rate."

Translation: Aram was having a wonderful time playing detective.

"Talk to me."

"Michael, I've set up a secure dedicated line to your private vid. When I say I'm ready, respond clearly with your house code. All right. It's done. We're secure. When I arrived here, Yuri waited outside. I told the owner that I was a freelance computer consultant who specialized in organizing and upgrading real estate databanks. He was skeptical. I asked him if I could examine his computer system for ten minutes, no charge. Thirty minutes later, after I'd pounded it into his thick skull how, even on this outdated equipment, I could cut his data retrieval time by almost half, and make it more productive as well, he offered me a job at ninety dollars an hour."

"Great."

"Have you lost your mind?" Aram said. "I'm going to increase his data retrieval by seventy two percent and the cretin offers me ninety dollars an hour?"

"Aram," I said. "Focus on reality. You're worth close to ninety billion dollars."

"What does that have to do with anything?" Aram said. "I told him that I wouldn't take a penny less than two hundred dollars an hour and, at that, I was giving him an incomparable bargain because in my own words, 'I don't know, Jack. You seem like a really nice guy.' I did that for you, Michael."

"So?"

"So everyone's out and I'm working on the system. Have Aurelian send over something to eat. Not too spicy. My stomach is already upset from looking at this database program which looks like it was written by a trained gorilla."

"It's done. I'll have him send over some silicon chips and spaghetti wiring."

"If you plan on making any more remarks at my expense when I could be home with my head on Kristin's lap, they better be more amusing than that."

"Agreed. What have you found out so far?"

"What do you mean? I've found out everything there is to know."

"So now you're actually doing the work for the realty company, aren't you?"

"Of course, I signed a contract under the same Sam Semi. So you can add forgery to the list of crimes I've perpetrated today. In any case, a contract's a contract."

There was no use discussing it further with him. I filled him in on Janison's visit and Callie's call. He agreed there wasn't much point tracing her call.

"I'm not inclined to take any unnecessary risks," he said. "Here's what I know for certain. Calena Lacerda passed the California Real Estate Exam about fifteen months ago and began working at Hill Realty. Since March of last year, she was paid a total of three hundred and twenty thousand dollars."

I whistled softly.

"Pretty good for a fledging real estate agent," I said.

"Extraordinary, considering that she never sold any property."

"What?"

"Exactly. She was paid that considerable sum, but not for the normal duties of a real estate agent. The payments and the taxes seem to be in order, but there are no hard transactions to justify those payments. While we've been talking, I checked on Todd Carrol. Carrol is a photographer and the CEO of Models Living Incorporated. Records here show that, in the past year, Models Living paid Hill Realty six hundred seventy five thousand dollars in fees."

"Let me guess. Models Living never bought any property."

"That's correct. A careful cross-indexing shows that the six hundred seventy five thousand was more in the nature of real estate expansion consulting fees. Wait a minute. I have to go. I call back."

Fifteen minutes later, my secure line rang.

"What happened?"

"The owner stepped in to see how it was going," Aram said.

"So you casually mentioned the name Carrol to the office manager to get his reaction."

Aram made a noise that sounded like *Puh*.

"Can you imagine I'd be so clumsy? I demonstrated some of the improvements I made in the software. I worked it so that the name Models Living appeared on the screen in a random test of client access. I watched his face inconspicuously when it happened."

"And?"

"He tried to be casual when he asked for a command that would necessitate a new screen. But he was clumsy."

"So Callie was being paid by a photography studio through a real estate company for doing nothing."

There was a silence at the other end of the phone. It sounded like the silence that might arise between a frustrated teacher and a dull student.

"There are a discrete number of things in this world of which I'm absolutely certain," Aram said. "One of them is that no one creates an elaborate corporate pipeline to pay a new employee over three hundred thousand dollars for doing nothing."

CHAPTER 18

~~~~~~~~~~~~~~~~~~~~~~~~~~~~~~~~~~~~~~~

MARIA

Chechnya
Winter, 2013

Maria's dark blond hair smelled of strong soap. The back of her head rested in the crook between Time's arm and his left shoulder. They were pressed together in order to squeeze onto Maria's single bed in her windowless bedroom. Minutes ago, she had cried out her pleasure. When they made love, even when he was on top, Time could easily lift her to bring her closer to him. She was thirty-one years old and not quite three-quarters his size.

They were naked. It was cold in the room. A scratchy woolen blanket covered them in the minutes before they reached the height of their pleasure. Afterwards, when Maria snuggled close to him, she pulled it back over them to keep their sweat-covered bodies from shivering.

She sighed deeply.

"Sometimes you make the world seem different," Maria said. "I forget for a while. Sometimes, when we make love, I imagine I can see through a window to the sky."

Time looked at the wall. Even if Maria could afford a room with windows, it wouldn't be wise. A Chechen rebellion was in full swing. A nearby explosion would shred them with flying shards of glass.

"I can't stay with you tonight," Time said.

"I didn't think you would," she said. "But will you stay here a little while after your business is done?"

"I'll try. But I have to go where the work is. It all depends how business goes for my current employer."

Maria smiled in the dark.

"Then I hope your business goes badly for him so you'll have to stay longer."

A month ago, Time had joined Treeves and General Tresain, already in the middle of a pre-mission briefing. Time wondered how much information they were keeping from him regarding the upcoming operation. The general was halfway through a Cuban Cohiba Robusto.

On April 17th, 1960, three months into John F. Kennedy's term of office, Martin Tresain was escorted to the president's private quarters. He found Kennedy dressing for dinner, his hair still damp after one of the many showers he took every day.

Tresain had great respect for Kennedy. He considered him a brave and brilliant man. However, the general felt the president was unseasoned and unqualified to be commander in chief. That night, Kennedy's appearance gave Tresain serious cause for concern. He'd seen the young president in excruciating pain, both mental and physical, however he'd never seen him so low.

"How did you know?" Kennedy said, without prefacing the question with any type of greeting.

"I didn't know for sure, Mr. President. But I knew the people running the operation couldn't be trusted to do it correctly."

"I should have trusted you, Martin. I will from now on. However, except for Bobby, I don't want anyone to know about it. I don't want you in on discussions or arguments. I want the two of us to go over all of it with you afterwards. You'll be at my right hand whenever I make my final military decisions. Nothing like what happened during the last two days can ever happen again during my watch."

"I understand, Mr. President."

The next day, ten boxes of Kennedy's treasured stash of Cohibas appeared in Tresain's living quarters. In 1962, during the Cuban Missile Crisis, he never left John Kennedy's side.

Tresain had taken great pains to properly preserve the Cubans for the next forty-one years. He only smoked one when he wanted to feel reassured that his judgment was sound. The fragrant smoke informed Time that he was walking into something bad.

"The two of you are going to separate," the general said.

Time and Treeves had never been apart on a mission.

Time surprised everyone by nodding towards Treeves and saying, "Who will take care of him?"

Treeves cocked his head slightly and looked at him with an expression Time hadn't seen before.

"Don't concern yourself with Dr. Treeves," the general said. "He'll be safe. He'll be out in the open and ten of my men, including five of my best snipers, will cover him at all times."

"And what will I be doing while he's taking this little vacation?" Time said.

"This," said the general.

He handed Time a photograph of a woman. She wasn't a classic beauty, but her features were alluring and even her photograph foretold the strong sexual magnetism that many eastern European woman radiated.

"Get close to her," the general said. "Find out everything you can about her, her friends and associates. Everything about everyone she knows. She'll have her guard up. It won't be easy."

"We've covered the subject of male-female relations," Treeves said, without a hint of humor or lechery.

"What is she?" said Time. "Chechen resistance? A spy for the Russians?"

"She's a school teacher," said the general. "It's not about what she is, but rather the circles she travels in. The people she grew up with. Some of those people occupy very important positions in the resistance."

"When you say 'get close to her,' how close do you mean?"

The general and Treeves exchanged a glance.

"As close as you can," the general said.

"So now I'm a gigolo?" said Time.

The general shot him one of his hard looks. He blew out the puff he'd taken on his cigar.

"You're whatever you need to be," he said.

"And, Time," said Treeves. "Be careful."

It hadn't been easy. It had taken Time a week before he was able to crack her shell and have a short conversation with her. They had grown closer over the course of a month. They'd been lovers for two days.

"You have bad scars," Maria said. "Were you such a bad soldier?"

Time could feel her smile on his chest.

"Would a bad soldier be here to do this?" he said.

He raised his head and gently kissed her willing lips. Even though Time had been smoking terrible Russian cigarettes without inhaling, he could still detect their foul odor on Maria's breath.

She had seen only his freshest scars. The Bunker's world-class team of plastic surgeons had been able to remove almost all evidence of many of his smaller wounds. Maria ran her finger over one large scar that remained. It ran from the middle of Time's chest, horizontally across the right side of his body, ending under his right armpit.

"What happen here? It looks as if you were cut almost in two," she said.

"I fell on a shovel while I was digging a trench," Time said.

"Ha ha," said Maria. "Did you find out the shovel's name?"

She paused.

"You have such a strange name. Ty. Who would call their baby, Ty?"

It had been a quick setup. Time only knew the basics of his cover. It wasn't a subject he wanted to explore.

"A school teacher, just like you. Except that she was a meth abuser in the American heartland. I don't want to talk about it."

They heard an explosion in the distance. Neither of them said anything for a while. Maria began shaking. Time knew this woman was not afraid for herself. She was one of the bravest and strongest women he had ever known.

"You're afraid for the children," Time said, finally.

Maria shifted her weight.

"Sometimes I look at them and think that they've never known anything but war," Maria said. "It's not a way to be young."

It was the first time he had broached the subject of the rebellion. Treeves' had studied her. He advised a great deal of patience. It would be impossible to make her talk. Time had to wait until she wanted to talk. He felt her relaxed glow after their lovemaking. He felt ashamed and kept silent.

"There has to be an end," Maria said. "They have to understand that there has to be an end."

"Everything ends," said Time.

He knew that was a ridiculous statement. Chechnya had been at war, in one way or another, since long before the fifteenth century. The latest dust up was only one in a long series of conflicts fought over this mineral-rich, but cold mountainous land. Chechnya was a pot into which had been poured religious intolerance, avarice, and political deceit. The basic elements of human conflict. Stir well and suffer.

Maria moved her slim leg in between Time's thigh. As she raised herself over him, he felt the nipples on her small breasts grow harder. She kissed his neck, his chin, and then his mouth. The pressure of her leg aroused him.

"Make love to me," she said.

She reached down and guided him into her. She pushed herself down and turned her head to the wall.

"Give me my window," Maria said.

That afternoon they went to a restaurant and ate Djepelgesh, a Chechen concoction of potatoes, dough, and smelly dark spices.

"Do you know what we call the Red Army?" said Maria.

Time shook his head.

"Chechen dog food."

They laughed.

Two tables away, Edgar Treeves sipped his tea. Later that night, Time slipped away to join Treeves at a safe house.

"I'm getting nowhere," said Time. "What are the hell are we doing here?"

"We're renegade Russian arms dealers. At least, I am. You're my protection. Our buyer, Makkhal, is a Chechen rebel leader."

Time grunted.

"Renegade Russian arms dealers? Aren't all Russian arms dealers renegades? What are we selling? Rifles? Handguns?"

"No, the Strela 9K32, a shoulder-fired, low-altitude missile system with a high explosive warhead and passive infrared homing guidance. You might recall NATO labeled it the Grail. What it lacks in range, speed, and altitude, it makes up for in portability. The Grail is a tail-chase missile system and its effectiveness stems from its ability to lock onto the heat sources of low-flying aircraft."

"So these won't be functional?"

"Really, Time, sometimes your lack of understanding of even the most basic human behavioral parameters is simply astonishing. The missiles must be functional. We're not interested in Makkhal. He's been compromised and he's a rather small fish. We want the man who controls him and several others. This sale is the first step in moving up the ladder. How could we get any further with Makkhal if we sold him non-functional missiles? Don't you think he'll test them?"

"I don't get it. How can we hand over weapons like that to a terrorist?"

"The missiles contain sophisticated homing devices. The general will be able to track the position of each missile to within six meters. They'll fail to operate properly against objects that exceed a size limit. They'd destroy a small helicopter or plane, but their heat-seeking systems would fail and they'd veer off course if fired at aircraft as large as a Blackhawk or passenger jet. Shortly after Makkhal takes the shipment, the general will offer him a target so tempting he won't be able to refuse. Makkhal will be convinced that a small helicopter is carrying an important Russian official. In reality, the helicopter will be unmanned. We believe that once Makkhal succeeds in shooting down that helicopter, he'll deliver the remainder of the missiles to his control. The general will scoop them up all at once."

"This entire operation seems ridiculously risky to me."

"You noticed the general smoking one of his precious cigars."

"The whole setup stinks. Why are we against people who are fighting for their freedom?"

"Don't be naïve, Time. There are plans within plans. Since the end of the cold war, Russian criminals have been selling nuclear materials and weapons. The Chechens don't have any. With which side should we align ourselves?"

"I don't like any of this," Time said.

"You actually care for her, don't you?"

"That part is not your business, Treeves."

"Before you become too fond of that woman, let me assure you that if you make the slightest slip, you'll wake up to the unpleasant sensation of feeling your throat being slit."

CHAPTER 19

<hr/>

BUSINESS

Todd Carrol's Studio
Summer, 2018

The next day, Jackson's assistant made a two-thirty appointment for me to meet with Todd Carrol at Models Living. The stated reason was to discuss promotional photography for The Ahh Baloney Café. Aram and I spent the morning in L-9 with SAM.

Aram had gathered a great deal of information on Carrol's personal and professional life. As a photographer, Carrol was mildly successful. He'd done a few shoots for national magazines, even a Playboy layout. His bread and butter was freelance advertising shoots of professional models, some of whom he also managed. He had a reputation for working with beautiful people, generally staying away from the kind of work that involved still lifes of cars and hamburgers.

He was thirty-two. Seven years ago, he'd moved to California from New York after finishing a fine arts degree at Queens College. By accessing his credit card receipts for the past five years, Aram discovered Carrol belonged to three health clubs. Between IRS records, credit reports, and things like health insurance forms, an American would have to live in a cave and exist by barter to cling to any hope of privacy. To someone like Aram, who entered and manipulated databases with the same ease that many people surfed the Web, a person's financial situation, purchases, and medical history were open books waiting to be checked out of a vast digital library.

As soon as he finished at Hill Realty, he went to work with SAM. There were times when I wondered if Aram ever slept. At some point during the short trip to L-9, Aram decided that if he was to be Archie Goodwin, the mobile half of Rex Stout's immortal detecting team, it was only right that he should have a Nero Wolfe, the obese genius who almost never left the confines of his New York Brownstone, but always solved the crime from a custom-made chair.

At seven-fifteen in the morning, I got call from Aram asking me to join him.

As soon as I arrived, Aram said, "As you know, SAM has been programmed with a great deal of practical knowledge. I've implemented expert systems in history, finance, medicine, psychology, law, and many other disciplines. Many of the best people in these fields contributed to his knowledge base. As a matter of fact, Paul Arons called me a month ago in order to update SAM's medical knowledge base regarding Paul's most recent work with genetically engineered viruses."

"SAM is definitely male now? That's new."

Aram smiled.

"I thought it might help developing the personality routines and, considering the amount of time I spend here, I thought Kristin might get a tad jealous if I continued to sometimes refer to SAM as a female."

"In any case," he continued, "I believe you're aware that an expert system is basically a set of facts and rules. A program can access the facts and apply the rules. The result can then be added to the available facts and new rules may be generated. Of course that's a gross over-simplification. In fact..."

I held up my hand.

"Thanks," I said. "I'm delighted with the simple explanation."

"As you wish. Considering that premise, it occurred to me last night that since detective work is basically logic applied to a set of known facts, why not write a program so that SAM could help us analyze the known data relating to Callie?"

"Sounds interesting. When can you start?"

"It's done," Aram said. "It wasn't difficult. The facts are limited and the rules are basic."

"You wrote an expert system overnight?"

"You've got that look on your face again," Aram said, pursing his lips.

"What look?"

"The same look you had on the day we met when I told you your score was sixty-seven percent and you came in third."

"Do you ever forget anything?" I said. "How does it feel to be able to use your mind like that?"

"It doesn't feel like anything. How does it feel to use your hand? Michael, really, I understand you're under a great deal of stress. However, I don't expect questions like that from you.

"You express amazement at the way my mind functions. Sometimes I wonder if you still believe it's some sort of trick. From the moment I realized I had something to work with, I've trained my intellect to be useful.

My mind functions as it does because I've continually challenged it, forced it to expand. For myself, I'm often amazed how other people, whatever intellect they possess, are content to sit for hours in front of a vid which has the sole purpose, in between short doses of insipid entertainment, of convincing them to accumulate products which they would either buy anyway or haven't the slightest intention of buying?

"Almost everyone is born with the priceless gifts of reason and insight. How can they allow themselves to be so easily manipulated? For the wrong reasons, they vote for fools and obvious liars. And when those leaders, through incompetence or worse, cause calamitous effects on our world, they're permitted to spill out a few more popular lies and continue along without consequences. We're staring at worldwide economic and ecological disaster and the very people who have contributed to it the most are allowed to go merrily forward."

"All this couldn't have something to do with what Kristin told me a couple of days ago?"

That stopped him cold.

"She told me she didn't want anyone to know for a while."

After a moment, he said, "She's truly fond of you."

Aram looked around.

"I hope SAM will make a difference. He can be a super-intelligent friend and advisor. Imagine having at your fingertips an unbiased vessel of all known facts, always available to help you make informed decisions, to let you know what's real and what's not."

"No world is perfect, Aram," I said. "And don't forget you'll have to use the vid to convince people to accept it."

"A necessary evil."

"Besides, I'm not so sure people want reality," I said. "Sometimes I think humanity is more like a giant bureaucracy. A lot of people are more content with a pleasant-sounding lie than a truth that doesn't fit into their forms."

"And you? Are you really looking for the truth?" Aram said.

"Meaning?"

"If we investigate further, you may be unhappy with what we uncover."

"My happiness isn't the issue. I'm only interested in the people who killed an innocent young woman and are searching for Callie right now. And we're burning time so, if you've no further objection, let's get on with it."

Aram slowly closed his eyes and then opened them.

"We'll use the wall screen."

The wall opposite the entrance to L-9 held a twelve-by-eight foot ultra high-resolution computer screen. We sat facing it.

Aram said, "SAM, wake up, please."

"Good morning, Dr. Cooper," SAM said.

"SAM, detective mode."

"Ready, Dr. Cooper."

"Let's begin with Todd Carrol's finances," Aram said to me. "For the past four years, he's been living way beyond his means. And he hasn't been sufficiently careful about it. A year ago, the Internal Revenue Service initiated an investigation. There was plenty to investigate, but after three months the process was suspended and his case hasn't been reopened. Naturally, SAM is fully programmed on our tax laws and the general operating procedures of the IRS."

"After that business a couple of years ago, I'm not surprised."

"Perhaps you shouldn't have contributed so generously to that organization."

"We've had that discussion. Let's move on."

"SAM, comment on the IRS actions regarding Todd Carrol," Aram said.

"Unusual," SAM responded. "Investigations of this nature are rarely terminated so abruptly."

"Possible causes for termination?"

"Usually the death of the subject," said SAM. "Other causes for termination include timely adequate settlements, courtesy requests by another government agency…"

"Wait," I said. "Janison said that the investigation into Callie's murder was suspended after members of our State Department spoke to his captain."

"SAM," Aram said. "Cross reference data regarding Carrol and the U.S. State Department."

"Carrol maintains a United States Passport and the United States State Department maintains a standard data set on him. There are no unusual connections."

"Does Carrol have dual citizenship?" said Aram.

"No."

"Is there anything that might indicate relations with or connections to a foreign government?"

"Accessing. No data of that type is available."

"SAM, check if he served in our armed forces," I said.

"Mr. Carrol has no military record."

"Does he have any criminal record?"

"Mr. Carrol has never been charged with a crime," SAM said.

"What about personal relationships and characteristics?" I said.

Aram answered for SAM.

"We know Carrol is homosexual," Aram said.

"That's pretty definitive conclusion. You extrapolated that from his lifestyle data?"

"Really, Michael, this is the twenty-first century. Mr. Carrol is not keeping his sexual preference a secret. He's vocal, but not militant."

"Let's try another avenue," Aram said. "Even though we know Carrol's preferences, it's not impossible that he's tested their limits at some point. Please don't take offense."

"Go ahead. There's more important things at stake."

Aram said, "SAM, was Calena Lacerda ever Carrol's partner, or even his wife? Did she have any type of intimate relationship with him?"

"No evidence or records," said SAM.

"So there's no evidence she was ever involved with him sexually?" said Aram.

"No data to support that conclusion."

"What does that mean?" I said to Aram. "How could SAM possibly know if they slept together?"

"Obviously, SAM can't," said Aram. "However, he can access all of Carrol's non-cash transactions. He can even access records where Carrol paid in cash and used his own name, perhaps to rent a hotel room. It's extremely rare, if not impossible, in our society for a man to have an intimate relationship with a woman without spending money on her in some way. Of course, that's just one of many factors. SAM also scans all Bay Area media for references…"

I held up my hand.

"I get the idea," I said. "SAM looks for any detail at all that might indicate a relationship and, since relationships between men and women tend towards the physical, that would raise the probability of intimacy."

"Well, yes, that would be it, very simply stated."

There was more. Much more, in fact. By the time I was on my way to Models Living, I knew a great deal about Todd Carrol, but none of it made any difference in what happened.

Models Living was located in a converted two-story warehouse in a section of San Francisco that had been industrial and was now trendy. There was a loading dock where, in other times, full-sized trucks had pulled in. It still smelled vaguely of the things that had been unloaded there, including a fair amount of human urine.

I walked up a ramp next to a space for two trucks and arrived at a sign that was so discreet it was almost non-existent. There was a bell and an even smaller sign that requested, in so many words, that I state my name and business with force and clarity. If I hadn't been looking for them, I might not have seen them. To be fair, I was concentrating on other things. I did notice that a plaque attached to the door read, *Monitored and Protected by Cooper Security.*

A woman's voice assured me I was expected. The large industrial elevator had a slatted wooden gate that slid up without any effort on my part. The inside of the old freight elevator was immaculate. Once the door closed and the elevator smoothly started up, I smelled only the fresh odor of lemon-scented cleaning products.

On the first floor, the door rose by itself again and, twelve steps ahead of me, a young woman was seated at a modern desk. She was the type that might look very good in photographs, but in real life, was so thin as to appear sickly. She had black hair, cut in a Prince Valiant bowl style, and she wore a plain black outfit with subtle white trim. She'd probably read somewhere that black was thinning. The dress hung off her and I speculated that dressmakers probably didn't make smaller sizes. She appeared to be vaguely aware that I'd entered.

"Mr. Case?" she said, looking up from her magazine.

The question seemed redundant since I'd just rode up alone in the elevator after identifying myself on the loading the dock. I was about to make a remark to that effect when I noticed she was looking at me and through me. Herometh, I decided. She probably put it up her nose so as not to mark up her skin.

"That's right," I said.

"Todd's finishing up a phone call. He'll be with you in just a second. Please take a seat."

I told her that I preferred to stand and asked if it would be all right to look around. She said to just be careful not to bump into the lights and then went back to work, meaning she went back to reading her magazine.

Beyond her desk was a large photography studio and, as far as I could tell, it was equipped with all the trimmings. A Hasselblad was aimed at a detailed and colorful set that looked like an advertisement for something you would absolutely need in order to survive in the jungle. I guessed it was an ad for swimwear, as there were several tiny tops and bottoms strewn about. While I pretended to study something that held no interest for me, I tried to prepare myself to present the right tone. This was my first chance at someone who might know something about Callie. I wanted to get it right.

Carrol's office had been carved out of the back right of the warehouse floor and formed a triangle. I turned when I heard him enter the studio and he apologized for keeping me waiting. A warm firm hand preceded a tall handsome athletic man. He was dressed in expensive casual wear, right down to his shoes.

"Please come into the office," he said, with a barely noticeable New York accent.

He spoke to the receptionist, "No calls."

She acknowledged him not at all. I felt better. It wasn't just me.

Inside his office, he said, "Would you like something to drink? Coffee? Water?"

I declined. He seemed relieved. He probably would have had to get it himself and that would have been awkward.

His office wasn't large, but it was certainly adequate. It contained very expensive leather furniture and tasteful lights. As expected, the walls were decorated with a choice selection of his photographs and, although they weren't anywhere near the level of, say, an Annie Liebowitz, they seemed professional enough. I could tell he noticed me looking at them as he sat behind his uncluttered glass and metal desk. I thought well of him when he didn't ask my opinion of his work.

"So you're Jackson Aurelian's partner?" he said, pleasantly. "I've eaten at The Ahh Baloney Café several times. That man's a genius."

"No argument from me. Actually, I'm only one of his partners."

"And you're interested in some publicity photos?"

"Yes. I saw your work in a recent issue of Bay Area Living. I was impressed, especially the way you integrated your models into the crowd. That's what we're looking for. We don't want shots of the restaurant filled with just beautiful people. Of course, we're looking for eye-catching models, but we'd like them to look like they're dining and having a good time with the regular crowd. You get the idea."

"I can see it now."

We went on like that for about ten minutes. If I had to use one word to describe him, it would be smooth. I could mention the dark blond hair and the slightly effeminate mannerisms. And, although maybe it was in my mind because I was studying him from a certain perspective, I also felt there was something off center about him. He wasn't quite what he was projecting. Perhaps he was tougher or cleverer or oilier. Although my original plan was to move slowly and gain his confidence, I decided to take a chance.

"Actually, I must confess to a minor ulterior motive for picking you for this assignment," I said, casually.

"And what's that?" he asked.

"About two weeks ago, I met this incredible woman at a party. I felt a real connection with her, but for some reason, well, let's say she didn't warm up to me right away. Then, a couple of days ago, I was chatting with the hostess, you must have heard of her, Kristin Cooper, and she said she'd ask around for me. She called me and said if I wanted to know more about this woman, I should mention her to you."

As I told my lies, his smile became less polite and more strained. I went on, as if I were a bit dim.

"Her name was something Hispanic. Yes. Now I remember. It was … Calena."

I probably could have gotten the same reaction by announcing that my religion demanded that all gay men be sent to sexual reorientation camps.

"Damn," he spat.

"Excuse me?" I said, with a puzzled expression.

He punched a button on his desk.

"Bitty, get me The Ahh Baloney Café. Now."

We sat in silence. I tried to look as if I was trying to comprehend why he had suddenly gone mad. The vid on his desk buzzed. He picked it up, put it against his ear, and asked to speak with Jackson Aurelian, adding that it was urgent.

After a few minutes, he said, "Chef Aurelian? Yes, this is Todd Carrol. You may not know me, but I'm a photographer here in the Bay Area."

He listened for a minute or two.

"Oh, you do? There's a Mr. Case in my office with me. Yes. I see. No, no, nothing. Yes, I'll be happy to do that. Fine, I understand. I imagine your sauce waits for no one. Right. Thank you. Goodbye."

He looked at me apologetically.

"I'm sorry, Mr. Case."

He sighed.

"There's been some unpleasantness and I'm afraid you're the victim of a coincidence."

"Really? Concerning this woman?"

"Calena was an acquaintance. I took some photographs of her here a long time ago. I thought she'd left the Bay Area. I really can't tell you anything about her."

"That's a shame. Do you remember anything at all? I do a lot of traveling."

"We don't keep up-to-date contact information for subjects that aren't regulars. Believe me, there's no dearth of young women wanting to be models. I can guess why you're interested in her. She was something special. However, I think I remember that during our last shoot, she said she was ready to move on from modeling. Like I said, I have a very long list of younger ones who are desperate to get into the business. Really, I know very little about her, except, that for some inexplicable reason, there are some unpleasant people who seem to believe I do."

He had referred to Callie in the past tense and must have realized it and hoped I wouldn't notice. He had gone on too long in order to cover.

"Well, I certainly don't wish to be involved in any unpleasantness," I said.

I rose, giving the impression that he'd just eliminated any possibility that we might do business together.

"As I said, it's all just a big coincidence," he said, quickly.

The Ahh Baloney Café was nationally known and photographing it would be an excellent career move. He smiled at me warmly.

"Listen, I know many other gorgeous women. The kind that would make my receptionist look like a scarecrow. I'd be happy to introduce you to one of them."

I smiled warmly in return.

"That's always a possibility, I suppose. As for the photographs, let me talk it over with Jackson. I'll get back to you."

"Please, anytime."

I walked out quickly and got in the elevator. As the door began to close, I saw Bitty look up at me.

I winked at her and said very softly, "Caw."

On the way to my car, I spoke dark thoughts to myself.

"Some detective. SAM could have done better."

I felt the frustration building inside me. What about Carrol? How long would it have taken to cultivate him, to gain his trust, to get him boasting, confiding in me about Callie? Much too long. Time I don't have.

However, above all, one thought wouldn't leave me. It ran over and over through my head.

How could Callie have spent any time at all with a pimp like Todd Carrol?

CHAPTER 20

MAKKHAL

Chechnya
Winter, 2013

The operation had been dicey from the beginning. Time was convinced that Treeves and the general were holding back vital information from him about the plans that led up to this meeting with Makkhal.

Time stood in a grade-school classroom that had suffered a direct hit from a drone. The resulting explosion ripped off the roof while miraculously leaving the most of all four walls intact. It didn't matter. The darkening afternoon of a Chechen winter was not an ideal time to engage targets.

Time felt like he was standing in an outdoor topless freezer.

The other men, including Treeves, seemed oblivious to the weather. Time felt as if his entire body was turning into an ice sculpture. He concentrated on moving blood through his extremities, convinced that he'd need them before long.

Makkhal had broken the agreement not to bring weapons to the meeting. He came with two men, twins in more ways than one. Both were holding state of the art R40 automatic rifles that fired both standard and wobbling rounds. Each rifle had two barrels. The top barrel was similar to those found on M40s. Directly underneath it, the second barrel was something entirely different. It fired rounds that exited the weapon with a slight wobble. The movement increased as they approached their unfortunate objective. Wobblers were not accurate at distances greater than three meters, but when they hit, they caused catastrophic damage.

Time and the twins formed a triangle. They both stood to his left. It was an excellent crossfire position. One twin was three meters in front of him, against the wall, possibly hoping to cut the edge from the icy wind swirling inside the classroom. The other was the same distance behind him. They held their rifle casually, with the barrels angled towards the ground. However, their fingers rested on the trigger guards. Everything Time had learned from Iain told him that the safeties on the R40s were disengaged. Professionals didn't remove the safety on a firearm unless they intended to use it imminently. But why? It didn't make any sense. Time and Treeves were providing an excellent product at a fair price. By killing them, Makkhal would risk his reputation and sully future business transactions.

Directly in front of Time, Makkhal and Treeves were engaged in a conversation in fast Russian. He couldn't understand their exchange, but they seemed to be in agreement.

Everyone was dressed in the type of rough peasant clothing that could be seen in any village in Chechnya: Heavy pants and shirts, short overcoat, fabric gloves, and boots. Makkhal's paranoia was legendary and before he appeared, Time and Treeves had been expertly searched. If they had brought any weapons to the meeting, Makkhal would have had them executed on the spot.

He and Treeves were delivering the shipment of Grail missiles to Makkhal. Time had expected this to be a low-key mission. Get in, make the sale, and get out. Time didn't even understand why the general had given them such a light assignment.

As always, Treeves was playing his part perfectly. But Time sensed that he was concerned. Fifteen minutes ago, Treeves had signaled Time to prepare for imminent combat. It was a clear indication that the situation had reached a level of highest possible risk. It was unusual for Treeves to hold his Weapon so long at the type of alertness required to react instantly. But since then, Treeves had not given him follow-up instructions.

Suddenly, Treeves scratched his left hand with his right. That signal was crystal clear.

It meant, "*Prepare for elimination orders.*"

Time had to devise a strategy to kill one or all three of the targets that surrounded him. In an ideal situation, Treeves would direct him to his best opportunities. Looking at the twins, their positions, and the added threat of Makkhal, Time couldn't devise a winning strategy. Eliminating one of the guards would draw fire from the other. If these men had already planned some type of assault, it would be even more difficult.

No matter how he played it out in his mind, Time couldn't imagine how he could take both brothers, not to mention Makkhal, before one of them killed either him or Treeves.

Time estimated the brothers to be six-three, about two sixty. Both men had their fingers near their triggers and were prepared to fire. Treeves shifted his weight and placed his right foot slightly in front of his left. That motion gave Time two minutes to prepare his strategy.

For some reason, a saying from a book about samurai culture that he had been ordered to read came floating into his thoughts.

Any man can be prepared to kill. A Samurai is prepared to die.

It meant a fighter will survive a mortal fight only when that fighter enters into it expecting to die.

Kaicho had taught him to consider distance and weight when engaging in multi-target hand-to-hand combat. When you're holding an opponent in your arms, the closer your knife is to the heart when it enters the body, the less time your opponent has to respond, and the more time you'll have to get on with other business. Weight can be strength in numbers. It can be using your opponent's weight against him. It can also be the ability to estimate the weight that can be applied to a large chunk of concrete embedded in the ground between yourself and your target.

Time planned each step and each breath. Within sixty seconds, he had developed a plan of action. It wasn't a good one, but it was the best of all the others that he'd considered. If he lived to make a report, neither Treeves nor the general would be impressed.

He saw Treeves close his left hand into a loose fist and move it slightly backwards. That signal was unmistakable. In his mind, Time clearly heard three words.

"Kill them all."

CHAPTER 21

ANGEL

Berkeley Hills
Summer, 2018

As I drove home from Models Living, a tornado of improbable and partially formed theories swirled around me. I fought to keep my mind clear so that any idea, or even a germ of a plan, might appear to me the way that a misplaced item would often appear the moment I stopped searching for it.

As I got out of my car, three men came towards me quietly and swiftly, moving with explicit menace. They walked together so much like the members of a gang, they brought me back to a place that I'd almost forgotten about, a world where I had to be careful not to be caught alone.

One was taller than me. He circled behind me and took up a position facing my right shoulder. Another was short. He moved symmetrically to my left. The third stopped directly in front of me, silently staring at me.

All of them were dressed eerily alike. It gave me the impression that they were some kind of classy Latin music group. However, they couldn't be mistaken for mariachis, not by dress or attitude. They all wore blue shirts, tan pants, and a dark blue sports jackets. All of them had on comfortable looking brown shoes that made no sound whatsoever when they moved.

The man in front of me was approximately my age and height. He looked very fit. Although he was lighter and his features were broader, there was no doubt in my mind he was Callie's stepbrother.

"You're Laura's brother," I said. "Please accept my sympathy for your loss."

His expression, which hadn't been friendly to begin with, changed only slightly. It became less friendly.

"Your sympathy doesn't interest me," he said, with hardly any accent at all. "I only care about what happened to Laura and where is Calena."

"We should talk," I said.

"I know about your house," he said. "The way you people live here. We need to go somewhere private."

"I have a studio in the back. There's no surveillance of any kind there."

"All right," he said.

I took them through the garden by the most isolated path. I wanted them to trust me. However, I made an absurd mistake. The events of the day made me forget what was in the studio.

Callie's statue was completely covered with a large canvas cloth, but it dominated the room.

When we went inside, Callie's brother turned his full attention to me. The other two men wandered aimlessly around. I knew that they were searching for any evidence that we were being watched.

"Now tell me everything you know," Callie's brother said.

"Callie never told me your name," I said. "You can call me Case."

He responded with a swift spin kick. I barely saw it coming. Perhaps I could have blocked it, but I didn't want to fight him. I moved my head away, succeeding enough so that it was more of a graze than a solid blow. But as I did that, one of them kicked me in the small of my back. I knew the technique. It was Jiu-jitsu, a deadly form of Brazilian kickboxing.

It must have been the short one who kicked me in the back, because the tall one stepped behind me, grabbed the hair above my ears in both his hands, and turned me to face Callie's brother again.

"I did not come here to chat with you," he said.

He was trying to project a cool, dangerous image, but his anger was so volatile that his body was trembling.

"The young detective, the foolish one, told me that maybe you killed my sister," he said. "We are not going to talk. You are going to tell me everything you know about Laura and Calena."

"I never knew Laura," I said, through the pain. "I don't know where Calena is. I want to find her as much as you do. I love her. We were going to be married."

The short one pulled back the canvas slightly to see what was underneath. He reacted with a soft whistle.

"Ferro," he said.

He pulled away the cloth to reveal my statue of Callie's naked body. Ferro turned and studied it. The longer he stared, the angrier he became.

"Cover that," Ferro said.

He turned to me.

"You have only one chance to leave this room alive," he said. "Tell me where Callie is."

I didn't believe him.

"I love your sister," I said. "I'm searching for her every moment with every asset I have. Hurting me would be hurting her."

"You love her?" he said, "Is that why you put her naked body on display?"

"That statue was meant to be a work of art, to honor her."

Ferro looked to his right and grimaced. He saw the short one staring at the canvas as if he could still see what was beneath it.

"Where are you looking, Pino?" he said. "Get over here."

I knew it wouldn't change anything, but I tried to explain.

"That was a wedding present meant only for Callie, not for public display."

He responded with a kick to my side that forced me to my knees.

"I'm not here to discuss what you consider art," he said.

"That young detective is a fool," I said. "You know that. I'm your best chance of finding your sister. If you hurt me enough to slow me down, you'll be helping the real killer escape and Callie will be in more danger."

He shook his head. Reason had left him. His anger had obliterated it.

"Enough bullshit," he said. "It starts now and it stops when I know how to find Calena."

The big one let go of my hair. I expected the blow to come from her brother and I started toward him, hoping to flatten his nose and make a run for the door. But it was the short one behind me who delivered a precise kick to my kidney. That immobilized me. When I hit the floor, I rolled into a fetal position, protecting my head and my internal organs as much as possible. I tried to find their rhythm and sway out of the blows to minimize them. They weren't trying to kill me. They must have thought I had something to tell them. The first five or six blows were bad. After that, I was covering up and pain was just a state I was in, like hunger, and everything they did to me was like adding water to a full bucket. Except for the damage they inflicted, there was no purpose to it.

"Enough," Callie's brother said. "Get him on his knees."

He produced a gun from under his jacket. It was a small caliber revolver. As it moved towards me, I could see the bullets.

"I ask you one more time. Tell me where I can find Calena and I will not kill you."

I looked at him. There was blood in my mouth. I spit it out.

"You're a damned liar," I said, with difficulty. "You're going to kill me no matter what I say."

I jerked my head towards the statue.

"If for nothing else, for that."

He cocked the revolver. He placed it almost flush against the top of my forehead.

"You're right," he said. "But that's only part of it."

I closed my eyes and, in the second before he pulled the trigger, I saw Callie's face in front of me. She looked at me tenderly. She forgave me for failing her. I couldn't help her anymore, but I was still her angel.

"Angel," I said.

The gun went off and my pain was all gone.

CHAPTER 22

NECESSITY

Chechnya
Winter, 2013

Time had to move.

When Treeves signaled, *Kill them all*, he meant, *Kill them all now*. It wasn't going to be easy.

To neutralize two targets holding R40s in ready position and still have a reasonable chance at Makkhal, Time would need more than his speed. He'd have to give the twins a reason to slow down.

Time exploded towards the twin in front of him and to his left. He'd been trained to achieve maximum acceleration in the shortest distance, ignoring everything around him. He concentrated on reaching the concrete driven into the ground a meter in front of the target. The brothers quickly raised their heavy R40s, but they weren't firing yet. They made the error of taking an extra moment to point their weapons before they pulled the triggers.

Time launched himself off the ground in order to make the target in front of him lose a split second adjusting him aim. He used it like the starting block of a fifty-meter race and pushed off of it towards his objective.

When he crashed into the first target, he made no attempt to wrestle the R40 away from him. There was no time for that. The target's finger was pulling the trigger and Time could feel him firing. He smashed the side of his foot into the instep of the target's right foot and drove the hard point of his knee into the soft side of the target's left knee. At that point, the target

149

was in too much pain to think clearly and he kept firing blindly. It was exactly what Time had hoped would happen.

He grabbed the hot barrel in his gloved left hand and the area of the stock just behind the trigger assembly in his right. Using his strength and his knowledge of balance, he rammed the end of the stock against the target's face while, at the same time, pulling the barrel towards the other twin. As he was doing that, he pinned the target's right arm with his elbow.

The other target had recovered from the initial hesitation of having to risk killing his brother in order to fire at Time. He was probably expecting some sort of stand off. He had no idea what kind of man was controlling his brother's rifle.

As soon as Time jammed the butt of the R40 into his brother's face, he could see what Time could feel. His brother was dead. The heavy recoil of the R40 had reduced his face to a flat, bloody mess. The second target reacted by firing too quickly. Time's rifle was already firing and all he had to do is adjust its line of fire about thirteen inches to the right.

The rifle was firing from the lower barrel. The further the bullets were from the point of exit, the larger they became. By the time they reached the second target, they were wobbling enough to make it seem as if more than half of his chest disappeared into a red cloud.

Behind Time, the body of the first target began to slump to the floor. His limp arms still held the R40. Time turned to face Makkhal, ripping the rifle from the dead man's hands. He expected to see an automatic pistol aimed at his forehead. He was prepared to die.

Instead, Time was astonished to see Makkhal raise his pistol to fire at Treeves, who had his hands up as if to say, *No*.

Time switched the rifle into single fire, normal mode. Since all cell leaders were to be taken alive if possible, he fired at the top of Makkhal's right shoulder, but as he did so, the body of the first target shifted under him in a post-mortem convulsion and it threw off his aim. The bullet entered just below Makkhal's armpit and ripped through his back.

Two shots sounded almost like one. Treeves fell to the ground.

The entire sequence from the moment Time had started towards the first target until Makkhal fell to the ground had taken less than twelve seconds.

Treeves was on the ground curled into a fetal position. Wearing the coppery smell of blood like some sticky cologne, Time quickly went to him.

"How bad is it?" said Time.

"I've been shot. There's no way you could possibly describe that as good."

"You're welcome for saving your life … again."

Time checked him and found a groove in the top of Treeves' right shoulder.

"This doesn't even deserve a pressure dressing," said Time, ripping off a piece of his shirt to cover the wound.

Treeves noticed the blood on Time.

"Is any of that yours?" he said.

"Yes. And, for the record, we aren't going to call this little scratch on your shoulder a wound."

Treeves took a moment to survey the carnage. His near-death experience caused an unusual reaction. He made a joke.

"You really are quite accident prone, aren't you?" he said.

"Next time I'll be more careful."

Makkhal was twisting slowly on the ground and moaning.

"Why did he want us dead?" Time said.

"Help me up," Treeves said, by way of an answer. "We only have about ten minutes. Unpack the missiles. We'll need them. Soon, we'll hear a small plane. You have to destroy it. It's traveling at a low attitude, but it will be a difficult shot."

Time shook his head.

"More like impossible and you know it."

"You may have time for two shots. We have no choice."

"Why are we suddenly shooting down aircraft? Not that it matters, but that wasn't in the pre-mission briefing."

Time didn't expect an answer. Treeves never explained his orders in combat. Questions were for the debriefing. However, Time felt that Treeves wasn't simply ignoring his questions. Although it was impossible to read anything Treeves didn't want to reveal, Time had the strangest feeling Treeves needed to end any further discussion regarding why they were about to attempt the almost impossible task of shooting down an small aircraft with trick missiles. Treeves was working hard at keeping information from him. Time put those thoughts aside. If it was necessary to prepare the ordinance and bring down a plane, there was no time for questions.

"You'll have to help me," Time said, preparing the launcher.

He heard the faint buzz of an engine.

"Can you see it?" said Treeves.

"Over there."

It was coming into view in the west.

Makkhal began chanting. Time couldn't understand all of it, but he recognized the words *homeland* and *victory*.

Soon the plane was within range. Time aimed the missile.

"Be careful," said Treeves. "Allow for all the variables."

"Did I tell you how to speak Chechen?" said Time.

"You don't know any Chechen."

"Exactly. Besides, I know a little. Remember who I've been with for these past weeks."

Normally, unless he was playing a part and wanted his feelings known, Treeves was as hard to read as an Egyptian tomb, but suddenly, a strange look crossed his face.

"Yes, I remember."

During this exchange, Treeves made the final preparations. Time led the plane and fired. He missed by nearly fifty feet.

"Shoot down that plane!" said Treeves.

"Do you think I'm trying not to?"

Treeves quickly prepared a second missile. Time considered what had gone wrong with the first shot. The plane was closer now, so it seemed to be traveling faster.

"Listen to me before you fire," Treeves said. "If you miss, at least a hundred thousand people will die and that may just be the beginning. Do you understand? Don't miss again."

Time went to the place that his teachers had taught him to construct. It was a small space where only the moment and the objective existed. He joined himself to the destruction of the aircraft. When he was as close as he could get to the moment before that would happen, he fired the second missile.

It rose into the sky and appeared to veer off course. Instead, it turned and rammed into the belly of the plane. The entire sky seemed to fill with a massive explosion. The blast knocked both of them to the ground and it was suddenly warm within the walls of the classroom. Whatever was on the plane, what ever it was carrying, was vaporized.

"Damn," said Time, his ears still ringing. "That was no missile. What the hell was that?"

"That plane was carrying Octanitrocubane, probably the most powerful explosive in the world. I'd say at least enough to level a square city block."

Dust was raining down on them. That was all that was left of the aircraft.

Treeves regarded Time the way a man might look at an artist capable of painting a masterpiece.

"I honestly didn't think you could do that," he said

Makkhal was moaning on the ground.

Treeves said, "Kill him."

That didn't make sense.

"Why?" said Time.

"What do you mean, 'Why?' Kill him because I said to kill him."

Now, Time was convinced that not only was Treeves hiding something from him, it was something that he should never know. He walked to Makkhal, who was repeating simple phrases over and over. In the past few weeks, Maria had been teaching him a little Chechen. Time could make out the words *children* and *paradise*. He picked up Makkhal and placed his head on his knee.

"Children?" Time said in Chechen.

Makkhal said, "My children. Maria. In paradise."

"Paradise?" said Time.

"Children, Maria, on the plane."

Time turned to Treeves.

"He put his children on that plane?"

Treeves looked at him. There was no way to avoid it.

"The entire class. Maria too," he said.

"Maria? Her class? Those children were only twelve years old."

"Yes."

"How many?"

"Listen to me. That plane was headed for Grozny. The plan was to crash it into the Russian Consulate. It would have left nothing there. The children were a tactic to slow down a response or make the Russians look like monsters. From the moment it left the ground, there was no way anyone on that plane could have survived. I discovered his plan. The twins were here to control us. I had no choice."

"How many?"

"Fourteen."

Time locked eyes with Treeves for a second.

"There was no other option," said Treeves.

"There's always an option," said Time.

Time drew a knife from a sheath on Makkhal's thigh. He grabbed Makkhal's hair, pulled back his head, and slid the blade two inches below his chin. The knife sliced through his neck and opened a long red crescent. Time tossed him aside and rose.

"You're the expert in human behavior," he said. "So you understand what comes next."

He began to walk towards Treeves. He felt dizzy.

"What I understand," said Treeves, "is that you're unaware of how much of that blood you're wearing belongs to you. Look at your side. Let me apply a pressure dressing."

Time kept walking towards Treeves, but only for a couple of steps before he collapsed from blood loss.

CHAPTER 23

DIANE

Berkeley Hills
Summer, 2018

I became aware of her in fragments. First, there was the softness of her lap and her cool hand stroking my forehead. That was nice. Then I recognized her voice, but I couldn't understand what she was saying. She smelled like she always did, as if she just stepped from a shower where she'd been covered in vanilla scented soap.

When I opened my eyes, I found myself looking up through the valley between her breasts to her startling eyes staring down on me. Even with her brow creased and her mouth tight, her face never failed to stun me when I hadn't seen it for more than a few days. Diane Milston been blessed, or perhaps cursed, with the type of symmetry and features every red-blooded boy dreams will inhabit the house next door. Her highlighted hair fell just over her shoulders and her short, uneven bangs hung above brown eyes, unusual for a natural blonde.

The dense fog between us was dissolving and, slowly, I began to understand what she was saying.

"Paul's on his way. Just stay here. Don't move."

"What happened?"

"I was hoping you could tell me. Your friends haven't been much help."

"Friends?"

"They were carrying you into the house when I got here."

Diane and I were on the couch. I turned my head. Five feet away, the small Brazilian was sitting on a chair taking a bite out of a sandwich. He favored me with a wide grin. He raised the glass of beer in his other hand and winked at Diane appreciatively. The beating he had helped administer came back in a painful rush.

I tried to get up and realized that would be a major mistake. The full intensity of the damage I suffered didn't kick in until I moved, and then it seemed like every bone and muscle in my body was screaming the same message: We're in serious distress. Don't even think about moving us.

I groaned. Diane leaned over and kissed me on the forehead. The small Brazilian seemed envious. I felt like telling him how much it hurt me when she moved.

"Don't try to move," she said, in concert with my nerve endings. "You don't look that bad, but maybe you broke something."

"I've broken everything," I said.

"Is bad," said the Brazilian, taking another bite.

"Almost it is worth it," he continued, with a thick accent. "To be where you are. Ferro was angry."

He chuckled.

"I never see Ferro so angry," he said. "Man, he was talking English to me and Paulo."

He had to laugh at the absurdity of that.

"What's your name?" I said.

"Name? Ah, Pino," he said, tapping his chest. "And you, Case. And the angel?"

"This is Diane. And trust me, she's no angel."

"Yuk yuk," said Diane, shifting her weight. "So funny. How funny would it be if I started laughing really hard?"

"Why are you here?" I said. "Why now? I never thought I'd see you again. Except on the screen."

"I've been having some trouble, Case. Everyone says what a great actress you are and suddenly you're finishing the biggest film of your career, the one that's guaranteed to make you a star. The only problem is that while I'm giving my powerhouse performance, I keep having the feeling that I'm hamming it up in my first high school play. Sometimes I felt like I was chewing so much scenery, I couldn't even get out my lines. The director was a hack and the studio massacred the script. It's being edited now and I'm terrified. I had to see my old friends. Oh, and by the way, I heard you had some trouble."

"After what you said the last time we spoke, I thought you hated me."

"Jackson called me a couple of nights ago. Did you know we kept in touch?"

I shook my head slightly.

"Well, we did. When he told me what happened, I didn't know if you'd want me to come. But then I decided, why should I suddenly care what you want?"

"In character," I said.

"No, you're the character. By the way, don't even think about bullshitting me about the money. I know it came from you. I almost sent it back, but I didn't for two reasons."

"What's the other reason?"

She made her face that signifies *smartass*.

"I figured, what the hell, if you wanted to be a sucker, who was I to say no?"

"Why can't you ever be honest with me?" I said. "You took the money because you knew that it would bother me if you didn't."

"You always think you know what I'm feeling."

"You married together?" said Pino, who had been trying to follow the conversation.

He looked worried. I realized he was probably thinking Ferro wouldn't like it if I were married. I knew Pino wouldn't like it if Diane were married.

The doorbell rang.

"I'll get it," said Diane.

When she lifted my head out of her lap, she wasn't rough, but she wasn't slow. Once again, the messages poured in. Even so, I noticed as her sheer blouse and tight jeans moved away, she hadn't gained anything and she hadn't lost anything. Pino was also noticing with all his might.

She came back with Paul Arons, who carried his medical bag. He was wearing a v-cut sweater, chinos, and a concerned expression. Next to Diane, he looked small, which was no easy task.

"They said he fell off a ladder in his studio," Diane was saying. "They carried him in here. Then two of them went for a walk and Pino and I waited for you. He came to about five minutes ago."

"His brain hasn't changed," she added, as if that wasn't necessarily a good thing.

"Hello, Michael," Paul said.

It was ironic that Paul would be described by society as gay because everything he did, he did seriously. He was a good friend and I'd always liked him, but the weight of his work had overpowered any personality he had once had. I hadn't seen him for at least six months. I doubt anyone had, except his colleagues and lab assistants. He was the central force at the Marin Research Center for Viral Diseases. His work caused him to look older than his thirty-six years.

For the next fifteen minutes, Paul performed like the excellent gentle doctor he'd once been.

"How did she get you?" I asked him, in between pokes, prods, and questions.

"My home vid gets routed to one of my assistants at the Center. He said that a woman named Milston was hysterical."

"That's ridiculous," said Diane quickly. "I was not hysterical. I was concerned."

Paul smiled. It made him look sad.

"My assistant told her that I'd left instructions not to be disturbed. Diane responded that if he didn't get Dr. Arons' ass to the phone in one minute, she'd come to Marin and make his dream of true sexual freedom a reality. Which is to say, she'd free me from ever wanting to have sex again."

"I could have gotten another doctor," Diane said. "But I always want the best."

Paul took out his personal vid.

"What are you doing?" I said.

"I'm calling for a room at the hospital. I still have privileges."

"Put down the phone. I'm not going to any hospital."

"You need tests. I can't tell anything until I see the results."

"I'm fine. I know my body. I'll be okay in a couple of hours."

"Couple of weeks would be more my guess. If you fell off a ladder, I fell out of the cabbage patch."

"That's what happened. I fell."

Pino nodded.

"Fell bad," he said.

"Is he bleeding inside? Is he dying?" Diane said.

"How do I know?" Paul said.

Diane and I stared at him. Pino was busy looking at Diane.

"My guess, from what I can see and feel, is no," Paul said. "The instruments I have with me don't reveal any severe fractures. You appear to be lucid, but without tests, there's no way to determine what's happening. Considering the beating you've taken, you could have a tiny hemorrhage in your brain."

Diane had been listening carefully.

"What beating?" she said.

Paul looked at me intently. His expression was clear.

Paul was thinking that he'd treated enough hate crimes to recognize a serious ass kicking when I see one.

However, the more important lesson of his life was to not stick your nose into other people's business. He turned to Diane, changing the subject and looking to her for support.

"Talk some sense into him," he said. "You're the only one who's ever been able to make him do what he didn't want to."

"I'm not sure I take that as a compliment," Diane said.

Paul was wasting his breath on Diane. When she was ten, her father had gone into a hospital for a minor operation and had never come out. I was sure Diane respected Paul, but I also had the feeling just having him talk about hospitals made her uncomfortable

157

"Thanks for coming, everyone," I said. "I appreciate your concern, but I'm fine now. Diane, Jackson will get you a suite at the Claremont."

"I'm staying with you," Diane said.

"Now that would kill me," I said.

"I'm staying," she said, as if once she'd said it, everything was completely decided.

It was her trademark. She turned to Paul.

"I'll keep an eye on him and, if anything happens, I'll call you. Keep a team ready at the hospital. Get the best people you can and tell them money is not an issue. Aram Cooper guarantees it."

"You can't stay here," I said.

"Take your pick," Paul said.

He was too smart to argue with Diane.

"It's either her or I call Cooper Security to bring an ambulance right away. And since I wouldn't risk STAY on you at the moment, it won't be a nice young lady to take you away. I'll force them to admit you by certifying that you're delirious from multiple blows to the head. Aram has to protect the company assets, you know."

"You know about that?" I said.

"Aram and I talk. He's my largest benefactor."

The front door opened and Ferro and his tall friend entered. He and Diane exchanged glances. Then he looked at Paul.

"Who are you?" he said.

His tone was abrasive. His anger was still so volatile it seemed to make his jacket vibrate on his shoulders.

"I'm Dr. Arons," Paul said. "And you, I believe, are the ladder."

"What?"

"Nothing. I have to leave now."

Paul gave Diane a small bottle filled with pills.

"For the pain," he said. "Only as directed. I'll check in later this evening."

He left. We all looked at each other. The only one who seemed to be in a good mood was Pino.

"Diane, would you make some tea?" I said.

She didn't look happy but, once she announced she was going to nurse me, there wasn't much she could do about it. She headed for the kitchen.

Ferro walked over and stood looking down at me. He didn't try to hide his frustration, making it obvious that he was a man looking at a half-finished job, an important task that he wouldn't be able to complete.

After a few seconds of that, I asked him, "Why am I still alive?"

CHAPTER 24

TRAITOR

Berlin
Winter, 2013

She was pretty, very pretty. As she floated above Time, he saw a halo of light around her long blond curls. She was dressed in white. The smile she gave him and the hand that touched his cheek were as gentle as any he had ever known. He felt grateful, and also deeply shocked, that he'd been allowed to enter heaven after all the terrible things that he'd done. It occurred to him that, if he'd been allowed to enter paradise, perhaps all the people that he killed were here as well, waiting for him.

The angel spoke.

"He's awake, but he's very weak," she said. "He must be in terrible pain. Can't the doctor prescribe a minimal dose of morphine?"

"This man's accustomed to pain. He is not to have any drugs that require triplicate prescriptions."

Time instantly recognized the voice. As his head cleared, he smiled to himself and thought that General Tresain's voice was about as close to the voice of God as he would ever get.

"Yes, sir, general," the angel said.

She floated away.

"How do you feel?" said Tresain.

"Like I've been shot with a wobbling round from an R40."

"Actually, you were shot twice. But you were lucky. The twin firing at you had his weapon in rotation mode. He was turned towards Makkhal and they didn't want any accidents. You just happened to hit the right brother first."

"No, I considered that. I figured the one facing me would be set to splatter me over the landscape. The other was for backup and to fire at Treeves, who was standing closer to Makkhal."

The general nodded.

"In any case, you lost a decent chunk of your right side. However, the impact wasn't significant enough to cause a massive shockwave to your brain. Also, you were lucky it was so cold and we'd taken out your spleen years ago."

"I'll head for Vegas as soon as I can stand. I will be able to stand, won't I?"

"Everything should be as it was."

Time stared at the general for a moment longer than he meant to.

"Not everything," he said.

"Treeves is dead," said the general.

"So I got to him after all," Time said, without emotion. "The last thing I remember was walking towards him."

"Don't be a fool. If you had killed Edgar Treeves, do you think that we'd be having this conversation? I would have killed you myself.

"Treeves activated an emergency homing signal. We were minutes away, but Makkhal had a man patrolling the perimeter. To say he was paranoid would be to damn him with faint praise. His man got there before we did. Killed Treeves. Probably heard us coming and thought that you were dead. He didn't have the time to make sure. He wasn't very wrong. Our medical team had to bring you back."

"As soon as I can stand, I want to see Treeves' body," Time said.

The general's expression hardened.

"He was cremated. Listen carefully. I'll say this once and only once. You are not to look for answers to any questions you may have regarding the death of Edgar Treeves. What the two of you did together must never come under suspicion because of your irrelevant inquiries. If I even suspect that you aren't following my orders to the letter, there's no place on earth where I couldn't find you and when I do, you'll disappear as if you never existed."

The general changed his tone.

"You still require a great deal of medical attention. When you're feeling better, take a furlough, Time. Let your mind heal as well as your body. We'll find another Medium for you. We'll pair you with the finest one that Dr. Treeves was training. Of course, there'll never be another Edgar Treeves, but she shows real promise."

Time studied the man in front of him. For the first time, he challenged him.

"I've listened to you," he said. "Now listen to me. I was a soldier. I had orders and they had to be followed. Then I became a Weapon. His orders had to be second nature to me. Even so, I fooled myself into thinking that I wasn't just some mindless puppet. But Treeves knew better, didn't he? He used me to execute innocent children and someone I cared about. He knew

I wouldn't have shot down that plane if I knew who was inside it. To him, I was never a human being, just a mechanism. And while we're discussing things that we shouldn't forget, let's remember that he knows exactly how I feel now."

The general studied Time. He looked as if he were trying to solve a difficult strategic conundrum.

"You're using the present tense when you talk about him. Edgar Treeves is dead."

"I haven't forgotten what you told me, if that's what you mean."

"Then don't forget this. We spent years training you. Another Medium is waiting for you."

"Not for me, general," Time said. "I'm done. A long time ago, you said that my last known position was at the bottom of the ocean. I'm ready to go there now. I'll never be anyone's Weapon again."

"All right," said the general. "For the time being, let's leave it at that. I'll speak to the committee and you'll know what we decide."

The general turned to leave the room.

Just before he reached the door, he turned and said, "We've known each a long time. You find me difficult to understand?"

Time said, "It's never been difficult to understand you, general."

CHAPTER 25

FERRO

Berkeley Hills
Summer, 2018

Ferro sat on the edge of my coffee table and studied my forehead.

"Calena was always the independent one, the one who laughed at rules," he said, almost whispering. "When we were very young, she became involved with a boy. She said she loved him. When I found out that he hadn't respected her, I paid him a visit and taught him a lesson, a serious lesson. Nothing happened to me. In our country, a man has a right, an obligation, to defend the honor of his sister. But Calena didn't speak to me for months. She behaved as if I no longer existed.

"I could not understand. What I did, I did for her. Finally, she spoke to me. She said she was afraid of my temper. She realized the relationship with the boy had been a mistake, but she asked me, 'What if I meet a man I really love and you go crazy and hurt him, maybe even kill him?'

"I told her that I would know the right man for her, but that wasn't good enough. So we made a bargain. If she was absolutely sure it was the right man, if she was absolutely sure he loved her, she could tell him that he was her *angel*. She swore that she would do this only once and only if there was no doubt in her mind. For my part, I swore upon my honor that I would not harm a man who was protected in this manner.

"I wanted to kill you. I wanted it very badly. But I heard you say, 'Angel.' You are fortunate that I have always been very, very quick. I pulled up the gun even as I pulled the trigger. You were a breath away from the end of your life. The bullet missed you completely, but the recoil caused the barrel to hit you on the forehead."

He smiled, but not warmly.

"Or maybe it wasn't the recoil. I'm not sure. In any case, it knocked you out. When we brought you in here, we met the blonde woman. I had to walk to clear my head."

He paused.

"Your English is excellent," I said, not only because I was looking for something to say, but also because I remembered that I'd said, 'Angel,' in English.

"My life has not been a simple one," Ferro said. "At one point, I actually served with your military. I suppose you know Calena and Laura are my stepsisters. She must have told you about me."

She never had, but there was no reason for him to know that.

"Calena called me on the telephone yesterday," I said. "She told me to tell her family that I was her angel."

As soon as I said it, I realized that my failure to convince her to trust me had driven everything else from my mind. I'd forgotten about being her angel. Perhaps some survival instinct had made me utter that particular word. Perhaps my life had been saved by my subconscious.

"You spoke to her yesterday," Ferro said, moving closer to me. "Where is she?"

"I don't know. She wouldn't tell me."

"Bullshit."

"No, it's true," I said. "She just wanted to let me know that she was alive and that I'd never see her again."

His expression changed from suspicion to contempt.

"How could you speak with her and not find out where she is?"

I understood exactly how he felt.

"Tell me what you know about Laura," he said.

"No," I said. "I don't know much, but what I know, I'm not telling you."

He tilted his head and his lips tightened.

"There must be a knife in the kitchen. The way you are, you couldn't stop me."

"That wouldn't work for you now. You said you're a man of honor and I believe you. I'm certain that you believe I didn't murder Laura and you can't kill me for what I did with Callie. You don't hold any threat for me."

"There are many unpleasant things that can happen to a man besides death."

I shook my head.

"I've had my in-house security off since the first night Calena came here, but I could turn it on with a word. Too many people have seen you. Diane would call the police. Would you hurt her too? And the doctor? You can't do anything for your sister if you're in prison."

"You think you know all about me."

"I love your sister. You came from the same house."

"You say you want to find the bastards who destroyed my family. Why won't you tell me what you know? We can work together."

"No. You're a hothead. We have different ways of doing things."

"To hell with you," he said. "I'll find her on my own. I don't need you."

"Pino, Paulo, come on, we're leaving," he shouted.

Both Pino and Paulo had drifted into the kitchen to help Diane with the tea.

Ferro went out the front door and left it open. Pino walked over to me.

"I am happy you are alive," he said, pleasantly. "I did not think Ferro is so mad he would shoot you. He is a good man, but he is not happy now."

"You work for him?"

"We work together. How do you say it, partners? Friends, since children."

Although their outfits were virtually identical, I saw now that their clothes were quite expensive. I wondered if the common look was some sort of camouflage.

"What business are you in? Export?" I asked.

"Export?"

He wrinkled his forehead, thinking about the word.

"Ah, you mean drugs," he said, after a moment.

He shook his head resignedly.

"Americanos, always the same."

"We are advogados, how you say? Lawyers!" he said, smiling proudly.

Ferro shouted his name from outside.

"I go," he said.

He looked wistfully towards the kitchen.

"I come back here in one day or two to see if you are okay. Okay?"

"Okay," I said.

I liked him. He left and he also left the door open. Perhaps no one closed doors in Brazil.

"Lemon zinger," Diane announced, as she carried in a tray from the kitchen.

She was wearing an apron just to rub it in. Jackson and Aram walked through the open door. Jackson had his head turned to look behind him. When Aram saw Diane, he grinned.

"Mr. Lightbulb," she said, happily.

For some reason, Aram laughed at all Diane's jokes, no matter how silly. It had nothing to with her looks. I've seen Aram look at beautiful women as if they were spills on the rug. Aram's susceptibility to her wit probably stemmed from the fact that Diane, who had been Kristin's friend first, was one of the few people who had liked Aram from the moment she met him.

"Look at you," he said, walking towards her. "If Grace Kelly had been three times as beautiful, she wouldn't have been as pretty as you."

They hugged each other tightly.

"Maybe the two of you would like to be alone," I said.

"It's my dream," said Diane.

Aram laughed.

"Hey, don't I merit a quip or two?" said Jackson.

She turned to him.

"I'm especially glad you're here," Diane said. "There's no food in the kitchen. I have to go to shopping and you're coming with me. Aram, can you stay with him while I'm gone?"

She gave him all the contact numbers and instructions.

"Don't worry," Aram said. "I've already spoken with Paul. There'll be a mobile hospital unit outside in a minute or two."

"You've got to be joking," I said.

"Michael, use your right hand and tell me how many times I've joked about something that impacts my company," Aram said.

"Maybe we can all have dinner?" Diane said.

I checked my face with hands. I could tell the boys from Brazil had concentrated on my midsection and that there wasn't much damage above my neck. Perhaps that's why Diane forgot that I'd just survived the beating of a lifetime.

"Kristin and I have tickets for the symphony, but we'll come by for breakfast tomorrow. She's dying to see you."

"Me too her," said Diane.

"Can I get someone to enter it into my calendar?" I said.

"Grouchy, much?" said Diane.

Jackson turned to me.

"What exactly happened to you?"

"I fell," I said.

"Fell bad," said Diane.

So she liked Pino too. Incredibly, against all sense or logic, I found myself feeling jealous.

Diane said to Aram, "Remember, if Case starts acting unusual in any way, call Paul. He'll tell you what to do."

"What exactly do you mean by *unusual*?" said Aram.

"You know, if he stops breathing or starts saying nice things about me."

Aram laughed. I started to say that there was plenty of food in the kitchen, but then Diane would have said, not real food, and I wanted to be alone with Aram in any case. We had many things to talk about.

CHAPTER 26

TARGET

Mexico
Fall, 2014

General Tresain never visited Time in the hospital again. After the general's final visit, Time underwent three surgeries and an extended period of rehabilitation. One morning, a young doctor, dressed in spotless starched whites, entered Time's room. He glanced over the chart at the foot of the bed.

"So how are we feeling today?" he said, without looking up.

"Well, for one thing, I'd appreciate it if you'd stop poking and prodding me twice a day."

The doctor smiled.

"Fortunately, I don't see any reason for that to continue. Your recovery has been truly remarkable. I'll write your discharge instructions this afternoon. You should be walking out of here by the end of the week."

Time awoke the next morning to find that a large manila envelope had been placed on the stand next to his bed. Inside was all the documentation necessary to support a new identity. Time would be an American Citizen. There were excellent recommendations from people he'd never met. The social security number, resume, and references that he found inside the envelope would make it easy for him to land a position as a highly paid personal bodyguard or even a chief of security at a mid-sized corporation. The envelope also contained an account number and the necessary authorizations needed to access sixty thousand dollars in a Caribbean Bank.

As he stepped into the sunlight outside the hospital, Time tried to imagine why the general and the committee had decided that eliminating him wasn't their best course of action.

Were they convinced that he understood disobeying orders from General Tresain was tantamount to suicide? Perhaps they concluded his training wouldn't allow him to become a threat. Maybe they decided the expense and effort of training him shouldn't be wasted so easily. They hoped the general would eventually find a way to return him to the fold. If they based their decision on any of those suppositions, they had made a rare mistake.

Over the next few months, Time patiently began to take small steps to disappear. The sixty thousand dollars was converted to stacks of small bills during several random visits to the bank. He knew he was being watched, but after so many years with Edgar Treeves, he could usually identify the men and women who were keeping track of him. Each time he had an opportunity, he attempted to convince his watchers that he had decided to shed all memories of, and all connections to, his past life.

When the moment was right, he vanished. He left no traces, going so far off the grid he believed, unless they got very lucky, he could not be quickly found. Long ago, Time had learned an identity needed a foundation. If there was nothing to support a person's existence, they simply ceased to exist. He changed his appearance often. Whenever he needed to travel, he stole the necessary documents. He communicated with no one, even avoiding random conversations with strangers. When he was certain he was as clear as possible, he did nothing for four months but hide and make plans. He nurtured an obsession. He was going to kill Edgar Treeves with his own hands.

However, before Time had any possibility of accomplishing that goal, he needed to locate Treeves. He considered his options. Although he trained inside the Bunker, he didn't know precisely where it was located. He and Treeves had been driven in and out of the Bunker in the back of beat-up pickup trucks, sitting on comfortable chairs and cots, hidden under windowless covers over the truck beds. Neither of them could see the surrounding countryside. They were taken to airstrips many miles away and quickly transferred to air transport. If Treeves or Time were discovered and captured, they couldn't possibly provide their captors with any useful information regarding the Bunker's exact location.

General Tresain had supervised the construction of the Bunker. He recruited men and women who were fanatically loyal to him and devoted to the work they performed. Treeves provided the general with potential candidates with the proper personality profiles and talents ranging from electrical engineer to sniper. He also conducted random interviews to make certain the hundreds of operatives who supported the Bunker had no knowledge of anything unrelated to the function they performed.

The general decided the best camouflage was to hide the Bunker in plain sight. It was located under a large barn in the American Midwest. The farm surrounding it was one of thousands of similar agricultural concerns owned by America's giant agri-corporations. Necessary funding for the Bunker was skimmed from low visibility slush funds of endless government research programs.

There were several levels of security to defeat before a large elevator hidden inside the barn opened and was ready to begin its descent a mile underground to the operations area.

The land surrounding the Bunker was chosen because of higher than normal land formations that were ideal for virtually invisible sniper hideouts. The only entrance to the Bunker opened onto twelve miles of private road. Strategic areas of farmland, monitored at all times, were rich with deadly anti-personnel measures that could be set off with a flick of a switch. In addition to their day-to-day duties as regular farmhands, everyone who worked above the Bunker was a trained killer. The general's Rangers followed a standing order. Discourage, with extreme prejudice if necessary, any unauthorized personnel from coming within four hundred yards of the barn that stood over the Bunker.

General Tresain had been officially retired with four stars, while at the same time he was awarded five. Tresain could count on his right hand the number of occasions when he had been forced to reveal and utilize his rank. The general and his team rarely interacted with other military forces or intelligence agencies. If he needed cooperation, the necessary orders came from partially informed sources with unquestioned authority. In concert with Edgar Treeves, the operations that the general deemed appropriate were planned down to the last detail and contingency.

Time accepted that, even if he could somehow find the Bunker, he had no chance of getting to Edgar Treeves when he was under that kind of protection. Therefore, as unlikely as it seemed, he had to hope that a situation would arise that was so crucial and volatile, it would be necessary for the general to employ the talents of his best Medium.

Time spent weeks searching for an answer to one question. How would Edgar Treeves go about uncovering information about an operation so delicate that the participation of the world's finest Medium would be absolutely necessary? Time had a unique advantage. He had participated in operations that the general had chosen when he was Treeves' only protection. The general sent Treeves out of the Bunker only when it was necessary to avoid a more devastating outcome than the possible loss of America's single most valuable intelligence asset.

Therefore, step one was to gather data and assess the risk quotas of situations that might require the intervention of Edgar Treeves. Time knew that other Weapons and Mediums were being trained inside the bunker. Of course, training new Mediums would have limited success at best. Edgar Treeves was born to be a Medium and he had perfected his gift with untold hours of study. There was a theory that ten thousand hours of practice were required for talented individuals to become exceptional in their chosen fields. Treeves had passed the ten-thousand-hour mark before he was a teenager. On the other hand, a Weapon simply had to be smart, focused, strong, and quick. He remembered Treeves' assertion that, regardless of the competence of his Weapon, he would always find a way to survive.

When they were together in combat, Treeves had never had to test that theory. He was about to get his chance.

Gerald McClaren had the CIA's highest security clearance. He worked as a computer analyst in one of the company's high-threat assessment divisions.

On a Wednesday evening, he kissed his mistress. He was careful to do so before opening the door to exit their hotel room. A few minutes earlier, he had reimbursed her in cash for hotel charges that she had placed on her credit card.

McClaren was a man who limited his exposure as much as possible. Rather than leave his car with the valet, he had parked four blocks away. As his thumb moved towards the button to unlock his doors, his world went black. He woke up in the back of a van, strapped to a chair that was bolted to the floor. A man was sitting across from him in the dark.

"I'm not going to hurt you, Gerald," Time said.

"You'll never get away with this. Do you know who I am? They keep track of me every minute."

"Of course I know who you are. You're an intelligent man, Gerald. Anyone who might be keeping track of you thinks that you're very far away from here."

"What do you want?"

"Direct to the point. I like that. A terrorist killed a woman and some children that I cared about very much. I want to find him. I plan to kill him."

McClaren would have never had risen to his current sensitive position if he were prone to cowardice or panic. His captor had a clear American accent and had used the word *terrorist*. McClaren made the assumption that he was talking about an enemy of the United States. In any case, it didn't matter. He was ready to say whatever was necessary to free himself.

"I see," he said, calmly. "I can help you with that. Why not give me all the information you have and I'll help you track him down. Don't worry. We'll make sure he pays for what he's done."

Time snapped out an expandable baton and tapped it almost gently against McClaren's elbow. He waited for the signs of agony that it caused to subside.

"There no need for that," McClaren said. "I'm on your team."

"I don't have a team," said Time. "I have a goal. I need information in order to resolve some unfinished business."

"Listen, I don't know what you think, but I can't help you if you hurt me. You have to trust me. You can kill me, but how would that help you? I'm an important man. Believe me, they wouldn't stop until they find you. And torturing me won't help. How would it look if I had to crawl into work tomorrow? Be reasonable. There's no way I could possibly access the kind of information you want from outside company headquarters."

"Torture you? Kill you?" said Time, slowly. "Who said anything about killing you? Tomorrow you'll go to work as if we'd never met and you will very carefully find some way to bring me the information I want. When I have it, you can go back to your life and your mistress and forget all about me. However, if you or I aren't the best of friends in the days ahead, well, look at what I have here."

Time leaned over and placed a board with three photographs on McClaren's knees.

"I've been watching you for a long time. What you're looking at are the three things in the world you love the most. Strange, isn't it, that she's not one of them? I have an associate, a Japanese man. I saved his life once, though I don't imagine that means very much to him. On the other hand, he'll do anything for the right price. I've paid him an exorbitant fee. He has to hear my voice every six hours. If you betray me, or fail me, or attempt to have me caught, he has one simple assignment. He will indulge his rather sadistic proclivities on what you see in those three photographs. If you cooperate with me, then no one will be harmed, no one except a murdering terrorist who deserves to die. But remember, if you and I don't get along, there's no way that I could stop him. He will never give up. I could tell you that he's a sociopath, but there's a better way to describe him. He thinks of himself as a samurai, with a samurai's sense of honor. Unless I cancel our contract, he will find a way to carry out our agreement. Can I make your position any clearer?"

Time got the information he needed. He studied it, going over every detail, looking for the most likely situation that might require the intervention of the finest Medium and his Weapon. He thought it could take months, but was startled when a most top-secret operation jumped out of the data provided by McClaren.

The drug war on the Mexican Border had threatened to spill over into United States Territory. The U.S. Government was fully aware that nothing could be done to eliminate, or even decrease, the growth of a business that was so fully supported by the citizens of the United States. If the flow of drugs could not be slowed, then the violence that accompanied the industry's growing pains had to be muted. Radical action was required. Through layers and layers of diversion, the assistant director of the DEA organized a meeting with four of Mexico City's most powerful drug lords. The presence of the director and his team would guarantee the security of the cartel leaders who attended. It was hoped that an initial agreement could be worked out to divide their operations into definitive territories and eliminate the minor competition.

When Time examined the support staff that was to accompany the director, the inclusion of a Medium and Weapon was an obvious necessity. Perhaps it wouldn't be Edgar Treeves, but the assistant director was a high-value asset. Multiple meetings were not an option. The Medium had to be good enough to know immediately and without any doubt which of the drug lords could be trusted to maintain a peace accord and which, if any, had to be targeted for assassination.

The situation was perfect. In order for the location to be completely neutral and have the greatest chance of secrecy, the meeting was to take place in the desert, miles from Mexico City. A conference table would be placed under an open-air canopy. The canopy's fabric was impervious to satellite surveillance. Each of the Mexican participants would be allowed two companions, an advisor and a personal bodyguard. The United States would provide overall security. There was no profit for any of the cartel leaders to cause trouble. A successful accord would ensure a reduction in profit-less violence and make each of them even more powerful.

Who could suspect that a rogue agent with advanced knowledge of the meeting would have the time to set up a sniper outpost with an outstanding view of a potential target?

Time chose the McMillan TAC-50, the rifle that had been used in Afghanistan to set the world record for the longest confirmed kill shot of 2,657 yards. He spared no expense to add the package extras that would make the TAC-50 the most effective weapon for his plan.

To calculate range, wind velocity, and other crucial factors, Time needed the services of an expert spotter, someone who had a strong desire for cash and a weak desire to know why he was being paid. Fortunately, the type of spotter he needed wasn't all that difficult to find. A large contingent of America's military presence throughout the world consisted of extremely competent mercenaries employed by private companies. Even with the finest technical support available, Time would have to be prepared and he would have to be lucky. There was never any guarantee of success with a long-range sniper shot.

They practiced in the desert for many hours using cantaloupes stuck on top of poles. As he successfully exploded target after target, Time became more confident that, with his first fifty-caliber round, he could do the same to the brain of Edgar Treeves.

The day of the meeting arrived. The gathering was to take place shortly after sun-up so that the heat of the desert would have as little effect as possible. No one wanted to meet in the dark. Even in this unpopulated area of the desert, artificial lighting would be an unacceptable risk. It had been arranged that the DEA Director and his entourage would arrive first. Time watched as the party stepped from the air conditioning of their SUVs into the growing heat of the desert. Their discomfort was necessary. It could never be revealed that the United States was colluding with Mexican Kingpins to facilitate a peaceful distribution of their products.

Time studied the group. It was easy to identify the director. His known aides and bodyguards were checked off. Then, suddenly, there he was. Time watched as a man who might be Edgar Treeves signaled a woman walking a few steps behind him. He heard the order in his mind.

Protection only.

He recognized the woman. She had begun training as a Weapon a year after Time had entered the Bunker.

The director sat at the conference table. The Medium sat behind him on his right side. The director's party waited for the other participants in this highly unusual conference to arrive.

Time studied the Medium. Edgar Treeves was the perfect chameleon, but every chameleon has individual characteristics. In a combat situation, there's significance to almost every movement that a Medium makes. A critic who has spent years studying a particular pianist's technique can easily identify their performance of a Chopin Etude.

The spotter was making the final calculations. Through his scope, Time saw the Medium cross his left leg over his right. His left toe was subtly tapping the air. He placed his right hand over his left in his lap and gently tapped the bottom hand with his index finger.

Time knew he was looking at Edgar Treeves.

Then a thought flickered through his mind.

That's a lot of movement. Where have I seen that combination before?

Time was too concentrated on making his shot to think about it too deeply or clearly.

"Let's get this done before the others show up," he said to the spotter.

"Right. What's the target?"

Time decided to aim for the center of Treeves' head. If he got lucky, the fifty-caliber round would explode his magnificent brain like a grenade. Even if the spotter's calculations were off a bit off regarding the bullet drop, the large-caliber round would still smash into Treeves' midsection. Any impact on Treeves' body would cause a massive and fatal shockwave to surge through his bloodstream.

Time placed the cross hairs slightly above Treeves' right ear. Suddenly, he watched through the scope as Treeves turned his head and stared into the barrel of the TAC-50. Time had the eerie unmistakable feeling that Treeves knew that he was there. He mentally shook the idea out of his head. It was impossible that Treeves could see him at this distance. Then Treeves spoke to him. His closed his eyes and nodded towards his toe gently tapping the desert air. Time clearly heard the voice of Edgar Treeves in his mind.

He was saying, "My left leg is over my right. My left foot is tapping. My right hand is over my left. What you're doing is wrong. Stop now."

Time suddenly realized that he would never make the shot. The spotter was compromised and probably the rifle as well. Even though he had broken it down and oiled it carefully earlier that morning, Time knew the TAC-50 would malfunction. He had never been a true expert like Iain and he hadn't taken an expert's care to make certain that his weapon would perform as expected. He remembered that the spotter had carried the case that housed the rifle from their ATV while Time had scanned the meeting place with binoculars.

Time was not suicidal. He clicked on the safety and began breaking down the TAC-50.

"What are you doing?" said his spotter. "You've got a clear shot."

Now Time was absolutely certain. He hadn't yet identified the exact target and yet the spotter knew the man was exposed.

"I've changed my mind," Time said. "Don't worry. You'll get paid the full amount."

The spotter produced a small automatic and pointed it at Time's head.

"Someone wants to talk with you," he said.

The spotter tossed a small communications device at him. Time watched the man change right in front of his eyes. He was no longer a mercenary for hire. He was one of General Tresain's Rangers.

Time picked up the device and opened a channel.

"Still fond of your tests, aren't you, general?" Time said.

He instantly recognized the voice that responded.

"That's correct," said General Tresain. "And you've just passed one that was conceived and executed by Edgar Treeves in order to give you a chance to prove that we should allow you to go on living. If you had pulled that trigger, you would have never known the mistake you'd made. After a great deal of discussion, the committee and I came to the conclusion that our best course of action was to have a painless substance injected into your IV tube. However, Dr. Treeves intervened. He convinced us that, even given the perfect opportunity, you would not harm him. We spent a great deal of time and resources to prove him correct. Dr. Treeves tells me that we should let you go. He tells me that, someday, something will prove to you that your selfish desire for revenge is nothing compared to what I've spent a great deal of my life building and protecting. So, for the moment, you're on your own. Do what you like, to whomever you like. But don't ever come within a hundred miles of Edgar Treeves again. Because that would be testing *me*."

The channel shut down.

The Ranger reached over and carefully pulled away the TAC-50. He rose and slowly stepped away. Time looked down towards where the meeting was to take place and saw clouds of dust kicking up in the morning air. He was sure that the Mexicans were actually arriving.

He was ten miles from the nearest village. The Ranger climbed into their vehicle and turned on the engine.

"What about me?" Time said. "Can I get a ride?"

The Ranger tossed out a canteen full of water.

"Not with me, you can't."

He drove away. Time started walking.

He arrived back in civilization, angry and covered in dust. On the walk back, he decided that he was done following orders. Never again would anyone tell him what to do or when to do it. He took a plane back to the states and arrived at Newark International Airport. He wandered around, enjoying a strange sensation of freedom for perhaps the first time in his life. He wanted to find a place where he could continue to feel that way. He'd always been instructed to travel to some country or region or city. And when he arrived, he always played a role while performing a function. For most of his adult life, he'd never really had the experience of simply traveling and enjoying his surroundings.

He walked past the Air France Counters. There was a small tourist information booth off in a corner. He strolled over to it, thinking he'd go somewhere on a whim, determined only by the outcome of the moment.

"Excuse me," he said, in French. "I'm looking for a town off the beaten path, some place quiet, perhaps somewhere in the south. Do you know of a place like that?"

The uniformed man behind the counter barely looked at him. Perhaps he was having a bad day. He spat out something in extremely fast French.

Time's French, though not perfect, was good. He caught some, but not all, of the man's response.

"I'm sorry," he said, once again in French. "Could you repeat that? Perhaps a bit slower?"

"Of course," the man said, very slowly, in English, with a pronounced accent. "I'll be happy to speak to you as slowly as I possibly can."

Time stared at him and his right hand began to tremble slightly. The anger and frustration that he had carried out of the Mexican Desert returned. It formed a dark cloud around the Frenchman's shoulders. Time looked around, checking the airport's surveillance setup. There was no doubt in his mind that he and this rude little man were standing in a blind spot. He considered reaching across the counter and crushing the man's throat. Afterwards, he would simply stroll away as his target quietly and quickly expired behind the counter.

As these thoughts raced through his mind, Time suddenly became aware that there was nothing to control his impulse. Not the old man, or his superiors in the military, or his need for vengeance, or, most perhaps importantly, Edgar Treeves. He realized that he needed to find some way to control the man that all of them had created.

"Merci," Time said, placing his hands inside his jacket. "I'll find a place on my own."

He quickly turned and walked away, leaving the man standing there, never knowing how close he'd come to an uncontrolled Weapon.

CHAPTER 27

FORGETTING

The Berkeley Hills
Summer, 2018

Later that evening, I managed to get off the couch and onto my bed. Diane brought me some of the exquisite chicken soup Jackson made before he left. She did her best to convince me that she should spoon it into my mouth. We had a small argument and she let me win. She was no fool when it came to picking her battles. She brought in another bowl for herself and we ate in silence. After we finished, she put the bowls on the bureau. She noticed my glance.

"What? You don't have a housekeeper?"

"She was just here. She'll be back in a couple of days."

"You mean, with all your money, you don't have a butler and a maid?"

"I like my privacy, remember? Besides, I'm not here all that much."

Diane nodded her head towards a photo of Callie on the bed stand.

"Is that her?" she said.

"Yes."

"She's really beautiful," she said.

"You have no idea," I said. "Look, I need sleep."

"Okay," she said.

Diane began taking off her jeans.

"What do you think you're doing?"

"I'm getting ready for bed."

"Like hell. Look, it was kind of you to start in here for old time's sake, but, do me a favor, finish taking off your clothes in one of the guest rooms."

"No. I'm sleeping in here with you in case something happens in the middle of the night."

After tossing her jeans in a corner, she opened a drawer and took out a tee shirt. She turned around, removed her blouse and her bra, threw them on the bureau next to the soup bowls, and wiggled into the tee.

"Is this some kind of punishment?" I said.

She grunted in a way that was meant to signify something, but only to herself.

"What?" I said, and not just because I was curious.

I was trying to occupy my mind with something other than her legs.

"I was just thinking about how you never know. If someone had told me in the first six months after we met, that one day you'd describe me getting ready to sleep next to you as a punishment, I'd have thought they were as crazy as those tabloid stories they run about me."

"I didn't mean it the way it sounded," I said. "Don't get me wrong. Really, it's good to see you again. But when you left, missing you was a full-time job for a long time. I understand you were probably right to go. I couldn't read you then, and I still can't. Whatever you felt when you left, I'm happy that you still care enough to be worried about me. I always want you in my life and you can always count on me, but I'm not sure I can hang out with you alone. Even though I finally came to accept it, it's still hard to look at you without thinking about what happened between us."

"You really are being an asshole," she said. "Maybe I might have stayed if you weren't acting like such a jerk back then."

"I was a jerk because I wanted exclusive rights?"

"You didn't know what you wanted."

"Yeah, right," I said.

I was angry, because if I allowed myself to think about it, I had to accept that she was right. I didn't know what I wanted until I met Callie. Diane calmed down. That surprised me. The Diane I knew would have thrown something first.

"Anyway, what's the point of talking about it now?" she said. "We can't change what happened and there's nothing left to fix. As soon as I'm sure you're okay, I'll be out of here before the door can hit my world-class ass. Now put your hormones back in your pocket and go to sleep."

She lay on the bed, rolled over so that her back was to me, put one arm over her head, and closed her eyes. In a short time, her breathing changed. She never had any problem falling asleep. No conscience.

I looked over and thought about another time when I had watched her. I had lied that night in my living room when I told Janison that Callie was the only woman I ever asked to marry me. One night in Mexico, in a dark hotel room, after a bottle of Tequila and a long time lost in Diane's body, I asked her if she wanted to get married. The soft clicking noise she made with her lips as she slept had been her answer that night as well.

Slowly shaking my head with my eyes closed, I ordered my brain to change the subject. It chose to dwell upon the damage that can be inflicted by hard blows to the head. Was it possible that somewhere in my brain, a trickle of blood was preparing to wipe away my thoughts, my memory? For the first time that day, I found myself truly grateful for Diane's presence. If I was responding to her in the way that my body was betraying me, I knew I was still functioning.

Think about something else, I told myself.

Todd Carrol. He had to have answers. What was the quickest way to get them from him? I didn't even know the right questions to ask. There was no point in blind speculation.

In the morning, I listened to Diane singing in the shower and reflected that she'd made the right choice when she decided to be an actress. I tested my body and it was better than expected. I reached over and took one of Paul's pills.

In a few minutes, she came out of the bathroom wearing a towel.

"Look, hormones or no hormones, I'll make a deal with you," I said. "I'll stop chugging down memory lane if you agree to wear a full set of clothes around me at all times."

"Deal," she said, smiling.

She looked great when she smiled. I worked at not noticing.

Later that morning, Aram and Kristin came. Then Jackson showed up with Mary St. James, his current girlfriend and everyone's favorite bet for a long-term situation. Jackson made vegetable frittatas, fresh popovers and muffins. Kristin brought champagne for mimosas. Diane had gone to the Cheese Board when she went to market the day before. I needed a day to heal and decided to let myself rest for a short time. For a while, it was easy.

Kristin and Diane put on a show when they first saw each other. Aram was standing around looking exhilarated.

Kristin stepped back, glanced at Aram, and blurted out, "I'm not supposed to tell. Not yet, not like this, but what the hell. I'm pregnant! I found out for certain last week."

Diane screamed. Aram beamed. We all hugged Kristin. No one was foolish enough to try and hug Aram.

"There's going to be a Mr. Lightbulb Junior?" Diane said. "My God, the world is saved."

"Everyone shouldn't be so excited," Aram said. "The baby could have my looks and her brain."

I stared at him, dumbfounded. Aram was suddenly making stupid jokes. He must have been blissful beyond comprehension. Kristin slapped him playfully.

"I'll love it anyway," she said. "And, hey, what's wrong with my brain?"

"Nothing at all, darling. It's quite lovely," Aram replied.

Diane laughed her I'm-with-my-old-friends laugh.

I took another pill and drank some champagne, and although I had to move slowly, the pain was reduced to a background hum that I ignored most of the time. We ate and talked and laughed.

Diane told a funny story about a romantic scene she had to play with her co-star, a famous sex symbol.

"I was pretending he was James Kelley and he was pretending I was James Kelley. Now that was acting," she said.

It was one of those mornings when the world seemed enclosed and comfortable. The warm sunlight that filled half the room was a reflection and a reminder of the feelings we had for each other. I sat next to Diane and every once in a while, she looked over, with a kind of half-smile that seemed to say, this is how it used to be, when it was really good between us, remember? I did remember. She was the kind of woman who was easy to fall in love with and yet hard to love. No matter how much I gave her, there was always the next day, and she wanted more. If not from me, then someone else. Like many actresses, Diane wanted everyone in the world to love her, even people who didn't know her. Perhaps everyone in the world would have been enough for her. I don't know why, but when she and I had been together, I always believed that somehow, if I tried hard enough, I could be enough. I had been proud to stand next to her. I had been favored by chance to hold her against me on both cruel and gentle nights. But as much as I might have wanted a life with Diane, what we had known together was only a part of what I felt for Callie.

Diane had told me she loved me and, sometimes, I believed her. I never had any doubt that Callie loved me. I tried to imagine what was happening to her that would make her believe she had to separate herself from me. By reflex, I reached over and took Diane's hand. She smiled at me and squeezed mine gently.

Kristin said, "Look at the two of you. I'm so glad you're together. You belong together."

Blinded by her own happiness, Kristin had managed to find exactly the wrong thing to say. The silence that followed was impenetrable. I got up slowly.

"I'm going for a walk," I said. "I need to stretch."

"I'll come with you," Jackson said.

"No. No, I'm all right. I'll be back soon."

Kristin said, "Shit. I think my hormones have already kicked in."

I went over and kissed the top of her jet-black hair.

"Kris, it's fine. I know what you meant. I'm happy for you. I'll see you in a little while."

I walked into the street and, even though it was a pale blue and golden yellow Berkeley day, I left all warmth and gentleness back in the house. I nurtured my anger, toyed with it, and let it form into a force I could use. I concentrated on who was hunting Callie. I steeled myself during that walk. I made a decision, so when the time came to act, I'd have no hesitation.

When I returned, I didn't go into the house, but walked around back to the studio. Inside I found what I'd been dreading. Ferro had taken a sledgehammer and reduced Callie's statue to jagged pieces. I walked over to where I kept a bottle of Black Bush on a top shelf.

Suddenly, I wasn't just angry with those responsible for Callie's disappearance, but with Callie herself, her foolishness, her decision to stay away. Why didn't she know that I'd protect her against anything that would hurt her, even against anything she'd done?

Damn her, I thought.

I took a long pull on the whiskey. The morning with old friends, the alcohol, and my anger and loneliness were excuses I gave myself for what happened when I went back into the house.

CHAPTER 28

———————————

LOVERS

The Berkeley Hills
Summer, 2018

Diane was sitting on the couch staring at something across the room. Everyone had left. The remains of the feast had been cleared away. Jackson wouldn't have left without doing that.

"They're all gone?" I said.

"A while ago," she said.

I sat down heavily next to her.

"How do you feel?" Diane said.

She reached over and gently pulled a lock of my hair.

"Top of the world, ma," I said.

"Check it out. You're smashed."

She seemed delighted.

"I am not smashed," I managed to say. "I'm medicated."

We were quiet for a while. It occurred to me that the fading sunlight in the room made the wisps of her hair in front look lighter.

"Kristin felt terrible. She didn't realize what she was saying."

"I'll call her later. Don't worry about it."

"It was just a slip of the tongue."

"A tip of the tongue. You know, you've got a very pretty tip of a tongue. A very pretty everything. Coming back here, walking around half naked most of the time."

"Oh, please," she said. "Give me a break."

"Yes, please."

I reached over and put my hand around the side of her neck. I was sitting with my feet up on the coffee table and my knees bent. With a soft grunt she slid into the space between my chest and my knees with her back resting against the top of my legs and her legs curled on the couch, pressing against my side. She looked at me with her head resting between my knees.

"Do you know what I like about you?" she said.

"My industry?"

She had on a white blouse buttoned down the front. I played with the area below her throat and her top button. Somehow it came apart.

"The fact that you never tried to impress me," she went on, ignoring me. "In bed or out."

"I'm not sure I take that as a compliment," I said, suddenly beginning to notice the next button on her blouse.

"Don't worry. You always impressed me like hell."

I felt a warm surge running up my spine directly to the top of my head, activating thoughts that an hour ago would have seemed crazy. I wanted to kiss her and I knew she wanted to kiss me. I couldn't make love with her. That would be wrong. But we were old friends and a soft kiss would be all right. There was nothing wrong in that. I leaned forward slightly and so did she.

"We never kissed hello," I said, though I was barely able to speak.

"Hello," she said, and she put her mouth on mine.

Diane always tasted good, like warm sweet cream. I kissed the front of her mouth and then the side. Then top of her lips and afterwards pulled gently on her lower lip. Unfortunately, I'd forgotten a key element of having her close to me. Each time I had a little of her, I wanted more. Our lips melded together and I ran my tongue across the top edge of her perfect teeth. She made a soft, growling noise at the bottom of her throat and nestled closer. Still kissing, we rolled over so that she was on her back on the couch and I was on my knees in front of her. She wrapped her legs around me just above my hips. I pressed the bottom of my belly into her and moved slowly side to side. I thought I'd kiss her just a little more.

I opened her blouse and pushed it aside. She was wearing the kind of bra that clips in the front and it followed the blouse. Rather than falling, her breasts seemed to lift after her bra was open. I buried my head in her belly and licked and kissed upwards towards one and then the other. Her skin was silk smooth and flawless. I knew what she liked. I bit her nipples hard and then moved up to suck on her neck just under her ear.

She was squirming fitfully under me, pulling me closer with her legs wrapped around my back. I know she could feel me between her legs. I couldn't imagine feeling any harder. We rolled onto the floor, grasping at each other.

Once we were lying on the floor, her on top, we began a slow rhythm together, our bodies reacting to each other. We kissed harder, with more insistence. She slipped her hands between us and undid the front of my pants. I was wearing a soft pullover and I pushed it up so I could feel my chest flatten her breasts. She reached around and tried to pull down my pants. I turned her over to make it easier. I moved my head down to give her pleasure on and between her thighs, but she pulled me up.

"Later," she whispered. "I don't want to wait any longer. I've been thinking about it since we went to bed yesterday. I need you now."

I caught my breath. I looked at her and suddenly it was if I was waking from a dream. As much as I was drawn to her, I realized that if this went any further, it would change what existed between Callie and me. And as much as I wanted Diane at that moment, I couldn't allow it to happen. I moved her hands and pulled away from her.

"Wait," I said. "We have to stop. I can't do this."

"Why? Come on. You want to. I can feel it. So do I. I really want to."

She looked like an erotic dream. Her hair splayed on the rug, her chest heaving. From her round shoulders to the ribs that formed into her slim waist, she was forcefully desirable.

"I'm sorry. I was drunk and hurting and I forgot myself. I can't be with you. I'm in love with Callie."

"And you don't love me? What the hell does it matter anyway? Listen, we're alive for just a short time and then it's over. What happens tomorrow or a week from now isn't important. Let's do what we want now. After it's over, there'll be time to think about whether it was right or wrong. I'm not looking to take you from her. I just want you now."

She moved her face close to my chest. She kissed me.

"I'll make you feel good, even better than you remember. Think of what I used to do for you."

"Believe me, I remember. But soon, I'll see her again. And when I do, I can't have a memory that would hurt her if she knew. I was weak to start this, but I'm strong enough not to finish it. Diane, you have to understand. I can't let this happen."

She fell back onto the rug and her body stiffened.

"Get the fuck off me, you bastard," she hissed.

"Diane, listen."

She punched me hard in the chest with her fist.

"I said, get off."

I sat back on the couch. She picked up her things quickly and left the room. Fifteen minutes later, she left the house.

I lay back and closed my eyes. Maybe I'd felt worse sometime in my life, but I'd have been hard pressed to cite an instance. If I hadn't caught myself, I'd have been making love with Diane that very moment. It was difficult to forget how good that felt.

To paraphrase Hemingway, a moral act is one that makes you feel good afterwards. By that reasoning, I'd just committed the most immoral act of my life. The only positive for me was that the pills were wearing off and the rest of my body hurt so badly, the pain in my groin really didn't add that much.

After a while, Jackson walked through the front door. He sat next to me.

"Diane showed up on my doorstep crying like a widow. I offered her the guest room, but I think she's going to Sausalito to be with Kristin."

"I guess she mentioned in passing what a prick I am."

"I got the impression you're not her favorite person at the moment. On the other hand, she did ask to me to come here and check on you. I believe her exact words were, 'If that son of a bitch dies now, I don't want any guilt interfering with how good I'm going to feel about it.'"

"Eloquent."

"But telling," he said.

Jackson sighed.

"Listen, I was never going to tell you this, but maybe you need to hear it now. Did you know that for a while I had, well, let's say, a notion about Diane?"

I smiled.

"Yes, I knew. It was pretty obvious, Jackson."

"A few weeks after the two of you started living together, you went to New York on a business trip. I was helping Diane move some of her things out of storage. I helped her carry some of her stuff up to one of the bedrooms. Some of those ridiculous stuffed animals she's so crazy about. I don't know why, but we started getting silly. You know, I started tossing them at her, running around, just kidding around.

"Anyway she was laughing, trying to get me to stop. We started wrestling, you know, playful. Somehow we wound up on the bed. I was holding her arms down and I had my leg between hers, and still we're just kidding. Then suddenly, I looked down at her and I realized I wasn't kidding anymore. Man, I wanted her so bad my toes ached. And I almost kissed her. And, between us, I don't think she would have stopped me. But I didn't do it. I got up and said, 'Let's clean up this mess and I'll make dinner for us.'

"She sat up in the bed and looked at me and you know what she did? She kind of laughed and said, 'Chicken shit.' I don't think I'll ever forget that for as long as I live. Even though you're my best friend, I'm going to wonder until the day I die, if doing the right thing for you caused me to miss out on what might have been one of the best nights of my life. On the other hand, if I'd done it, it'd just be a memory now and I'd have to sit here knowing that I betrayed you.

"Anyway, the reason I told you that story is there's one thing I'm sure of. We haven't known Callie a long time. I don't know what's happened to her or what she did, but I know this. Nothing like what happened that day between me and Diane could ever happen with Callie and another man. After she fell in love with you, you're the only man she'd ever let touch her. I can't tell you why I believe that, but I can tell you that I know it."

"You know why you're my friend, Jackson?" I said.

"I let you eat for free at the restaurant, even though you only own twelve percent?"

"Because sometimes you know the exact right thing to say, even if it's a confession about fooling around with my ex-lover."

"It's a gift. So, what now?"

"So now I find out what Todd Carrol knows."

"When?"

"In the next few days."

"Are you going to be okay by then?"

"I'll be okay. I've been stupid. I've been letting things happen to me. That's over. Starting tomorrow, things are going to start happening to other people."

CHAPTER 29

LING

The Berkeley Hills
Summer, 2018

Later that evening, I tried to check on Diane, hoping she'd speak with me. Kristin answered the vid with visual on.

"She's not here, Michael."

"Is she all right?"

"I believe she's enjoying the company of a certain Brazilian gentlemen," Kristin said, with more than a hint of satisfaction.

"Pino."

Diane probably gave him her vid info in the kitchen when she went to make my tea.

"Why, yes, I seem to remember that was the gentlemen's name."

"Kris, how long are you going to talk to me like you're Kate Hepburn in a forties movie?"

"Probably until I figure out why you behaved like such a shit to my best friend. And, as I recall, Katherine Hepburn never uttered the word *shit* in a forties movie."

"Kris, I have to go, someone's at the door."

"Ta."

The vid went dead.

Class. The woman was lousy with it.

I went to the door and looked through the small window. I'm not sure how he managed it, but my visitor was standing there looking like a composite of every man on the face of the earth, a walking definition of nondescript and noncommittal, the type of man who would fit in just about anywhere. His suit was good, but not too good. The colors of his suit, shirt, and tie seemed to blend into the landscape. His hair was short and well groomed, but not excessively so. His expression was bland and pleasant. Everything about him gave the impression that he was a perfect diplomat. I opened the door.

"Mr. Case? My name is Jon Ling. May I speak with you for a minute?"

"Why not? Come in."

Without any wasted motion, he seemed to float into the living room. He glanced around and nodded his approval.

"Very nice," he said. "Very spacious."

"Selling carpet?"

"Excuse me?"

"Nothing. Care for a drink?"

I watched him think about it for a split second. My guess is he wasn't thirsty, but his training must have included a lecture on not insulting the locals by refusing their hospitality in regards to food and drink.

"A sparkling water might be nice," he said.

I brought him one and a beer for myself. When I returned from fetching the refreshments, he was standing in exactly the same spot as when I left.

"Have a seat," I said.

"Why, thank you," he said. "Mr. Case..."

"I represent the government," we both said.

He smiled.

"Is it that obvious?" he said.

"Coyness works best for starlets, Mr. Ling. What's this about?"

"Let's begin with the strange fact that a man vaguely resembling Aram Cooper recently took a consulting job at Hill Realty, the former employer of Calena Lacerda. Also, it seems that certain unauthorized activity has been noted on federal computer systems. And, finally, you had a superfluous business meeting with Todd Carrol."

"Superfluous? Hardly. I had a meeting with Mr. Carrol to discuss the possibility of him taking some pictures of The Ahh Baloney Café. As for the other things you just said, I have no idea what you're talking about. It is amusing to imagine Aram Cooper working as a consultant at a realty firm. However, I am curious about one thing. Why is the state department interested in a local murder investigation?"

His eyes widened for briefest moment.

Then, very softly, he said, "Janison."

Damn, I thought, that was a stupid mistake.

The pills and the liquor had to stop. Janison wanted to help me and I'd put him at risk. Although there was something completely disarming about Ling, I sensed that he wasn't a harmless man. I'd dropped my guard for a moment, made an error, and he was instantly there to take advantage of it.

"I'm going to ask you to trust me, Mr. Case. Not only me, but trust your government as well."

"Please," I said. "I pay my taxes. I even vote when there's any kind of choice. But don't ask me to trust you or the government."

He seemed amused. I began to get the feeling everything about him was unreal, a performance. More disturbing was a nagging suspicion that I felt that way because he wanted me to feel it. His performance was flawed only because he was allowing it to be that way. For some reason, he wanted me to know he might not be as innocuous as he seemed.

"What exactly do you do for the state department?" I said.

"Oh, this and that. Mainly, I keep volatile situations from getting out of hand. These unfortunate events are part of a larger mosaic. Overall, there are more important issues at hand."

"Nothing is more important to me," I said.

"Of course," he said. "But please allow the proper authorities to take care of it. You and your friends blindly stumbling around will only muddy the waters. I'm here to assure you that steps are being taken."

"What are you?" I said.

"Please, Mr. Case, who's being coy now? I believe you can imagine exactly what I am."

Suddenly, the façade came down and he let me see behind the curtain. There was a casual deadliness to him that was terrifying in both its ability and the lack of restraint with which he would apply it. This man had been trained to go anywhere and get to anyone. He allowed me to know that he was a man who had the resources and the temperament to drown a young woman in a swimming pool and leave no traces.

I readied myself to rise.

"Don't," he said.

I relaxed back into the chair. Jon Ling wasn't a man I wanted to take on without a weapon.

"Before a few days ago, I had no interest in either Calena or Laura Lacerda. I'm here for you. I came here as a courtesy. You're involved in an affair you couldn't possibly understand. Let it be."

"Get out of my house."

"Of course," he said. "Thank you for the water."

He left without another word.

"Vid up," I said.

"Aram? Don't say anything. I need to talk to you, now. I'll meet you at Scully's at the end of University Avenue."

Scully's was a pick-up bar, pure and simple. It was large, loud, and crowded. Perfect for what I needed to do. A crazy impulse made me scan the crowd for Callie's hair. The back of one woman's head might have been Diane's, but she turned and canceled the impression. Winding through the crowd, I inundated myself close to the bar with my back to the large blaring vids. A woman drinking to my right sent an appraising glance at me, but her radar was working perfectly and she ignored me for more fertile game.

Aram was disguised when he walked into the room with his bodyguard, Yuri. His expression made me think of an Alka Seltzer tablet entering a room full of leaky water glasses. I waved. He grimaced and began fighting his way toward me, Yuri opening a path for him.

"Why?" he said, when he was finally in front of me.

I pushed backward slightly to make room for him. There were no complaints from him. He was truly miserable.

"I just had a visit from our state department. It's not safe for you to continue. I wanted to be sure we could talk where no one could hear us."

"This is good then," he said. "I can barely hear you."

"The powers that be have picked up activity on their computer networks."

His eyes glazed over. He was going over his moves.

"They can't possibly prove it was me. Of that, I'm sure. However, I must have made a mistake somewhere."

"Don't blame yourself. Ten to one, the only reason they found anything was that they were expecting it. In any case, now they'll monitor everything you do."

"I could loop..."

"No," I said, firmly. "You've done enough. I have to visit Todd Carrol again and I need to know everything he knows. Whatever's going on, for some reason the government wants us out of it. They may even plant false information. From now on, I want you to be a model of integrity."

Aram was looking over my shoulder. His expression had changed. I turned around.

A news announcer was talking over the words *triple murder* in large, gruesome letters. I struggled to hear.

"This triple murder occurred at approximately eight o'clock in an alley near MacArthur Boulevard in Oakland. Repeating, three men were gunned down less than two hours ago. Although there were no eyewitnesses to the killings, bystanders say the gunfire sounded like an automatic weapon. The police have not revealed any names, but it's believed the three men were Colombian Nationals. A police department official on the scene is quoted as saying the killings appear to be a drug-related execution. More details on this breaking story at seven."

I turned to Aram.

"Colombians?" I said.

"The vid never gets anything right."

"Stay here. I'm going to find a quieter place."

It was a frustrating six minutes before I got Janison.

"I just heard something on the vid," I said.

"I just got off with Oakland," Janison said.

"Well?"

"Her brother and his two friends."

It felt as if someone pulled a belt tight around my chest.

"Damn."

"Yeah, damn. Where are you? I want to talk to you now."

"Later. I have to go."

"Listen to me, you're not going…"

I hung up.

I thought, Diane.

I raised the vid.

"Kristin?"

"Yes, Michael, what is it now?"

"Where's Diane?"

"Look, you can't have it both ways."

"Goddamn it, Kris," I said. "If you know where Diane is, tell me now."

I'd never spoken to her like that before. It must have shocked her.

"I'm looking at her now," she said, quietly. "Pino got a vid from one of the others and he had to go to Oakland."

For the first time since I'd spoken to Janison, I felt I could breathe.

"I'm sorry, Kris. Please listen carefully. Don't say anything to Diane. Keep her busy until Aram arrives and don't turn on any vids."

"I must say, Case," she said, "I'm concerned about this new side of you."

"That's good. Pretend that I'm jealous or something. There's nothing for you to be afraid of, but a level-one security team will arrive any second. Aram will explain everything."

"I really don't have time for this."

"Just like that. I always said you were the smart one."

I hung up. Aram was staring at his foot when I returned. It looked like he was counting the number of times it had gone up and down since I left.

"Was it them?" he said.

"Yes," I said. "Her brother and his friends. The ones who were at my house."

Aram didn't say anything for two seconds while he considered it.

Then he said, "Diane?"

"She's at your house. I just spoke with Kris and told her that you're coming home."

"And you?"

"Go home, Aram. Stay with Kris and Diane. Tell Yuri to keep his weapons ready and not let you out of his sight."

"What are you going to do?"

"I don't know," I said. "I guess I'll go home and get some rest."

"You expect me to believe that? Michael, don't be foolish. If you act without thinking, you'll play directly into their hands."

"Whomever they may be," I said.

"Come home with me. We'll work this out together."

"No. I have to leave. Tonight."

"You're leaving? When will you be back?"

"As soon as I can."

I put my lips close to his ear and spoke very quietly.

"Aram, don't do anything else to find Callie until you hear from me. I can't put you in any more danger."

"I'm not afraid," he said.

"I know," I said.

"At least, tell me where you're going to be."

"Sorry, Aram," I said. "I don't know."

CHAPTER 30

<hr/>

REQUIREMENT

The American Midwest
Summer, 2018

Time parked his rental car outside his motel room. His voicecard opened the door to his room and he sat on the bed. He turned towards the vid screen.

"Vid up," he said. "Audio. Information."

"How can I help you?"

"I want to report suspicious activity."

"Nature of activity, please?"

"It concerns a man. I have reliable information that he's ignored legitimate warnings by our government to cease certain activities."

"I see. To which agency are you reporting this activity?"

"Well, I'm not sure. I knew someone a long time ago. He was a special individual. If I could find a way to speak with him directly, I'm sure he'd know exactly what to do."

"His name, please?"

"His name isn't important. Neither is the name I'm registered under. I suggest you forward my voiceprint to the closest anti-terrorism agency along with a notation that I'm aware of a high-level and imminent threat. I'll wait here."

Time closed the connection. He lay back on the bed and closed his eyes. He hadn't realized what a long trip it had been and how long he'd been awake. He was asleep when he heard a quiet knock on the door.

He said, "Unlock."

Two men entered the room. One moved into a corner. The other stood at the foot of his bed. Time didn't try to stand up. He didn't want to hurt them. He sat up on his pillows.

"You fellows wouldn't happen to know how to get to Madame Jane's Mustang Ranch?" he said.

"We're not known for our sense of humor," said the man standing at the foot of his bed.

"Then let's all move very slowly," Time said.

A forty-five-caliber automatic appeared in the man's hand as if he had been holding it all along.

"Slow enough for you? Our orders are to bring you in. Don't give us a reason to slow you down."

Another man stepped into the room.

"I'm a doctor," he said. "I'm here to begin the process of taking you inside. You'll have to undergo a series of examinations. Believe me, you don't want to be conscious during these procedures. Some of them are rather invasive. If you agree, I'll put you under after you're in the truck outside. You'll wake up after you've been cleared."

"And if I don't agree?"

The doctor repeated the message without expression.

"If you agree, I'll put you under after you're inside the truck. You'll wake up after you've been cleared."

"Well, since you've all asked nicely," Time said.

He slowly rose from the bed. He walked outside, careful not to get too close to the Rangers. He smiled when he saw the beat-up pickup truck that was parked next to his rental car. It was exactly like the one that had transported him out of the Bunker the final time. When they were settled in the truck bed, the doctor pushed a pen against Time's arm. The next thing he knew, someone was shaking his shoulder.

"So you decided to come back," said General Tresain.

"It's been a while, general," I said. "I wish I could say it's good to see you again."

"All right, the pleasantries are over. Why are you here?"

"You know why I'm here. I want to talk with him."

His eyelids narrowed and I actually thought he was about to strike me. I wouldn't have stopped him. Getting physical with Martin Tresain in the Bunker was about as smart as jumping naked off a skyscraper.

I endured his stare for a few moments.

"Who taught you tactics?" he said.

"You did."

"And according to me, what are the four basic principles of tactics?" he said.

"What? You want me to recite them for you?"

"That's exactly what I want."

"One, know your enemy. Two, know yourself. Three, have both a long and short-term plan. Four, be flexible enough to change your plans when it becomes necessary."

"I have a long-term plan for you. That's why you're still alive. However, when you tell me you want to talk with Edgar Treeves after what I said to you in the desert, you're forcing me to be flexible enough to change my plans."

"But you won't just yet, will you, general?"

"Why do you say that?"

"Because I'm still talking to you. You're not a man who wastes his time or reminisces with old friends. Something's going on with Treeves, isn't it?"

"Damn," he said. "Yes. You're right. Treeves has gone down hard. Of course, it's happened before, but this is the worst I've seen."

Shortly after I began working with Treeves, I had an interview with an Army psychiatrist. He explained that Treeves had medium bi-polar disorder. Most of the time, he was in total control of his emotions. However, there were other times when he experienced intense mood swings, from a type of chemically enhanced hyperactivity and joy in his work to the most horrible sorrow and regret a person can know.

Because of his knowledge and emotional training, it was not apparent to the outside world when he was in these states of mind. But there were signs. Both the general and I knew them well.

"How long has it been?" I said.

"About four months. He can't work and we need him. The president wants him in his entourage when he goes to China for the financial summit."

"The summit is four weeks away. What if I can help?"

"And what if you make him worse? I can't prove that you've really stabilized. What if you tried to harm him? In that case, you know I'd have no option."

"It doesn't matter, general. I need him."

Tresain closed his eyes for the briefest moment.

He said, "No matter what you've thought of me in the past, you know I'm as good as my word. I believe you when you say that you need him. Naturally, we've kept track of you. I can tell you this. She's a smart girl. Even we don't know where she's gone. I can't see her disappearance as some elaborate trick you've thought up. No matter. Whether you think that he can help you find her or you're just trying to get near him, remember this. If you pose any kind of threat to what I've built, you'll disappear off the face of the earth. And it won't just be you. That goes for anyone who's helping you. Anyone. You find me difficult to understand?"

I considered his words. Martin Tresain wasn't a man to make idle threats. In fact, in the years that I'd known him, the only other one I could remember was to a young lieutenant on the day I'd met the general.

Somehow, even though I knew he'd hate it, it seemed appropriate to respond, "As clear as a bell ringing, general."

"So what do I call you, now? You're not a Weapon. As far as I'm concerned, you don't deserve the title."

"That's all right. Case will do."

CHAPTER 31

AGREEMENT

An Open Field
Summer, 2018

I was taken to a helicopter and blindfolded. I hadn't seen Edgar Treeves in years. I wondered if he'd changed in ways other than his physical appearance. I knew one thing for certain. The general had run out of options when he agreed to let me speak with Treeves. It was a desperate attempt to lift him of the darkness.

I considered what approach to take. There was nothing I could say or do to manipulate Treeves. I had to be honest and hope for the best. An old habit kicked in and I began silently counting minutes. Each time the helicopter made a turn, I memorized the duration and direction. After thirty-five minutes of that, I felt the chopper beginning to descend. We landed and my blindfold was removed. Two Rangers and I hopped out onto a grassy field and the helicopter took off. I stood in the middle of nowhere in the company of dangerous men. I felt as if I'd been dropped into another life.

"He's on his way," one of the Rangers said. "It won't be long."

I wanted to ask exactly how long we'd have to wait and decided against it. It's not usually wise to make unnecessary conversation with a man holding a laser-sighted rifle with the safety off.

The Ranger said, "After he arrives, we'll walk behind you, out of earshot, but never out of range. Stay at least one meter away from him at all times. We have very clear orders. If you so much as raise your voice, we'll both open fire. Don't be concerned. Neither of us has ever missed anything we were aiming at. He'll be safe. You'll never know what hit you."

I broke my own rule by saying, "You're quite a jolly fellow. Has anyone ever told you that?"

"The general told us you had a smart mouth. I'll make certain my first round goes straight through it."

After that comment, there wasn't much to talk about. We spent the better part of an hour waiting in silence. Treeves may have been five minutes away, but there was no way of knowing. At last, we heard the sound of a helicopter. After it landed, everyone waited until the blades stop rotating. Finally, Edgar Treeves, the man who had been once been the center of my world, emerged.

"I believe it's Mr. Case at the moment," he said. "You've changed."

I was curious.

"Changed in what way?" I said.

"Let's say it seems as if you've lost a layer of ferocity."

"Perhaps. I have friends now. I don't remember having any before I arrived in California. It seems to me you've changed as well, Dr. Treeves. Unfortunately, I can't remember when you've looked worse."

It was an honest appraisal. He'd never been a natty dresser. However, in the past, he'd been careful about presenting a professional appearance when he wasn't in the field. Of course, in the field, he blended into whatever character was appropriate for the situation.

"Well, there was an unfortunate bit of business with my last Weapon," he said. "Some plastic surgery was required."

He paused. His eyes closed and then slowly opened as if he felt a spasm of pain. He smiled with only his lips.

"From the day you met me, you thought of me as some type of biological machine, a man without emotions. That's not the case. I assure you that I do have emotions. It was necessary to suppress them in order to achieve my goals. I have not lived the comfortable life that you've enjoyed the past few years. Masking my emotions has become more difficult. After my last assignment, the general insisted that it was time to take a forced retirement from the role of Medium. I had to agree."

As we walked next to each other, he had no reason to be anyone but himself. He wore a rumpled grey suit that seemed too big for him. There was no tie around his button down blue shirt. He had neglected to button one of the collar buttons. His hair appeared somewhat greasy and poorly combed. He rarely bothered to stand up straight when he wasn't in character, but he was noticeably stooped over as he walked beside me. His eyes reflected an inner pain that only people afflicted with a certain kind of misery can ever understand. At its worst, people often wished for an end to it.

Even Edgar Treeves, with his tremendous self-control over his physical presence, couldn't arrange his features to fully disguise what was happening inside of him. I had seen like this once before during my second year of training. I asked him what it felt like and he was weak enough to answer.

"Imagine a hypothetical situation. A man has a child, a teenager," he said. "One evening they have a bitter argument. The man says awful things, angry words, words that once spoken cannot ever be fully erased. He cannot control his rage. Even as he says these terrible words, he realizes he doesn't really mean them, but he literally cannot stop himself. The teenager rushes out. Soon the man calms down and realizes that he overreacted. He plans to set things right as soon as his child returns. However, an hour or so later, he receives a visit from the police. His child has been terribly injured in a car accident and will probably never regain consciousness. Imagine that moment, the rush of grief, of regret, of shock. Now imagine what it's like to relive the emotion of such a moment over and over again without pause, every waking minute, for days on end. The pain comes in waves, each one racking your mind and body, and you often feel that the latest is the worst, until another washes over you that is even more unbearable. Sleep is your only respite, but as soon as you awaken, the same waves come crashing down upon you."

Thinking about what he'd said, I understood why someone would spend days curled on a bed in a fetal position or leaning against the nearest support. Treeves only appeared to be uncomfortable, as if he were suffering from a toothache. That's all he allowed himself. That's all he gave away.

"I understand you've amassed quite a fortune," he said, as we walked aimlessly through the clearing.

"I've been lucky."

"Aram Cooper is a brilliant man. You would have never been able to earn that kind of wealth on your own. No offence to you. You simply didn't have the interest or the drive."

"I have only one interest at the moment," I said.

"Calena Lacerda," he said, quietly.

"Yes, Calena Lacerda. I need you, Treeves."

Although it was a warm day, he shook for a moment. He turned to me with a bitter smile on his lips.

"Do you think I belong to myself?" he said. "They would never let me help you."

"You forget who you are, how important you are, and what you can do. You can make them do what you want."

"Not at the moment, Mr. Case."

I turned to him. I could feel the Rangers tense up behind us.

"Don't worry," said Treeves. "They're just window dressing. The general is fully aware that, at this distance, if you decided to kill me, there's really nothing they could about it."

"On that same subject," I said. "Why did you warn me that day in the desert?"

"You were correct when you told the general I would know how you felt," he said. "You didn't deserve a death sentence for those feelings. On the other hand, I couldn't constantly be looking over my shoulder and still hope to work effectively. There was no guarantee you would see and understand my signal. But you deserved a chance."

"You know, there was also a chance that the Ranger posing as my spotter would make a mistake. In fact, he did. It was just bit too late. If he'd made a mistake like that earlier, I would have taken him. In that case, I would have had a decent shot at removing your head from your shoulders."

Treeves was silent. I thought it over for a minute or two.

"Somehow, you convinced the general that was impossible, didn't you? You told him there was no chance at all that I'd see through your test, that I was too concentrated on my goal and I would believe whatever the two of you wanted me to believe."

Treeves shrugged.

"But you knew that there was a chance, didn't you?" I said.

"Of course."

"So you calmly sat there, knowing that I might have your head in my cross hairs and a live round in the chamber. Why would you do that?"

"I calculated the percentage that you'd see through my test and I came up with a rather small quotient of success, even factoring in the strange and unpredictable variable that you had always been rather lucky in combat. Perhaps that's why you survived when other Weapons didn't."

"I don't understand. Why didn't you just let them put me down while I was in the hospital?"

There was no emotion in his voice when he said, "As I said, I felt you deserved your shot."

"How did you know how I'd go about it?"

"Please, who do I know better than you? You'd want to control it, to see it happen. There was no possible way to get close to me. Providing you with an opportunity to put me in the sights of a long-range sniper rifle was an obvious conclusion.

He shrugged.

"I don't have a perfectly logical explanation for everything I do," he said. Our relationship is not a simple one. There are many variables. At the moment, I'm not prepared to explain all of them to you."

"You don't sound as if you're prepared to explain much of anything at all."

I said it as a challenge, a desperate attempt to make him snap out of it. I wanted him to know what I was thinking.

I considered saying, "You aren't camouflaging your emotions, Treeves. Aren't you the least bit ashamed?"

There was no reaction from him.

He must be in hell, I thought.

I tried something else.

"Why don't you take the drugs?" I said.

"For me, it's not so simple. When my brain turns against me like this, it uses its knowledge on me. What would drugs do for me? What would they do to me?"

Treeves was silent for what seemed like a long time. He was a man so closed into himself, so concentrated into his calling, that to leak his thoughts to another person was as terrifying to him as it would be for an engineer to randomly blow cracks in a massive dam. Then he began speaking, as if I'd walked away and he was talking to himself. It was the first time I'd ever heard him speak about his past.

"When I was a boy, I realized I was hyper-sensitive to what people were feeling and what they were thinking. I could tell whenever my mother lied to my father. Of course, he knew that she was lying, but he pretended not to know. I come from old money. Our house was very large. No one really bothered about me."

He smiled wistfully, as if he were enjoying the memory.

Then he said, "From the moment that I realized I could see things that seemed invisible to the people around me, my only interest was to learn everything I could about men and women. I wanted to unravel their behaviors. I studied psychology, physiology, anatomy, and, in fact, any subject that I even suspected was relevant. I memorized the muscles of the face and what their tiniest movements revealed. What some people call *body language* was child's play to me. I wanted to fully comprehend the language with which every man or woman communicates, to understand movements that were beyond a human's ability to hide or control. I even spent a year or two absorbed in magic. I knew the study of human behavior would be my life's work and I embraced it, not really caring that my own relationships suffered, as you can well imagine. You cannot correctly conduct experiments unless you maintain a scientific objectivity. I had to distance myself from my subjects, to remove my own emotions from the equation. I had no friends and no connections of any kind. My own family set up a trust fund and, after that, they wanted nothing to do with me. I'm sure that I frightened them."

Treeves slightly waved his hand before him as if he were entirely dismissing that part of his life.

"Then, suddenly, my own humanity betrayed me. In my third year at Princeton, I wandered out of my basement lab and met Elizabeth. I quickly found that she was someone with whom I couldn't maintain my objectivity. She didn't seem to mind that I could read her thoughts and emotions. In fact, it fascinated her. She revealed herself to me and, incredibly, I couldn't stop myself from allowing her to see who I was and what I was doing."

"You fell in love with her," I said. It was hard for me to imagine.

"I suppose you could put it that way. But I think it was more. For almost three years, we were like one person. Then, one evening, she received a phone call. Her mother and her sister had been killed by a car bomb while having lunch in a café in Televiv. To the world, it was a forgettable incident. No one even took credit for it. It was a random, senseless, useless act of violence. It changed Elizabeth profoundly. It wasn't long before her sorrow turned to anger and she directed it at me. She demanded to know why I didn't go to the Middle East and use my abilities to root out and punish the people who had destroyed her family. I tried to explain to her that I had no connections, no training, but she was obsessed. She said that if I wasn't man enough to go, then she'd find someone else. The irony of it was that, while I had spent years studying human emotions, I couldn't find the right words to comfort the only person I ever truly cared about. The more she withdrew from me, the more agitated I became. Her anger turned to bitterness. I'd let her know me too well. She knew exactly what to say to cut me as deeply as possible. One day, as I was fighting against a hyper-manic state, her words went to a level I didn't know existed and I slapped her hard in the face as she screamed things at me that I could not bear to hear."

Treeves stumbled. He may have stepped in a hole in the grass. My instinct was to reach out to steady him, but I caught myself just in time.

He regained his footing and turned to me.

"Can you imagine that, Mr. Case? I almost knocked Elizabeth down. I completely lost control."

I was engrossed in his story. I stepped a bit closer to Treeves. I heard the Rangers level their weapons and I quickly adjusted the distance between us.

"She left that day and I never saw her again. To be honest, I was relieved. I thought that she had driven me insane. I couldn't accept any other explanation for what had forced my hand. I immersed myself in my work. I hardly slept. I made breakthroughs. I could clearly see things that had been only shadows before. However, it wasn't long before I began to doubt my results. Was the data supporting my conclusions or were they based on suppositions I had simply accepted as true to support brilliant new theories?"

A cloud covered the sun and the field got slightly darker. It was a fitting preamble to his next words.

"It was then that the darkness began to close in around me. I saw it. I used all my will against it, but I couldn't stop replaying over and over the moment when I slapped Elizabeth, as well as the expression on her face the moment after. It played in my mind like a film loop, but instead of a soundtrack, there was an emotional track, filled with guilt, regret, and horrible sorrow. It crippled me for days and I was unable to move. I considered suicide, but by studying my own thoughts, I became aware that a chemical imbalance in my brain was causing my emotions to torture me. The diagnosis was simple. I had an incurable disease. However, who better to deal with an emotional disorder than an expert in human emotions?"

His voice filled with bitterness when he said, "It wasn't long before I knew I was losing the battle."

It was impossible to miss the irony in his words. After a lifetime studying the behavior of others and controlling those around him, his own thoughts betrayed him.

"I concluded that the only way to give myself a reason to go on living was to do what Elizabeth had asked. But how? Even if I could find the persons responsible for killing her mother and sister, I had no physical abilities. So I went searching for someone who could supply me with what I was missing. Of course, the man I found was General Tresain. When I met him, he was skeptical. It was easy to prove to him that I had the talent, but I also had to show him that I possessed the will. The general told me not to waste his time. He said I looked like a walking dead man. He told me if I intended to remain that way, I should do it properly. He offered me one of General Patton's pearl-handled automatics."

Treeves stopped walking and rubbed his cheek. It was obvious he was recreating all his emotions from that moment.

"I took his pistol and pointed it at my temple. But it was only bravado. I'd never held a firearm before. I wish I could tell you if it was loaded. I honestly don't know. I can only tell you that I couldn't press the trigger. So the general gave me a different option. Instead of wallowing in regret over something that I could never change, why not risk my life preventing damaged individuals from doing even more terrible things? Together, we created the concept of a Medium and a Weapon. The general was quite reassuring. He told me the chances that I would survive in the field were extremely low. I'd probably get killed soon enough without any further effort on my part."

"I thought the same thing," I said. "I also thought you'd take me along with you. But you didn't."

"Strangely enough, during the times I was up or down, I think I was actually better. I was sharper, because I couldn't afford to let my attention stray from the task at hand for even one moment."

"I repeat my question," I said. "Why not take the drugs?"

"Did Winston Churchill take the drugs? Or Lincoln? Or Hitchcock? And if they had, would they have been Churchill, Lincoln, or Hitchcock? Playing with the chemistry of your brain is for men who don't live for the uniqueness of their brain. My drug is my work, just as their drug was theirs. Should an expert on how humans think and behave need to drug himself to control his own thoughts and behaviors? I know what causes my pain the way a cancer specialist knows that nausea comes with chemotherapy. I should be able to deal with it."

"Then why do you look like you're ready to hang yourself?"

"You still blame me for what happened that day in Chechnya. It's true. I didn't tell you that Maria and those children were on that plane because I knew you wouldn't have fired that missile if you'd known. Nothing I could have said or done would have made you do it."

He stared at the ground in front of us.

"After you finished Makkhal, you turned to me," Treeves said. "I knew immediately that, if you could reach me, I was a dead man. You collapsed less than a meter in front of me. The general's extraction team arrived and they wrapped you up and took you away. The doctors told me you were dead."

"I came close. They told me my heart stopped a few times."

"Yes. But I knew you too stubborn to die. Not with unfinished business. I also had a recovery period. General Tresain visited and told me that I'd never see you again. That you'd become unstable. Did he tell you that the committee also considered trying an experimental memory removal procedure on you? Our mission in Chechnya had given the general just enough power to veto that."

I thought about the men in white coats in the Bunker and their little drills and probes. I silently thanked Martin Tresain.

Treeves said, "I asked the general to have a computer expert set up secure connection. I wanted to examine cross sections of Makkhal's cerebral cortex. They clearly showed that he was indeed a severely paranoid schizophrenic, a human time bomb. A computer expert gathered data and I began one-way video interrogations. I studied all aspects of our mission. I needed to know if I'd made the correct and logical decision. Could we have done anything else in time? Was there any way of stopping that plane without harming those children?"

Treeves slowly shook his head from side to side.

"Honestly, I don't know. I only know what Makkhal revealed to me inside that schoolhouse. The teacher, Maria, was key to the overall plan. It was her job to get the children on the plane. Fortunately, you were reasonably good at your job or we'd both be dead right now."

My anger came rushing back. Everyone in the field stopped.

"So you knew about the plane beforehand?"

"Don't be ridiculous. Do you think that I would have taken us into an operation as disorganized as that in the face of such a threat?"

"Makkhal told you that afternoon?"

"Not directly. The general and I knew that a catastrophic event was imminent. While you were with Maria, I was conducting my own research. During my conversation with Makkhal in the schoolhouse, I led him down the right path. By that time, he was eager to demonstrate his commitment to the cause."

"How could he sacrifice his own daughter?"

"We uncovered the details after the fact. His wife was terrified. She was planning to leave him and he had killed her the day before. He believed his daughters would be better off in Paradise."

"God. And the other children?"

"Maria had been brainwashing them, but who knows what they thought when they boarded that plane? Perhaps they thought they were going on a vacation, a school trip. Perhaps she thought it was best for them."

Treeves shook slightly.

"I looked at their faces and read their histories over and over. I tell myself there was no way those children could have been saved once that plane had taken off, but I'll never forget any of those children. If your rifle shot had hit Makkhal a few millimeters in a different direction, he would have died instantly. If you'd killed him as I ordered you to, we would have been debriefed and quickly moved back to Bunker. You would have been told that Makkhal had killed Maria as a traitor before he came to our meeting. It's very likely that you would never have known who or what was on that plane. You insist that I treated you like an ape that day. I only wish that I'd had the same opportunity. In that case, I wouldn't be responsible for making that decision."

We walked in silence.

"Treeves, help me. Do this for me and everything will be square between us."

He stopped.

"When you left the Bunker program, you told the general that you'd never function as a Weapon again. Now you're asking me to go into the field with you as a Medium."

"If you're concerned about my ability to protect you, let me assure you that if we find anyone involved in hurting Callie or her sister, I won't hesitate to end them."

"Don't be ridiculous. Remember what I said to you on the day we met? Your basic characteristics cannot be changed. You're as dangerous now as when you were Time. My concern is exactly the opposite. What if I ordered you, as your Medium, not to harm someone involved in this affair? Would you follow that order? Without question?"

I couldn't lie to Edgar Treeves. That would be a fatal mistake.

"I honestly don't know," I said. "It's a risk. But we've taken risks in the past."

Treeves grunted softly.

One of the Rangers shouted, "A helicopter is on the way. You have fifteen minutes."

"Treeves, the way you felt about Elizabeth, that's how I feel about Callie. I can't find her in time without you. I've never asked you for anything before. Please, help me."

"Mr. Case, as I once said, we are not friends. However, in many ways, we are more than that. So I offer you an agreement."

I waited. Somehow, I wasn't surprised by what he said next.

"I will attempt to help you find Calena Lacerda if you will do something for me. As soon as we're sure that Ms. Lacerda is safe, you will kill me, in such a manner that one moment I'll be conscious and the next I'll have oblivion. I believe that you're the only man in the world who could get close enough to do it. So, understand, the cost of my service will be your own life."

"No," I said. "I don't care about myself, but I couldn't kill you. Not now. You must know about the old man. He once told me that there are only two kinds of men. Those who act on what they believe should be done, even if they have to wait for years. I'm not one of those men."

"Perhaps you no longer have the desire to kill me for Chechnya, but what about Ms. Lacerda? Are you willing to trade your life for hers?"

"There's more to it. The general once told me that you're a national treasure."

"I'm not a Medium anymore," said Treeves. "General Tresain has organized and standardized the training program. It functions so well he hardly needs my input at all. I live underground and spend most of my time working up personality profiles and statistics for high-level meetings. There are other Mediums who are quite capable of detecting lies. I'm incapable of the kind of fieldwork we once did. I'm sure the general can get along quite well without me. Besides, he took that chance every time we left the Bunker. Circumstances forced him to do so."

"Treeves, You're not well at the moment, but you'll feel better. Perhaps much sooner that you think."

Treeves stopped. He turned towards me very slowly and invited me to looked closely at the man standing before me, removing all barriers between us.

"You think you understand pain? You have no idea what real pain is like. I want it to stop."

"It will pass. You know that."

"Yes, you're right. However, it will come back, each time I'll remember the things I've done and why I did them."

I heard the sound of a helicopter approaching. Thoughts raced through my mind. Then suddenly, the question became quite clear and simple. Edgar Treeves and I had boarded commercial airliners knowing that there was an excellent possibility that neither of us would ever step onto the ground again. We had risked our lives for strangers. Was his life and mine worth sacrificing so that Callie would be safe and secure? It wasn't a hard question to answer at all.

"This is what I'll do," I said. "If you help me find Callie and any danger that she's facing is eradicated, and you still want me to do what you asked, I'll kill you when you least expect it, regardless of any consequences to me. I'll make certain you won't feel a thing."

"Agreed. Let's go and make arrangements with General Tresain."

CHAPTER 32

BLACKMAIL

General Tresain's Office
Summer, 2018

"It's not going to happen," the general said with the kind of emphasis he might have used if I had asked to borrow one of Patton's pistols so I could shoot a cigarette from Treeves' lips in a Wild West Show.

Treeves and I sat on the other side of his desk and considered his response.

"Why not?" said Treeves. "We won't be boarding any hijacked airliners. We won't be strolling into vermin infested cafés. I'll simply be performing some evaluations for Mr. Case."

"Potentially in the field," said the general.

"Yes, possibly in the field," I said.

There was no profit in lying to him.

"Neither of you has been in the field for a long time," said the general. "With all due respect, Dr. Treeves, you're going through a rough patch. As for you, Case, you haven't functioned as a Weapon for several years. You look fit enough, I suppose, but you couldn't possibly be in peak condition. And, all that aside, a Medium and his Weapon need more than mental and physical ability. They must share a bond. Each must respond without hesitation to the slightest signal from the other. Do the two of you possibly expect me to believe you're capable of that? And, Case, you need the will and concentration necessary to protect Dr. Treeves at any cost. Try and convince me that you still have those qualities after all that's happened."

"We understand your concerns, general," Treeves said. "However, I repeat that the operation won't be that delicate. I don't see where I'll be in any real danger, nothing Mr. Case couldn't handle, if necessary. And let's not forget that if he allows anything to happen to me, he'll be endangering

Ms. Lacerda as well. That's the reason he's here. He certainly has enough incentive to keep me alive. However, we do have one other request that you might find more disconcerting. You'll have to keep your agents at a reasonable distance from the two of us."

"You can't be serious," the general said.

"Why do people keep asking me that? Do I appear to be constantly making attempts at humor? To keep the operation simple, we need to minimize the variables. Your agents would only muddy the waters. Aram Cooper has one of the best security organizations in the world. Following the murders of Miss Lacerda's brother and his friends, he has added extra measures. As a cover, he's announced that he's made a breakthrough in artificial intelligence and the new security measures are necessary to protect his data. Naturally, we may ask for some logistical support when needed."

"All this is just chatter anyway," said the general. "The president would never allow you to go out in the field at this time and you know it. It's too close to the financial summit with the Chinese. Do you think he'd allow an affair like this to interfere with his plans to have you with him in Beijing?"

"Please get him on the phone," said Treeves. "Now."

The general didn't seem surprised, but I was. I'd always suspected General Tresain had that kind of power, but I wasn't aware how far Treeves had risen until that moment. The general turned to me.

"Case, put aside your emotions for a moment and consider what you're asking, what you're risking."

"I know what's at risk," I said. "You have no idea what I'd do for her."

Treeves shot me a warning glance, but it was unnecessary. The general didn't care.

"If you're about to spout some romantic crap like those damn English poets made up, let me tell you what I've given up for my country. Men like us should care about only two things – our nation and our fellow soldiers. In that order."

The slightest smile formed on Treeves' face. It was the one he used when he was about to say something he thought might be amusing.

"I believe the general also loves his dogs," he said.

"Damn right," said General Tresain. "But I wouldn't send my best Medium after them if they went missing."

Nonetheless, it was a small weight that tipped the scales. There was a tiny, but clear, shift in the general's attitude. It was probably the first time in weeks Treeves had shown amusement in anything. Perhaps a pinpoint of light was beginning to glow at the end of his personal long black tunnel. The general pushed a button on his desk. There was no vid in sight.

"Is Mustang available?" said the general.

A disembodied voice responded, "Ten minutes, General Tresain."

The general told me, "It's an automatically secured channel."

We sat in silence for nine minutes and forty-seven seconds. There was a quiet beeping noise. The general pushed the button again. A very familiar voice with a slight southern accent came out of the air.

"I have twenty minutes for you, general. Will that be sufficient and will you require anyone to join us?"

"Twenty minutes should be sufficient, Mr. President," he said. "Thank you for taking the time."

"I always have time for you, general. How's our mutual friend doing?"

"I need to inform you immediately that Dr. Edgar Treeves is in my office along with a man who once supplied him with tactical support in the field. We've been keeping track of him. You have the briefs. It's Michael B. Case, a business associate of Aram Cooper."

"Oh, yes, Aram Cooper's a great American, Mr. Case. You be sure to tell him that the next time you see him."

The president paused so that his next remark might be interpreted as a joke.

"And let him know there's always a chair for him at one of our fundraisers."

"I will, Mr. President," I said.

I wondered for a moment if this president would be susceptible to a large campaign contribution in exchange for the services of Edgar Treeves for a few days, but I caught the slightest head shake coming from my former Medium's direction.

"Mr. President, this is Edgar Treeves speaking."

Pause.

"Good afternoon, Dr. Treeves. How are you these days?"

"Well, frankly, sir, I have been better."

"Well, I'm certain in a couple of weeks, you're going to feel much improved."

"Mr. President, our time is limited, so allow me to jump straight to the point. As General Tresain mentioned, my first Weapon is here with me. I don't think I exaggerate when I say that he may have been my best Weapon, especially considering the sub-par performances of my last two."

"Brave young soldiers. May they rest in peace."

"Yes. The two of us, Mr. Case and I, would like to take a short furlough, less than ten days or so, I imagine. Mr. Case has a personal concern and he believes I would be invaluable in helping him resolve it. This isn't a high-risk assignment. I'd be quite safe. In essence, I'm simply asking for some personal time."

There was a very long pause. The president was a man who knew how to say *no* without making it sound like *no*."

"Dr. Treeves, I'm sure you're aware that this request comes at the worst possible time. Although I have tremendous empathy for Mr. Case and I wish him nothing but the best, how can we possible consider putting his personal interests above those of our nation? Certainly, after you and I return from China, we might revisit his request and I promise you that we'll put the full resources of General Tresain's unit at his disposal. Within reason, of course."

"Mr. President, I fully intend to fulfill my responsibilities in China, but this is something I must do," said Treeves.

We heard the president take a deep breath. He was about to make a political speech. General Tresain and I stared at each other as Treeves preempted him.

"All the preparatory work for Beijing has been done and we are now as ready as we'll ever be," said Treeves. "We both know, that with three bills coming to the floor of Congress, you'll have very little time for me until we're on Air Force One. And, let's not forget, Mr. President, that I'm not a member of the military. Although I sometimes have the unpleasant sensation that I'm more of a prisoner than an asset, I do have rights as a citizen. The fact is that I can come and go as I please. I don't require your permission. Therefore, it's my hope that you'll consider this call as a courtesy. Don't you think it would be to everyone's benefit if you gave this small venture your blessing."

Pause.

"Mr. Case…"

Treeves gave me a signal to keep silent. I was taken aback how clear it was after so many years.

"I'm speaking for Mr. Case," Treeves said. "After all, it's my decision to stay or go."

The president was not accustomed to that type of dismissal.

"Dr. Treeves, surely you're aware that such a decision cannot be made lightly. It has great impact. This is a question of national security. There are powers I could invoke if you force my hand."

"I'm certain you might find a legal loophole that you could use to restrain me, but do you really feel that's your best course of action?"

There was a long pause.

The president said, "Are you actually suggesting to me that you would act against the interests of the United States in China?"

I couldn't imagine where Treeves was going with this line until he used his tone of voice to shove a knife in.

"Haven't you acted against my interests?" he said. "You should know that I'm aware of the additions to my diet."

"I have no idea what you're talking about, Dr. Treeves."

"Come now, Mr. President, my new personal assistant, who is obviously a doctor of some sort, has been adding various doses of some psycho-pharmaceutical drug, probably a Lithium derivative, to my evening meal in some misguided effort to treat me."

Treeves added a subtle touch of condescension to his tone.

"The label may read tasteless and odorless, but it's difficult for me to imagine that anyone would believe that I wouldn't notice my assistant studying me. I'm not sure what effect he imagined the drugs would have on me, but I can assure you that I was planning to inform you at an appropriate time that I do not appreciate this sort of manipulation. Therefore, as you've probably been informed, I've been eating less and less. If we don't come to some agreement today, I'll stop eating altogether."

"Really, Doctor Treeves, let me assure you..."

"No, let *me* assure *you*," Treeves said.

General Tresain did not look pleased. This was not a conversation he wished to join. However, he wasn't sure that he should simply stand by and allow Treeves to interrupt his boss, the most powerful man on the planet.

"Your assurances might work somewhat more effectively on a voter, Mr. President," Treeves continued. "Since you're familiar with my file, you must be aware that I don't vote. My particular talents removed the attraction of that activity years ago. However, all that aside, even if you could force feed me or use some type of feeding tube, what use would I be to you in China under those circumstances?"

Treeves continued in the same tone.

"If, for one second, I believed that you thought that I wasn't free to make my own choices, that this clumsy attempt to medicate me without my knowledge was nothing more than a criminally stupid plan conceived and carried out by one of your underlings without your knowledge. That this invasive procedure had been implemented without General Tresain's knowledge and approval. Well, in that case, I wouldn't hesitate to cease any further efforts on your behalf. I'm aware this is an extremely busy time for you and I apologize for disturbing you. Do we have any further items to discuss?"

"Gentlemen," said the president. "I'd like to speak with General Tresain privately, if that's agreeable with you."

The general reached down and picked up what appeared to be an antique telephone. He listened without a word for at least five minutes.

Finally, he said four words, "Yes, sir, I understand."

He closed the connection and regarded Treeves as if he were inviting him to read his expression.

"I didn't know anything about the drugs," he said. "I never would have allowed it."

"Yes, of course," said Treeves. "I didn't know about it either."

We both stared at him.

"Where do you get the stones to pull a bluff like that with the president of the United States?" I said.

"A bluff? Hardly. Call it a highly educated guess. I wasn't certain about the medication, but there were some clear indications. However, the clearest indicator was that I know this president quite well. If he believes something important is broken, he'll take any shortcut he can to fix it. He's incapable of a measured solution."

"If you weren't sure about the medication, why did you stop eating?" I said.

"Oh, that," Treeves said. "I haven't been very hungry lately."

General Tresain grunted. I laughed.

Treeves said, "To be honest, I don't think I'll be able to help him very much in China. Even with me by his side, the Chinese will most likely devour him like a spring roll."

The general caught my eye. My left profile was towards Treeves. I winked at the general with my right eye.

"Don't do that," Treeves said.

CHAPTER 33

PRESSURE

Alameda, California
Summer, 2018

I was driving with Treeves in the back seat of car provided by General Tresain. If I had passed Treeves on the street earlier in the day, I wouldn't have recognized him. His hair and eyes were a different color. He wore a thick pair of glasses. His ears and nose were disguised by the latest undetectable prosthetics. He sat as straight as Prussian Military Officer.

The license number of our car would come up on any law enforcement computer as: *Do not interfere.* It was the kind of license number reserved for high-level undercover activity. Unless we did something incredibly stupid, we'd be left in peace.

I picked up Jackson, who was waiting for us on one of Berkeley's darkest streets. Thick clusters of trees killed the light from the streetlamps and the moon. Just to be sure, Aram had neutered the street vids.

As Jackson walked towards the car, Treeves said, "We might have used one of the general's drivers for this."

"No," I said. "I don't want any of his agents involved. I want to control the situation as much as possible. That means only people that I can trust."

"What a quaint concept," Treeves said.

He grunted.

"When you think of 'people you can trust,' you had better be thinking, 'people that you have to trust.' And I'm possibly the only person on earth who fits that description until we complete our bargain."

I slid over and Jackson got behind the wheel. He turned to greet Treeves, who nodded in a neutral manner. I introduced Treeves as Mr. Temple, an associate whom I'd hired to lend us a hand.

Todd Carrol's home was located on street close to the Alameda Border. When we were about five blocks away, I sent a coded text message to a secure vid. I received a reply consisting of one word, *clear*. Aram had taken control of all surveillance within a four-block radius of Carrol's house. I lost count of how many laws we were breaking.

I told Jackson to park at a hydrant about ten yards from Carrol's front door.

"What if a cop comes along?" he said.

"Don't worry, you won't have to move. No one's going to bother you. But Jackson, listen, whatever you do, don't leave the car."

He started to protest, but I squeezed his arm.

"If you really want to help, listen very carefully. I need you to stay here. I know you'll stay here. However, and this is most important, if you see anyone going near Carrol's door, press this button. It shouldn't happen, but just in case…"

I handed him a simple reliable communications device.

"If you hear anything out of the ordinary, any loud noises or sirens, press that button, then get moving immediately. Leave the keys in the car and walk about a mile towards University and take a cab home. Stay there until you hear from me. Don't worry about how Mr. Temple and I will get home. If you need to leave, I've made other arrangements. But if everything stays quiet, don't get out of the car, you understand?"

"It's not complicated," he said, with a trace of annoyance in his voice.

"It's not as trivial as it sounds. I need you to watch my back so that I'm absolutely certain we won't be disturbed. Tonight, I need my friend. I know that you're smart and tough enough to help me do what has to be done. But, this is important. No matter what happens, don't forget that you're only here to watch the door."

"How do you even know he's there? What if he's having a party?"

"He's there and he's alone. I have it on good authority."

Jackson understood immediately. Aram was never far away.

"What are you going to do?"

"I just want a few minutes alone with him so we can talk privately."

I put my hand on the door handle and paused.

"Jackson, if you don't feel right about this, we can leave now and I'll make other arrangements. No blame, no loss. Don't feel you have to do this because we're friends."

"Look, it's pretty easy to tell Carrol isn't going to be overjoyed to see you. You won't tell me what you're planning and I don't like that. Not to mention, mister mysterioso in the back seat kind of creeps me out, you know? So, if you want me to say it's all just fine, well, that's not going to happen. But you're the best friend I've got, so stop telling me to sit on my ass and get on with it. Just don't take all night. I have the feeling the longer I hang around here, the more I'll have to explain to the first cop that comes along."

"Trust me, no one will ever know we were here," I said.

"Why doesn't that make me feel better?"

"Sit tight. Think about food."

"Always do," he said. "Except when I'm thinking about Mary."

Treeves and I walked towards the warehouse where Carrol lived on the second floor. As we did, I sent another text message, *hot*.

Aram had prepared the area. Any recording device or security apparatus in or around Todd Carrol's home would be recording nothing but an empty normality until we were finished. After we'd gone, any record of our words or our presence would be permanently erased.

Treeves and I had formed an overall plan. There was no sense in introducing complexity into a simple contact. I rang the bell for Carrol's two-story residence and his voice came over the intercom.

"Yes, who is it?"

I nodded at Treeves. He'd do it much better than I could.

"Hello, Todd," Treeves said. "It's M.B. Case. I'm sorry to drop in on you like this. I had some thoughts about The Ahh Baloney Café photos. I was in the neighborhood and I thought I'd kill two birds with one stone."

I had forgotten how good he was. Suddenly he wasn't talking about a photo shoot. Without significantly altering his tone, he made it clear to Carrol that the visit was simply a ruse to come up and spend some time with him, special time.

"Well, I suppose I have few minutes to talk."

"Wonderful."

The door unlocked. Treeves took off the glasses and removed a light, but opaque mask from his pocket. He pulled it over his head. Only his eyes showed thru two small holes. The remainder of his outfit was equally eerie. He wore a loose shirt, cotton pants, socks, and shiny shoes. All of his clothes were the same dark-blue color. Thanks to Aram Cooper, if Carrol was checking the door's vid feed, all he would see was a smiling M.B. Case, dressed in casual evening wear.

I chuckled lightly.

"What?" he said.

"You look like death dressed up like a Salsa Dancer."

"General Tresain was correct," he said.

His eyelids narrowed for emphasis.

"You think you know this man. That he'll roll over as soon as you apply pressure. I heard his voice. There's a fear in it that's deeper than anything a relative stranger could bring him. The Weapon I knew wouldn't have made a mistake like that, and Weapons who do, don't last long. Don't forget he believes that he knows what you are. There can be no half measures to what we do. You cannot act like the man you think you've become. Put your mind to the task at hand."

Carrol was walking towards the door as I entered. He was wearing jeans and a comfortable house shirt. He had on light wool boots that were pulled over his pants and ended about halfway between his ankles and his knees. His hair had been freshly combed.

"It's nice to see you again so soon," he said.

His tone implied that it was very nice.

"I hope I haven't interrupted anything," I said.

I didn't allow the door to close all the way.

"No, I'm all alone," Carrol said, smiling. "I was just tucking myself in."

He tried to appear relax and intrigued, but Treeves was right. There was a clear undertone. Carrol was on the razor's edge and it had nothing to do with my unexpected visit.

"So, would you like a drink before we begin talking business?"

"No, actually, I think it's best if we begin right away."

I stepped forward and Treeves stepped into the room. He allowed the door to shut and we all heard the lock click. It was loud in the silence following Treeves' entrance. The shift from my pleasant greeting to the appearance of hooded man was a simple, but chilling effect.

Carrol stepped backward as he said, "What the hell?"

I stepped forward and grabbed his throat with my left hand and pushed him quickly backward until the back of his head collided with the wall. The impact was great enough to knock several magazines off a nearby table. Then I slapped him hard twice across the face, once with my open palm and then with the back of my right hand.

I let him go and stepped back about three feet.

"I'm upset," I said.

"Jesus," he said, his voice rising, his left hand going to his throat. "You've hurt me."

"Yes, that was my intention. In fact, I'm intending to hurt you quite a bit, Todd. That is, unless in the next few minutes, you tell me everything you know about Calena Lacerda."

"Who? I don't know what you're talking about."

He turned towards the nearest stand and said loudly, "Vid on. Level One."

"That won't work," I told him. "Calena Lacerda?"

"Not this again," he said. "I told the police, I told those three sons of bitches, and now I'm telling you. I don't know anything about what happened to her. That's all I can tell you, no matter how many masked freaks you sneak in here."

"That's all you can tell me? I don't think so. I think you have a lot more to tell me."

Something flashed in his eyes. I caught Treeves in my peripheral vision. He blinked twice.

I reached out, caught Carrol's left wrist, turned his arm until the angle was right, and slammed the sensitive area of his elbow against the wall. I stepped back just as quickly. He let out a scream and grabbed his arm with his right hand.

"Oh God," he said, he said through his teeth, rubbing his arm.

Treeves and I waited calmly for the pain to recede somewhat. I nodded towards Treeves.

"The masked freak told me to do that," I said to Carrol. "I wonder what he'll tell me to do next."

"Who the hell is he?"

"Him? He's the one who told me you're lying about Calena Lacerda. That, in fact, you know an enormous amount about her."

Carrol was about to move towards me. I may have been out of practice, but he seemed as slow and clumsy as a square rubber ball. I kicked him in his left knee in a spot guaranteed to cause him the greatest pain. He doubled over with a howl.

"Why are you doing this to me," he said through his gritted teeth.

"It appears you're confused. I ask the questions, you provide the answers."

I nodded towards Treeves.

"He'll let me know if you're telling me everything you know. If he tells me that you're lying or that you're holding something back, I'll hurt you in many different ways. Soon, I'll begin hurting you in ways that will cause permanent damage. You won't just feel the pain tonight. You'll feel it for the rest of your life. Each time you lie to me, I'll do something worse to you. You're probably scared. Probably thinking about the pain that you're suffering at the moment, but the good news is, that up until now, the things I've done to you won't hurt tomorrow. Believe me, Todd, you don't want that to change."

I waited a minute or two. He remained bent over rubbing his knee.

"Straighten up," I said. "Or I'll kick you in the head. Hard."

He rose suddenly and a blade appeared in his right hand.

"You fuck," he said. "Do you know what happens to people who fuck with me?"

I thought about it for a second.

"They have to throw up afterwards?"

His brow furrowed.

"You're begging for it," he said. "You think I'm just a soft piece of shit, don't you? Let me tell you something. I've had to fight more times than you can imagine. I've studied Karate because of pricks like you. I'm an expert with this thing and don't think I haven't used it before. Back off or I'll show you what I mean."

I nodded at the knife.

"You had that ready when you let me in, didn't you? So what are you afraid of, Todd?"

"I'm thinking you're the one who should be afraid," he said. "Those assholes running around thinking they were tough, thinking they could scare people, look what happened to them."

He stopped himself when he saw the look on my face.

"Listen, I had nothing to do with that. But I can tell you this. If you keep running around, harassing innocent people, just like they did, you're going to wind up the same way."

"It's quite a coincidence that you think someone is planning to kill me, because I was thinking the exact same thing about you."

"They've got no reason to hurt me."

"Your story is falling apart, Todd. Who are they?"

He brandished the knife closer to me. I was careful. There was no sense in taking chances, but I didn't move back. His back was to the wall and that's where I wanted him. I didn't want him to have room to maneuver. The wall was my partner.

"Fuck you," Carrol said, his voice rising. "I want you and the goddamn lone ranger to get out of my house right now before I…"

"Don't be foolish, Todd," I said. "You don't want to threaten me with that knife, especially the way you're holding it. That's a crime both in a legal and a physical sense."

"You're insane."

Treeves was never out of my line of sight. He began a silent sequence. It was if I heard my native language again after living for years in a foreign country.

"*We don't have time for this*," he signaled me. "*I'll calm him down. Move through the levels as I instruct. He'll break at level four.*"

"Todd, put that knife on the table," Treeves said.

There was kindness and overtones of deep sympathy in his tone.

"What?"

"I said that you should put down the knife. You could throw it over in the corner if you like. You really don't want to hurt anyone, Todd. We can see that. You realize it was a mistake to pull that knife. I can see that you really don't want to use it. I can tell by the way you're holding it."

"I never wanted to hurt anyone," Carrol said. "It was just business. And it was good for everyone. Especially her."

I moved towards Carrol.

Treeves signaled, "*Freeze.*"

I did.

"Of course," he said out loud to Carrol, with a hypnotic calmness permeating his voice.

I maintained my edge. I'd been trained to be immune to his standard array of tricks.

"Let's all be reasonable," said Treeves. "If you force Mr. Case to take that knife away from you, someone could be seriously hurt. We don't want that. Why, someone might even be killed by accident. No one wants that. It was a bad lapse in judgment to pull that knife out. There's really no reason to be waving it about. So why not just put it down on the table?"

I watched him think about it. Treeves' had reassured him that I wasn't a mortal threat. He heard Treeves say I didn't want to kill him. He knew he was in trouble, but he was desperate to believe he could tough it out. He had seen how fast I moved. His bluff had failed. He knew he had no chance against me, even though he was wielding a knife.

Treeves signaled, "*He'll do it.*"

I stood there silently waiting. Carrol tossed the knife away from us.

"Look, I just want you to..."

I took him on the word *you*. I smashed his left wrist onto the edge of the table, breaking it. He had started to swing at me with his right. By the time it reached me, the blow felt like a tap on my shoulder. I don't think he even formed his hand into a proper fist.

Even with his body screaming at him, he tried to move around me to the front door. I hooked his ankle and he went down. I stepped away and bent down to pick up the knife off the floor. I felt differently. There had always been a rush of adrenalin in combat, but tonight was something else. After all the frustrating hours that had weighed on me since that awful moment in the pool, for the first time since I'd lost Callie, I felt some release. I was finally giving pain to someone who had a part in taking Callie away from me. Todd Carrol wasn't an opponent. He was a whimpering punching bag. And I was enjoying the workout.

Treeves did something extraordinary.

In my own voice, he said to me, "Not like that."

As for Carrol, he was finished. He backed against the wall and sat with his knees together, covering up. I stood over him, holding the knife.

"This has been a pleasure, Todd. But it's getting late. Talk now."

"The hell with you," he said. "All right, so you're big and quick. But what can you really do to me? You're just a big corporate jock who knows how to fight and is acting tough. So, go ahead, beat me up. Hell, I've been beaten up before. If I tell you anything, I'd be as good as dead."

"Corporate jock?" I said, my eyebrows going up.

I wondered if Treeves found the description amusing. If he did, he didn't show it.

Instead he signaled, "*Level four.*"

I said, "I think I've given you the wrong impression, Todd."

I leaned over and drove the knife almost to the hilt into the top of Carrol's left shoulder. With a look of pain and horror, he turned his head to see the handle sticking out. His nose almost brushed against it.

He began making a rhythmic high-pitched grunt. His right hand went up reflexively to grab the handle and pull it out. I slapped it away.

"You know, that's a mistake most people make. The knife does much more damage coming out than it does going in. Think of all the blood vessels you might leave severed and where's all that blood to go? You really need to have it removed in an operating room under controlled conditions. If you or I pull it out now, you'll probably bleed to death rather quickly. But, if you talk fast and I activate your vid, you'll probably make it."

"Jesus. Call an ambulance."

His face reminded me of a boy about to burst into hysterics.

"No. First, I want to hear it. All of it."

I leaned my head towards Treeves.

"And keep in mind that he'll know if you're telling the truth or if you leave anything out. Do it quickly. Then we'll see about getting you some help."

"I can't tell you anything. He'd have me killed."

I leaned over and flicked the knife handle with my index finger. He responded with a high, whiny moan.

"What do you think I'm doing right now, Todd?" I said. "I'm killing you and, unless you start talking, you'll be dead in just a few minutes from now."

"All right, all right, dammit. All I did was find her and then arrange to pay her. I did it for a man named Bai Ju Hong. He invited me to a diplomatic reception. Said he was interested in financing my work, my real work, my art. He's very, very rich, high up in the Chinese government. Still young, in his thirties. He likes women, especially western women. But he wanted to be sure they're, you know, healthy. He's paranoid about making his body impure or some kind of crap like that. I don't know. Also, his wife's family is very powerful. If she found out what he was up to, there'd be hell to pay."

Carrol stopped to take several deep breaths.

"I'm going to die," he said. "Get me some help."

"Keep going," I said.

"Bai can be pretty damn charming when he's trying. He twists things around, makes everything normal and natural. He wanted me to find women that were especially beautiful and had little or no experience. I was supposed to get to know them, find out their secrets. He thought, for some reason, they'd confide in me. And they did. I was safe, for them and for him.

"If they seem to fit the bill, I'd introduce them to him. He had his own people check them out. After a while, he'd make them an offer. It was like they entered into some kind of harem. He paid them a lot of money and set them up. They only had to do two things. Be willing to be nice to him when he wanted it and agree not to be intimate with other men. But I'm telling you, he was crazy about it. He told them if he ever found out that they were screwing around anyone else, he'd have them killed. And, believe me, they took him seriously. He travels with this bodyguard. Scary motherfucker. You wouldn't believe it."

He began moaning.

"Time's running out," I said.

"The deal was the women could leave if they wanted, but they couldn't cheat on him," Carrol said. "Everything was great, everyone was happy. Then he met Calena and, suddenly, the rules changed. It was like he became obsessed with her. Calena wasn't like the others. I really liked her. I think in the beginning she actually cared for him or she wouldn't have even considered it. Maybe she looked at the money like he was helping her. Who the hell knows? She had a lot of pride. When she was a kid, her family was poor as dirt. Then, suddenly, she changed her mind. She wanted to leave, but he wouldn't let her. She came to me. He was giving her some crap about having a contract for a year and she'd have to stay for a year. But we both knew he was just stalling, holding on. You ask me, I think he fell in love with her."

My head was throbbing.

"You're a lying son of a bitch," I said.

For the first time since we'd walked into his house, I broke my connection with Treeves.

"If he loved her, why would he kill her?" I said.

Carrol looked at me with disgust.

"Don't you know? She must have told him about you," he said. "Why'd you do this to *me*, you bastard? You're the reason her sister's dead and her brother. You're the reason she's running."

He began crying.

"I need help," he pleaded. "I don't want to die."

I pulled out my device and texted, *vid on, 5 minutes, audio only*.

"I can't move," Carrol said.

"Your vid will be active in five minutes. If I were you, I'd say a man followed you home and you made the foolish mistake of inviting him in. He did this to you. If my name comes into it in any way, I'll make certain to tell Mr. Bai how I found him."

"I won't say anything," he said.

Treeves nodded.

"I know you won't."

When we got close to the car, I saw Jackson leaning on the fender. He looked at me with an expression I'd never seen on his face before.

"Is that blood on your hand?" Jackson said.

"Forget it. It's not mine."

To answer his look, I said, "Do you hear the siren? That's an ambulance. He'll be fine. Let's get out of here."

"Where do you want to go?" Jackson said, when we were all back in the car.

"I don't know," I said, cleaning Carrol's blood off my hands with wipes from the glove compartment. "Take us to Cooper SHW. I have a feeling Janison may be waiting for me at home and I don't want to talk with him right now."

Jackson started driving. I knew there was no point to it, but I turned around anyway.

I said to Treeves, "Well?"

He nodded.

"All of it," he said.

"The two of you were gone a long time. I was worried," Jackson said.

It sounded as if he was explaining why he was outside the car.

"It wasn't that long," I said.

I was numb.

Jackson glanced at me and then quickly looked back at the road.

"Long enough," he said.

CHAPTER 34

BAI

Cooper SHW
Summer, 2018

Jackson, Treeves, and I drove back to Cooper SHW in silence. Jackson began to say something every so often, glanced over at me, and thought better of it. Treeves was silent in the back and, and as far I could tell, he was thinking about pie. I wasn't sure what I was thinking. My teeth were clenched and my eyes were burning. Every few minutes, I had to push down an impulse to smash in the glove compartment.

Security had never been an issue at Cooper SHW. However, as we approached the front gate, it was obvious that it had been taken to a new level. There were four men patrolling the reinforced front gate.

One of them shown a flashlight into the car and said, "Good evening, Mr. Case."

"We're here to meet with Dr. Cooper," I said.

He bent back to check something written on a clipboard in his hand. He placed the light squarely on my face.

"I'm sorry about this, Mr. Case, but Dr. Cooper gave me specific orders. He says I have to do this before you come in. I have a question for you. What did the angel say to the lawyer?"

I remembered SAM's joke.

"The jury will back in about four seconds."

He straightened up, turned and nodded to his men. They were standing on either side of the front bumper. One had taken a position to his right. They looked like former secret service to me, the kind who could make automatic weapons appear out of thin air.

"That's correct. Go on in."

We drove through the fortified gate and Jackson parked in my spot. Three more men were waiting inside the front door. I didn't recognize any of them. The one in charge had the hard, no nonsense demeanor of a drill sergeant. When he spoke, it was clear he was a man who wasted no words and whose mind was razor sharp.

"Evening, gentlemen," he said. "My name is John Copinger. I'm Mr. Cooper's new chief of security. This facility is locked down. All employees have been re-located to a temporary location. You're cleared to enter, Mr. Case, but I'm currently waiting for final authorization for your companions from Dr. Cooper."

"Cooper's authorizing me?" Jackson said. "Next time he wants takeout after midnight, I'll authorize him."

Copinger felt something go off on a device he was holding in his right hand, put it up to his ear, and received his instructions. His expression remained as stony as it had been when we walked into the lobby. He signed off.

"I have authorization," he said. "Dr. Cooper is waiting in your office, Mr. Case."

"Damn," Jackson said, as we walked down the hall. "I feel like Case Corleone's evil twin."

"Four people are dead, Jackson," I said.

"Maybe five," he said, looking at me.

Aram was sitting in my chair studying the air in front of him. When we walked in, he put his finger to his lips. He got up and we followed him to the entrance to L-9, where he opened the door by going through his elaborate security precautions. SAM was on and soon as we'd entered, I felt as if another presence had joined us. For some illogical reason, I felt a pang of satisfaction that there was finally there was someone in the room that Treeves couldn't possibly read.

"Where's Yuri?" I said.

"His mother suffered a serious heart attack," Aram said. "He didn't want to leave, but I insisted. He'll be back soon."

Treeves and I exchanged a quick glance. Neither of us believed in coincidence.

"I didn't recognize any of the guards out there," I said.

"They're from a company called Star Power," Aram said. "I've confirmed that they're the best available. The survival rate of their clients, even in the worst of situations, is ninety-eight percent."

"I'm sure that's a great comfort to the other two percent," said Jackson.

Aram ignored him.

"Despite their organization's unfortunate choice of name, I'm satisfied that we're secure. They've provided protection for the wildly popular and unpopular. There are two men and a woman on the boat with Kris and

Diane. And, of course, I've upgraded my own electronic security. I believe no one could possibly get to any of us."

Treeves smiled. Aram's conviction that we were totally secure could easily be a fatal error.

"How is Diane?" I said. "How did she react when you told her about Pino?"

"Badly," Aram said. "She liked Pino. They were having dinner when he got a call from Callie's brother. He didn't want to go, but Ferro said that he needed him to follow up on a lead in Oakland. Pino put her in a cab and promised to call."

Aram smiled sardonically.

"From what I've gathered from Kris, this hasn't been a particularly good week for Diane. Paul prescribed something for her and Kris made sure she took it. She should sleep for quite some time."

Jackson looked around L-9.

"I never thought I'd see this place," he said. "So where's SAM?"

"Everywhere," Aram said. "He's in rest mode."

Aram was clearly uncomfortable. He didn't like to have people in L-9 who weren't directly involved in SAM's development.

"I thought it best to talk in here. We're entirely cut off from the outside world. No surveillance of any kind. I guarantee it. We can speak freely. I see you've brought a visitor with you."

"Aram, this is Mr. Temple. He's an associate of mine from the days before I arrived in Berkeley. I brought him in on this because he has a great deal of experience finding missing persons. As a consultant, he's assisted several police departments ..."

"That's enough, Mr. Case," Treeves said. "These men aren't dunces. They're also unquestionably loyal to you. They would not be standing in this room, let alone find themselves traveling in the same circle, without your friendship to bind them.

"Gentlemen, I'm here to assist Mr. Case and, perhaps, protect your interests as well. However, you must understand that I am, without question, the most dangerous man you've ever encountered. Although I personally mean you no harm, once I've finish my work here, it would best if you forget every word that's passed between us, everything that I intend to have us accomplish. Circumstances have forced us to meet. All of you will only know exactly what you need to know. What I need from you is to understand that this encounter goes above and beyond any loyalty you may feel for Mr. Case. It must be burned into your senses of self-preservation. Once I'm gone, you must erase any memory that I was a part of your lives in any way. To do otherwise, would be to risk not only your own life, but also the lives of everyone who is close to you. There is no room for misunderstanding."

Jackson looked as if he didn't understand.

"You're telling us to forget you were here," he said. "What about those men outside? What about the security tapes from this place? What about Todd Carrol?"

Aram was looking at Treeves. His eyes clouded over.

"Those men outside don't work for Star Power. Do they, Mr. Temple? And I'm sure Todd Carrol didn't get a good look at you either."

"It's good to meet you, Dr. Cooper," Treeves said. "I've heard you're an interesting man. I'm pleased to note how easily you live up to your reputation."

"So, you work with computers," Aram said.

"No," said Treeves. "I'm not fond of computers."

Aram's forehead furrowed. It didn't seem to faze him that Treeves had claimed to be the most dangerous man on earth, but what kind of man would walk into his lab and casually say that he didn't care for computers?

"I assume you don't have any objection to communications devices," Aram said, reaching for the only one in the room.

"What are you doing?" I said.

"Now that you're here, I'm assigning three of those men out there, whomever they are, to stay next to you at all times. I assume that since I'm personally paying their ridiculously high fee, I still have the prerogative to do that."

"Not a chance, Aram," I said. "Put that down."

"Michael, be reasonable."

"I am being reasonable. You can't convince me and you can't safely protect me without my permission. Those guards would only get in my way."

Aram sighed. He looked at Jackson, but he didn't seem to be paying attention. He was staring at Treeves. Aram realized he wasn't going to win the point.

"Were you able to gather more data from Carrol?" Aram said.

Jackson grunted. I ignored him. I was realizing that I wanted to draw on qualities from all of them. I needed Aram's intellect, Treeves' knowledge of behavior, and Jackson's integrity.

"What I'm about to tell you about Callie goes no further," I said, carefully. "That means everyone else in the world, including Kris. Understood?"

Jackson nodded.

"No, I can't promise that about Kris," said Aram. "I don't keep secrets from her. She's damn intuitive and if I hid anything from her, it could have consequences for our relationship."

"Then you're out of it," I said. "Thanks for what you've done. The rest of us have to go."

Jackson didn't move.

"Goddamn it, Aram," he said.

Aram looked at his feet.

"I'll do the best I can. But I can't promise."

"All right. Do the best you can. But if you have to tell Kris, you must hold her to the same promise."

"I can assure you about that. Kris and I keep our secrets."

I told them what Todd Carrol had told Treeves and me. I left out nothing but Bai's name. I referred to him as a rich bastard from China. There was no reason not to name him, but when the time came, my throat closed and I couldn't get it out. When I finished, Aram was quiet and Jackson looked dumbfounded.

"The son of a bitch is lying," Jackson said.

Edgar Treeves had been in the room when Carrol told his story.

"Not a chance," I said. "As absurd, ridiculous, and obscene as it sounds, everything Carrol said was the truth."

"Michael, you must walk away from this," Aram said.

"Not even a remote chance I'll do that," I said.

"You're not thinking clearly," Aram said. "The man you intend to challenge is not only powerful through his wealth, but also through his position in his government. Our own government seems intent on protecting him. No doubt he has diplomatic immunity. He'll never be brought to trial and you'll never get a chance to get close to him. If you do get close enough to harm him in some meaningful way, you'll be branded an assassin, hunted, not only by his people, but our government as well. And for what? You've only known this woman for a short while. She lied to you again and again. I can understand that you were fond of her, but you didn't even know her. Would you have asked her to marry you if you'd known that she hadn't been honest with you for one moment? That in fact, she was nothing more than a well-paid prostitute?"

I started towards him on the word *nothing*. Treeves was already moving. He stood between Aram and me.

"Don't stand there gawking," he shouted at Jackson. "Get over here. Now!"

Hearing Treeves shout was jarring. It broke my momentum and I stopped.

"It's all right," I said to Treeves.

"Aram, you've made a serious error," I said. "I'm going into SAM's other room for a few minutes. When I come back, it's going to be as if you never said that. And, of course, I don't expect you to ever make that kind of mistake again."

I crossed the room and shut the dividing door behind me. I got down on one knee. There was a shiny surface over one of the many servers. I looked into it and saw a man who a few moments ago had almost attacked Aram Cooper. I didn't recognize him. I wanted myself back. I wanted Callie back. I wanted what we had, what we were, in love and untroubled. Of course, it had never really been like that. Callie had never been untroubled. But she had loved me. She had risked her life to be with me. I released the tension in my neck by twisting my head from side to side. I willed myself to be Case again, the man who was not a killer, a man who had friends. As I opened the door to step back into SAM's living room, I heard angry voices. When Aram did something, he did it all the way. He had soundproofed the server area.

"You must be insane," Jackson shouted. "Do you have any human parts at all or have you made yourself into a goddamn machine?"

"You're hysterical," Aram said. "Calm down or get out."

"Oh, yeah, there's genius for you. Why don't I just leave you and Case alone so you can goad him into breaking your neck."

"What are you talking about?" said Aram. "Michael would never harm me. He isn't capable of that."

"Before you get too damn sure of what Case is capable of, you should know that less than an hour ago, I saw him go into Todd Carrol's place with mister 'I'm the most dangerous man in the world' over there and when they came out about twenty minutes later, Case had blood all over his hands. You want to know what I think. From what I've seen and heard, I think he murdered that son of a bitch."

I stepped closer and they both looked at me as if they'd forgotten I was in the building. Treeves was looking, without any apparent interest, at the lights on the plasma screen.

"I only stabbed him with a knife," I said. "It missed his major veins and arteries. He's not going to die."

"You stabbed him?" said Jackson. "What if he's a hemophiliac? Or he has a weakened immune system? What if the ambulance didn't get to him in time."

"He's not a hemophiliac," said Aram. "He's quite healthy."

Suddenly, I saw the same smile appear on Treeves' face that he had in the general's office.

"Well, at least he was until tonight," he said.

"Jackson," I said. "We know a lot about Todd Carrol."

"Who are you people?" said Jackson. "I feel like I just stepped into one of those idiotic movies where all the villagers seem normal, but then they turn out to be witches and warlocks. Are you telling me that you think what you did was okay?"

"Carrol was scared to death of this man, Bai," I said. "Worse still, he had formed an opinion of me that prevented him from taking the situation seriously enough. I might have tried harder to finesse him, but we're running out of time. What's Callie going to do when she finds out her brother is dead as well as her sister? I have to find her now. It has to be now."

"Bai?" said Aram, his head snapping back slightly. "Are we talking about Bai Ju Hong?"

"You know him?" I said, astonished.

"I know of him," Aram said. "There's a message from him waiting for you. He wants to talk to you about a software upgrade that would have been worth untold millions to us. Dammit."

In all the years I'd known him, that was the only swear word I'd ever heard him utter.

"Michel, it's over," Aram said. "You can think or feel whatever you like, but I can assure you that you have no chance whatsoever against Bai Ju Hong. You're aware that I personally perform background checks on all potential clients over twenty million dollars. This man is untouchable. Don't take my word for it. Read yesterday's *Financial Times*. Bai is a member of the Chinese delegation that's scheduled to meet with the president in Beijing. There's no way on earth that you could breach his security. Not to mention the fact that he has full diplomatic immunity. Bai Ju Hong has absolutely nothing to fear from you. You'd be a mouse attacking an elephant."

Treeves had been silent since he stepped between Aram and me.

"Don't they say that elephants are afraid of mice, Dr. Cooper? Trust me, Bai does have fears connected to Mr. Case or Laura Lacerda would not be dead. Also, why does he wish to do business with a man whom he knows to be working against his own interests?"

"Probably to tell Case to his face to keep his nose out of his business," Jackson said.

"I'm sure there's some validity to that," said Treeves. "But there's also something else. Yes, something else.

"In any case," he continued. "I've begun formulating a plan of action based on what we know so far. I'll need Dr. Cooper to help with some of the technical details. Also, we'll need the cooperation of Dr. Paul Arons. However, to have a reasonable expectation of success, I need to meet Mr. Bai in person. I'm not busy Friday evening. How about Mr. Case and I have dinner with him at your restaurant, Mr. Aurelian? Oh, and one more thing. My plan requires an outlay of a sum of money. Fifteen million dollars should be sufficient. Naturally, you could divide up that cost as you see fit, however money is always an issue, even among the closest friends, so I suggest you allow me to arbitrate who contributes what amount. An equitable arrangement should be five million from Mr. Case, eight million from Dr. Cooper, not only because he can well afford it, but also because Mr. Case is a valuable asset to his business, and the other two million from Mr. Aurelian, because I'm certain he wants to make a contribution."

We all stood there silently for a minute.

"Okay, just who the hell are you?" Jackson finally said.

I smiled.

I said, "I'll take that one. Let's just say Mr. Temple is someone who isn't shy about letting people know who's in charge."

CHAPTER 35

DINNER

The Ahh Baloney Café
Summer, 2018

Jackson was dead set against it. I wanted to meet with Bai at the same table where I proposed to Callie. However, this time, it would be set for four.

"No," Jackson said. "It's a stupid move. And what does it get you, some twisted sense of irony?"

"He's right," said Treeves, after Jackson had stomped off towards the kitchen. "We manipulate other people's emotions. There's no profit in playing with our own. Tonight is a combat operation, just like any other. It's unrealistic to hope you can fully function as my Weapon, but I won't work with an amateur. The slightest lapse in concentration will put the entire plan, not to mention all of our lives, in jeopardy."

"This isn't just another combat situation," I said.

"Remember your training, Mr. Case. How many times were you told that allowing emotions to effect your actions increases the probability of catastrophic failure by an unacceptable margin? You must remember nothing but my signals tonight."

"I don't want us to sit at that table because of an emotional connection," I said. "I want to be reminded that tonight can't be about revenge. It has to be about finding Callie."

"If you need a table to remind you what you're here for, then walk away now. I guarantee you that Mr. Bai is clear about why he's here tonight."

Treeves studied the room.

"We'll use that one in the corner," he said. "It works to our advantage."

I reminded myself that there was no point to working with a Medium if his orders weren't followed without question. However, in the end, it was Jackson who had the last word. He told us that it was his restaurant and he had the final word on where his patrons sat. He chose the same table that Treeves had. So much for the customer always being right. Whenever you have something unique to sell, you can afford to be tyrannical. However, the entire discussion turned out to be a waste of time. When Treeves and I entered the restaurant that evening, Jackson handed me a piece of paper.

"So much for what we want," he said.

Later in the afternoon, Bai's secretary bought out The Ahh Baloney Café for the entire evening. Bai's staff would work with Jackson's people to reschedule all reservations. All cancellations would receive complimentary meals, with all the trimmings. It seemed like poetic justice that Bai chose the same corner table. He would sit with his back against the wall. His bodyguards would occupy the tables on his right and left. His head of security would join us at our table. I didn't tell Jackson that, as we were leaving the restaurant that afternoon, Treeves told me not to concern myself with other patrons because there wouldn't be any.

At eight o'clock that evening, Treeves and I sat waiting for Bai with our backs to the door. I looked down at my hands and willed them to remain calm. They seemed to feel that they should grab Bai by the throat as soon as he appeared and squeeze until his face turned blue.

"You are not here for yourself," Treeves said quietly, folding his napkin into his lap.

Suddenly, the room grew dimmer. I turned my head to discover that the source of the illusion was a man standing directly behind me. I'd forgotten how big he was. He was wearing a custom-tailored suit, white shirt, and blood red tie. His slicked-back hair, still black, framed his well-proportioned features. He was looking at me and behind me at the same moment. I couldn't tell if he recognized me. The last time he'd seen me, I was sixteen years old.

Ko didn't look much older. He looked slightly bigger and a hell of a lot richer. He regarded me as if I were something unpleasant crawling across the table, but said nothing. He stepped to his right and the room grew brighter again. As if it were one of Ko's tricks, a smaller man appeared from behind him.

He was a slightly pudgy, but not unattractive, specimen also dressed in a dark-blue pinstriped Armani suit. A patterned blue tie was knotted expertly over his cream shirt. He had a small, well-trimmed moustache and his straight dark hair was persuaded towards the top of his head like a crown. As for his height, he was standing directly in front of me and I could see what was behind him. Throughout the introductions, he maintained a gentle smile. There were small bows. No one shook hands.

With a slight, but noticeable accent, Bai said, "It's a pleasure to meet you, Mr. Case. This is Ko. He won't be participating in our discussion, however he never leaves my side when I travel outside my country. He oversees my personal security. We can speak freely in front of him."

"Of course," I said, confident that I gave away nothing. "I'd like to introduce James Temple. Dr. Cooper has employed Mr. Temple in the past for transactions with our most valued clients. He's here tonight to acquaint himself with the principals and get an overall view of the particulars."

Treeves assured me earlier that Bai would not have any questions for him. Bai turned to Treeves.

"I have no doubt that any CDL who works for Aram Cooper must be extraordinary. It's a privilege to have you aid us in moving forward."

Treeves effortlessly responded in Standard Mandarin. Bai listened and chuckled.

"Why, thank you. I wish I could speak English as well as you speak Mandarin. In fact, I've never heard a westerner speak it better."

Treeves acknowledged the compliment by slightly bowing his head.

At that moment, Henry arrived at our table with four glasses that were half full of a yellow-orange liquid. For the occasion, he wore a stylish tuxedo and white gloves. Ko studied him intently. Bai's staff had requested photographs, along with complete resumes, of the wait staff. They also asked Jackson to suggest which member of his staff should serve our table. Naturally, Jackson had chosen Henry, AB's well-known veteran headwaiter, and he was approved. Bai was a man who limited his enemy's opportunities to an absolute minimum.

"I took the liberty of bringing you one of Chef Aurelian's famous appetite stimulators," Henry said, as the glasses were placed before us.

Bai sipped his drink. He pronounced it delicious. According to our data, Bai never touched alcohol. He hadn't felt the need to remind us of that before he drank. He trusted Henry to know it. That kind of judgment and restraint was a foundation of personal charm.

"Henry," I said, as he filled the water glasses. "Would you bring us a bottle of the Viognier?"

I turned to Bai.

"I understand you don't drink alcohol, but I hope you don't mind if the rest of us have a glass or two. Viognier is a white from here in California and it's too good not to enjoy with one of Chef Aurelian's creations."

"Please," said Bai. "I'm not a judgmental man. I simply never developed a taste for alcohol."

Henry returned, stood by as I approved the wine, and then began to pour for Treeves. Ko put his hand over his glass.

"My security chief and his men have already eaten," Bai said. "He doesn't want to have their hands encumbered while they're working."

Henry stepped back. I took a deep draught of the wine and smacked my lips. I tried to give the impression it hadn't been my first drink of the evening.

"To begin with," I said. "I wanted to convey Dr. Cooper's most sincere apologies. As you know, he rarely meets with clients, but in your case, he would have gladly made an exception. He was planning to join us, but he was taken ill at the last moment."

"How unfortunate," Bai said, politely. "Please convey my hope that he'll feel better soon."

"Oh," I said, and blinked nervously. "I hope I haven't overstated it. It's only a nasty little rash that's been plaguing him for a few days. Probably some kind of bug he picked up from a scratch he got on his boat. God knows what's in the water these days. More annoying than anything else, really."

There was an uncomfortable silence. Treeves sipped a thimbleful of his wine. Henry was standing by.

"Shall we order?" said Bai. "Naturally I would like to try the famous abalone."

"Of course, sir," Henry said.

"After that," Bai said, "I'll have whatever Mr. Aurelian feels is appropriate."

I thought that rat poison seemed appropriate. Treeves and I gave the same order. Henry filled my nearly empty wine glass and glided away.

Bai turned to me.

"Let me begin by saying my education was focused on economics and political science. Although I'm not a computer expert, I believe that Dr. Cooper's services could be an essential component in the technological development of my country. Are you an electronics wizard as well, Mr. Case?"

"Hardly. However, I am capable of explaining some of the options available to you within the guidelines you've requested."

Bai held up his hand.

"Please, not this evening," he said. "I've been told that, to a great extent, you handle Dr. Cooper's professional relationships. I have complete faith in his technological skills, which have been proven time and again. However, there are several other companies that have provided me with excellent proposals. As you can imagine, I'm a busy man. If I choose Cooper SHW over another, it would be because I feel that I can easily communicate my desires to you and have my requirements fulfilled with as little effort as possible. Tonight, let's simply be two men sharing a meal. I hope we can get to know each other. Let's see if we can develop the beginnings of a relationship where both of us can profit."

He turned his attention to Henry arriving with our food.

"Ah, at last, the beginning of our feast."

It was that simple. If I knew of his involvement in Callie's troubles, he had just delivered a warning as precise and neat as a good business letter. If I posed no threat, I'd go unmolested. I would even be enriched. If not, I'd join her brother and sister. I felt a cold rage. Every ounce of my will was directed towards arranging my face and relaxing my upper body. My features fell naturally into my gameface, a pleasant, neutral expression, with the slightest hint of vacancy. There was no cleverness in it, only cooperation. No hint of cunning, only a desire to remain open to suggestion. If Bai wished to initiate a gambit that would lead to my eventual checkmate, I would stumble right into it. If he wanted to raise into what he was sure was a bluff on my part, I'd throw good money in after bad. Inwardly, I concentrated on Treeves' plan for Bai's annihilation. I took a healthy gulp from my wine glass. Treeves glanced at me with the slightest hint of disapproval.

Henry placed the plates before us.

He said to Bai, "Mr. Aurelian has prepared this blending of spices especially for you."

I noticed Ko studying the plate.

"Is Mr. Ko your food taster as well?" I said a bit too loudly, chuckling at my own cleverness. "I'd be happy to switch plates with you if you like."

Ko looked away. Bai smiled.

"I hardly think that's necessary," he said. "It is a perplexing world, however, and, unfortunately, it's necessary to for me to take some precautions. As you know, I'm a strong supporter of the United States' position against some of the more extremist elements in my country. There's no lack of misguided individuals who wish me harm."

"That must be quite difficult for you," said Treeves.

"Yes," I said. "And your family, too."

Bai paused with his fork halfway between his plate and his lips.

"What exactly do you mean by that?" he said.

"I simply meant that it must be nerve racking for them to know how easy it is for a man in your position to collect enemies."

"Yes, well," he said. "We all must make sacrifices."

I turned my attention to Jackson's crusty bread and baloney. He was very good many years ago when we both lived on Blake Street the year I arrived in Berkeley. Since then, he had ascended to an entirely new level. The flavor, texture, and the nuanced spices of the thick slices of Jackson's creation bore as much resemblance to the supermarket variety baloney as an art student's copy of Michelangelo's David might bear to the real thing. It spread on my bread like a creamy mousse. As I savored the melting combination of spices on my palate, I glanced over at Bai and saw that he too was enjoying the experience.

I thought about his relationship with Callie. Todd Carrol had said he thought Bai had fallen in love with her. Clearly, her betrayal had induced strong emotions in him. He was rich and venerated. Callie must have affected him in a manner that went beyond the betrayal of their arrangement. What she'd done had gnawed at him. If he allowed her to go unpunished, it would fracture the protective shell he had built around himself.

We finished our portions. Treeves let me know he was done with Bai and it was time for our next move. He put me in ready position.

"I really feel this meeting merits a toast," I said. "In fact, it demands one. Henry, bring us a bottle of Bollinger Special Cuvée."

Bai and Ko exchanged a glance. Henry very quickly placed three champagne flutes on the table and popped the cork.

"How about just this once?" I said to Bai, slurring my voice slightly. "For this very special meeting of new friends?"

"No, thank you," said Bai, curtly.

"C'mon," I said. "It's bad luck to toast with an empty champagne glass. Henry, pour some water into Mr. Bai's glass."

Bai said, "I don't believe in luck."

Henry quickly poured water into his champagne glass. Treeves let me know that Ko was about to move.

Now, he signaled.

"To…" I said, and raised my glass and, like an awkward fool, knocked Bai's tall champagne glass of water towards him. Some of it spilled across his hand and onto his suit. I had just managed it. Ko's hand was an inch from mine.

"I'm terribly sorry," I said. "How clumsy of me."

Henry rushed over with a towel. Ko waved him away. For a moment, Bai looked at me as if my head should be separated from my shoulders.

Then his features relaxed and he said, "Think nothing of it, Mr. Case. After all, it's only water."

"Still," I said

I was doing well. My face was flushed.

"This is very embarrassing," I said.

Ko was staring at me. I looked directly into his black eyes.

"I'm sure we can all be grateful it was just water," I said.

"In any event, I cannot sit here in such a condition," Bai said. "Please convey my apologies to Chef Aurelian. Tell him we'll return another time."

Bai's security moved like a drill team as they made preparations to leave. I was sure that Ko hadn't recognized me. However, before he left, he leaned over so that his lips were close to my ear.

"You're still soft," he said.

With those three words, he made it clear that he remembered me.

Treeves watched them leave.

"You did well," he said. "The alcohol inhibitor worked, I see."

"Yes, Paul really is an invaluable resource, isn't he?"

As in the old days, Treeves seemed to read my mind.

"Don't waste time thinking about it. It was a fruitful evening. Now you understand that you could have never gotten to him with that kind of protection."

"Not in the way I wanted to."

Henry came over.

"What should I do about the water?" he said.

"Leave it," I said. "It'll evaporate."

"Will that be all for this evening?"

"Yes, thank you, Henry," I said. "You performed perfectly, as always."

I shook his hand. When we were done, his contained a slip of paper.

"Check that offshore account tomorrow. Aram made it virtually untraceable. Leave the money there for at least a couple of months. And thank you."

"No," he said. "Thank you, sir."

He left. Jackson came out.

"What's going on here? I understand our guest just stormed out without paying."

"Put it on my tab."

"Why is the table wet?" he said.

"Don't touch it," I said. "That's important, do you understand? Just let it dry."

"Okay. You insult my food. You mess up the place. The kitchen is going down and I'm going home."

"Like hell. We're moving to that table over there. Get back in the kitchen and finish our dinner."

"For tomorrow there's an excellent likelihood we may die," Treeves said.

Jackson winked at him.

"Cheery fellow," he said.

After Jackson went back to the kitchen, I said, "Will it work?"

"That man controls almost every aspect of his world, but everyone fears something. The rate that his eyes blinked changed dramatically when you said the word *rash*. The movement of twelve key facial muscles and a minor shifting of his weight made it a certainty. He is devoted to and protective of his family. I would say that after what I've observed tonight, we should proceed."

"How do you feel?" I said.

Treeves thought for a moment.

"I'm hungry. You know, the food here really is quite good."

CHAPTER 36

REUNION

Cooper SHW
Summer, 2018

I made certain we weren't followed and drove Treeves to a motel in Marin. I went in alone, paid cash for a room, and bribed the appropriate staff with more money than necessary, but not enough to make them suspicious. Then I snuck Treeves into the room as if he were a beloved dog where pets weren't allowed. He tested the bed.

"Too soft," he said.

"If you'll recall, Goldilocks, field work requires sacrifice. I took you out for a nice meal, didn't I?"

"Interesting company, as well. We'll make the call tomorrow afternoon."

"Do we have to wait that long? Paul said it would begin tomorrow morning."

Treeves stared at the pillow.

"We have to wait," he said. "Be careful until then. Tonight was a charade. Both of those men want you dead, the big one perhaps more than Bai. He doesn't simply want to kill you with his own hands. He wants to see you suffer in the process. He'll be coming for you. Bai is not a man who uses a battle axe when a stiletto will do. And Mr. Ko appears to want the assignment very badly."

"I know him."

"Yes, I'm aware of that."

I smiled.

"Of course," I said. "In another lifetime, we worked for the same man."

"He was a source of competition between the two of you, wasn't he? And it came to a bad end."

Treeves studied me.

"It was you who failed."

"I tried as hard as I could, but I couldn't kill an old friend."

I realized what I said.

"Back then," I added quickly.

"You never have been and you are not now a cold-blooded murderer," Treeves said. "You were a soldier, then a Weapon, and now you're doing what has to be done to defend yourself. And her."

I looked into his eyes. It wasn't easy.

"If I had the chance this moment, I'd make Bai talk and then I'd murder him. In the coldest blood you can imagine."

"No, you wouldn't. You think that you would, but you wouldn't."

"Do you really believe that you know me better than I know myself?"

"Don't make ridiculous statements. I know what I know. I know the fundamental characteristics that make up your personality profile. Perhaps better than anyone has ever known you. You've changed and you aren't aware how much."

"There's no point arguing with you."

"I wasn't aware we were engaged in an argument."

The secure audio device that Aram had supplied activated.

"What is it, Aram?"

"My program has uncovered some essential data," Aram said. "You need to know it before you do anything further. Can you come to L-9 now?"

"Yes. I'll be there within an hour."

I closed the connection.

"You'll be safe here," I said to Treeves. "I'm sure we weren't followed."

"Call him back," said Treeves. "I want to hear his voice again."

"No. Too dangerous. Aram's no fool. I don't want him getting any notions about who and what you are. I can't put him in jeopardy."

"I said call him back."

"Why? Aram would never betray me. You're being overly cautious."

"And you are being careless. I told you that everyone is terrified of something. As soon as an operative discovers what it is and has the will to exploit it, the target is finished. Behavioral Science One Oh One. Has your training completely faded?"

Treeves interrupted himself.

"Wait, no."

He closed his eyes for a moment.

"I see it. You want the big man to be there, don't you?"

"When you dreamed up Bai's nightmare, you didn't factor in Ko," I said. "Your plan will never work as long as he's alive."

"Perhaps. But, trust me, you're no match for him. He's as quick as you are, is much stronger, and he's maintained his combat readiness. If you go up against Ko one on one, he'll almost certainly kill you. Cooper SHW is obviously compromised. Let's call for support."

"No. We can't do that. Ko has the instincts of a jungle cat. He'll retreat and wait. He won't let Bai out of his sight. We don't have time for that. I have to take a chance. Treeves, if he succeeds in killing me, promise that you won't stop until Callie's safe."

"Don't be foolish. I don't make idle promises. Not unless they're to my advantage."

"Get some sleep," I said. "I won't be alone. Remember that Aram has the best security money can buy. Better. Ko doesn't know that he's up against the general's Rangers."

Treeves had the last word on my way out, "Money cannot buy security."

I stopped at my house, opened my hidden floor safe, and drove to Cooper SHW. It looked like a new shift had taken over. I didn't recognize any of the men who questioned me, but the security procedure was essentially the same. In fact, it was easier since I was alone this time.

"Dr. Cooper?" I said.

"He's waiting for you in L-9."

It was late and the facility had that hollow office feel. Some computer screens were still lit, but everyone had gone home. The door to L-9 was slightly ajar. I readied myself and stepped inside. Ko was leaning on a desk across the room with a forty-five-caliber automatic in his right hand. He pressed something on a console. The door clicked shut behind me.

"Well, here we are, alone again at last," Ko said.

My gut did a somersault, but I managed a little smile. I meant what I said to Treeves. I expected Ko to find me and I knew that he'd want us to be alone. But I never thought for a moment Aram would let him into L-9.

"Security?" I said.

"Don't make me laugh. Did you think that would be a problem for me and my people?"

"Actually, no. But how did you get in here?" I said.

My chest tightened up and blood rushed to my head.

"Why, Dr. Cooper let me in, of course."

"Where is he?"

"Don't worry. He's locked in the bathroom of his office. We won't kill him. That would be bad publicity and Mr. Bai doesn't care for that, especially this close to his meeting with your president. Of course, there's a good man standing outside the bathroom door and if I'm not done with you in half an hour or so, he has clear instructions to inject Dr. Cooper with something nasty. Your friend will be out of action for quite some time. Who would've thought that the great Aram Cooper would turn out to be a secret drug abuser? So, little boy, you've blundered into a situation that's very neat. You're going to die tonight."

"You're going to shoot me? Why didn't you do it when I walked in?"

"Don't be stupid," Ko said, as if I'd insulted his taste in suits. "The gun is only so that we'll have a few quiet minutes so that you can tell me all about the little plan you've cooked up for Mr. Bai. You're friend, Cooper, told me everything he knew, but, unfortunately for you, he didn't seem to know all that much."

I silently thanked Treeves for his methods. Everyone involved only knew what they needed to know.

"Not that it matters all that much. I've locked down Mr. Bai. There's no way on earth you could get to within a mile of him."

"How did you get Aram to make that call?" I said.

"How do you think? One of my men was holding a knife to the throat of his sweet little ride. Actually, by now, he's left and she's tied up in a closet. Mr. Bai didn't want her hurt either if it wasn't necessary. Also, too high profile. But to get Cooper to make that call, I had to send my sickest freak. I certainly hope he didn't lose his head and do something nasty to her and the movie queen before he left. No matter. She won't say anything."

Treeves was right, of course. Everyone is afraid of something.

"So you see, little boy, there's no need to worry about your friends. If you cooperate, you're the only one who interests me."

"You've changed, Ko. I never knew you to be so chatty. Do you really think I'm going to tell you anything?"

"Oh, you'll tell me things. Remember how good I was? I'm much better now."

"How did you know it was me? I can't believe that you recognized me in the restaurant."

"Do you remember what I said in the old man's hallway? Patience. Patience is always rewarded. Believe it or not, by now, killing doesn't mean a whole lot to me. Just another chore. But with you, it's different. I wanted this time with you. I wanted to tell you what happened after you left."

"You know, in the movies, that's always a mistake."

I shifted my weight and his finger tightened on the trigger of the automatic.

"I don't watch movies," he said.

The barrel of the automatic was unwavering.

"I know you're quick," he said. "But don't forget how quick I am. I'm aiming at center of your head and I could squeeze off three rounds with my eyes closed and still put you down. And while I'm thinking about it, move your hands away from your body, palms down, and open them slowly. My guess is that you've got some sort of device in the left one."

I did as he said. The small plastic flash grenade that I'd been holding dropped to the floor and rolled away. I'd been waiting for the heat of my closed hand to activate it. It would have felt hot a second before it was ready.

"That's good," Ko said. "Now stand perfectly still for a moment."

Without diverting his focus on me for a second, Ko picked something that looked like a large vid from the desk next to him. He pointed in my direction with his left hand and waited. In a moment, there was a single pinging noise.

"Handy little gadget. Scans for objects that have the general outline and density of hundreds of known weapons of a certain size. Hard to believe you would stroll in here unarmed."

I shrugged.

"I don't usually carry guns to the office."

"Still pretending to be hard, aren't you? Well, enjoy the act during the next few minutes of your life. I know that I will. I know that you remember that I don't respect many people and I'd be hard pressed to name someone I like, but the old man was different. It wasn't that he didn't judge me. I don't care about that. It was that he valued me."

He paused and smiled his graveyard smile.

"For what I am," he said.

For the first time, I felt a strong emotion coming from Ko. It was unmistakable. He was angry.

"After you left us, they came at us like wolves. Your disappearance fooled no one. Just as he predicted, they thought he'd gone soft. I still can't figure out why he didn't let me put you out of your misery after you bungled that simple job."

"You couldn't stand it that he cared about me, could you?" I said. "He cared about me and he just used you."

Ko grunted.

"The only thing that bothered me were knives and bullets that got under my skin after he let you go. I fought for almost a year, blood and then more blood, but the old man never had a chance. I couldn't kill them all. There were just too many. It wasn't long before I knew it was only a matter of time before he'd make another mistake."

I put myself into combat mode. I'd been trained to believe that every situation has a solution. But no matter how I choreographed it in my mind, the outcome was always the same. I'd be dead on the floor with Ko standing over me.

"Did you know that I'd been with him since I was a boy?" he said. "In the end, I had no choice. I retired him myself and, after all the blood that was spilled, they wanted it done in a bad way. That was the price I paid for my life. I could have come after you then, but I wanted to honor him. So I waited. I knew that eventually there would be the perfect moment, perhaps when you were fussing about with some whore. I must say, for a whore, she is a knockout. I wanted to have her myself that night I pushed her down into the pool so I could tell you all about it, but Mr. Bai was very clear that I wasn't to *molest her* as he put it. I wish I'd known it was her sister."

I felt my anger rise, ready to overtake my training. Then I heard Edgar Treeves' voice in my mind – emotions have no place here. I forced myself to be calm and go to the place that Kaicho had shown me. My anger and fear couldn't reach me there. Ko's voice became a soft humming in the background.

"You want to know how I knew it was you?" he said. "I tracked you for years, but I have to give you credit, you were good. I knew you went into the military, but then you just disappeared into thin air. I never believed you were dead. Then, about two years ago, I had a breakthrough. I realized my resources weren't enough. So I offered my services to a high-level official of the Chinese Government. You can't imagine the doors that opened for me. Mr. Bai has people everywhere."

I wondered if he was talking about Jon Ling.

"I might not have recognized you," Ko said. "But no matter how much a man changes, there's one thing that stays the same. His voice. I had people checking millions of vid conversations and then, one day, I got a gift I couldn't believe. Our software matched a vid recording between you and her."

I moved.

"Don't be stupid," he said. "It wouldn't be close."

I thought about how many times I'd said that to other men. And how few of them had survived. Ko glanced at his watch.

"Well, it's getting time to wrap this up. You know, I don't believe you're going to tell me anything useful because I don't think you know anything that I don't. Or can't handle if it comes up. Ah, but perhaps you'd like to know that after that little stunt in the restaurant, Mr. Bai is really annoyed with you. And with her. Did I mention that we've almost found her? I'll probably be on my way tomorrow. See what I mean by patience? Killing you tonight is not only going to be profitable, it's going to taste extra sweet because now you know that soon she's next, right after I've had an hour or two showing her how she wasted it until I happened along."

While he was talking, I noticed subtle changes on the computer screen behind him. I had years of practice dividing my attention between two things. I tuned him out. He couldn't imagine the level of access I'd had to information that interested me. I had known for a long time what he thought he was divulging to me.

As Ko was talking, SAM was talking as well. Aram was talking to me through SAM. I recognized an icon that signified my presence in L-9. It would no longer be necessary to identify myself to SAM. Words began appearing at the top of the screen: *YOU* for distraction; *PLEASE* for darkness; *ME* for sound.

Aram was letting me know that I could control the atmosphere of L-9 simply by speaking the appropriate words. SAM would only recognize my voice.

Then Aram added, *Three-second countdown.*

Under *THUNDERSTORM*, I saw variables.

Lightening: maximum;
Thunder: maximum;
Water: maximum;
Interval: zero;

Ko had finished and was waiting to enjoy my reaction. As soon as he felt satisfied, he would begin killing me.

"You tell an interesting story," I said. "But please don't kill me."

Ko smiled. He aimed the automatic at my left arm.

"I won't all at once."

"Over here!" SAM shouted from behind him.

The atmosphere in L-9 exploded into a three-dimensional holographic thunderstorm. There were flashes of lightening and an ear-shattering roar of thunder as the room went black. Holographic rain fell as if we were caught on a mountaintop downpour.

Ko turned for an instant, but he was still able to put two shots where my chest had been. I'd already jumped to my right and, by the time his second shot had hit the door, I was on him.

I wanted to be close to him to minimize his power. I jumped onto him and got lucky with my left foot. I smashed his wrist against the edge of the desk, forcing him to drop the gun. He swung his left arm around to catch me with an elbow to the head, but I ducked under that and came up around him, trying to work my forearm under his neck. He was too strong. He clamped down with his jaw and threw me off as if I were a child.

I rolled across the room to regain my balance. When I got up, I saw what was coming. He was waiting for a steady target for his throw. I waited too. I'd been taught by the best to how avoid thrown objects. However, Ko was so incredibly swift, his knife got a piece of my shoulder as I turned out of its path.

Both of us had the same thought and we looked for the automatic on the floor. By that time, the holographic rain had filled the room to our ankles. The illusion was spectacular. It looked like real water. It was so convincing that my mind played a trick and I almost felt wet.

I grabbed one of Aram's notebooks and threw it hard at Ko's knee. It connected and I saw him wince, but I could see it hadn't done any damage.

I ran for the door. He was right behind me. I knew the door wouldn't open from the inside while the program was in progress, but I also knew Ko and how he fought.

At the last second, I stepped to my left and let him crash into the door that he planned to crush me against. I connected well with a roundhouse kick to his kidney, but he just grunted. A roundhouse kick with the forward leg is for speed and not as powerful as a back leg kick. Still, the impact of my foot would have sent a normal man to his knees.

I reset as soon as my foot touched the ground and sent a left roundhouse kick towards the front of his head aiming for his nose or his Adam's apple. The problem was he was ready for it. He caught my leg in the classic forearm hold and prepared to rip it out of its socket. I only had one chance. Using his hold on my leg as a brace, I spun my body up and kicked him in the ear with my right foot. It stunned him and he let go as my leg turned, but not before he'd done some damage.

My landing was clumsy and I wound up on my ass. Ignoring the pain in my ankle, I slid away from him as fast as I could. It was then that I noticed that the holographic water had risen almost to his crotch. I knew something he didn't. It was impossible to see through the water from above. However, from underneath the surface, you could just make out shapes above you. Aram called it a flaw in the program.

I straightened my body on the floor, hiding under the holographic water. Because it wasn't real, I knew any movement would not disturb the effect above me. I was invisible to Ko, but I could still see him above the top of the water. He was more or less a large outline, but I could follow his movements as he searched for me. I heard a crash. He was trying to disable the computer. He was wasting time doing that. SAM had multiple failsafe systems.

The gun had to be near. I thought I saw its shadow in approximately the right area. I was on my way to get it when I saw that Ko had given up on SAM and was moving towards me. As soon as he realized he couldn't stop the storm, he knew he had to come looking for me. He entered the water and was on the floor very close to me. It would be seconds before he stumbled upon me.

I had only one chance. I jumped up as fast as I could and planned to crash down on his back near his kidney with my knee, putting all of my weight behind it. It didn't matter how strong he was, such a blow would cripple him. But I didn't land on his back. He rolled, caught my knee with his hands, deflected it off the hard muscles of his chest, and kept turning. He held me until I was under him and then pinned my arms with his enormous legs. My head was under the water. His hands found my throat. He squeezed until my breath was cut off. I was looking up at him and, suddenly, it was as if I was being held under real water.

"I enjoy a nice workout before bed," he said. "You've learned a few tricks, little boy. I'll give you that."

I felt his fingers slowly tighten on my throat. The sounds in the room grew dim and the light became brighter. Then, something extraordinary happened. The holographic water suddenly became real. It felt as if a bucket of it was thrown against my face. Ko loosened his grip and, using all the strength and leverage I had left, I pushed him off of me. After a second or two, I could breathe again.

"SAM," I said in a hoarse whisper. "End program."

L-9 instantly returned to normal. Ko was lying on his back on the floor with a large pool of blood expanding around his upper body. His throat had been slashed in two parallel lines. He was coughing, trying to expel the liquid from his ruined esophagus. He reminded me of a slaughtered bull. My face and upper chest were covered in his blood.

Jon Ling was standing above me, looking at Ko's body with a mild curiosity.

"You cut his throat," I said.

"Seemed like a good idea at the time."

I tried to get up too quickly.

"I've got to get to Aram's office," I said.

Ling held up his hand with a mild expression.

"That's already been taken care of. The ones in front as well. Dr. Cooper is still locked in his bathroom. He's quite safe."

"You left him locked in there?"

"Do you want him wandering around at the moment?"

I turned over on my side and rose. Ko was dying. I put my face close to his fading eyes.

"Ko? Ko? Look at me."

I stood up and made sure I would be the last thing he saw. Then I smashed my heel into his throat.

"I guess that proves someone isn't always right. I am a murderer."

"I don't know about that," said Jon Ling. "He was pretty much dead anyway."

I looked at the wounds on Ko's neck.

"What did you use?" I said. "A stiletto?"

He examined the parallel lines in a professionally curious manner.

"Actually, I used a rusty old safety razor from Dr. Cooper's office drawer."

"You're joking."

"Absolutely not. I don't think that man ever throws anything away. Did you know there are old candy wrappers in there."

"I meant you were joking about the safety razor."

"No. They're really quite useful if you know how. You see, first you carefully crack the plastic. Then you remove the blades. Put a little tape…"

"I get it. What about all the bodies?"

"Not my department, but there's a new highway project not far from here. I believe a certain general will have his people cart them over there."

"You know General Tresain?"

I couldn't detect any emotion when Ling gently smiled as an answer my question.

"So you were sent here to protect me?"

"Hardly. Dr. Cooper is a very important man. Much more than you could possibly imagine. Someone suggested he might be in danger. I wasn't far away. I convinced one of the men out front to tell me where he was. When I spoke to Dr. Cooper through the door, he asked me to remove another threat that was in his lab. He described him quite graphically. He activated an emergency door release for L-9 from the hidden terminal he'd installed in his bathroom. Actually, I wasn't even completely sure what the big one was doing when I cut his throat."

"Well, thanks anyway."

Ling nodded. He turned to leave. Then he stopped.

"Like they say at the banks and the vid companies, this is a one-time courtesy," he said. "I'm not a judge. I only carry out the sentence. But it seems to me you've been placing good people into bad situations. I imagine that if we ever find ourselves together again, you won't see me. You understand?"

Ling nodded at Ko.

"Just like he didn't," he said.

CHAPTER 37

<hr>

TERROR

Marin County
Summer, 2018

I slept in the same room as Treeves that night. In the morning, we had breakfast delivered from a local diner. Treeves ate it, but I just moved my food around the plate. My throat still hurt. We still had some time to wait.

"I suppose I should thank you for saving my life," I said.

"Yes. Perhaps we're even."

"I've never counted. I'd say we're probably at twenty or thirty times for each of us. You called General Tresain?"

"Shortly after you'd gone. As soon as you'd left, I sat back and reconstructed Dr. Cooper's words and tone. He really is quite extraordinary. Even under the pressure of that situation, he was able to tell you that you were walking into a trap deeper than you could imagine."

"How did you know?"

"To quote him precisely, he said 'my program has uncovered some essential data.' Then he said he was in L-9. He has the unbreakable habit of referring to that thing in L-9 as SAM. Dr. Cooper would have never called it *my program*."

"Of course. So he was trying to warn me. But how could you know how bad the situation was."

Treeves finished chewing a piece of toast.

"I heard him speak didn't I? To a trained ear, the human voice is like a stringed instrument. It contains overtones and nuances. If one listens carefully, Time, it isn't difficult to hear when it's being played so out of tune."

"So now I'm Time again?"

"After last night's fiasco, I think it's a requirement. We're entering the most delicate phase of a dangerous situation. Either you agree to be utterly controlled by me or we don't proceed. I can't have you making your own decisions, running off on errands that I don't approve. From this point on, you will control your emotions and I will control your actions. Either you're my Weapon or you're not. Decide now."

I didn't hesitate. He knew I wouldn't.

"Tell me what to do and I'll do it without hesitation."

"Good."

"May I ask a question? I know you called General Tresain last night. Did you also tell him to send Jon Ling?"

Treeves stared at his plate. I didn't have to be a behavioral scientist to detect the shift in his demeanor.

"Suffice it to say," he said carefully, "the less you know about Mr. Ling, the better it'll be. He's not a policy maker. Mr. Ling does only one thing and he does it with a casual single-minded ferocity. He's a talented individual, devoted to perfecting his gift. When he goes up against opponents, he focuses only on the most efficient and elegant way to achieve his goal. He is an artist in his field."

"And a real humanitarian, from what I've seen," I said.

Treeves ignored the comment. I considered what he said.

"So the general sent Ling to wipe out what might have been his own team based on your phone call?"

"The general wasn't eager to send him. He thought a squad of his Rangers would be sufficient if you needed them, but I convinced him otherwise. Remember what I've said about the right tool for the job? In this case, I thought a force of nature would be the right choice. The general made his final decision based on my assessment that Ko would make his own decision regarding Dr. Cooper's ultimate fate. He dripped arrogance."

"Force of nature is a good description for Ling," I said. "But before you become a fan of Mr. Ling, you should hear me describe what he did to Ko's men before he got to L-9."

"Yes. His methods of extracting information are not what I would describe as subtle."

"If someone is too slow with information he wants, he's about as subtle as a potato peeler. By the way, do you know that he stole a police helicopter? It was in the parking lot. That's how he got close to the men outside. And then he used it. Nice trick."

Treeves smiled a bit.

"One thing," I said. "Why didn't he bring any firearms?"

"You didn't usually employ firearms because they weren't available to you when you needed them. Mr. Ling was trained differently. He's the most covert of assassins. He eliminates targets without the use of conventional weapons. I'm sure he knows how to use a gun, but I imagine it's been quite some time since he had one in his hand. Almost everything that surrounds us in day-to-day living is capable of mortal damage if it's utilized with the proper force and will. People are rather fragile, as you well know."

Treeves gave me a meaningful look.

"When his targets are more high profile, Mr. Ling specializes in accidental death. Shall we talk about Dr. Cooper now?"

"You mean he how he's dealing with opening L-9 for Ko and then calling me to come down there?"

"What else could I mean?"

"My expert opinion," I said. "I really don't know. After Jon Ling left, the general's cleaners arrived. Lots of them. I went to Aram. He was on the floor of his bathroom crying. He told me Ko had put Kris on a vid and, after that, he forced him to talk with the maniac who was holding her. Aram could hear Kris whimpering. There was nothing he could do. He kept telling me again and again that there was nothing he could do."

"What did you say?"

"Say? I picked him up, pushed him against the wall, and slapped him enough to get his attention. Then, I told him that he saved my life. That if he hadn't been strange enough to install hidden controls for SAM in his bathroom, and if he hadn't been brilliant enough to figure out the right way use them, I'd be dead instead of thanking him for removing our biggest obstacle."

"Basic, but decent psychology."

"Yes. Well, it didn't make me feel any better for getting him into this. The scars will be there for a while. This morning I put everyone, including Diane, on a corporate jet. They'll spend a month recovering in pleasant places, unknown to anyone but me. Of course, Aram wouldn't go. He's locked in with SAM, waiting."

"He really is exceptional."

Treeves glanced at my watch.

He said, "It's time."

We settled ourselves with the secure audio vid between us. I added a simple listening device to so I could hear the conversation.

"Are you sure you should do this instead of me?" I said. "You could tell me what to say."

"No. I need to use my tone of voice as well. He has to believe the story beyond a reasonable doubt. You don't have that kind of talent. You could make a mistake. We both know that I won't."

I thought about how many times I'd heard variations of that statement. It must be an amazing feeling to have that kind of confidence in your abilities.

We had to go through several levels at Bai's headquarters. We were on hold for a long time. Treeves kept repeating that he was an associate of Mr.

Ko and needed a moment of Mr. Bai's time to convey an urgent and personal message. Finally, Treeves got him on the line.

Using a flawless imitation of my voice, Treeves said, "Mr. Bai, do you remember me from the other night."

"I remember you, Mr. Case, however this isn't a particularly good time for me to talk. Perhaps I could get back to you later."

He was very good. If he knew anything about Ko's attempt on my life, I couldn't tell from his voice.

"If you could give me just few moments of your time now, I know you'd be interested in what I have to say."

Treeves' voice was calm and reasonable, the perfect important businessman.

"I have some sensitive and urgent information for you. I'm prepared to tell you over the phone, but I want you to turn off all recording and monitoring devices. Also, you should stop any tracing you might be doing on this line. I know you have that capability. However, I assure you that it would futile. Do it now, please."

"I'm sorry. I don't have time for this. Besides, what you're asking is ridiculous."

"Is it? Because I'm not asking," Treeves said.

Bai's voice came back still under control, but tinged with anger.

"Who do you think you're talking to?"

"I'm talking to a man who noticed something out of the ordinary on his body this morning."

There was a pause.

"What do you know about that?"

"I want to talk with you privately. When I'm sure what I'm saying is just between us, then I'll tell you. Trust me. It's to your advantage."

We waited. I looked at Treeves. He nodded slightly.

"All right, it's just us."

"It was nice speaking with you," Treeves said. "I don't care for childish tricks. I'm going to hang up now."

"Wait," said Bai. "Give me a moment."

In a minute or so, Bai came back on the line. His voice was tight.

"It's done," Bai said. "No one can hear us. There'll be no recording."

"Good," said Treeves. "You're waiting to hear from Mr. Ko. I'm afraid you won't be hearing from him any time soon."

"Is that so?"

"I ran into him by accident last night. Did you know we were old friends? We had quite a conversation. He confided to me that he felt his life was a complete failure. He was quite despondent and told me that he's decided to take an extremely long vacation."

"Well, that's unfortunate. Thank you for letting me know. I'll have my assistant arrange for a replacement immediately. And now, if you don't mind, I have some important business…"

Treeves interrupted him.

"I'm going to speak with you for exactly seven minutes and, if we can't agree, I'm going to disappear. This morning, you noticed a rash on your hand. It's gotten worse during the day. It's beginning to spread. In approximately seventy-two hours, it will cover more than two thirds of your body. It will itch and blister and then it will burn. Large areas of your skin will literally peel off. A short time after that, your skin won't be able to breathe and you will die of suffocation."

"You're insane. What have you done?"

"I introduced a genetically altered bacteria into your nervous system the other night in the restaurant. I did it when I spilled water on you. In liquid form, it's absorbed through the skin and it's programmed to begin as it did this morning."

Bai exploded.

"I'll kill you. Whether I live or die, I'll make sure you're dead. You and everyone around you. That chef, the woman, Cooper, everyone."

"You can try and kill whomever you like, but it won't have any effect on what's happening to you. Also, it would be a foolish waste of what is now your precious time for two reasons. One, no one had any idea about it except for myself and the doctor who provided me with the bacteria in exchange for several million dollars. Reason number two is that I don't care about any of those people you mentioned. Do whatever you like to them. I only care about one person."

There was a pause.

"What do you want?" he said.

"Ah, now you're beginning to think clearly. Why would I call you instead of just letting you slowly fry to death never really knowing what happened to you? It's very simple. I have in my hand a tube of the antidote to the bacteria. Apply it three times a day for a week and you'll never be bothered by those nasty little bugs again."

I looked at Treeves. I thought he was overdoing it. I never would have said "those nasty little bugs." On the other hand, when Treeves said it, I could almost feel something crawling on my skin.

"In exchange for?" Bai said.

He knew the beginning of a negotiation when he heard it.

"As of this moment, you will stop any efforts you are making to locate Calena Lacerda. Tomorrow at ten in the morning, you'll drive up the coast highway. You'll be alone. A car will begin following you and then pass you. I'll give you its license plate. You'll follow that car to a rest stop. You'll have with you all the information you have about Calena Lacerda, including everything you know about her current whereabouts. You'll also bring me the names, addresses, and photos signed by you of all the other women who currently work for you in that capacity. That's my security. You can't realistically take any further action if I have those photographs."

"Do you really expect me to meet you alone on the coast highway?"

"That's exactly what I expect. If you don't come or if I even suspect that anyone else is with you, I'll drop the only tube of the antidote into a jar of acid and you can spend the next two weeks of your miserable existence checking out various herbal cures. That is, until you're too weak to stand."

"Let's discuss this reasonably," Bai said. "How do I know this is really a fatal bacteria?"

He was born a negotiator. He was negotiating with his own life. Only Edgar Treeves could convey the exact mixture of sincerity, apathy, sympathy, and menace in the next few words he said.

"If you choose to believe that what I've told you is a lie, then I'm afraid we have nothing further to discuss. Have a nice day."

"No, wait," said Bai, quickly, "I believe you. But what assurance do I have that you won't just take the information and kill me?"

"Why would I kill you?"

"Because of what you think I did to her, of course."

"You think I care about you? About her?" Treeves said. "You think I care about that lying cheating whore? I only care about one thing. I want to be sure that I'm the one who kills her."

"Listen to me," Bai said. "You're right. Something is terribly wrong. But I can't be on the coast highway tomorrow. They would never let me get away alone. I'll give you fifty million dollars for that antidote. My country and yours are about to enter into trade agreements. I could make you one of the richest men in the world."

"I'm already rich," Treeves said. "You're a clever man. Figure out a way to get away. The directions are simple. You have a pencil? Coast highway. Ten in the morning. We both walk away with what we need."

Treeves hung up. He cleared his throat.

"You're certain Dr. Arons said there was no chance Bai could spread that bacteria to other people?"

"Highly unlikely, exposure requires a prolonged dampness on the skin. The surfaces on that table were prepped with a reagent. It was also on our napkins and the silverware. It activated the bacteria."

"Sounds extremely complicated. How did he whip it up so quickly?"

"Well, he didn't invent it. The United States still maintains robust biological weapons research facilities. Insane, really. You'd be surprised how easy it is to bribe an underpaid government scientist if you have several million dollars. I explained the basic parameters and he gave Paul the recipe for the stew."

"Even if Bai doesn't show up, that rash will disappear in a few days?" Treeves said.

"It will spread and get progressively worse over the next few days. He'll be terribly uncomfortable, but the rash will eventually fade like a common cold. So what if Bai doesn't come? What's Plan B?"

Treeves looked at me as if he were challenging me to remember other times.

"Case, Plan B is that you accept that sometimes life decides there isn't a happy ending, simply the lesser of two evils. I wouldn't worry about that too much, however. It's quite rare that I make that kind of error in judgment."

"It was quite a performance," I said.

I had faith in Treeves, but the stakes were too high and our options were too limited.

"Are you sure he'll come?" I said.

"Think about who Bai is. Remember his voice. Consider that although I told him he was been infected with a deadly biological weapon, he expressed concern for no one but himself. Then tell me. Will he come?"

I didn't have to think about it for very long.

"He'll come," I said.

CHAPTER 38

KNOWLEDGE

Coast Highway
Summer, 2018

We picked up Bai's Mercedes on the coast highway and followed him for long enough to make sure that no one followed us. When I was absolutely certain, I passed him and sounded my horn. He looked over at me. Treeves was hunkered down in the back seat and couldn't be seen. A short distance after that, I put on my blinker and pulled into the spot that Treeves had chosen. It was a small area off the highway just big enough for two cars. No one would bother us there. I quickly got out of the car. Bai began to open his door.

"Stay in your car," I said to Bai.

He got back in. I went to his window and took a moment to enjoy the expression frozen on his face.

"Open the trunk," I said.

I searched his car thoroughly. I used a device Aram had given me to check for transmissions. Bai was alone. At least, for the moment.

"Get out and bring the information."

We walked to a place between the cars. I was wearing jeans and cotton short-sleeved shirt. He was in a suit and tie. He walked with an uncomfortable gait, but said nothing about it. He reached out to hand me a portfolio.

"Wait," I said. "I'm going to search you first."

I really didn't expect him to be armed, but there was no reason to be careless. Not when I was so close. He had a wallet inside his jacket and a thin vid with a panic button in a hidden jacket pocket. I didn't find any weapons.

"Take out the contents of the portfolio and hand them to me," I said.

"I want to see the antidote."

I took a large tube out of my pocket and handed it to him. It had no markings on it. He immediately pulled up his sleeve and rubbed some of the ointment on his hand and forearm. What I saw did not look pleasant. The medicine seemed to give him almost instant relief. Paul had told me the burning and itching would be driving him mad.

"Now follow my instructions," I said. "And don't forget that you sent Ko to kill me and I'm standing here in front of you instead."

"I'm not afraid of you," he said, trying hard to mean it. "Obviously, someone knows that I'm here. If I don't return unharmed, I guarantee that you and your friends will be hunted for the rest of your short lives."

He opened the portfolio, reached inside, and took out several sheets of paper and some photographs. He handed them to me and I glanced through them.

"Everything seems to be in order. Have you called off the search for her?"

"Yes," he said. "I've done exactly as you asked. Can I leave now? I no longer have any interest in this. This entire affair has been an annoying distraction from the moment it began. You have the upper hand. I simply want all of you out of my life so I can continue with my business."

"It's interesting that you would describe the death of four innocent people as a distraction."

"Innocent? Who is innocent? You have no idea what I've seen. You have no idea what kind of man you've chosen to play games with."

"Well, of course, that's always a possibility, but, just for a moment, just for the sake of argument, let's consider the possibility that it's actually you that doesn't have a clue about who you're playing with."

He looked at me and I watched the suspicion spread across his face. Then came the fear.

"Relax," I said, wanting to be sure I got an honest reading from him. "All I want is to be certain that I won't be disturbed when I'm finally face-to-face with her."

"Don't be a fool. You've won. Do what you like. I'm going to forget you exist."

Treeves got out of the car.

"What is this?" Bai said. "You told me we'd be alone."

"We are alone," I said. "This Dr. Edgar Treeves. He doesn't exist."

"What are you talking about?" Bai said, quickly. "What is this?"

"Relax. We're not going to do anything to you," I said. "This is simply an introduction."

I said to Treeves, "Was he telling the truth about not bothering with Callie and me anymore?"

Treeves' eyes closed and he shook his head from side to side. He studied Bai for a moment.

"Don't think about scratching it," he said. "That will only make it worse."

Bai took a small step forward, but he stopped when I did too.

"Are you the insane doctor who's done this to me?"

"Did I engineer a weaponized bacteria complete with a unique antidote? I hardly think so."

Bai said, "What I have in my pocket. Will that cure me?"

"Absolutely," said Treeves.

When he spoke in a certain tone, there was no way to doubt his sincerity.

"Then there's no reason for us to remain here," Bai said. "We both have what we want."

"There's just one more thing," I said.

Bai tensed. His breathing quickened.

"Relax," Treeves said. "We aren't going to harm you."

I walked over and opened the trunk of my car. Inside was a sensitive microphone, a set of speakers, and a connection to a Cooper SHW Satellite that employed an encryption code that couldn't possibly be broken in a short period of time. Our voices would be transmitted through SAM, who was coding the signal in real time using a set of generated keywords in the most random manner possible. There were only two devices capable of decoding Sam's scrambled signal. One was in the trunk of the car I was driving. The other had been delivered to General Tresain that morning. Within the hour, the set of keywords Sam had generated would be deleted by destroying an external hard drive, rendering any recording of our conversation sounding like nothing but annoying static. Our words would cease to exist. I picked up the device and punched in a code. In a moment, I heard General Tresain's voice.

"Dr. Treeves?" he said. "What is this?"

"This is Time, General Tresain. I'm with Mr. Bai and Dr. Treeves."

"Is that you, Case? Where is Treeves?"

"Dr. Treeves is standing next to me. He's perfectly safe. As I said, we're talking with a man named Bai Ju Hong."

"It's true, general," Treeves said. "I'm here and I'm quite safe."

I said to Bai, "I don't believe you know General Martin Tresain, but trust me, he's aware of you."

Bai said, "If you really are a general in the United States Military and you know this man, I want you to know that he's insane and he's brought me here against my will. I'm a respected businessman and a high-ranking minister in the Chinese Government."

"I don't know what you think you're doing, Case, but shut down this connection immediately. Allow Minister Bai to leave unmolested. Bring Dr. Treeves directly to the Marin Naval Station. We'll discuss all this then."

"Time and I will be happy to do that, general," Treeves said, very calmly. "However, before we do, I have some information I'd like to share with Mr. Bai. You can't prevent me from doing so, therefore please be quiet and listen carefully."

We heard General Tresain's voice come from the speakers in a calming tone.

"Mr. Case, I don't know what you think you're doing, but you shouldn't have helped Dr. Treeves to leave here. Please bring him back now. Imagine what will happen if you don't return immediately."

"I imagine that I'm committing suicide," I said.

I turned to Treeves.

"Go ahead," I said.

"Mr. Bai," Treeves said. "For several years, Mr. Case and I were undercover operatives working under the direction of General Martin Tresain. I functioned as a Medium and Mr. Case was a Weapon, code name Time. Mr. Case's orders were to understand my silent signals and neutralize any threat that I identified. His ability to survive last night's encounter with Mr. Ko should be all you need to know regarding his ability to inflict damage and persevere against capable opponents. As a Medium, a student of human behavior, I was invaluable to General Tresain. Not only am I able to discern, through disciplined observation, what people are thinking, but I can also predict, with an extremely high probability, actions they are about to take. You can imagine how valuable such an ability would be in any urban combat situation."

The general said, "Treeves, have you completely lost your mind? Minister Bai, allow me to assure you that this man is delusional. He was a contributor to our intelligence services, but only in a minor capacity. Recently, he's been under observation, but Mr. Case helped to free him in order to cook up this ridiculous story."

"Really, general," Treeves said. "Do you believe that such a banal, obviously improvised story will hold water once I share with Mr. Bai just a fraction of what I know?"

"All this is fascinating," Bai said. "But what does any of it have to do with me? My government, does not, under any circumstances, engage in acts of terror of any kind."

I grunted. Treeves signaled me to remain completely silent.

"Perhaps you don't find the knowledge that I've just given you to be of great import. However, you're about to take a bite of an apple that will change your life forever. In four weeks, I will accompany our president to China. I'll appear to be simply another minor member of his support entourage. However, the reality is that I will be the most valuable asset that he takes with him to your country. I'll advise the president on every plan and every deception that your people have hatched up for this summit. I will uncover your weaknesses and allow our economic team to attack them directly with a maximum of intelligence. Obviously, in order to utilize my invaluable advice to full effect, my abilities must remain most top secret. And now, unfortunately for you, you are aware of them."

There was a silence. At last, the voice of General Tresain came over the speakers.

"Minister Bai, please accept my apologies for this terrible inconvenience," he said. "I repeat. This man, Treeves, is delusional. You cannot believe this absurd story."

Treeves effortlessly switched to my voice.

"Really, Martin, give it up already," he said, condescension dripping from every word.

It caused General Tresain to make one of his extremely rare mistakes.

"Bring Dr. Treeves in immediately. That's an order, Case."

"Thank you, General Tresain," Treeves said, in his own voice. "That's all we require from you at the moment."

He signaled for me to break the connection. Bai was staring at Treeves. Treeves looked back with a mild curiosity.

"Why not give him a demonstration?" I suggested.

Bai continued to stare at Treeves.

"Your prospectus offers a one-point-three percent index, however your government has no intention of honoring those figures," said Treeves. "I observed that as I studied your preliminary negotiators. By having our negotiators present targeted facts and scenarios to your people and gauging their reactions, I was able to extrapolate that the true figure will be much closer to approximately point-nine percent. Quite a difference, wouldn't you say?"

Bai looked confused.

"There's only one way you could possibly know that," he said. "There's a traitor in the ministry."

"Absolutely not. However, even as I give you that assurance, you're thinking that the traitor is your brother-in-law, Li. That would be a blow in more ways than one. Now you're telling yourself that it's almost a certainty that he's loyal to you. However, let me assure you that you're incorrect. I've had plenty of opportunities to observe Li. He feels trapped under you. His ambition is gnawing at him. How could you be so blind?"

Bai's eyebrows went up as he pulled his lips inward.

"What are you?" he said.

Treeves said, "I'm your death warrant."

He signaled me.

"That's right," I said. "I've committed treason here today. I'm a dead man. And you're as dead as I am. General Tresain will kill me for what I've done. And he will not allow you to go on living, knowing what you know."

"What are you talking about?" Bai said. "The United States does not assassinate men in my position."

I didn't need to be Edgar Treeves to see Bai's fear.

Treeves said, "At this very moment, General Tresain is reaching out to a man who specializes in accidents. How quickly could you convince anyone that what happened here today actually happened? What would you say? That you met a man who travels with the president in order to read minds and that an American General wants to have you killed because you found out about this mind reader while you were trying to clean up a mess you created by forming a harem? How would that appear to some of the more staid members of your ministry? No. Our agents or your own people would assassinate you long before you could find some way out of this trap that you've constructed for yourself. You could apply the antidote and try to hide, but I doubt that there's any place on earth that the general couldn't find you."

Treeves gestured at me and said, "Mr. Case has your vid. The moment you leave, he'll call the general and give him the necessary parameters to pinpoint your coordinates. General Tresain will know precisely where you are. That antidote also contains a nano transmitter. Think about it. Think hard. It isn't only you. From this moment on, if you use a vid or any communications device, the general will make certain the person on the other end of the call will also die. If you use a public vid, the general will check the records and he'll know where you've been. If you speak to your family, they'll die in some horrible accident. You're a walking, leaking canister of fatal nerve gas. The general cannot afford to take chances. Wouldn't your people do the same if they were in his position? From this moment on, you, and anyone who comes in contact with you, are as good as dead. The general will clean this up quickly and thoroughly."

Treeves clapped his hands together twice as if he was shaking something unpleasant off of them.

"Of course, you can throw that antidote into the ocean and try to run for as long as you can," he said.

Then Treeves hammered the final nails into Bai's coffin.

"However, I don't suggest tossing it away. Your body will eat itself within days. I've seen them experiment with that kind of thing on some rather nasty people in our biological weapons labs. You can't imagine…"

It was a warm day. Treeves shook slightly, as if he were cold. I felt my skin crawl. Panic began to spread across Bai's features. Treeves' attitude changed. He put on a sympathetic air. His voice was soothing.

"Really, there's only one option," he said. "Get in your car, turn around and drive it off the highway. Many people have accidents on these curves. I promise you that I'll tell the general you did it quickly and that my identity is secure. Your death will be honorable. Your family will be safe."

Treeves smiled reassuringly. He continued as if he was presenting Bai with a wonderful gift.

"Minister, men like us must always be ready to die. So many women. Surely, you must have thought about your death. And, in a very real sense, wouldn't it be a release, a respite? All the pressure we live under every day. Knowing that one fatal mistake could be the last."

"Do you think you can make me into a fool so easily?" Bai said.

I recognized the bravado. I'd seen it on the faces of other men in the past. Treeves knew exactly what to do. He filled his voice with contempt and he used it to cut into Bai like a knife, twisting and lifting it.

"You think that *I'm* trying to make *you* a fool?" he said. "You've made yourself a fool. You were weak and you know it."

Treeves waved his hand at the photographs that Bai had delivered to us.

"How long did you think that sort of nonsense would last?" he said. "Forever? Your life is over. You have this one chance to save your reputation and your family. Accept it now…or suffer."

It pushed him closer to the edge. Treeves told me it was time. I stepped in and found a nerve bundle in Bai's neck. His body tensed, but he wasn't able to make a sound.

"No trouble," I whispered.

Treeves took Bai's vid from me and examined it. He placed a voice frequency scrambler over the microphone. It wouldn't affect the sound of his voice. However, minor fluctuations would appear to be glitches in the transmission and make it impossible to guarantee that it was actually Bai who was speaking. He manually activated it, held it to his ear, and listened. After a moment, Treeves began speaking and Bai eyes widened to their fullest.

"All's well," Treeves said, in perfect Mandarin, perfectly imitating Bai's voice. "I'm on my way back now. I have new information. Cancel the orders I gave before I left. I'll have new orders when I return."

Treeves listened to the response.

"Good."

He hung up.

Treeves said, "I think I did that rather well, don't you. Right down to the way you sign off."

"Come on," I said, releasing Bai and taking his phone from Treeves. I put it in my pocket. "We're finished here."

"Wait," said Bai, as Treeves and I walked back to our car. "I want to defect."

Treeves waited. I enjoyed watching the spark of hope that came to Bai. Then Treeves pronounced a final judgment in a tone that couldn't be mistaken.

"In order to defect, you have to be useful," he said. "You're defective."

We left him standing by the side of the road. I drove further up the highway. In about an eighth of a mile, I pulled over.

"Do you think we'll hear the crash from here?" I said.

"Probably. In about six or seven minutes," Treeves said.

We heard it almost immediately. Treeves shrugged.

"Nobody's perfect," he said.

I watched the ocean.

"It's a nice day," I said. "I'm going to take a walk down the road, find the site of the crash, and throw his vid into it."

I paused.

"It's a nice day. Do you feel like coming along?"

I knew he would understand. As far as I was concerned, he had fulfilled his end of the agreement. I was ready to pay my debt.

He thought it over for a few seconds and then he said, "No. I'll think I'll watch the ocean from here."

CHAPTER 39

JUDGMENT

General Tresain's Bay Area Headquarters
Summer, 2018

There was no way to avoid or delay facing General Tresain. I made sure Aram received the information we had gotten from Bai. Then I returned with Treeves as the general had ordered. I harbored no illusions. More people than you can imagine quietly rest under our nation's highways and in the foundations of office buildings.

Rangers, dressed in plain clothes, met us outside the gate. Half of them escorted Treeves politely to a nice evening meal. The other half practically carried me to a waiting room. Waiting was exactly what I did for the next six hours. I was told to sit in a hard wooden chair and my ankles were shackled to the wall. At the furthest end of the room, a Ranger stood as rigid as one of those fancy guards outside of Buckingham palace. He was well armed, but didn't keep any of his weapons handy. I think he was there to make sure I didn't get comfortable. That meant no food and no water. About seven o'clock, I told him I need to take a piss and he nodded at a bucket by the side of my chair.

I didn't care. I knew Aram was sharing Bai's data with SAM. I smiled, realizing that I was thinking of SAM as a personality, not a computer. I wondered if I'd ever be able to get a message to that effect to Aram.

As for Callie, I never expected to see her again. What I'd done was worth it, just knowing that she'd be safe. Somehow, Jackson would find her and he'd let her know that there was nothing else to fear. I smiled again. Across the room, my Ranger companion said nothing, but an expression flashed across his features. I could tell he was thinking that I had broken and gone over the edge.

I'm turning into Edgar Treeves, I thought.

And I smiled again.

By nine o'clock, my mood had changed. I wondered what was taking so long. Was the general so angry that he felt I needed to suffer before I was put down? If that was his plan, it was working. I was grinding my teeth, desperate to know if SAM and Aram had made any progress.

I considered it a good sign that I wasn't transferred immediately to the Bunker. Of course, that's where they'd taken Treeves. There was no reason to be concerned for him. The general wouldn't even give him a dressing down regarding his actions. Treeves was much too valuable an asset. They had always handled him with kid gloves and they always will.

Finally, a Ranger opened the door, walked over to me without a word, and unlocked my shackles. I was taken into General Tresain's office. Except this time, after I sat in another hard chair facing the general's desk, I was shackled again. The general didn't look up. He sat at his desk, arranging some folders, clearly letting me know that I wasn't worth his immediate attention.

The Ranger left.

The general looked up and said, "You realize that you've left me with no option after that stunt you pulled this morning."

"I was fully aware of the risk, general. I'm ready to face the consequences."

"Risk? Risk?" the general said, his voice rising. "Time, a risk is something you take when you choose to perform an action that has a reasonable chance of success. It's not a risk to commit treason as I listen to you doing it."

"Treeves is safe," I said. "His identity is protected."

"Yes. I've made sure of that."

I raised my brows involuntarily.

"I've had my next best Medium blind interview everyone he might have come in contact with while he was outside the Bunker. Fortunately, only one person had even an inkling of who or what he really is."

The muscles in my chest tightened up.

"Aram Cooper," I said.

"Yes, of course, Dr. Cooper. Did you imagine that you could callously parade Edgar Treeves in front of someone with Aram Cooper's intellect?"

He allowed that knowledge to fully sink in. My blood pounded through me and rose to my head.

"General, Aram Cooper's entire life has consisted of keeping secrets from the world. Treeves' identity is as safe with him as it is with you or me."

The general exploded.

"Well, now we know exactly how goddamn safe that is! What was all this for, Time? A woman?"

"It wasn't about a woman for you, general," I said. "It was about a malfunctioning piece of invaluable military hardware. You wanted me to fix Treeves for the summit. Well, I fixed him. What's more important? The result or the means?"

We stared at each other. The general's breathing began to slow.

"Don't concern yourself with Dr. Cooper," he said. "Aram Cooper is much more important to this country than you can possibly imagine. He's been doing work for us for years. I don't suppose you were aware that a young Aram Cooper wrote the program that identified potential identities for you? He's actually already submitted a proposal to study Dr. Treeves' methods and incorporate them into his brain child."

"SAM?"

"Yes."

I slowly shook my head from side to side. I tried to imagine Treeves' reaction when he heard about Aram's proposal. It made me forget for a moment where I was and what I thought was about to happen. Then I remembered.

"So are you planning to keep me here all night, general?" I said. "Or can we get on with it? By the way, I haven't eaten since yesterday and I haven't had anything to drink for at least six hours. I believe a last meal is traditional."

I smiled.

"I'd like a pizza, with lots of fresh vegetables. And a beer, please."

"Wipe that smile off your face, Time. If it were up to me, you'd have a bullet in your brain at this very moment."

I raised one eyebrow. I only did that on special occasions.

"But it's not up to you?"

"Both Aram Cooper and Edgar Treeves personally assured the president that they would refuse to work for our government in any capacity if you were harmed in any way. Of course, you knew they'd do that, didn't you? You were counting on it."

"I never asked either of them to intercede on my behalf."

"More importantly, you did help Treeves achieve a higher level of functionality in time to accompany the president to China. The president was pleased about that. However, I think you should know the most important reason that you're going to walk out of here with your brain intact is that Treeves made it clear to the president that it was a great advantage that he'll be negotiating with Bai's brother-in-law, Li, rather than Bai. Treeves put it in terms of a successful military operation."

I thought of Jon Ling.

"What I don't understand, Time, is why you never asked me to trade your talents in exchange for my resources to find and protect Ms. Lacerda. We would have found her within two weeks."

"I didn't have two weeks, general. When we looked over the data we took from Bai, it was clear we didn't have two days, let alone two weeks. Bai had already been using his considerable resources to track Callie and he was close. The only way I could ever find out what he knew was to use Treeves."

The general shuffled the folders on his desk.

"Five minutes before you came in, I spoke with the president. He's decided that to ensure everyone continues to perform at peak capacity at this delicate time, it's best to consider this a sanctioned operation for a Medium and his Weapon. Those were his exact words. Politicians will be the end of us sooner than any of us imagine."

"So? I'm free to go."

"Free?" the general said.

He leaned across his desk towards me.

"I wonder if you actually believe that someday I'll forget that you used me for your personal ends. Get this straight, Time. You'll walk out of this facility, but no matter what Treeves or Cooper or even the president says, I would kill you right now if I didn't have a use for you. If you never understood it before, understand it now. I control you, Time. I have from the first moment I saw your name on a dossier. You find that difficult to understand?"

I stared him down. It wasn't easy.

"You've never been difficult to understand, general. I guess we'll be seeing each other."

Forty hours later, I took a flight to Seattle and rented a car. I drove about fifty miles to a small town that serviced a logging company. I stopped at a diner for a cup of coffee. I gave the waitress who served me fifty dollars and asked her to tell the Latin girl working in the kitchen that Case was waiting in the parking lot.

Callie was scared when she came out. Her expression didn't change all that much when she saw me.

"It's over, Callie," I said. "He's dead. Anyone who might hurt you is dead. I came to tell you that. You're safe now."

"You have to go away," she said.

"If that's what you want. But not before I tell you something."

"I don't understand. What are you doing here? You must know about me. You know who I am. You know what I've done. I murdered my sister and my brother."

"You didn't murder anyone. It wasn't your fault. You made a mistake."

"That's just talk," she said. "Nothing can ever be the same. I wish I had the courage to end it. Every day I wake up and I wish I had courage. One day, I will. Please, go away."

She turned and began walking back towards the diner.

"Wait," I said. "You think I can't forgive you, but it's easy to forgive you for what happened before we met. What's hard to forgive is what happened after Laura was killed."

She stopped.

"What do you mean?"

"Instead of coming to me, you ran. You didn't trust me. You didn't let me defend you. To fight for you and keep you safe."

I walked over to her and put my hands on her shoulders. She was shaking.

"Don't ever do anything like that to me again," I said.

She turned around and, at last, I was holding her again.

She smelled of bacon grease.

She felt like Callie.

CHAPTER 40

<hr>

FRIENDS

The Ahh Baloney Café
Spring, 2019

Jackson Aurelian exploded out of the kitchen, nearly knocking over two waiters and a table. Standing inside the front door was a tall man. Jackson hadn't seen his younger brother, Jess, for more than four years. When they'd finished hugging and loudly greeting each other, they settled at a table and Jackson called for a bottle of *kleren*, the Haitian cane liquor steeped with weeks-old, red-hot peppers.

"Ah, my, my," said Jess.

"Food for the spirit," Jackson said, his smile stretching his features.

As they drank, a waiter began piling food on the table.

"It's good to see you, my brother," Jackson said. "I'm sorry I couldn't be at the airport to pick you up."

He was mildly surprised to hear himself slip so naturally into the French of his homeland.

"No problem. It was better to see that fine limo waiting for me."

They laughed. Both of them realized how much they missed each other. They were the only family they had left. On the mean streets of Port Au Prince, where voodoo and violence were a volatile combination, they had watched each other's backs.

Jess had been living in Europe for five years, exiled from Haiti because of his politics. Facing the machetes of those who disagreed with him or walking the streets of Paris was not a difficult choice for a man of his temperament.

"How long will you stay?" Jackson said.

"Just long enough to get my older brother into trouble. Always, you are too safe, too conservative. That's no way to live."

"You make me laugh, like always. It was never that I was conservative, it's that you were reckless. Remember when you dropped that water balloon full of your piss on that bastard's head?"

"Remember it? I did the same thing to an art critic in *Montmarte* about ten days ago!"

As Jackson loudly laughed, Jess was distracted by the entrance into the restaurant of one of the most beautiful women he'd ever seen. His first thought was how he would love to paint her, in several different poses.

"Oh, my, my," he said. "Look who just walked into my life."

A tall man, walking next to the woman, looked over at Jackson and nodded. Jackson smiled and nodded back.

Jess noticed it and said, "You know them?"

"We were once great friends," Jackson said. "But, it turned out, I really didn't know him that well."

"Better still, *mon frère*. Anyway, he's not the one who interests me. Come on, let's go over and you can give me a nice introduction."

"I don't think so," said Jackson.

His mood had changed. His brother didn't notice it.

"What I wouldn't give for an enjoyable evening with her," Jess said.

He was a bold man, confident in both his looks and his personality. He continued to stare at the woman and her companion.

Then he turned as he felt his brother's hand on his arm.

"Don't even think about it," Jackson said. "Look at me. Not at her."

Jess was surprised. He and his brother had lived in the *Cite Soleil* slums. They had walked some of the most dangerous streets on earth together. Now Jackson was worried because some businessman in his fancy restaurant might get annoyed that his lady friend was being admired.

"I can dream, can't I?" said Jess.

He looked over just in time to catch the eye of the woman and he gave her a little wink. At the same moment, the man looked up to see him do it. Jackson squeezed his brother's arm hard enough so that Jess's features showed the pain he felt.

"Why aren't you listening to me?" Jackson said, in an angry whisper. "I told you to look away. Now look away."

ABOUT THE AUTHOR

John J Heartfield was born in New York City.
He lived for many years in Berkeley, California.

The Italian Towns of *Sestri Levante* and *Cavi di Lavagna*
are his second home.

He's an entrepreneur and a songwriter,
as well as an author.

His previous published book was
Make Your Small Business Website Work,
Easy Answers To Content, Navigation, and Design
(Rockport Publishers).

For more about
John J Heartfield:

www.johnheartfield.com